STILL
DOING TIME

WANDA ADAMS FISCHER

Copyright © 2024
Wanda Adams Fischer
STILL DOING TIME
All rights reserved.

No part of this publication may be reproduced, distributed, or transmitted in any form or by any means, including photocopying, recording, or other electronic or mechanical methods, without the prior written permission of the author, except in the case of brief quotations embodied in critical reviews and certain other non-commercial uses permitted by copyright law.

Wanda Adams Fischer
Published by Spring Training Media
htpps://wandafischer.com
X:authorwfischer

Printed Worldwide
First Printing 2024
First Edition 2024

10 9 8 7 6 5 4 3 2 1

ISBN: 978-0-9995049-7-0

This is a work of fiction. Names, characters, places, and incidents either are the product of the author's imagination or are used fictitiously. Any resemblance to actual persons, living or dead, events, or locales is entirely coincidental.

This book is dedicated to the people who dream for a better world and do everything they can to make it happen.

Other Books by the Author

Empty Seats (a novel)
Handprints (a short story)
The Genius and the KGB (a short story)
The Audition (a short story)
A Few Bumps (a novel)

Table of Contents

Introduction 1
Chapter One 3
Chapter Two 8
Chapter Three 11
Chapter Four 13
Chapter Five 15
Chapter Six 17
Chapter Seven 25
Chapter Eight 28
Chapter Nine 30
Chapter Ten 35
Chapter Eleven 41
Chapter Twelve 44
Chapter Thirteen 52
Chapter Fourteen 55
Chapter Fifteen 57
Chapter Sixteen 59
Chapter Seventeen 71
Chapter Eighteen 75
Chapter Nineteen 78
Chapter Twenty 81
Chapter Twenty-One 83
Chapter Twenty-Two 85
Chapter Twenty-Three 90
Chapter Twenty-Four 93
Chapter Twenty-Five 95
Chapter Twenty-Six 98
Chapter Twenty-Seven 102
Chapter Twenty-Eight 109
Chapter Twenty-Nine 113
Chapter Thirty 121
Chapter Thirty-One 124
Chapter Thirty-Two 128
Chapter Thirty-Three 130

Chapter Thirty-Four 132
Chapter Thirty-Five 136
Chapter Thirty-Six 142
Chapter Thirty-Seven 145
Chapter Thirty-Eight 148
Chapter Thirty-Nine 151
Chapter Forty 154
Chapter Forty-One 160
Chapter Forty-Two 164
Chapter Forty-Three 168
Chapter Forty-Four 171
Chapter Forty-Five 174
Chapter Forty-Six 176
Chapter Forty-Seven 179
Chapter Forty-Eight 183
Chapter Forty-Nine 187
Chapter Fifty 189
Chapter Fifty-One 191
Chapter Fifty-Two 193
Chapter Fifty-Three 200
Chapter Fifty-Four 203
Chapter Fifty-Five 207
Chapter Fifty-Six 212
Chapter Fifty-Seven 214
Chapter Fifty-Eight 216
Chapter Fifty-Nine 220
Chapter Sixty 223
Chapter Sixty-One 226
Chapter Sixty-Two 228
Chapter Sixty-Three 234
Chapter Sixty-Four 236
Chapter Sixty-Five 239
Chapter Sixty-Six 241
Chapter Sixty-Seven 243
Chapter Sixty-Eight 244
Chapter Sixty-Nine 247
Chapter Seventy 248

Chapter Seventy-One	250
Chapter Seventy-Two	252
Chapter Seventy-Three	255
Chapter Seventy-Four	258
Chapter Seventy-Five	260
Chapter Seventy-Six	261
Chapter Seventy-Seven	265
Chapter Seventy-Eight	268
Chapter Seventy-Nine	274
Chapter Eighty	277
Chapter Eighty-One	280
Chapter Eighty-Two	284
Chapter Eighty-Three	286
Chapter Eighty-Four	288
Chapter Eighty-Five	290
Chapter Eighty-Six	293
Chapter Eighty-Seven	299
Chapter Eighty-Eight	303
Chapter Eighty-Nine	307
Chapter Ninety	309
Chapter Ninety-One	311
Chapter Ninety-Two	315
Chapter Ninety-Three	323
Chapter Ninety-Four	325
Chapter Ninety-Five	329
Chapter Ninety-Six	333
Chapter Ninety-Seven	337
Chapter Ninety-Eight	339
Chapter Ninety-Nine	342
Chapter One Hundred	347
Chapter One Hundred and One	356
Acknowledgements	361
About the Author	362

Introduction

Still Doing Time began as a sequel to my first novel, *Empty Seats*, which featured Jimmy Bailey and his two friends, Bud Prescott, and Bobby Mangino, as they worked their way through minor-league baseball, aiming to make it to the big time. However, as the novel developed and the characters matured, the characters themselves—specifically, Jimmy and his sister Debbie—took the story in a different direction. Baseball still plays a role in their lives; however, many other factors come into play, and this is not simply another baseball novel. While it's still located in Massachusetts, specifically, North Weymouth and other parts of the Boston area, the book explores other aspects of Jimmy's and Debbie's worlds.

Wanda Adams Fischer
Schenectady, New York
August 2024

Dear Jimmy,

Thank you for your note. I have heard from the guys about your situation. From what they tell me, it doesn't seem fair. Let me know when you're out of that place. I'm sure we can find something for you to do around here at Fenway Park. I'll find a job of some kind for you. Call my secretary as soon as you're able to, and we'll set something up. My wife and I wish you all the best.

Sincerely,
Tom Yawkey
May 7, 1975

Chapter One

I've folded and unfolded this piece of stationery so many times, it's a wonder any print remains at all. The edges are frayed from being handled repeatedly, but distinctively at the top is the name **THOMAS R. YAWKEY**. Not as clear, is his title: *President and Owner, Boston Red Sox*, with the logo underneath.

I have so few things to my name that mean anything to me. This I cherish. *A job offer from the president of the Red Sox. The Boston Red Sox, for Pete's sake. For me. A convicted felon. It's almost like having a get-out-of-jail-free card. I'm ready, willing, and able to work at Fenway Park.*

In five days.

And counting.

I've been in this hellhole for what seems like eternity, yet the calendar says it's been four years.

Only four years.

A lifetime inside this cell.

I remember the first day the door slammed shut. The worst noise I've ever heard in my life.

Before that, I thought the worst noise was when the judge crashed his gavel on his colossal, oak desk, as I stood before him next to my lawyer, hoping against hope that he'd realize I was telling the truth and change his mind about what he planned to say.

Instead, with the stroke of wood on wood, he sent me to this godforsaken place, this nightmare of noise, this complete torture chamber. If I hadn't found ways to cope, I don't think I'd still be alive. If I'd had a different cellmate, I might not be here today, counting down the days until I walk out the front door into the arms of my freedom.

Freedom. Even the word sounds like music. Only five days to go.

My name is Jimmy Bailey. Once I believed I'd be playing Major League baseball. Thought it'd be a piece of cake. After all, I had the best teacher in the world—my dad. He'd been in the big-league pipeline himself.

Because of how my dad coached me, nurtured my skills, passed on his experience, I was the best pitcher on my Little League team. In Babe Ruth ball. All-star high school champion. Scouted by Major League teams. Drafted in the fourth round by the Montreal Expos. Sent to play Single-A ball right after I graduated from high school. Even got a signing bonus.

Yep. I was flying high.

When I was in high school, I was a starting pitcher. In Jamestown, they put me in the bullpen as a reliever. Somehow, they realized that I didn't have the confidence or composure to start games. I admit, when I first got to the team, I was anxious when I surveyed the talent.

Dad always said I had the talent, work ethic, and the drive to do it. He would know—he was on the cusp of being called up to *The Show* when my mother made him choose between baseball and her. Yes, that's right. She made him give up baseball for her. And he did it. I'm not sure I know many men who would.

But he did. Instead, he decided to groom me, his son, to take his place. I didn't realize that when it was happening. I didn't appreciate the full extent of his sacrifice until I spent these last four years, sitting in a cell, with so much time to think—hoping against hope that I would survive the ordeal—four years in prison for a murder I didn't commit. Involuntary manslaughter. Right. How about involuntary imprison-ment?

So much has rattled my brain over the past four years. In some ways, I'm fortunate, because I have a good cellmate. Keeshon and I became good friends. He's going to be here longer than me. We've kept to ourselves mostly, so that we don't have to deal with the general population much. We do our jobs in the kitchen, we go to the library, and I convinced him to take GED classes so he can get a high school diploma. It's going to be hard enough to get a job when we're outside of this joint with a high school education, let alone without one.

I've come to realize so many things since I've been in.

Institutional food—especially in prison—ain't ma's home cooking. I gagged for weeks when I saw what was on the plates. I lost weight, and then re-gained it, because whatever it is they feed us is so filled with salt and starch, that it's fattening without even tasting good.

The human voice can make unrecognizable noises—guttural, ugly utterances that come from deep down inside, expressing anger, pain, emotions I don't understand. Also, these guys—and the guards—know words I've never heard before, and I don't know what they mean. I know when I get out, I never want to hear them again.

When men are angry simply because they're no longer free, they can be cruel, outraged, unreasonable, and furious over simple things, such as not having a spoon at dinner, or not having enough detergent when working in the laundry.

Receiving a piece of mail in here is like getting a block of gold from Fort Knox. Even though mail is screened and pre-read before we see it, and everything we write and send out is also scrutinized, I've seen even the most indignant inmate melt into jelly when he gets an envelope. Sometimes, it's hard for a man to hide tears when a card or letter comes through the prison mail system. I'd guess that's when it's from a wife, sweetheart, or a child.

We have little or no idea what's happening in the outside world. Every now and then I see a newspaper, but it's usually several weeks old.

Same with magazines. Sometimes people bring old magazines to the prison library, but they're usually so outdated, it's a joke.

Music? What's that? I have no idea what's going on in the music world. Haven't heard a radio for so long. Can't have FM antennae here. Guess they think we'll turn them into weapons. Some guys would, I suppose.

Five days.

In so many ways, I hate to leave Keeshon here by himself. Who knows who they'll put in here with him? He's small—not a bad bone in his body. I still can't believe he was convicted the way he was. These Black guys... if they have no money, they don't get good lawyers. Hell, I had a good lawyer, and I still got four years for a crime I didn't commit. Keeshon, he got money from an old lady he was taking care of—she gave it to him—and her memory wasn't too good. Her family accused him of stealing it, so here he is. No evidence. No way to prove one way or another that he did or didn't take the money from the lady. He was assigned a public defender who was so overloaded with cases, the guy barely paid attention to him.

He told me the lady liked him, that she thought he was funny, that they watched "The Cosby Show" on TV all the time and laughed, laughed, laughed. He said she was nice to him, especially when he wheeled her out to the park on nice days. She liked to feed the pigeons, he said, so he'd take stale bread and chop it into tiny pieces for her to throw into the air. She liked the way the birds cooed as they hopped over each other to get to the bread. He said she smiled and laughed the whole time they were in the park.

Keeshon likes to make people happy. He's kind and soft-spoken. I stepped in a couple of times when guys in here tried to take advantage of him. Guys thought we had a "thing" going, but the only thing we had in common was getting convicted for crimes we didn't commit.

He never had anyone to talk to, the way he talks to me. He said he'd never known a White man who didn't look down on him. Of course, I joked with him and said, 'That's 'cause you're so short, Key.' And he is—only about 5'4," and here I am, 6'3," almost a full foot taller than him.

He frets every day about my leaving. He paces around the cell. Keeps saying, 'Jim, I don't know what's gonna happen to me when you gone. I mean… I mean… I mean, man, you saved my life in here.' Pacing. 'I mean, you got me to get that GED done, and maybe that means I can get a job when I git outta here.'

"Yeah, you gonna get a job when you're outta here, Key," I tell him. "We'll both be fine. Once we get out, we'll be able to breathe."

"Breathin.' Yeah. Looking forward to that, man."

Five days.

Chapter Two

Four days.

Can't decide if I love or hate baseball.

It was my life for so long. Everyday. Every night. And then this. This place. No baseball here. In fact, I didn't want these guys to know I had anything to do with baseball. As soon as someone found out, though, it spread through this place like wildfire.

"Hey, Bailey, throw me a fastball! Or are you better at curves? You got some great curves there!"

I hate this stuff. Leave me alone. Get me a book from the library and let me read.

"Whatsamattah, Bailey? You shy or sumthin'? You don't like it when a guy tells you you're good-lookin'?"

And of course, I blushed. Red-faced. I could feel it from the tip of my toes to the top of my head. Scarlet skin, through and through.

Leave me alone. Get me back to the cell with Keeshon.

"Ooohhh, he gotta get back to his home base with his little Black boyfriend!" Then they made all kinds of hooting and hollering noises, as if Keeshon and I were, you know…

Can't they get this through their thick skulls? Keeshon and I aren't doing anything in our cell except reading. I help him with his GED stuff, and sometimes he reads to me for practice. He's getting better with his reading. For God's sake, I have no idea how he was ever promoted from one grade to another. He couldn't read! He could barely identify the alphabet! Wow, how lucky was I to have such great teachers in Weymouth. And I didn't even think I was smart. At least I could read.

Four days.

How will I handle this whole thing? I've learned a whole new way of breathing, of coping since I've been here. Will my lungs even be able to manage fresh air?

Mr. Yawkey said he'd get me a job at Fenway Park. Can I even stand to walk into the place, to watch guys who went through what I was beginning four years ago? Can I go from one prison, being on the inside looking out, to another, where I'll be on the outside looking in on the world of Major League Baseball?

I just don't know.

I'm beginning to have the same kind of doubts I did when my first professional pitching coach told me to warm up in the bullpen and said I'd be the next pitcher to go into the game. I didn't have butterflies in my stomach; I felt like there were vultures down there, ramming my insides with doubt. Then I got to the pitching mound and settled down after throwing a few wild pitches—a curve that didn't break, a fastball in the dirt, that sort of thing.

My catcher would come to the mound and help calm my nerves. He put his hand on my shoulder, told me to follow his lead, and I did. Before those days, I'd always been able to look up into the stands and throw a glance my dad's way. He'd nod at me, and I'd be okay. He wasn't in the stands way out in western New York when I was playing. My catcher—my friend—knew all the right words to appease me and set me on the right road.

When I walk out that door in four days, will anyone have their hand out to help me relax as I begin a new life?

Baseball was my life. Will I have a shot at getting back to playing professionally? Or is that over? Will the Expos even talk to me again?

Would I even know what to do if someone handed me a baseball and asked me to throw it?

Four days.

Chapter Three

Three days.

Keeshon is becoming increasingly anxious. But then again, so am I.

"I got a letta from my sista today, man. She's goin' to the govna again to see if he will commute my sentence. Get me out of hea soona. Ya' think I got a chance?" he asks.

"I don't know anything about that stuff, Key. I can talk to my sister when I get out. I can call my lawyer. He might know."

"That'd be good, Jim. Good."

Keeshon calls me Jim when it's just us. When we are around the general population he does as they do and calls me Bailey.

He's choking up. I can see it. I can feel it. Now I'm starting.

"You think you'll go lookin' for the guys who witnessed that night on the beach?" he asks.

"I don't know where I'd start."

"Yeah. Kinda a long shot, I guess. You gon' go back to that beach? Eva?"

"Don't know. Never thought about it."

What a lie that is! I think about it all the time. Go back to Wessagusset Beach? Not any time soon. I don't think I could take it. I want to see the ocean, yes. But there's a new section down by the neck on the other side of the beach. They call it the "new" beach. It's where the old fertilizer plant used to be. I might go down there. Don't think I can go down where the old bath house was, where Terry and Eddie used to bring the booze and we'd drink. And then, that night…

"It might be a good place to start. You might 'memba somethin' if you went back."

"Or I just might get more nightmares."

"Prob'ly so. You know betta than me, Jim."

"I've got enough nightmares from this place. Only thing I got lucky with is that you were my cellmate. Worked out good. Wish you were coming with me."

He's sitting on the edge of his cot. I've learned his huge eyes bug out when he gets stressed. They're bugging now. I see tears welling up as he wipes the side of his face.

"Worked out good for me, man. Learned some readin,' some writin,' thanks to you. You shoulda been a teacha, not a ball playa."

"A teacher? Me? Oh no, I'd never survive. Buncha little kids running around? Nope. Never happen. I got no patience with kids. None."

"Thanks for having patience wit' me, man. The GED teacha said I did good becuz' you made me study."

"Yeah. Important stuff. Never told you I never did my homework in school, did I? But I made you do yours. My teachers in Weymouth would never believe it."

"Teachas I had wuzn't wuth crap, Jim. Thanks to you, now if I have to sign somethin,' I know what it is because I kin read."

I'm speechless.

We just sit on our cots, staring at one another, not knowing what else to say without becoming sappy.

"I wish I was goin' wit' you, too."

Three days.

Chapter Four

Two days.

I'm starting to sweat. It's not even hot in here. It's cold and damp. I've got sweat pouring down my face, salt inching into my eyes, the back of my hair soaking wet. I'm not even moving.

I'm going over my books with Keeshon. They let me keep a few of my sister's old novels, and I'll leave them with him. It's not always easy to get stuff past the censors. They look at our books and magazines. They say it's because they don't want us smuggling anything in—contraband, drugs, other stuff we're not supposed to have. Keeshon and me, we don't want to get in trouble. We toe the line.

He only wants one of the five books I still have. It's Claude Brown's *Manchild in the Promised Land*. My sister gave it to me right after I got here. I think she expected me to get some understanding about Black people. I don't know. We had no Black people in Weymouth. The first Black people I met were in Jamestown on the baseball team. Joey Tidwell played second base. He was quiet at first. He was starting to open up to all of us, just as the season ended.

It's all a blur now, in some ways. Tidwell. Stevie, the bullpen catcher. Richie, from California, who took a line drive in the leg and was out of commission for a few weeks. The pitching coach called me "Bos-tone," and Richie was "Surfer Dude." Funny to think of these things right now. Funny how my mind's working today.

Two days.

Brown's book didn't make much sense to me until I came to this place. So many Black people. So many could have stepped right out of the pages. After I read it a second time, I started asking questions about why so many of the guys in here are Black and so few are White, in proportion to how many Blacks and Whites are in the general population. And why are the few Whites in here always the ones who seem to get the cushy jobs—the ones where they get to push everyone else around?

I never wanted one of those jobs. I don't care that I mostly ended up washing dishes and folding laundry. I kept my head down and stayed near Keeshon. Felt like I had to protect him. Who's going to protect him when I'm gone? I can't get that out of my head. He's got at least one more year in here unless some miracle happens. His sister's been working on getting the governor to pay attention to his case, but I don't know. He should be able to get out early because of good behavior. No one in this place behaves better than him.

Two days. Forty-eight hours. Frightening and exciting at the same time.

Chapter Five

One day.
Tomorrow. Twenty-four hours.
Yikes! July 19, 1976.

I don't even know if someone will be at the gate waiting for me. My sister said she would be, but who knows, if she can't get out of work. My mother never learned to drive. I still can't believe it. She continues to rely on her friends to take her everywhere. I guess at the age of sixty-four, she's too old to take driving lessons with teenagers.

Sweating, again.

Everything I need to take with me is in a small pile. Four books, three changes of underwear, one of those marbled, black-and-white composition books like we had in elementary school, where I've kept notes and some diary-type entries. I'm sure when we go to the dining hall the guards look through our notebooks and have some good laughs. My writing isn't prize-winning stuff; it just has some things that have happened to me since I've been here.

Civilian clothes. Don't know if they'll give me something, but I know they won't send me out into the non-prison world with this get-up I'm wearing. I've got a pair of dungarees they have us wear when we go out in the yard on cold days, but they're kind of beat up. I guess I could wear them home.

Home? Where's home? Do I go back to live with my mother? Will she have me? My sister in Georgia still blames me for Dad's suicide. My mother doesn't. At least, I don't think she does.

My bed. That little, twin bed from high school. Gotta say, even it will feel good after sleeping on this cot. An actual mattress with real sheets.

I'm feeling so guilty about leaving Keeshon. Never thought I'd get to know a Black man. Growing up in Weymouth, I never even saw a Black person in our neighborhood. Now I have a Black friend. A real one. He's an amazing guy. Never had a break in life, and now he's in here. Tomorrow he'll be by himself.

One more day.

Chapter Six

Today's the day.

I'm not going to eat the food here. I'm planning to eat when I leave. Key's gone down to breakfast, but I hope I'll get to see him before I leave.

Guard comes to the door. "Bailey, Warden wants to see you." Door clanks, slides open, creaking the whole time like it always does. Needs a good squirt of WD-40.

Guard grabs my elbow so he can guide me down the catwalk. Most guys are down at the mess hall, so it's quiet. "Can you give me a little break?" I ask. "It's my last day."

"Yup, I know, but I gotta follow rules."

Seems like he just wants to have one last time to control me. I just nod, the way I've always done, just to cooperate. *Don't make any waves. Don't cause trouble. It's your last few hours, for God's sake.*

Guard takes his big wad of keys from his belt as we get to the warden's door. He follows a routine of keys into various locks until the door opens. Guard takes my elbow again and guides me to the seat at the desk of the warden's secretary.

"Okay to have him wait here? He's not dangerous. It's his last few hours here. Don't need to put him in shackles."

"If you say so, Mel," the secretary replies. She doesn't even look up from her typewriter.

I look around the office. Lots of things hanging on the wall. Aerial photos of the prison grounds. Team photo of the 1975 Red Sox. Autographed photo of Bob Cousy. An *unautographed* photo of Bobby Orr. An oil painting—a paint-by-number thing—of a seagull, maybe something on Cape Cod. No family photos, though. Guess they don't want anyone who's in here to know what their family members look like.

Buzzer rings. "Yes, sir?"

"Please send Mr. Bailey in."

"Yes, sir."

She finally looks up. "He will see you now."

"Okay."

I get up and head to the door, which I soon discover, is a little warped and needs a bit of an oomph to open.

Warden stands up. "Good to see you, Mr. Bailey."

Mr. Bailey? That's what everyone called my dad. I am not used to this.

"Yes, sir."

"Sit down, sit down. Just want to have a few words with you, you know, before…you know, you leave us."

"Yes, sir."

"I know this has been difficult for you being here. You've done well, and it's time to go home. I have a few things to say, and I don't always speak to inmates when they're leaving, but in your case, I feel I need to."

"Yes, sir."

"You have made a tremendous contribution to your cellmate's ability to work on his GED, isn't that right?"

"Yes, sir."

"The teaching staff tells me you might have been a good teacher if you'd gone to college. Is that right?"

"I never thought I could do that. All I ever wanted to do was play ball."

"But you worked with him on his reading. Is that right?"

"Yes, sir. And I found I liked to read while I was here."

"It sure made a difference with him. May mean a difference when he gets to leave."

"Sir? May I ask a question?"

"Go ahead."

"When do you think Keeshon will be able to leave? I've watched out for him since we've been cellmates, and I worry that he'll get behind on his studies and that…"

"That he might not be safe when you leave?"

"Yeah. He's such a little guy, and some of those guys out there…"

"Some of them can be dangerous. I know."

"He's become a bookworm, you know, and I don't want them to be making fun of him or taking his books away."

"I'll see what I can do."

"When do you think he'll be going home? He's really done enough time, you know."

"That's not up to me, son. It's up to the courts."

"Can't you recommend he get credit for good behavior? He's got good behavior."

"I'll see what I can do."

I feel my face getting more and more red. I feel moisture in my eyes. I'm sweating again. "It's just, sir, I paid my dues, and I think he has, too. I think we should be walking out of here on the same day."

"I can't make that happen, but I will keep an eye on him. I will do my best to keep his cell a single for as long as I can."

"And sir? Is it possible that I can see him before I go? We are good friends."

"Do you have your belongings together? Your sister will be here in about half an hour."

"Yes, sir."

"I'll have Melvin bring Keeshon back here while you wait for your sister. And Mr. Bailey—"

"Yes, sir?"

"You have been nothing short of a model inmate. Everyone you've come in contact with inside this administration has commented on how well you've done here. I think you're right when you say you've paid your dues."

Paid my dues? You think I've paid my dues? I have no career left, my father's dead, one of my sisters won't speak to me, a guy died at Wessagusset Beach, and I didn't kill him, but I still had to spend four years of my life here. You're right, I paid, but I didn't do anything to deserve this.

Then again, neither did Keeshon. He was framed. A kind, gentle soul. He wouldn't hurt a fly. At least now he knows how to read better. I just hope he makes it out of here in one piece.

"Yes, sir."

"Do you have a job or anything waiting for you when you leave here?"

"I-I-I don't know. I think I have some possibilities. My sister, Debbie, knows a lot of people. She went to Harvard, you know."

"Yes, I think I knew that. What about baseball, though? You think you'll go back to that?"

"I don't know if they'll take me back. I'll have to get back in shape. Mostly here I sat around and did a lot of reading. Didn't do much in the way of exercise. Feel very flabby."

"You'll get it back…if you want to…"

"Yes, sir."

He goes to his telephone and buzzes his secretary. "Will you get Melvin to bring Keeshon Washington to my office?"

He looks back at me. "We'll get him up here soon. I gotta admit, Mr. Bailey, I didn't know what was going to happen with you when you came in. And that situation with your father…I almost didn't know how to handle that."

He had to bring up my dad's suicide. He thinks he didn't know how to handle it. Is he serious? It's not as if a day goes by that I don't think of it a hundred times. I just remember coming into this office—that may even be the last time I was in here, come to think of it—in shock, seeing my two sisters in here, crying their eyes out, with Donna screaming at me that it was all my fault. Then, going to the funeral in shackles and wearing an orange jumpsuit. With two guards. Walking into the church in front of all those friends. How embarrassing.

"No, sir, I didn't know how to handle it, either."

"I didn't mean…"

"No, sir, I didn't think you did. It just brings back lots of…memories. That's all."

I'm having a real conversation with the warden. This man controlled my life for the past four years, and, except for when I learned of my dad's suicide, he hasn't even acknowledged my existence. Maybe that's a good thing. I haven't gotten in trouble with him. Or anyone else here.

He seems human enough.

We hear a knock on the door. It's Melvin.

"Sir, you asked me to get Washington and bring him up here? Here he is."

Keeshon comes in, looking at the floor.

"Come in, Mr. Washington…have a seat. Your friend, Mr. Bailey, asked me if you could come up here before he leaves."

"Yes, suh."

I stand up. Again, it hits me how much taller I am than him.

"I'll leave you two in here for a couple of minutes. Sound fair?"

"Yes, sir/suh," we both say, simultaneously.

Silence. Seems like a long time, but probably for only a few seconds.

"Key, I don't know what to say."

"Me, neitha."

"I wouldn't have made it without you to support me."

"Me, neitha."

"I don't know where I'll be when you get out."

"I don't know if I'll get out without you hea' to make sho' no one messes with me."

Silence.

"Yeah." I sigh. Long sigh.

I'm feeling guilty. I was put in for involuntary manslaughter. He came in for taking some money—not even all that much—from an old lady, who really gave him the cash, but her family said he stole it. He had a bad lawyer—got much more time than he should have.

"I'll send you my address when I get out. I'm probably going back to my ma's house. You want me to contact your sister or anything when I get out?"

"I dunno. I'm havin' a wicked hahd time with this, Jim."

"I'm feeling wicked guilty, leaving you in here."

"But you gotta go. Massachusetts ain't gonna pay yo' room and boad if yo' time's up."

He's trying to make me laugh. He does that. I feel moisture in my eyes. I can't cry. Stop it.

"Time's up. Yeah."

I figure the warden's coming back soon, so I grab him, hug him, and tell him I'll miss him. I feel him sobbing.

"Oh, man, Jim, you changed my life. You been my frien' and teacha. Don't know what I'll do when you gone."

"I'll be here in spirit, especially when you go to the library and get new books."

"That liberrian can't keep me in books."

"And you got your GED."

"Couldn't have done it without you."

How about that? Those teachers in Weymouth who just passed me so I could play ball, would just flip out if they heard that I'd turned into a teacher! Or maybe I was his coach.

The warden knocks on the door and comes back in with my sister, Debbie, in tow.

"Debbie, this is my friend, Keeshon. He's been my roommate since I've been here."

She reaches her hand out to shake his. He's a little taken aback—most White people around here don't make physical contact with Black people, even now, in 1976.

"Nice to meet you, Keeshon. I'm sure you and my brother had a lot to talk about."

"Yes, ma'am, we did. He taught me how to read."

"Are you serious? Are we talking about *my* little brother? The guy who always hated to read when he was in school?"

"Yup, we kept takin' books outta the liberry. He helped me get my GED. I neva got a high school diploma befoe' I came hea'."

She looks at me and says, "Wow, you did that?"

A scarlet rush overtakes my face. "Um, yeah…"

"I'm impressed. You should think about going to college and getting a teaching degree. We'll talk about it. You got all your things together? I'd like to get going."

She's always in a hurry. I always thought I'd be in a rush to get out of here when the day came, but I hate leaving Keeshon. I feel so guilty. He should have been the first one to leave, not me.

"Yeah, I don't have much. Didn't have much when I came in, don't have much now."

I reach out my hand and shake with the warden. "Thank you, sir." Then I turn to Keeshon.

"Thank you, my friend. Never met anyone like you before. Probably never will again." I reach out to shake his hand, and he grabs me—hugs me tightly.

"God bless you, Jim. See you on the outside. Let me know wheah you at, heah?"

"I hear."

Melvin comes back and escorts him out. He looks over his shoulder as he walks down the hallway.

I have a bad feeling about this. He's so small, so vulnerable.

"Uh, Jim?"

Debbie's voice brings me back to Planet Earth.

"Yeah? Okay. Guess we better get going."

The warden interjects. "There are some papers to sign—my secretary has them at her desk. Miss Bailey, you have to sign some as well."

"Soon to be Dr. Bailey. I'll be getting my PhD in a few weeks."

"I stand corrected…*Dr.* Bailey. Congratulations."

My sister, the doctor. Her brother, the jailbird. My best friend, walking down the hallway with a prison guard, being thrown to the wolves.

Chapter Seven

Debbie drives a brand-spanking-new 1976 Volvo. She said she always wanted a Swedish car—very stylish, in her words, just like she is.

She had a full scholarship to Harvard to study urban planning and earned a doctoral degree. She wrote her thesis on how to build, what she calls "mixed-use housing for people of all income levels, by minimizing income distribution issues in major cities." I don't even know what that means.

I'm pretty sure her car's perfect, just like everything else about Debbie. She looks so much like our mother, it's almost scary. Very tall—almost as tall as I am—and statuesque. She carries herself with a rare and refreshing elegance and confidence. She never needs a stitch of makeup to look ravishing. She's not model-thin, but when she walks down the street, men and women alike turn to admire her. Just like with our mother, it was never simply her looks; it was the complete package.

She tells me she's met a guy who she's serious about. Immediately, I'm suspicious. He's from Long Island, kind of rough around the edges, without a real job, so he's driving cabs in Boston right now, and sometimes gets called to substitute teach in the Boston Public Schools. "Things will work out for him," she says. "It's kind of a rough time for people looking for jobs, even if they have a college degree." I don't think he deserves my sister, but I'll give him a chance to see if he passes my litmus test. She's about to get her PhD, and he doesn't even have a real job? Doesn't add up in my mind.

My thoughts return to my situation. If it's hard for someone with a college degree to get a job, what hope is there for folks with a felony record and no college degree? Great. I'm doomed. I probably couldn't even drive a cab. I haven't driven a car in so long, I probably don't remember how. Plus, I don't know my way around the area anymore.

"What do you think my chances are of getting a job?"

"I don't know. Where do you think you're going to be living?"

"I expect I'll be with Ma until I can get a job and get my own place."

"She'll let you stay around for a while, but she still hasn't gotten over Dad…"

"You mean she still blames me?"

"She blames the situation—your hanging out with Terry and Eddie, drinking and stuff like that."

"I guess."

"She's so lonely, Jimmy. She still doesn't understand why he'd do what he did. Some of the neighbors still don't talk to her, and you know she's such a social person. She keeps thinking *she's* going to go to hell because *he* killed himself. The Church and all its rules. She spends a lot of time wondering what she could have done to prevent it. Some days she doesn't even put on makeup, you know. And without her Revlon, she doesn't even look like herself."

"Ma? Without makeup? Really? I can't even imagine that. She's always been so concerned with her looks."

"A lot of that was for Dad. She wanted to be perfect for him. It wasn't for us. It was for *him*. She always made sure she got enough sleep, that her clothes were just so, that the meals were perfect. You know what I mean? Now…she's, well, different. You'll see."

I'm not sure I want to see my mother the way Debbie is describing her. I've spent the last four years remembering her the way she'd looked the day I'd gone into that place. Perfectly coiffed. Not a hair out of place. Ringlets on top of her head, held in place by invisible bobby pins. Prominent red rouge on her cheeks, but understated eye make-up. Red—I mean, striking red lipstick. Tasteful clothing that complimented her figure, hiding some of those little bumps that come with age and having given birth to three children. She found ways to accentuate her looks, despite what the years had done. She looked better every time I saw her. But then, I'm her son. I'm not exactly looking at her with neutral vision. She always looked like she'd stepped off the cover of *Good Housekeeping* or *Redbook Magazine* to me.

She's perfect in my eyes. She always will be. She doesn't need cosmetics or beauty-shop hair. She's my ma, The Filly, the one who'd tempted my dad so much that he gave up professional baseball for her.

Debbie touches my right arm—my pitching arm. "Are you okay?"

"Uh—yeah, I was just thinking."

"About?"

"Just some things I have to take care of when I get out of here."

"You're not thinking of getting back with Terry and Eddie, are you?"

"No! Not a chance! Those bums! Hey, don't we have some paperwork to do?"

"That's what the warden said."

"Let's get it over with and get out of here."

Chapter Eight

As we walk out through the corridors, hearing prison doors clank behind us, I jump as each one closes.

Debbie looks warily at me but keeps walking at a steady pace. She quickens her steps as we go from one checkpoint to the next. The guards, of course, take one look at her and undress her with their eyes, going from her head to her toes with lewd glances that make me want to lash out at them, but I know better than to do anything that could interfere with my getting out of here.

She knows. She knows what they're doing, but she's got too much strength, too much presence of mind, to let it bother her. One of them tries to reach out and pat her on the rear, and she grabs his hand.

"What do you think you're doing, bustah?"

"Me?" he asks, feigning innocence.

"Yes, you! Keep your hands to yourself!"

"It was an accident, Miss! I swear!"

"If you're ready to swear that it was an accident, I'd hate to see what else you'd be willing to swear to, especially under oath. In court. Like I said, keep your hands to yourself."

The other guards, in chorus, utter something that sounds like, "ooooooooooo," in unison, and someone in the back pipes up, "She got you good, Rossi."

"Shut up, idiots!" Rossi shouts back.

Debbie looks back over her shoulder at the five of them clumped around, and quips, "Goodbye, boys, nice to have met you," in a Katherine Hepburn-esque way that shows *she's* in control. They're stunned.

Yes, that's what it's like. *Katherine Hepburn comes to take her errant brother out of prison. They walk out the front door, straight to the brand-spanking-new white sedan, glittering like snow on a Christmas card, and then drive south on the highway.*

If it really *were* Hepburn, I'd be some famous actor, and we'd be going to a mansion along Cliff Drive in Scituate.

Instead, we are going to a bungalow in Weymouth.

The one where we both grew up.

The one we left every day to go to school.

The one where our mother cooked us Sunday dinner.

The one where our dad taught me to play ball in the backyard.

The one where our dad killed himself the day I went to prison.

Chapter Nine

I'm having trouble breathing when we finally leave.

The hot, muggy, July air chokes me. I'm not used to the atmosphere on "the outside."

I can't see straight, either. The sun's so bright, it's burning my eyes.

I pause briefly and ask Debbie to lead me to the car.

"You can't see?"

"No… you gotta understand, I've been in a dark place for four years. Not much sunshine inside that prison."

"Do you mean that literally or figuratively?"

"Both, I guess. Just get me in the car. Let me sit for a minute."

She reaches into her purse and hands me a pair of cheap sunglasses. "Here, put these on," she says. She, of course, sports elegant, tortoise-shell sunglasses.

Probably got them at Lord & Taylor. Or at least Jordan Marsh, or upstairs at Filene's. Debbie would never be caught dead shopping in Filene's Basement.

What a wimp I am. I finally taste freedom, and I need my sister to lead me to the car like a blind man. My legs are turning to jelly, and I can't see.

She unlocks the door and ushers me into the passenger seat. I settle in, let out a huge sigh, and pull down the visor.

"Okay, okay. So much better. You better get us outta here before they come running after me because they've changed their minds."

"They're not going to change their minds, Jimmy. You're out. You're on parole, but you're out. Done with Walpole. For good."

For good. Except I need to keep in touch with Keeshon. I'm so worried about him.

"You're right, sis. For good. Let's go."

The last time I was in a moving vehicle was almost four years ago, and that was in the van that brought me to prison. I bounced around with a bunch of other prisoners in the back of that van, and we all got hurt during the ride.

Debbie isn't talking. She's listening to the radio. Paul Simon's singing about "Fifty Ways to Leave Your Lover."

"Get on the bus, Gus... Make a new plan, Stan... No need to be coy, Roy... Just listen to me..."

I'm fascinated by the passing sights, things I'd always taken for granted—never thought these everyday things would look so good to me.

I look around at landmarks. The Channel 5 building on the right. Route 95, south to Providence. Then Route 24, heading to Brockton or New Bedford. The hotel on the right that looks like a castle.

Ah—South Shore Plaza. I'd like to go there sometime soon. It has a movie theater, I think.

We pass where the road splits, where Route 3 to the right goes south toward the Cape, and Route 95 off to the left heads toward Boston.

We get off at the first exit past South Shore Plaza, take a right, then a quick left, up by Archbishop Williams High School. We then drive through Faxon Park, toward the Quincy Quarry, and lastly by the Fore River shipyard, where Dad used to work. I feel a lump in my throat, thinking about Dad in his coveralls and steel-toed safety boots, working his fingers to the bone in that place.

We drive into North Weymouth, over the Fore River Bridge, past McDonalds and the Chinese Restaurant, Cazeault's Hardware, Wrye's Fish

Fry, Thayer Pharmacy, Beale Park, St. Jerome's Church, and then turn right onto the street that leads to our house.

Deep breath, Jim. Just take a deep breath. It will be okay. The Filly will be happy to see you. No matter what.

Debbie pulls up to the house.

"Well, here we are."

"Yeah."

I open the car door and swing my legs out, putting one foot after the other on the ground. My legs are shaky, but I'm pretty sure they'll hold me. I *have* to stand up. I almost feel drunk without having had as much as a whiff of alcohol in four years.

"You okay?"

"Maybe…yeah. I'll make it."

We walk up the path, and there she is, The Filly, standing behind the screen door. She looks like the most beautiful person in the world. The Mona Lisa, Whistler's Mother, Woman with a Pearl Earring, Madame X— all have nothing on my ma. I haven't seen her in person, without a piece of plexiglass between us, for almost four years.

She puts her hand up to the screen, palm up flat. I reach out and do the same, touching hers, through the crosshatched metal.

"Jimmy? Is it really you? It's not a dream, is it? I've been dreaming you'd be back. Is this really happening?"

"Yeah, Ma, it's me."

She opens the door, and I see she's crying. What else could I expect?

She opens her arms and hugs me so tightly, I can barely breathe.

"Oh, Jimmy, Jimmy! I didn't think you'd *ever* come home! I thought something terrible would happen to you in that place. But you're here, you're here! Come, sit down, sit down! Let's get some food for you. Wait! Stand up! Let me look at you!"

She takes my face in her hands and looks over every inch—hair, eyes, nose, mouth, ears—then down to my shirt, my arms, my waist, my legs, my feet.

"You're all there, still," she declares. "I was so worried you'd come back with parts missing!"

"No, Ma, nothing's missing, except maybe my pride."

I look over in the corner and see Debbie rolling her eyes back at me. *Corny. Right?*

"Well, you can get that back, Jimmy. Just sit down. What can I get you to eat?"

"I'm fine, Ma... but do you have any tonic?"

"How about some Coca-Cola? You want some?"

"Perfect. It'll hit the spot."

She almost skips to the kitchen in her slippers to grab a glass and Coke. She calls to me, "Ice or no ice?"

"Ice is great, Ma."

"See, she's going to cater to you, Jimmy," Debbie says. "You know she loves it when she can wait on people. She loves being in the entertainment business. It's who she is."

"I don't want her to be waiting on me, Debbie. It's not like I'm helpless."

"Let her do it for a while. It's what she needs."

"Yeah, but it's not what I want."

"Just humor her. It'll work out."

"If you say so. You staying here tonight?"

"No, I'm going back to my apartment in Cambridge. You're on your own."

"Just make sure I've got your phone number. Okay?"

"Ma has it. Sometimes I think it's the only number she knows."

We smile at each other.

"Here you are, dear, a nice, cold Coca-Cola for you. Now you can sit back and relax, maybe watch some TV?"

"Sure, Ma, that would be nice. Maybe as soon as Debbie leaves."

I survey the living room and realize nothing's changed. Same recliner chair, same rocking chair, same couch, all with crisp, white doilies on the arms. Same rug in the entryway. Same runners on the stairs leading up to the second floor. Same television set with the radio on top. Same two-tiered telephone table with the phone on the top and phone books on the shelf under the phone itself.

It's a time warp. Everything's just like it was, four years ago.

Except one major hole in our lives…Dad's gone.

Chapter Ten

Three days later, I'm settled in a comfy chair in the living room, watching Peter Falk in "Columbo" when the phone rings.

"May I speak to James Bailey, please?"

"May I ask who's calling?" I respond, cautiously, because I don't know who even might know I'm home, and who would call me "James."

"Yes, this is Officer Hogan, calling from Mass General Hospital. I was asked to call you by a Keeshon Washington…"

"Keeshon? What's he doing in Mass General?"

"He had a *problem* at Walpole State Prison…"

"What do you mean, a 'problem,' officer?"

"He wants to tell you himself."

After a short pause, a barely intelligible voice comes through the phone.

"Jim—it's me, Key…"

"What? Can you speak up a little?"

"No, I can't. I got beat up pretty bad last night. Got a coupla broke ribs, my nose is broke, and maybe mo'. Can you come see me? Heah's the officer…" his voice trails off.

"Mr. Bailey? He's on a lot of pain medicine, and he's pretty banged up. I can get permission for you to come see him tomorrow. He has guards outside his room."

"What happened? Do you know who did this?"

"Several inmates were involved, Mr. Bailey. I fail to see what good it would do for you to know who was involved."

"Officer, I was just released from Walpole myself. Keeshon and I were cellmates."

A long pause at the other end of the phone, and I detect a distinct difference in attitude in Hogan's tone. "You…were…his…cellmate?"

"Yes. Yes, I was. What difference does that make?"

"I need to make sure it'll be okay for you to visit. I don't know if it would violate your parole."

"So, how will I know if it's okay?"

"I'll call you back."

I hang up the phone and call Debbie.

I don't even let her say hello when she answers. "Debbie, Keeshon was beaten up at the prison, and he's at Mass General in bad shape! I gotta go see him! I knew something bad would happen. I just knew it!"

"Slow down, Jimmy. How'd you find out about this?"

"He called me. No, a cop called me, and I spoke to Key for a couple of minutes. He said they broke some ribs and his nose. Now they gotta find out if he can have me as a visitor without it violating my parole."

"He's at Mass General?"

"Yeah, the guy said he's got guards outside his door. He's not dangerous, Deb. He wouldn't hurt a fly, really. I need to see him!"

*I **knew** this would happen. I knew they were lying in wait for him once I left. I gotta get him out of there. I have no money, but I need to find a lawyer to get him out of there.*

"Do you think this cop will check things out? Let you know if you can see him?"

"He said he would."

"Let me make a couple of phone calls. I'll call you back."

The phone goes dead. Fast. When my sister says she's going to make phone calls, she gets right on it. Who knows, she might even call the governor himself. She has so many connections with her Harvard connections and that urban planning thing she does.

Pacing. I begin pacing. At least, here in my parents' living room, I've got more room to walk than in that little cell.

My mother descends the stairs stopping at the bottom. "Oh, baby, what's wrong? You're going to wear a path in my rug! You're not practicing for baseball, are you?"

"No, Ma. The guy who was my cellmate in jail, he got beat up bad and is in Mass General. He called me—no, an officer called me—a little while ago. He's got some broken bones and is in tough shape. I want to go see him, but the guy who called me said I might violate my parole if I do."

"Well, I don't want you to do *that*."

"I don't either. The guy said he'd ask about it. I called Debbie. She's making some phone calls. She seems to know people."

Ma rolls her eyes back, as if she was a teenager. "That she does, Jimmy, that she does. Some days I think she's getting ready to run for president. Wouldn't that be something? First woman president? My daughter, Debbie Bailey? You know, I think she could do it, too! She's on TV all the time. I'm so proud of her!"

She's looking at me, pity in her eyes, but still with a mother's love, something that can't be explained or taken away. Somehow, she knows in her heart of hearts that I'll never be a success like Debbie. She walks over to me, putting her hands on my shoulders. I'm looking down at the floor, but at least I've stopped pacing.

"Oh, I'm proud of you, too, my Jimmy, my baby boy. You made it through a terrible time, and I wasn't even there to help you. Your mother's supposed to be with you, by your side, in times of need, and I wasn't."

She takes my face in her hands and looks directly into my eyes. "You look just like him, you know. The spitting image. How handsome. How tall and handsome. If you walked down the street right now, the girls, they wouldn't be able to resist you. Just like him. We—all the girls in the office—noticed him right away when he worked in the shipyard. Out of all those guys who worked there, he stood out. And I knew. I knew I wanted to see his face on a child of mine, and here you are." What could I say to *that*?

I can't help but look straight into her eyes as she grips my face, gently but firmly, and tears begin streaming down both our faces. Today she has put her make-up on again. Her mascara's running into her rouge and foundation, making a Picasso-esque mess out of her cheeks. She's sobbing and trying to say something else, but nothing comes out of her mouth, just sounds that don't form real words.

My hands, flopping at my sides, reach out to her shoulders and pull her into a full-blown hug. She buries her head into my chest. I'd forgotten how tall she is—not that much shorter than me—but she's more fragile now than she was just four years ago.

She's a widow now.

What a strange word. *Widow*. It's like something you hear on a TV western, when the hero goes out to the cabin on the outskirts of town, to help the "Widow Jones," who's having trouble maintaining the house she and her deceased husband built together. He politely knocks on the door, kicks the dust off his chaps, removes his hat, and says, "Ma'am, I'm here on behalf of the town to help you with whatever you need. I'll bring the boys out and we'll fix your roof and your fence so's the cows don't get out anymore. And don't worry about them rustlers. We'll get rid of them, too."

Widow. My mother's a widow. Because my father killed himself the day I went to prison.

My fault? The prison counselor told me my dad was probably depressed, and because he refused to admit it, something awful might have happened anyway. *But suicide*, I asked her? *Maybe, maybe not, but don't forget, Jimmy, he was living vicariously through you.*

Vicariously. What the hell does that even mean? He was trying to play baseball again through what I was doing, because he couldn't, and I could? Something like that. And because I threw my baseball life away, hanging out with Terry and Eddie, drinking at the beach, I essentially threw his life away? He was depressed because of that?

'No,' the prison counselor said, *'he was depressed before that, probably because he felt he'd thrown his life away by giving up his own future in baseball, and he watched you making progress as a professional ballplayer, but you weren't doing everything his way. He wanted you to do everything he told you to, the way he told you to, and if you strayed in any way, shape, or form from his direction, he thought you were insulting him, taking things away from him personally.'*

How would she know? She didn't know him! How would she know about my baseball career compared to his? How would she know about our times in the backyard when I was a kid, and how much it meant to me? Or how much it meant to him? The bond we had. How much I relied on him to be at my games. How hard we both worked to make sure I was drafted. How would she have a clue?

Back to reality. Debbie's on the phone.

"Jimmy, I called a friend of mine in Governor Dukakis's office. He says he'll make sure you can get in to see Keeshon. He knows the former corrections commissioner. He'll make sure you don't violate your parole. I'll go over there with you tomorrow. He told me he'll supply us with a letter, and we can use his name if we have any problems. You on board?"

"Yeah—I—"

"You what? You got a problem with me intervening?"

"No, I was just thinking about a lot of stuff. Lots of things going through my head. Lots of memories, you know?"

"I can imagine. I'll pick you up at one. Get some lunch before we go in there. Hospital food is notoriously bad."

"It's probably gourmet, compared to what I've been eating in prison for the past four years."

"Could be, could be. But be ready. I'll drive in there all the way. Usually, I'd take the train, but I'll drive in. Don't want to get caught in expressway traffic on the way in."

"Okay. I'll tell Ma what we're doing."

"Good idea. She'll want to know."

I feel better after the call. I can see Keeshon, and maybe Debbie and I can come up with a plan to get him released from Walpole. Since she knows that guy in the governor's office, maybe he's got some ideas.

Then, I have another thought.

"Hey, Ma, you have any books I can take with me tomorrow?"

"What? Where are you going tomorrow?"

"Debbie arranged for me to see my friend at Mass General. When we roomed together, I helped him learn to read better. I read to him a lot. If you have any small books I could read to him, I think he'd like that."

"You *read to* him? Really? That was nice, dear. Well, there's a pile of books in the cellar. They might smell a little musty but go take a look. You might find something you like."

I head down the basement stairs to find a bunch of books stacked next to a pile of Dad's old tools. I find one I remember as being pretty funny—*Veeck—As in Wreck*, about the guy who used to own the Chicago White Sox. He did all kinds of crazy publicity stunts, like when he brought a little person up to bat, gave him the number 1/8 on the back of his uniform and had fun with that.

Key will probably get a kick out of it.

Now I'm pumped. Angry about what happened to him. But pumped.

Chapter Eleven

Getting to Mass General involves taking two buses and a train, and I hadn't navigated that for a long time. I'm glad Debbie agreed to drive. I'm shaky about going places alone. My first meeting with my parole officer won't be until Monday. I need to keep my nose clean until then and beyond. Don't want to drive. Don't want to risk getting even so much as a parking ticket.

Debbie will be my escort. She's the one with connections. She knows people in the governor's office. Hell, she may even know someone in the president's office for all I know. Maybe she knows people who could get Keeshon out of prison altogether.

Pacing. I start pacing again, waiting for her. Again. Wearing a path in my mother's carpet. Again. It's almost as if I am back on the running track outside Weymouth High, getting in shape for baseball season. Seems as if I'm becoming a pacing specialist.

Baseball. There's that word again. Seems like yesterday, but seems like decades ago, too. Don't know what it would even feel like to pick up a ball, a glove, a bat. Don't know if I'd even remember how to hold one, look in for a sign, go into a windup, and throw it, expecting it to go where I want it to, and how I'd want it to land into a catcher's mitt.

Baseball. It was my life. From the time I was four years old. Right here, in this house. Go through the kitchen after dinner to the backyard. Dad, with his yellowed teeth and shipyard-worn hands—weariness disappeared as soon as he picked up a ball.

Baseball. The newly-mown grass, the sun on the field, the dirt, the way it all comes together, creating an aroma, a special, intoxicating, captivating perfume—a siren's song to young boys, promising a ticket to a high-riding roller coaster that only an elite few get to experience, while holding a well-worn piece of leather in one hand, a white, yet scuffed ball in the other, squinting in the sun, sweating, dreaming of one day playing in the big league.

Baseball. The promise I threw away. The way I cavalierly chose bad company and booze over hard work and focus. The way I refused to listen to Dad—the way I took him and his talent for granted—the way I disregarded all he gave up for me so that I could take his place in the world of champions—the way I drove him to mental illness and death—the way I tore my family apart.

Baseball. The simple kids' game (three bases, home plate, a brown-dirt mound, green grass) that some kids play for fun, but it was always serious for me because it's what earned me praise, lifted me up on a pedestal, at home, at school, in front of girls, got me noticed by scouts, helped me walk tall and earn a place on this earth.

My head feels like a nor'easter inside, with all these memories, these uncontrollable feelings, swirling, taking me in one direction one second, another direction the next. My mind's bopping between Little League and Babe Ruth ball, between getting an award for the best player in the Commonwealth of Massachusetts, to being sent to the bullpen in Single-A ball, between my hometown, where everyone knew my name, to the far reaches of New York State in Jamestown, where I knew nobody and nothing.

Then, I was between a rock and a hard place.

Paulie Donovan, some two-bit guy from Southie, died at Wessagusset Beach one night.

People said I did it. Pushed him into the ocean and drowned him. I didn't. Couldn't prove it. Couldn't disprove it.

I went to prison for something I didn't do.

Baseball couldn't save me; I couldn't save myself.

No one and nothing could.

Can I ever love baseball again? Will baseball ever let me back into her arms, her embrace, surrounded by her sweet perfume on a fine summer day, smelling of sweat and leather? Will she forgive me for being away for so long? Will she think I've been cheating on her with another love, another obsession?

How will I explain this to her when I can't even explain it to myself?

Chapter Twelve

We drive down Wollaston Beach to connect with the Southeast Expressway. So many seagulls screeching and swooping down by the seawall, trying to swipe bits of food from discarded wrappers in the parking area.

Debbie's car is nice and clean. Just a hint of that new car smell. She's had it for a few months now. In the Boston area, it's amazing not to have dents in your car, even after only a couple of months, but Debbie manages to keep hers without even a scratch. She has a parking space at her apartment in Cambridge. Neat trick. She doesn't have to park on the street like most people.

Going up the ramp at Neponset is like navigating the Indy 500. She plows her way through the merging traffic, pushing her way into the line as if the other cars don't exist. I have to close my eyes because I am convinced we're going to hit another car and be dead soon. Headline in tomorrow's Boston Globe: *Former Baseball Player Survives Prison, Can't Handle Southeast Expressway*. Somehow, Debbie's in control, because when I open them, we're in the middle lane on our way to Mass General.

"I wonder what kind of shape Key will be in," I mumble.

"Probably not the greatest. But I'm sure he'll be glad to see you."

"Yeah. I brought him a couple of books. I used to read to him when we were cellmates."

"You told me that."

"I didn't know that I *was* a good reader until I found out how bad *he* was. He almost didn't know the alphabet. I read to him and then worked with him, so he started learning how to recognize words. Then he would read to me sometimes."

"You became his teacher. You already told me that, too."

"I guess so. I'm repeating myself again. He was too shy to get into classes at the prison, until he learned a little bit. Then I talked him into getting into the GED class. I helped him with the homework he got from that, too. Debbie, I had no idea that I even learned anything when I was in school, but those teachers in Weymouth must have sunk something into my thick skull."

"Or his teachers were so bad that they just passed him along."

"He said the teachers were afraid of the kids, so they just let them do whatever they wanted to. He said they had no books in the library, and they just ran wild in the school."

"Now that the schools in Boston are well on the way to being desegregated—"

"What does that mean?"

"There's a court order that Blacks and Whites must go to school together. The courts found that the neighborhood schools where most of the Black people live have no resources like books, and that the White schools have all they need, so the White kids were, of course, doing better. At one point, the head of the school committee said the reason Black people aren't learning is because they're stupid. There have been lots of riots and protests, and the worst were in '73, '74, but it's still going on. If they could afford it, lots of the Irish families from Southie pulled their kids and sent them to Catholic school."

"Wow. That might explain a lot about Key's situation. But I gotta tell you, Debbie, he's not stupid. He's just not had many chances."

"When they passed the Civil Rights Act in 1965, most people in this country thought segregation issues were only in the south, but we've got problems here, too. Major ones. I did a lot of work with some of the government agencies when I was pursuing my master's degree. No one seems to know what the answers are, but there are a lot of issues."

A lot of issues. Between Black and White people. It was like that in prison, too. More Black people than Whites in prison. I didn't think anything of it. I was too busy trying to protect Key.

"Like what?"

"Housing. Jobs. If people aren't getting even a basic education, they can't get jobs. And your friend, Key, if he's got a felony on his record, he's going to have an even harder time than you finding employment when he gets out. The Black Vietnam veterans who came home—have a terrible time finding jobs. They can't find housing unless it's in a *Black* area. People around here don't want to have a Black family move in next door to them. We don't have Black people in Weymouth, as far as I know. If we do, they're well-hidden."

"I don't remember seeing Black people in our school, come to think of it."

"We had one in my class, but he was an exchange student from Kenya, so we all used to say he didn't count. He was more of a celebrity than a regular student, you know? They loved him on the track team."

She veers off onto Storrow Drive—another road I hate—to the end by the bridge that leads over to Charles, then Kendall Square. She navigates this road with such ease that I almost feel as if I am in a taxi. She drives to the Mass General parking lot marked *Patients and Visitors,* gets a ticket, and parks the car.

"Well, let's go. Don't forget your books. Ma said you spent enough time in the basement last night looking for them."

"Thanks for the reminder."

I grab the paper bag, and we make our way through the cement structure to the front desk.

Debbie takes over from there.

"Good afternoon! We have permission to visit Keeshon Washington. Would you be so kind as to contact the people who are overseeing his room?"

The receptionist gives her a blank stare. "I have orders that no one is allowed to see him, ma'am."

"Really? I have a letter here indicating that *we* can see him. It's from the governor's office." Debbie reaches into her pocketbook for the envelope with the return address embossed in gold.

"I have to call my supervisor."

As the woman dials a number, setting off an overhead page, Debbie starts tapping her fingernails on the counter. She mouths the words, "I don't have all day, you know," to me.

I nod. "I know."

A security guard appears out of nowhere. Debbie's still tapping.

"Ma'am, may I help you?"

"Yes, sir. We are here to see Keeshon Washington. We have clearance from the governor's office." She reaches for the letter.

"Well, ma'am, Mr. Washington is having a little surgery right now. You might have to wait for about an hour. Would you like me to escort you to the cafeteria?"

Big sigh from Debbie. No, huge sigh.

"No, sir. I'm pressed for time. My brother is a friend of Mr. Washington's, and I am more concerned that *he* can visit with him. He has some books for Mr. Washington. I will wait for an hour, but if it's longer than that, I would request that you enable my brother here to see his friend."

Oh, no you don't! You're not leaving me here alone! I don't even know how to get home. I've only been out for a short time. How is this all going to work? I'm petrified here. Plus, I'm not too keen on hanging out with a guy in a security uniform.

"Yes, ma'am. Please wait here and I'll see if I can get a progress report."

We find seats by the window.

"What are you doing to me, Deb? You're going to leave me here? Alone? How will I get home?"

"You'll take the *T*. Sooner or later, you're going to have to do it on your own. Charles Street Station is right over there." She turns and points to a bunch of stairs outside the glass window. "You go up those stairs, buy a token, put it into the token machine, and go to Park Street. Then, you go downstairs and take the Red Line to Quincy. Then you can get a bus right down Bridge Street. Take the Hingham bus, just to be sure."

I begin sweating, even though the air conditioning is blasting inside the hospital. I feel heat come up from the tip of my toes to the top of my head. "You really think I can do this?"

"Yes. Of course. If you can teach someone to read, you can read yourself. If you can read, you can find a train and a bus. If it'll make you feel better, I'll write it down."

"Yeah. That would make me feel better."

She pulls a piece of paper out of her pocketbook and scribbles instructions about which train and bus I need to take, all the while shaking her head.

We sit in silence for about ten minutes before Mr. Security Guard comes back, making a beeline to Debbie.

"Ma'am, Mr. Washington will be back in his room in about ten minutes. I'll escort you up there. It will take us about that long to get there. Please follow me."

Like two, little sheep following our shepherd, we walk behind him along a yellow line to an elevator, arriving at a room with a guard stationed outside the door.

This must be his room. Why do they bother with a guard for him? If he's hurt as bad as he seemed when I tried to talk to him on the phone, he's not going anywhere. Maybe they think someone's coming here to get back at him, finish the job. Maybe that's it.

The room guard examines both of us from head to foot. "Ma'am, I need to look in your purse before you go in. And you! I need to pat you down to make sure you have no contraband."

Debbie looks annoyed but hands over her pocketbook. He rifles through it and nods for her to head on into the room. He tells me to empty my pockets, which is easy, since I have nothing but a wadded-up Kleenex, a comb and the scrawled directions Debbie wrote, then he pats me down. I think he got too much pleasure out of that because he smirked throughout the process.

Is this guy from Walpole? Does he know me from there? I don't recognize him, but maybe he knows me. Or maybe he just knows my name.

"What's in the bag?"

"Just a couple of books for Keeshon."

"Gimme the bag."

He rifles through the bag and pulls out *Veeck: As in Wreck*.

"What's this one about?"

"Baseball. The guy who used to own the Chicago White Sox. He was a prankster and liked to do wild things to get people into the ballpark."

"Maybe the Red Sox should try some of that stuff 'cause the team ain't so good, 'cept for last year's guys. They're going downhill again."

I don't know enough about the current Red Sox team to respond.

"Yeah, I guess so," is about all I can muster.

"Go on in. He just came back from the OR, so he's probably not 'with it,' if you know what I mean."

Debbie was already waiting inside for me, but she'd squirreled herself in the corner.

Key's face is all bandaged up, with just his eyes and mouth visible. His nose is broken, his jaw pretty-well bruised. I can only see a few bits of his hair through the bandages on top of his head, but not much. He's wearing a hospital gown, and underneath I see rib bandages and an intravenous line.

I lean in and whisper. "Key? Key? Are you awake?"

"Unnnnn."

"Key, it's me, Jimmy. I came with my sister to see you. Is it okay if I sit for a few? I could read to you. I brought a coupla books."

"Unnnn."

A nurse comes barging in, asking us to leave for a few minutes. "I have to check his blood pressure and temperature. I need to make sure his IV is working. Please step outside a moment."

We're outside with the guard again. He's looking Debbie up and down.

"You're a tall one, aren't you? Pretty and tall."

"I'm smart, too, and I have connections in the governor's office. If you don't stop leering at me, I think I'll have to make a call to my friend over there."

"Whoa, whoa! Can't a guy say a girl's pretty without her going over the ledge?"

"Nope. Not *this* one."

He looks over at me. "Sheesh, she's one of them 'women's lib-bahs,' eh?"

"No, she's just herself. She's always been like that. My big sister."

The nurse comes out and tells us we can go back in.

I pull a chair over next to the bed. The heart monitor is beeping in regular rhythms, the underlying beat for a soundtrack. I reach into the bag and pull out the top book, take a seat and hold his hand. "Key, I'm going to read to you about a guy who was a great showman in baseball. His name is Bill Veeck. His name is spelled 'V-E-E-C-K.' The book is called *Veeck: As in Wreck.*"

"Unnnn."

"Page one…"

I look over at Debbie. She nods, walks over from her corner, and hands me a $10 bill. "You have the directions, right? Then I'll see you later. You'll be fine," she whispers.

Key squeezes my hand.

He knows I'm here.

Chapter Thirteen

When I leave the hospital, I'm focused on making my way home. Debbie said it would be easy; I'm not convinced.

I walk to Charles Street Station, then up the stairs to the booth. I hand the $10 to the guy inside.

"How many tokens?" he asks.

"How many do I need to get to Quincy?"

"Two. One you put in now, the other you need on your way out at Quincy Station."

"Okay, then, two."

He gives me two, gold, MBTA-inscribed tokens, and my change. I pop one into the machine and go downstairs to wait for the train. I examine the gold token and finger it through and through, almost as if I were feeling the leather on a baseball, back in the old days.

Debbie said if I could read, I could find my way home. On the platform, I have to make sure I'm headed to Park Street. *I can do this. Really. I can.*

Train's coming in the direction I need.

I haven't been on one of these for so long, I decide to stand. I look at the map above the door, and I'm only going one stop anyway.

Hey, wait a minute! Is this a Braintree train? Some of these trains going through Charles go right to Braintree via Quincy! How will I know if I should get off at Park Street?

I hear an announcement over the intercom—but it's static noise, not clear. Sounds like, "This is a Blallalalal tain." Sounds like the word starts with a "b," but can't tell if it's a Braintree train. I'll get off at Park Street just to make sure and wait for the right train.

God, Debbie, why did you make this so hard? Why didn't you tell me that the train from Charles could be going to Braintree?

Squeal. The sound of train brakes on iron. We pull into Park Street Station, where lots of people are waiting. I get off, turn around, and look to see if I've just gotten off a Braintree train.

There it goes. A Braintree train. Without me on it.

I'll just wait for the next one. I'm not in a hurry.

A train comes roaring down the line. This one says Quincy. Nope. Have to wait for Braintree. Got this. Debbie might have been right.

A boatload of people get off—big crowds head up the stairs to trolleys to who knows where. I stand like a deer in headlights, waiting for my Braintree train.

"Hey! You! What're you starin' at?"

Some guy is yelling at me.

"Me?"

"Yeah! YOU!"

"Nothin.' Waitin' for a train."

"Yeah? You better stop starin' at me."

I wasn't even looking in your direction, pal. I'm minding my own business, waiting for the train. Don't want any trouble.

"Hey, don't I know you from somewhere?" he asks.

"Don't think so."

"Yeah. Yeah, I do. Can't place you, though."

"Look, buddy, I'm minding my own business. So just go your own way, okay?"

"Or what? What'cha gonna do if I don't?"

"Nothin.' Just waitin' for a train. Like I said."

A bunch of people are looking at us now. The guy is small—up-to-my-mouth small, but he's got a big mouth and talks tough.

"Nobody pushes us guys from Southie around. Don't you forget it. Capeesh?"

I must have rolled my eyes back because he came right at me.

"I said, 'Capeesh!' You know what that means?"

"Yeah, I know what it means. It means you should bug off and leave me alone."

He raises a fist at my face and his tongue rolls up in his mouth as if he plans to hit me. "Tough guy, huh? I don't like your kind," he says.

"Hey, Joey, leave him alone. What'd he do to you, anyway?"

"He was starin' at me, Lenny. Don't like that."

"So, you're gonna pick a fight because you thought he was starin' at you?"

"Yeah."

"Let's go," his friend says, grabbing him by the arm. They climb the stairs, bickering the whole time.

"What was *that* all about?" a middle-aged woman next to me asks.

"Darned if I know, ma'am. I was just standing here, waitin' for the train."

"Some of these guys who hang out down here…Well, you just never know. Some of them are looking for money, some looking for trouble. Most of the time, when you mind your own business, like you were doing…you're okay, though," she says.

Capeesh. Russ, our catcher in Jamestown, used to say that to us when he wanted to make sure we knew what he had in mind when he was calling games. Yet another baseball memory comes to haunt me today, right out of the blue. Out of the mouth of a thug who was trying to cause trouble. Capeesh. Yes, I understand.

Chapter Fourteen

"Lenny, I tell you, that was the guy on the beach the night Paulie died."

"Come on, Joey, how would you know? You were pretty drunk that night."

"No, I wasn't *that* drunk, Lenny, not at the time Paulie drowned. I know that was the guy. I got close enough to his eyes. I have nightmares about that face…those eyes. He's the guy who went to prison for us. We pushed Paulie in the water, and he never came up."

"But him and Paulie had a fight and Paulie fell in."

"But Paulie went after *you* when that guy passed out and fell on the beach, and I grabbed him off you, and we pushed him back into the water, and he never came back up. We killed him, Lenny…and that guy, he went to prison for us."

"Come on, Joey. Of all the people in Boston, how could you know it was *him*? Isn't the real guy still locked up?"

"I dunno. How can we find out?"

"No clue. You got any connections at that prison?"

"No! I don't want to get any, neither! If I tried to get in touch with anyone out there, they might get suspicious."

"Maybe it was in the newspaper. You get the newspaper?"

"You gotta be kidding. I wouldn't even *read* a newspaper if someone gave it to me."

"Maybe you could ask your ma."

"Yeah, maybe. My ma reads *The Herald*."

"So, let's ask her. Tomorrow. Maybe she'll know."

"Yeah. Lenny, I *know* it was *him*. I just know it."

Chapter Fifteen

I make it to Quincy Station and wait for a Hingham-bound bus. I feel as if I've climbed a mountain—a small one, but a mountain, nevertheless. It's a big accomplishment, especially just three days after getting out of prison.

To be honest, I didn't think I could do it. I thought I'd get lost and end up somewhere in Framingham or near the airport or something.

Here in Quincy, I smell Wollaston Beach a couple of miles away. Such a distinctive aroma, that Atlantic Ocean. For those of us born and raised on New England's East Coast, it feels like home, surrounded by seagulls and clamdiggers, high tide and low tide, northeast blowing wind off piles of barnacle-encrusted rocks. I take a deep breath, absorbing the complete sensation in my lungs and throughout my body.

Home. It smells like home. Freedom. The perfume of freedom. From the tip of my toes to the top of my brain. Breathe in. Breathe out. Open your mouth. Close your eyes. Bask in it. Don't let it go.

With my hands in my pockets, I realize I'm rocking back and forth, almost like pacing, standing still, making small circles with my upper body while keeping my feet solid on the ground. I feel a strange sense of euphoria I can't explain.

I'm not in a prison cell anymore. I'm free from the jailer's keys. My mother still loves me. My best friend is in a hospital, although I'm not convinced he'll be safe when they send him back. I have hope for him. I can visit him because I can navigate public transportation again. Maybe I'll find a way to spread my wings... again.

I reach into my shirt pocket where Debbie's written instructions show me how to get home, and there I find the dog-eared note from Mr. Yawkey, reminding me of his promise to find me a job at Fenway Park when I get out.

This is my "get-out-of-jail" card, my key to earning some money, and I need to get in touch with him. How could I have forgotten this? I know. It's not as if I haven't had other things on my mind.

Chapter Sixteen

As I get off the Hingham bus, right past St. Jerome's Church, I smell another beach.

This time it's Wessagusset, the place where that two-bit hood, Paulie Donovan drowned after I fought him over a beer—a stupid *beer*—and then got blamed for his death.

I can't bring myself to even drift over in that direction, toward *that* beach.

Debbie says there's the "new" beach and the "old" beach now. What they call the old beach is where the Donovan incident took place. People don't go there to swim anymore, Debbie says, because the old bath house is dilapidated, falling apart, and the town decided to just let it go. They removed the old docks, where we learned to swim, and now everyone goes to the "new" beach, where the town invested money, brought in tons of sand, installed a new seawall, and added a boat launch.

I'm not sure I can even handle going to a beach that bears the name Wessagusset, whether it's the old or the new Wessagusset. As far as I'm concerned, they're connected, thanks to the Atlantic Ocean.

And the contamination of Paulie Donovan's death. In *that* water, *that* section of the ocean. No matter who caused it. Even if he caused it himself. I don't care right now. All I know is, Paulie Donovan died in the water, they charged me for it, I went to prison, and my life floated right out to sea with his spirit and the changing tide. All those years, working to become the best I could be on the baseball diamond, gone, under the waves, washed out like a piece of driftwood with the tide, never to return. And it all happened at the beach where I'd learned to swim when I was seven years old.

I begin walking up the street toward my parents' house. When the scents of the sea begin to fill my lungs, my legs buckle under me. *Have to stop. Can't walk. Close my eyes. Have to get this out of my brain. Have to get home. Lightheaded. Can't think. Can't focus.*

The next thing I know, I'm on the ground. Three people—two old ladies and a kid about eight years old—are staring down at me.

"Sonny, are you okay? Mildred, he doesn't look too okay to me," one of the ladies says to her friend.

I try to form words, but they won't come out of my mouth.

"Nana, what do you think happened to him?" the young boy asks.

"Tommy, I don't know. Maybe you should go see if there's a police officer at the donut shop and have them call an ambulance."

"Great idea," Tommy says, as he runs off toward Mister Donut.

Police officer? No! I'm on parole! I haven't seen my parole officer yet! Please, don't get a police officer!

But the words won't come out of my mouth.

"Mildred, does this boy look familiar to you? He does to me, but I can't place him. You got any ideas?"

"He does look familiar, Sally, but I can't place him, either. Maybe I've seen his picture in a newspaper. No...Yes...Maybe?"

"We'll just stay here until Tommy comes back. Maybe he'll find a police officer who can help us."

"Sonny, can you hear me?"

I manage to nod my head. My right hand, though, really hurts. My pitching hand. Maybe I fell on it. Can't move my fingers. Maybe I broke it. *Focus, Jim, focus, dammit!*

Tommy returns. "Nana, the guy at the donut shop called an ambulance. He said they'd be here soon. And Nana, he asked me if we thought the guy was—er—drunk."

She leans down to smell my breath. "No, I can't smell anything like liquor, but let's see what they say."

Sirens. Flashing red lights as the ambulance wheels around the corner. Back doors open and two people jump out, a man and a woman. Immediately they spring into action.

"Can you tell us your name?" the man leans down to me on the ground and asks.

Still can't get words to come out of my mouth.

"He seems alert, but he's not talking. Let's see...he has a couple of pieces of paper in his shirt pocket." He reaches into my shirt pocket and pulls out the note from Tom Yawkey, and instructions on how to get home from Debbie.

The woman leans right down on top of me. "Can you hear me?"

I'm able to muster a slight whisper. "Yes."

"Okay. What's your name? Can you even tell me your first name?"

"Jim," I say, inaudibly.

"Jim," she repeats to her colleague. "He says his name is Jim."

"That's a start," the guy replies. "This letter he has in his pocket is from Tom Yawkey of the Red Sox. It's addressed to James Bailey at Walpole State Prison."

"Walpole? For real?"

"That's what it says."

Mildred, Sally, and Tommy are still standing around. A few others have since arrived.

"Any of you know of a family named Bailey in this neighborhood?"

"Up that street," someone points. "She's a widow. She has a son in prison. He used to play baseball for the high school."

"What color's the house?"

"Gray, with black trim…It's on the left side of the street."

"Okay. Guess that's where we're going."

They bring over a collapsible stretcher, push it down to ground level, then they boost me on top.

"Let's go, Jim Bailey. We're going to try to find where you live, then we're taking you to the hospital to get checked out."

"He's in no real distress, I don't think," the guy says. "Blood pressure, pulse, all seem normal. I'm thinking maybe his right wrist might be broken, though. Gotta get an X-ray on that."

Broken? He thinks it's broken? That's funny, I think it's broken, too. But I'm not laughing.

They put the stretcher in the back of the ambulance, slam the back door shut, and drive toward the street where I'd been walking when I passed out.

"Jim…Jim Bailey? Is that your name? I don't expect an answer, but that's who we think you are. That's what it says on that letter in your pocket. We're going to find out and then take you to the hospital."

Oh, great. They found the letter from Yawkey in my pocket. I hope they didn't lose it. Now going to the hospital. I'm on parole. No health insurance. What am I going to tell them? 'Oh, hi, I'm a jailbird and I just got out of a maximum-security prison. I have no job, no money, and I think I broke my wrist. My pitching wrist. Yeah. I was a pitcher. Minor-league baseball. Only I got sent to prison. Now I don't think I can throw a ball, even if my wrist wasn't broken. Will you take pity on me and tell me if it is broken? And then will you do something about it so I'm not useless?'

All happening too fast. Can't think. Try to get words out of my mouth, but a big lump on my head gets in the way… and besides, my lips aren't moving the way I command them to.

"Yeah, my name's Jim Bailey. Where… where are we going?"

Finally.

"Oh, he DOES speak!" one of the EMTs says. "Bailey, you got any ID? Driver's license, anything like that?"

"No...I..."

"Okay. You live up this street?"

I try to lean up on the stretcher to look out the window—only there aren't any windows in this thing.

"What street are we on?"

"Oh, never mind. We better go straight to the hospital. South Shore. We already called them and told them we're coming."

I lay my head flat again on the stretcher. "Whatever you say, man, whatever you say."

God, this thing hurts. My head, too. Feels like I got a rock on top of my forehead. You clumsy idiot! What did you do? Trip on the sidewalk? Catch your foot on a crack? Slip on a pile of leaves? Walk on dog poop? Why did I fall? Why did I get dizzy just then?

The ambulance screeches to a halt. The EMT flings the door open, and his partner comes to the back to help get me, the big magilla, out. They wheel me in, stopping at the ER desk.

"We got a guy here—looks like he's in his mid-twenties, I'd guess, Caucasian male, fell on his right wrist, looks like it may be broken. Looks like he passed out. We can't be sure. He hit his head when he went down, too. He's not too communicative, so he may have a concussion. He needs to be checked out. Can you get him in triage, Lynn?"

"You picked a good time to bring him in, Doug. Take him to three. We're not too busy."

They push me down a hallway into a room, pull back some curtains, followed by a nurse, who tries to ask me some questions. She takes my blood pressure, pulse, sticks a thermometer into my mouth. "Uh-huh, uh-huh," she repeats, over and over again, reaching for a clipboard and making notes.

A doctor pokes his head in. "I'm Dr. Schmidt, and I'm ordering some X-rays. When we get the results, I'll be back in, Mr. Bailey. I've got to tend to another case down the hall. Okay?"

What do you want me to say? 'No, it's not okay with me, Dr. Schmidt. I want you at my beck and call.' Of course, it's okay. You're going to do it, anyway. I have no say in this matter.

"Sure. I guess."

"Okay, good." He glances over at the nurse and says, "Order an X-ray of his right wrist and neck, and later we'll see if we need a CT scan of his head to rule out a concussion. But for now, I want to see if he's got a broken wrist. That's the first step."

I watch him fly out of the room, closing the curtains behind him, with his long, white lab coat open, floating as if it were a superhero cape, all in one motion, as he rushes away.

"That's the way it goes here in the ER," the nurse says. "Never a dull moment, never a minute to breathe."

She finishes gathering information, calls the X-ray Department, then informs me we're going for a ride. "I'll get you a chariot," she says, "disguised as a wheelchair. In other words, I'll be your driver to your next destination. My name's Lynn."

She leaves, returning shortly with a huge wheelchair, probably made for someone who weighs 400 pounds. She notices I'm surveying the situation. "It's all I could find. It'll work," she says.

She brings it to the side of the stretcher and guides me, carefully, into the seat. First, she has me swing my legs over the side of the bed, then asks if I can stand up. "I think so. I'll try." She brings the chair behind me, helps me up so I can stand, wobbling, then plunks me down into the vinyl seat that could hold two other passengers along with me.

"Okay, you did it. I'm going to strap you in, though, because this seat is so big."

She pushes the wheelchair down the hallways, and we move fast, making me even dizzier than I was before I got into the thing. Hospital corridors flash by so quickly that I feel like I'm inside a kaleidoscope. Everything is swirling. Name plates on offices. Vending machines. The darkened gift shop. Signs directing people where to go. A bank of elevators.

We arrive at the X-ray Department, the only one here. She knocks on the door.

"Eileen? Eileen, you there?" She glances over at me, even in my dizzy state, expecting me to understand what she's saying. "She may be on break right now. We never know."

I make a feeble attempt at a smile in return. I'm still woozy—roller-coaster-style—so all I can muster is a crooked, shaky smile.

"Stay put."

Does she think I'm going to leap up and go running down the hallways? Train for the Boston Marathon next year?

"I-I-I'm...not...going...any...where."

"Probably not, but just to be sure, I gotta tell you to stay put."

She dashes out, nearly colliding with another woman who's coming around the corner.

"Lynn!"

"Eileen!"

"Well, that was a close call! We might've needed X-rays ourselves if you hadn't moved at the last minute."

"No, if *you* hadn't moved..."

They burst into laughter; catastrophe averted. I'm still waiting.

"Listen, Eileen, this guy needs X-rays of his wrist and neck. We may need to send him for a CT scan later to rule out a concussion, but we need the right wrist and neck now. He seems like a nice guy, but he's still a little confused."

"Okay…"

Eileen puts her hand to the side of her mouth and whispers, "Lynn…is he drunk or anything? High?"

"I don't think so." Lynn muffles her voice as well.

They think I can't hear them. I broke my wrist, not my ears. I want to jump out of the wheelchair and scream, "NO, I AM NOT DRUNK OR HIGH!" But I can't move much. I'm afraid if I try to undo this seat belt and then make some feeble attempt to stand up, I'll fall flat on my face again, with this oversized wheelchair on top of me, and break the other wrist.

Both women approach the gigantic wheelchair that's swallowing my sore backside.

"Jim, this is Eileen."

Yeah, I figured that out.

"Jim, I'll be doing a couple of X-rays. It may be painful, but I have to get some pictures so the doctor can determine the best course of treatment for you. Okay?"

Yeah, so let's do it.

"Okay."

"I'll leave him in your capable hands, Eileen. Gotta get back to the ER. It wasn't busy when I left, but you know that can turn on a dime."

"Boy, do I know. Hope you have a slow night."

I look up as well as I'm able. "Thanks, Lynn. I hope I don't see you again."

"Wise guy, huh?"

"No, just don't like emergencies. Or emergency rooms."

"I don't like them much myself—unless I'm the one providing the care."

"Well, I'd feel better if it was you providing the care, Lynn," Eileen says. "She's the best nurse in the entire hospital."

"You probably say that to everyone who brings you a patient."

"Nope. I've got high standards. Now get outta here. Go back to your ER. I've got work to do."

Lynn smiles and throws a wave goodbye as she dashes out the door.

"Let's get down to business, Mr. Bailey," she says, lifting my working wrist to read the wristband.

"Jim. Call me Jim."

"Okay…Jim. Let's do the wrist first. We'll get that out of the way."

I'm beginning to get my bearings back, looking around the room. Dark. Stark. Cold. Big X-ray machine looming over the gray table, looking like the head of a Tyrannosaurus Rex, or a big giraffe, waiting to bite the head off an unsuspecting caveman.

Eileen runs around the room, gathering pieces of flat metal, lining them up under the T. rex head. She moves quickly and efficiently as if she could do this in her sleep, organizing everything she needs to take X-rays. I notice a small window behind the T. rex head, and she goes in and out of that, wielding a pen, making notes on the desk under the window. She returns to the room and places a flat metal plate on the table, under T. rex. I hear plates clicking as she puts a plate under the table where she has positioned my wrist.

"Okay, Mr. Jim, I need you to keep your right hand on this plate, as flat as you're able to, without too much pain. Is that something you can do without too much trouble?"

"I'll try."

Focus, Bailey, focus. Forget the pain. It won't last long.

I put my hand flat on the numbing, steel plate. The pain takes my breath away for a second, and I feel a muted wheezing sound coming out of my throat. Eileen frowns. "I don't mean to hurt you. I just have to…"

"Don't worry. I can take it." I close my eyes. She pulls the T. rex over the hand and places it over the top.

"Spread your fingers, if you can, and hold it. It won't be long."

She runs into the room behind the window, closing the door behind her. "Here we go."

Buzz. Buzz. Buzz.

She comes flying out. "Okay, that angle's done."

She repeats this procedure several times so that she gets the angles she needs on the wrist. Then, she gets busy on the neck. Plates in and out, Eileen in and out of the room, buzz, buzz, buzz, and then she says, "I have to take the plates to be developed."

"Developed?"

"Yes, these plates turn into X-ray film. Then the radiologist reads them to determine what's on them."

"You mean you don't know what they say? Someone else has to do it?"

"Yes. That's how it works."

She leaves for what seems like an hour. I look around the room, counting the square tiles on the ceiling, the eyelets on the hanging curtains, then the dots on the linoleum floor.

Eileen knocks softly on the door, letting in light when she reappears. She sits down next to me.

"So...how did all this happen to you? You weren't drinking, you weren't doing drugs, do you think you had a seizure?"

"No...it's kind of a long story. It would take me hours to explain the whole thing, and I'm not sure I'm even ready to talk about it. Yet."

"Oh...well, I don't want to pry. I'm just trying to figure out how a big, strapping, healthy-looking, young guy like you would be in this position. Mostly when someone like you comes in like this, it's a car accident or drinking or drugs or a seizure, something like that. That's all."

I'm watching her speak. She's beautiful. Maybe not in a classical sense, but a wholesome, "girl-next-door" type. Not like my sister, Debbie, who carries herself like Queen Cleopatra, like a woman who should be running for president, or at least senator. No. This Eileen wears no make-up, has a bunch of freckles that scream of her Irish heritage, twinges of auburn in her chin-length, brown hair, and twinkling, blue-green eyes. She's confident in her job, almost prancing around the room instead of walking, undaunted by the darkness T. rex requires to take a clean X-ray. I think she likes people, too.

I don't usually notice women. Maybe it's because I was in that stupid prison for so long. Maybe it's because I had to contend with three of them in my household when I was growing up. I'd expected if I became a baseball player, I'd have women throwing themselves at me, much like what my mother always thought would happen to my dad. I wasn't in baseball long enough for that. Somehow, this woman—this Eileen, whatever her last name is—piques my interest.

I will check her finger for a ring, the next time she comes close enough to me.

A knock on the door.

"Eileen? Are you there?"

I recognize Lynn's voice.

"Are you done with our patient? Schmidt's looking for him."

"Oh, you mean *Dr.* Schmidt?"

"Cut it out, Eileen! Not in front of a patient! Are the X-rays done?"

"Yeah, you take the patient, I'll get the X-rays."

"Deal. Mr. Bailey, are you ready to go?" Lynn asks.

"Jim. Call me Jim."

"Okay, Jim. Let's go."

I feel better as she's wheeling me back to the ER. I'm not as woozy now. My head's not spinning, and I feel like I can speak in sentences. At last.

She takes me to one of the ER rooms. I sit for a few minutes but not enough time to start counting ceiling tiles. Dr. Schmidt makes another grand entrance, with a huge envelope under his arm.

"Mr. Bailey, you do have a hairline fracture in your wrist, but it's not too bad. The good news is that nothing's broken in your neck. I would like you to go for a CT scan of your head to rule out a concussion. I'll give you an order for that and you can arrange that yourself," he says.

He whips one of the films out of the envelope and slaps it onto a light box. Taking a pen from his pocket protector, he explains, "See that small crack, right here?" He runs the pen over the place on the film, as if it were a pointer. "That's your break. It's not too bad. Should heal on its own, although I'd like you to use a brace and a sling for a while. I want you to go to an orthopedic doctor for follow up. You know any orthopedists in your area?"

"No—I—"

"The discharge nurse will give you some names you can check out. She'll give you all the information you need. I'd shake your hand, but...well, you know..."

"Yes, my right wrist is broken."

"And you should follow up with your primary care doctor, too."

"I don't have one of those, either."

"You need to get one soon."

"Okay. Soon."

"Glad we could help you out."

"Thanks."

He breezes out in much the same way he entered. In a hurry. On to the next patient.

Who's going to pay this bill? I mean, Keeshon's bills...

Oh, my God! I forgot all about Keeshon! I need to call Debbie! And my mother doesn't know where I am, either!

What a disaster I am.

Chapter Seventeen

How am I going to get back to North Weymouth from the South Shore Hospital in South Weymouth? Doesn't sound like it's all that far away, but it is. I can't walk, not in the state I'm in. I spent half of the $10 bill Debbie gave me to get home from Mass General. I have no idea how much a cab will cost.

I'm sitting on a bench outside the ER entrance, exploring ways in my head on how to make the two-to-three-mile journey, when Eileen from X-ray emerges.

"Hi, Jim. What's going on? Are you waiting for a ride?"

"No, I have no ride. My mother doesn't drive, and my sister lives in Cambridge. I only have about $5 to my name right now, and I'm trying to figure out how to get back to North Weymouth."

"Well, you can't walk. Not in the shape you're in. I'll give you a ride."

"You don't even know me. Are you sure?"

"Of course, I'm sure. I can't leave you here. If I do, you'll probably end up being here all night and maybe even tomorrow morning when I come back to work."

"Possibility."

"Where do you live in North Weymouth?"

"Down by St. Jerome's."

"Easy. I live in Quincy, so it's not far out of my way. I'll go get my car and come back around to pick you up. Stay here."

"I'm not going anywhere."

She flashes me a smile and hurries across the street to the employee parking lot. I still have a headache, but watching her walk, with a lilt in her step, her almost-auburn hair glowing in the yellow of the hospital lights, makes the pounding temporarily calm down, although it doesn't make it disappear completely.

She pulls up in front of me in what looks like a '72 or '73 VW Beetle. Light blue. Cute. Just like her.

I rise slowly and grab the door handle. It sticks a little because I'm forced to use my left hand to open it.

"That was a really good trick, using your left hand to open the door," she says.

"I thought it was pretty slick myself," I reply.

"Slick? You think you're slick?"

"Most days."

"Uh-huh."

"What? You don't believe me?"

"I really don't know much about you, Jim Bailey. Just that you have a broken wrist, maybe a concussion, that you collapsed on the street, and that you live near St. Jerome's Church. I also know that you need a ride home, and that's about it."

"What do you *want* to know?"

"What do you do for a living? You already know what I do."

"I'm between jobs right now."

"What *did* you do when you *had* a job?"

"I played baseball. Minor league. In Jamestown, New York. A team affiliated with the Montreal Expos. During the offseason, I worked at Mister Donut."

"Baseball? That must have been fun."

"It was. And now I've broken my pitching wrist and who knows what else is wrong with me. I probably won't ever play again."

"Why would you say that?"

"Because I…You need to turn right over here, up this street."

"Okay…by the way, how do you like my little buggy here?"

"I love the color. It goes with your eyes."

"You noticed. That's why I bought it. Marina blue. That's what the VW catalog calls it. It's the first car I ever bought new, and I drove it right out of the Charles Street Garage."

"That's near Mass General Hospital, right?"

"Yep."

"A friend of mine—my best friend—is in there right now. He was beaten up. I was coming from visiting him when I collapsed."

We pull up in front of the house and sit, talking for about ten minutes. Ma peeks out of the front door, then comes running out.

"Jimmy! Jimmy! Thank goodness you're home! I was beginning to worry about you! Oh, who's your little friend? Do you want her to come in? I have supper waiting for you."

By this time, it's almost 10 pm. And Ma still has supper waiting for me.

Using my left hand again, I roll down the window, which was no easy feat from the passenger seat. "No, Ma, this lovely lady was kind enough to give me a ride home from the hospital. I'll be right in."

"Okay, baby. I'll be waiting for you. I'm watching 'Hawaii Five-O' right now."

"My ma loves that show, Eileen," I say, when my ma turns to leave. "It's kind of funny. Sometimes she says, 'Book 'em, Dan-o' when she's walking around the house and doesn't know anyone's listening. I just shake my head when she does that."

"That is funny. Is your dad around?"

"No—he's not. That's another long story."

"I have an apartment in Quincy Point with a couple of other girls. My mother and father live in Hingham, just over the line, not far from here," she says, pointing toward Route 3A.

"That's the high-rent district from here." I laugh.

"Not where they live."

"Eileen, maybe you're not supposed to talk to patients and stuff, but you're wicked easy to talk to. I haven't talked to a girl in a long time. Maybe…when you're not working sometime, we could have lunch or something?"

"I'd like that."

Really? She'd like that? That must mean she doesn't have a boyfriend and isn't married.

"So would I. But first, can you tell me what your last name is? It's gotta be Irish."

"How'd you guess? Was it the hair?"

"That was the first clue. And the freckles."

"Maloney. Eileen Maloney."

She digs into her pocketbook to find a piece of paper and a pen. She scribbles out a phone number and hands it to me.

"Give me a call sometime. Don't lose it. Promise?"

"Promise. And thanks for the ride home."

"No problem. I didn't want to see you still waiting to go home when I got to work in the morning."

Chapter Eighteen

"Who was that nice girl in the little car, Jimmy? And what happened to your hand?"

"Before I tell you, Ma, I need to tell you about the hospital..."

"Oh, Debbie took you to see your friend, right?"

"Well, she did, but..."

"That sister of yours, she's such a help!"

"Yeah, Ma, she is, but she had to leave for work and sent me home on my own. She gave me bus fare and I was almost home when I blacked out and fell, right down the street. I broke my wrist and hit my head. I was taken to South Shore Hospital. The girl who brought me home was the one who took the X-rays. I had no other way to get home. Guess she felt sorry for me."

"That was nice of her, dear, and in her cute, little car."

Is my ma that dense, that she doesn't realize I was hurt? That I'm wearing this sling? That I might have a concussion? I think she's still in Honolulu watching McGarrett and Dan-o and not in the real world.

"Yeah. She lives in Quincy Point, over by the Dairy Queen, with a couple of other girls, she said. Her name's Eileen. She gave me her phone number."

"What? Wait. *You* blacked out? *You* were in the hospital? I thought you went to see your friend who you knew from that place you lived in."

"I did, Ma. But Debbie had to leave me because she had something to do for work. She gave me some money to take the train and bus home, but I blacked out at the end of the street, down by Mister Donut, and got taken to South Shore in an ambulance. I broke my wrist, too. Didn't you hear me when I told you all that a minute ago?"

"Well, I was thinking about that nice girl who drove you home…"

"She was the person who took my X-rays at the South Shore Hospital. The doctor read them and told me my neck wasn't broken but my wrist was. My pitching wrist."

"But you're not playing baseball now, Jimmy. You're just looking for a job, right? And maybe visiting your friend at Mass General? And maybe now calling that nice girl who brought you home in that cute, little car?"

My mind was ready to explode.

She just doesn't get it.

"Ma, I hit my head. I broke my wrist. I'm lucky I know who I am or could give her directions to the house. I have to call the Red Sox about setting up a job interview tomorrow, and I need to get myself together. That's my top priority. I can't be thinking about that nice girl who brought me home in a cute, little car."

The Filly raises one eyebrow at me, the way she did when I was a kid, and she was wary of what I had to say.

"That's nice, dear. Maybe you could call her sometime and go for lunch or something."

I could see the wheels turning in Ma's head.

I've never had a girlfriend, really. Never even thought about it. Was always too busy with baseball when I was in high school, then to Jamestown to play ball, then I found myself in jail for four years. I don't even know how to act with girls, really. That's why it was kinda nice talking to Eileen because it wasn't like that. It was just talking, just being friendly. That's just a nice way to carry on in life.

I know it's no use to change the subject back to what's going on with me.

"Yeah, that's what she said, too. I don't know much about her besides that she works with X-rays."

"Well, you'll get to know her. From what I could see, she's cute."

Cute? Wish you could see her eyes sparkle, Ma! She has that blush on ivory skin with freckles, too. And that reddish-auburn hair. It's a killer. Cute.

"Yeah, she's cute, but the best thing I found was that it was easy to talk to her. You know, Ma, I've never really dated anyone. Not seriously, I mean. I went to the senior prom, but it was only as a friend—not really a date."

"Yes, dear. Your senior prom photo is right on the, right next to your baseball championship picture." She points to the photo on the huge, oak mantel, crowded with pictures and memorabilia depicting Debbie, Donna, and me, and our various milestones.

"I don't know if I'll ever see any of my children married," she sighs. "Debbie's too busy making her connections and becoming important. Changing the world, I guess. I don't know what Donna's doing. She's so far away. She sends me a card here and there, but I don't know if she's dating anyone. Now that you're home, maybe you'll find someone…"

I can't confirm or deny if she sees me roll my eyes.

Chapter Nineteen

Baseball season is almost over. I wonder if Mr. Yawkey will even take my call and still consider giving me a job at Fenway Park. I retrieved the letter from the EMTs and had it back in my pocket. I need to call the Red Sox office.

I go downstairs to find the number in the phone book.

"Boston Red Sox. How may I direct your call?"

"I'd like to be connected to Mr. Yawkey's office, please."

"Mr. Yawkey? You must be mistaken, sir. Mr. Yawkey passed away."

"Passed away? As in died?"

"Yes, sir. Twelve days ago. Can I help you with anything else?"

"It's just that…just that…Mr. Yawkey promised me a job a year ago when I was… Oh, I'm so sorry to hear this."

I didn't know what else to say.

"I will connect you with our personnel office, sir. They might be able to assist you."

"Thank you."

Mr. Yawkey, dead? Of course, I wouldn't have heard about this. The Boston Globe *doesn't really make the rounds in prison until it's old news. How would I ever have known?*

"Red Sox Personnel Office, Dorothy speaking. May I help you?"

"Hello, Dorothy. My name is Jimmy—James—Bailey. I have a letter from Mr. Yawkey, and I just heard he has passed away. I'm very sorry to hear that."

"Yes, we were sorry to lose him." She pauses for what seems to be a long time. "He was very nice to the girls in the office. But what do you mean, a *letter,* Mr. Bailey?"

"Mr. Yawkey sent me a letter promising me a job when I became... available..." I stammer. "I am looking for a job now because I am now...available."

"What sort of position are you looking for, Mr. Bailey?"

"Well, of course, I'd love to be a starting pitcher," I joke, "but I'll take anything you have available where you think I might fit."

She doesn't laugh.

"Would you work in a concession stand?"

"I would."

"Or as a janitor?"

"Yes, ma'am."

"Let me look at my calendar. Could you meet with me next Wednesday at two, sharp?"

"I look forward to it."

"Come to the ticket office on Jersey Street and tell them you need to see Dorothy Malone in personnel. They'll direct you from there. And Mr. Bailey—please bring that letter with you if you don't mind."

"I never leave my house without the letter, Miss Malone. I always keep it in my shirt pocket."

"Terrific. And it's *Ms.* Malone."

"Oops, sorry. See you on Wednesday, *Ms.* Malone."

"Indeed, you will."

I hang the phone back up on the wall and do a little dance.

Maybe I can get my life back together again.

Then I look down at my broken wrist and the sling holding it close to my chest.

You're an idiot, Bailey. You told that woman at the Red Sox that you'd like to be the starting pitcher! What a riot! What a joker you are! Of course, any kid in all New England would love to be the starting pitcher for the Boston Red Sox! At one time, it might even have been you! But now, you're straight out of prison, your best friend is in the hospital after nearly being beaten to death, you're living with your widowed mother, you have no job, and the career you thought you had, is down the tubes.

That may change on Wednesday. If you play your cards right. But that's a big if.

Chapter Twenty

Keeshon opened his eyes in the hospital and moaned slightly as the nurse took his temperature and blood pressure.

"Where am I? Where's Jimmy?"

"You're in Mass General Hospital. Who's Jimmy?"

"Jimmy's my cellmate. He should be here. Who are you?"

"I'm Linda, your nurse for today. This is the hospital, not the prison. I think Jimmy may have been here yesterday, and he's probably the one who left you some books in this paper bag, here on your nightstand."

Sounds like something Jim would do. Seems like I remember his voice talking about a wreck or something about Chicago and the Red Sox.

"Yeah. Yeah, that could be him. Did you talk to him? Will he be back? I gotta see him again soon. Man, this headache is somethin' else. And I'm awful hungry, too, nurse."

"Linda. Please call me Linda."

"If I remember your name, Linda, it'll be a miracle. I can hardly remember my own."

She chuckled. "I wrote yours on the blackboard in front of you. If you forget, just look up."

"It hurts when I look up."

"You're pretty banged up. Those guys who came after you must've had it bad for you."

"Yeah. They did. They been waiting for Jim to be released to come get me."

"This is the Jim who left the books?"

"Yeah. Him and me, we used to read when we was incaucewated. Them guys who beat me up thought Jim and me was some sawt of sissies, but they wouldn't go afta Jim 'cause he was big. I heard they was coming afta me when he left. Didn't take long."

"I don't understand why men do these things."

"Just pure evil, ma'am, and pure meanness. I don't know if I can go back there."

"I don't know how you could, either."

"I hope Jim comes back to see me soon."

"I think that would be good medicine for you."

Chapter Twenty-One

"Eileen, what are you daydreaming about?" her roommate and childhood friend, Trisha, asked.

"I'm just looking out the window, that's all."

"There's more to it than that, kiddo. I've known you since second grade, and I've never seen that look on your face before."

"It's just…it's…"

"Spit it out!"

"I did X-rays on a guy yesterday, then gave him a ride home. He blacked out in the middle of a street, and when he fell, he broke his wrist. He doesn't have a car and has no job. And to top it off, he lives with his mother. How many strikes does that give him?"

"Ten. At least. That's more than three outs."

"The problem is, he was so easy to talk to. And talk about cute…"

"The cute ones are the ones who can sweet-talk us, Eileen. You gotta be careful. Don't tell me you gave him our phone number here."

Eileen looked at her roommate with her blue-green eyes.

"Of course, you did. And now you're hoping he'll call."

"Something like that. Trisha, I can't remember the last time I even spoke to a guy who talked to me on that level. It's always, 'Sir, please hold your knee in place while I take that X-ray,' or 'Yes, Dr. Schmidt, I'll have that for you in ten minutes,' or 'Thank you for bringing me more film—we were running out.' Everything's related to my work. Everything. I feel like I dream in X-rays."

Trisha sat next to her friend, put her arm around her, and pulled her closer. "You know, we've been through a lot together. That last guy you liked took you for a ride. You know, the engineer from MIT? Where did he work?"

"Draper Labs."

"How long did you date him?"

"Six months. He even met my parents. I thought he was *the one,* you know, and then he didn't call me for a few weeks. No warning. Nothing. You remember?"

"You didn't think anything of it, and then we went to that party at Alvin's house, and he showed up with that bimbo, right?"

Eileen's eyes filled with tears. "Yes, and he had the nerve to tell me that he'd always been nice to me. How could you treat someone the way he treated me and consider yourself as being nice to them? That party was the last I saw of him, and good riddance."

"Good riddance is right! If he wasn't interested any longer, he should have had the decency to tell you! And then, to show up at Alvin's party, knowing full well you'd be there—what a jerk!"

Eileen dabbed her eyes with her shirt. "It's so hard to meet anyone in this town, especially since I seem to be married to that hospital, working behind a lead screen. I need to get out more."

Trisha nodded. "Ain't that the truth! But I don't know if going to clubs and bars is the way to go. If only there were some way we could find decent guys without relying on places that focus on booze, smoke, and noise."

"Yeah, if only," Eileen agreed.

"Hey, let's go out and get some dinner. I'm starving. How about pizza?"

"Works for me."

As they grabbed their jackets and headed for the door, Eileen's thoughts focused on a call that she hoped wouldn't come through while she was away from the phone.

I really would like to talk to him again.

Chapter Twenty-Two

It had been a few days since I fell and broke my wrist, so at the ER doctor's suggestion, I find an orthopedic doctor. This was my first appointment with him. Should I tell him I once used this hand to throw baseballs? What good would it do? I'll never pitch again. I'm convinced of it.

I walk into a crowded—if not overcrowded—waiting room, right up to the sliding-glass window, waiting to be acknowledged by the receptionist. Finally, she looks up, opens the window, and asks if she can help me.

"Yes, I'm here for an appointment. I don't know which doctor, though."

"Name?"

"James Bailey."

"Date of birth?"

"March 18, 1954."

She hands me a clipboard with a few forms. "Here's a pen. Take a seat and fill out these forms. We'll call you when the doctor is ready to see you."

"Okay. Thanks."

Almost like a robot, she nods, closes the window, and returns to whatever is on her desk. Not exactly friendly.

It's not easy filling out forms with my right hand wrapped up. I remove it from the sling and begin writing.

Wow, my handwriting looks like it belongs to a doctor! Maybe that means the doctor will be able to read it. I'll try to make it legible, but this is the best I can do.

I look around the room. People of all shapes and sizes, all ages, wearing casts, holding canes, leaning on crutches, all gathered in the same place. Waiting. Waiting. Waiting. Every so often, a staff member opens a door and calls a name, and a hobbling or cast-wielding person makes his or her way to the exam room area. As I wait, I overhear many conversations:

"We've been waiting for hours. What's taking them so long? Did we get here too early for our appointment? Did they forget about us? Should we check in again?"

"Ma, I'm hungry! When can we eat?"

"Why are these magazines so old? Can't this doctor get something newer than three years ago in this waiting room? Sheesh!"

"After we're done here, Nana, will you take me to the toy store? I'm bored!"

Hard not to listen.

One by one, they're called in. I was sure my turn would come.

Waiting, waiting, waiting. Daydreaming about something.

"Bailey? James Bailey?"

I wake up from my brief daydream. "That's me!"

The entire waiting room looks at me. Must've said it way too loud.

"Come with me." She opens the door and ushers me down the hall. "You'll be seeing Dr. O'Connor. He specializes in hands and wrists. Which hand is it, again?"

I almost respond, "My pitching hand," but instead, I manage to say, "The right one."

She opens the door to an exam room and motions for me to sit down. It's obvious who is in charge. She doesn't speak again until she wants to shove a thermometer into my mouth and take my blood pressure. She pumps that little bulb thing until she gets it to work. "Pressure's good. No fever, either. Good." She makes little notes in the folder, then assures me the doctor will be in soon.

More waiting. Waiting. Waiting. Should've brought a book.

I start counting the ceiling tiles, then the floor tiles. They are out of sync. They don't match. Who installed these things, anyway? This exam table should be moved back so that it's centered against the floor tiles. It would make the room look bigger. When you've lived in a place as small as a cell, you think about ways to make places and spaces look larger. Yeah. Make it *look* bigger, even though it *isn't*.

As I continue daydreaming and posturing about the layout, the door opens. Enter Mickey O'Connor, MD, with his flowing, white lab coat. He's about 6'3", 195 lbs., light, brown hair beginning to recede at the top with just a hint of gray. With round, ruddy, Irish-heritage cheeks, he's got what Ma would call "the map of Galway on his face."

I stand as he enters, while he reaches out his hand to shake mine, then quickly pulls it back.

"Oh, sorry, I forgot, it's your right wrist. Don't want to shake that, you know. Saw your X-rays. It is definitely broken. You must have taken a tough fall there, Jim."

"I did. I blacked out and ended up on the ground."

"Blacked out? What do you mean?"

"I think it was because I hadn't eaten for a while. I don't know. Nothing like that has ever happened to me before. I also had a lot on my mind."

"Okay, let's talk. This wrist will most likely heal up nicely, given that you're young and healthy. I'm not worried about that. I am worried about this blacking out thing. What do you do for work?"

"I don't have a job yet. I have an interview tomorrow. At Fenway Park."

"Oh? Doing what?"

"I'm not sure. It's an open interview. I told them I wanted to be the starting pitcher for the Red Sox, but they weren't buying that."

"I'll bet they laughed."

"No, they didn't. But I wasn't exactly kidding. I pitched in the minor leagues a few years back, for an Expos team in upstate New York."

"Really? Was it fun? I played ball until I got to college, and then the academic pressures got to be too much."

"I was drafted right out of high school, but then I got into some trouble after the first season and never went back…"

Why am I telling him this stuff? I just met him. It's not like he cares about what I did or didn't do, or how I got where I was or am.

"Trouble? What kind of trouble?"

Is this guy a therapist or what?

"I was accused of a crime I didn't commit and ended up in prison for a few years. I took a plea deal. They just let me out last week. I'm trying to get back on my feet. I'm living with my ma again. I'd love to get back into playing ball, but I doubt I could get back in shape again."

"How'd you get the interview with the Sox?"

"When I was in prison, Mr. Yawkey wrote me a note that I carry with me, promising me a job at the park when I got out."

"But he died before you got out. Did you know that?"

"Just found out when I called for an appointment. They said to come in and bring the letter."

"Hmmm… sounds like they may give you a job. That would be great for you. So, let's get back to the wrist." He takes my hand and wiggles it around a little. "Any pain?"

"Yes, but not as bad as a couple of days ago."

"Wiggle your fingers for me."

I follow his orders. A little more pain.

"How's that?"

"Better than it was."

"Okay. I'm going to have you wear that sling for a couple of weeks, then I want to see you again after that. We'll do another X-ray. I think you'll be fine. But it's best to check.

"And Jim," he adds, "I've done some work with the Red Sox in the past. If you have problems getting through to them, in getting a job there, let me know. I'll make some calls. I might also have other ideas for jobs for you if that falls through."

"Thanks, Dr. O'Connor. I appreciate that."

Wow! Can't believe he made that offer. He doesn't even know me. And yet, he might be willing to go out on a limb? Mighty generous of him.

Chapter Twenty-Three

Debbie saunters back into the house and flops down on what used to be Dad's comfy chair. She grabs the newspaper, making comments about the headlines. I have no idea what she's talking about, but it must be good, because my sister, ever the expert, makes definite statements about what's happening in world, national, state, and local politics. Take your pick, she knows it.

"Are you staying for dinner, dear? I have pork chops tonight. The Filly asks.

"No, just for a little while," Debbie replies. "I'm meeting a couple of my friends from high school for dinner. A couple who live out of town have come home for a few days. We're going to the Red Coach Grille in Hingham. Can you believe it? Haven't been there in years."

I sit on the couch and tell her about my last visit with Keeshon. "He's in tough shape, Sis. I don't think he should go back to Walpole. I think he's a marked man. When I was there, no one would go after him. I don't know what the deal is. Maybe it's a gang initiation thing or something."

"I'm working on it. Give me another week. We may be able to take care of it," she says.

When big sister says she's 'working on it,' don't ask questions. Just let her 'take care of it.' I've learned that over the years.

"Another thing, Sis. I met a girl…"

"You WHAT? Seriously? That's great, Jimmy! Tell me more." She leans down, putting her elbows on her knees so she doesn't miss any of the details, as if we're back in high school and she doesn't want the cliquey girls to hear.

"This X-ray technician at South Shore Hospital. She gave me a ride home in her VW bug after they treated me for my wrist. I was sitting outside the hospital trying to figure out how I was going to get home, and she offered me a ride. We sat outside the house for a long time, just talking. She lives in Quincy Point with a couple of roommates. Her name's Eileen. She gave me her number."

"And have you called her?"

"No…"

"No? Are you nuts? If a girl gives you her number, don't you know that means she wants you to call? Wait! If you call her, you have no money to take her out on a date, right?"

"Right."

"When's your interview with the Red Sox?"

"Tomorrow."

"You gotta call her, Jimmy! If she gave you her phone number, she's interested." Debbie grabs her pocketbook and pulls out $50.

"Here, take this. Do something nice with this girl. Take her to dinner and a movie."

This is more money than I've seen since I went to prison.

"She'll have to drive, right?"

"Right. She's got a car. A Marina-blue VW bug."

"Marina blue? Aren't we getting all up in the details, now?"

"That's one of the things she told me. She's got near-red hair and blue-green eyes. I told her the color of the car matched her eyes. She told me that's why she bought that color car."

"Oooohhh, you're quite the romantic, aren't you? My baby brother, playing Romeo to a red-haired Juliet from Quincy!" She jumps up and grabs me, hugging me and jumping all over the living room. I feel like a baby kangaroo in its mother's pouch.

"What's going on in here?" The Filly asks. "The whole house is shaking!"

"Nothin,' Ma," I reply. "Debbie's just excited because I told her Eileen gave me her phone number."

"That girl who drove you home from the hospital?" The Filly asks. "And have you called her yet?"

"No."

"What're you waiting for? You know where the phone is! You know how it works! No one's stopping you, right?"

"No."

Debbie and Ma just look at each other like Cheshire cats, grinning and smiling at me, as if I'd just made a major public announcement.

I haven't even gotten to know this woman, and they've already got me walking down the aisle to The Wedding March, at St. Jerome's Church. Wow. Gotta tamp this down. But I do need to call her. Maybe in about an hour. Yeah. That works. As soon as Debbie leaves. Don't want her around when I make the call.

Chapter Twenty-Four

Interview day. Time to head to Fenway Park. It's a project: two buses, a train, and a trolley ride, even more than what it would take to get to Mass General to visit Keeshon.

I decide not to wear the sling into the interview. I bring it with me, folded up. I'll put it back on after the interview. My wrist feels pretty good, so I am confident I can get by without it.

I need to make a good impression. I only have one tie and one white shirt. The Filly ironed it for me, and I have clean, khaki pants. That's what I'm wearing, by default. My goal is to look clean and neat, not to be overanxious or appear too nervous, or to look as if I really need a job. Trouble is, I really need a job. No, I really need *this* job.

I look in the mirror. Hair's reasonably neat. No cowlicks. Don't need a haircut. Face is clean-shaven. Can't have facial hair for a job interview. "Can't look like a hippie," Debbie says. "Wouldn't go over well, especially with the Red Sox."

Tie the tie, pull on the pants, buckle the belt, tie the shoes. Check. Ready to go.

I take the stairs two at a time, getting excited, and maybe even a little anxious.

Calm down. Take a breath.

"Ma, I'm getting ready to go. I have to be there at two."

"Jimmy, did you get anything to eat?"

"No, Ma, I had some coffee, but that's about all I can handle right now. Maybe I'll stop at Dunks when I'm finished with the interview and pick up a regular, but I'm too keyed-up to eat anything heavy."

"Well, dear, how about a piece of toast? That's pretty light."

Sigh. *She's not going to give up.*

"Okay, Ma, toast is good. But no jelly. Just a little butter. I can't risk getting jelly on my shirt, okay?"

"Sure, dear." She presents me with two pieces of toast, lightly buttered. She'd already made them, even before she'd gotten the go-ahead from me that I'd eat them.

She hands me a $20 bill.

"I want to make sure you have enough money to get to your interview and maybe even stop on the way home to see your friend at Mass General," she says. "And then maybe you can get yourself some lunch or dinner before coming home. I know you will get this job. I know Mr. Yawkey won't let you down."

"Ma, Mr. Yawkey is dead. It's his wife who owns the team now."

"Oh, that's right, dear, I forgot. But don't forget your letter from him. Make sure you show that to the people who interview you."

I pat my shirt pocket. "Don't worry, Ma, I never leave home without it."

I put the money in my wallet. Then she hands me two MBTA tokens.

"Take these so you can get on the bus with them," she counsels. "Then you don't have to break the twenty."

I can't resist the urge to lean over and kiss her cheek. "Thanks, Ma, for taking care of me. I can't tell you how much this means to me."

"You are my baby boy," she says. "How could I not take care of you. I love you, baby."

I am speechless. What can I say to *that*?

Chapter Twenty-Five

"Mr. Washington, how are you feeling today?" the nurse asked.

"Uhhhh... still hurts."

"It's going to hurt for a while. I need to check your vitals, and I'll try not to cause you any pain during the process."

Her gentle touch calmed him, although he flinched when she moved his arm into the blood pressure cuff. He knew that she was only doing her job.

"Do you know who did this to you, Mr. Washington? I mean, this is terrible. They should pay for what they did."

"Uhhh... Can't say..."

"Can't? Or won't? Are you afraid they'll come after you and hurt you again?"

"Hurt? No. Kill? Yeah."

"You think they want to kill you?"

"Yeah. That's what they want. To kill me."

"Why?"

"Why? Because they don't like me...didn't like my cellmate... couldn't wait for him to be let go so they could come afta me. It's all about powa. That's what it is."

"Did you do something to make them angry?"

"Nope. Ain't done nothin' to none of them. They just neva liked me. They thought me and my roommate was sissies. You know, fairies."

"I don't know what you mean, Mr. Washington."

"They thought we was men having sex wit' each otha. You know, gay."

"Were you?"

"Hell no! We was just tryin' to do somethin' to pass the time. Jimmy, he taught me to read. Stawted out readin' to me, then he showed me how to read myself. I neva thought I could learn to do that, but when you got time on yo' hands, you know, you do things you ain't neva thought you could."

The nurse sighed. "People are awful quick to judge others, aren't they?"

"'Specially in prison, Miss. Hard to 'splain. But Jimmy, he found some books I liked. His sista, she's a big wig, in gov'ment. She found us some books to read. I ain't neva thought I'd like to read storees, but we didn't have no TV, so we read books. Jimmy got one I really liked. I read it a few times."

"Do you remember the name of that book?"

"Yes, indeed! It's *The Adventchuhs of Tom Sawya*. I love that rascal, Huck Finn. He was always thinkin,' you know, gettin' in and out of trouble. Always. Then Jimmy found a story called *The Celebrated Jumping Frog of Calaveras County*. Jimmy said the same guy who wrote about Huck Finn wrote about the frog."

"That's Mark Twain, I think."

"Yeah, that's his name. Jimmy said he had anotha name, though."

"Samuel Clemens."

"You wicked smawt, Miss. You like to read?"

"I do, but I haven't read those books since I was a schoolgirl, Mr. Washington. That was so many years ago!"

"My teachas neva gave us good books to read when I was in school. Guess that's why I neva learned to read befo' Jimmy came along."

"You were fortunate he was your roommate, then."

"Yeah. I was lucky. He saved my life, really. I lost that luck the day he got out. They came afta me. The gawds didn't help me at all."

"You're safe here, Mr. Washington. We'll make sure of that."

"I hope so, Miss. I just hope so."

Chapter Twenty-Six

Debbie Bailey waited impatiently to see a top aide to the governor. She made the appointment, not without trepidation, but with the realization that she had to do something to bring Keeshon's case to the forefront.

The secretary came to the door and peered out. "Mr. O'Malley will see you now."

Debbie jumped to her feet. "Thank you!"

Dusting herself off, she touched her hair to ensure it was still in place. She'd been waiting for more than forty minutes, so she had no idea what she looked like.

Of course, she looked fine. She always did. Crisp, professional, navy-blue suit. Three-inch, polished heels, punctuated by light-tan, nylon stockings. Flawless make-up. Impeccable, shoulder-length blonde hair—not one strand out of place—not one wisp errantly looking for where it belonged. She walked in cool confidence—straight, tall, focused.

She was on a mission.

John O'Malley, Special Assistant to Governor Michael Dukakis, stood to greet her.

"Debbie! Haven't seen you since we took that class together a couple of years ago. Who was that professor again?"

"Benjamin Hawley—'Haughty Hawley'—we called him."

"Oh, right! That was him. He was one pompous ass, wasn't he?"

"Pompous is an understatement, John."

"So…What brings you here today, Debbie? I know how busy you are, so I know it's not just a social visit."

"You're right, although we *should* have lunch or dinner one of these days."

"What's the deal?"

"Here's the scoop. My brother—"

"The one who played ball for an Expos farm club, right?"

"Yup. The only brother I've got. He just got out of prison—"

"Prison? He's not playing baseball?"

"No. It's kind of a long story, John. He was convicted of a crime we're sure he didn't commit, but he served his time. He's home, living with my mother. He seems okay."

"Doesn't sound like he needs help."

"*He* doesn't. But he had a cellmate whom he became close to while he was in Walpole."

"Walpole? He was in freakin' *Walpole*?"

"Yes. But let me finish, please."

"Okay."

"His cellmate, this small Black guy from Roxbury named Keeshon Washington—my brother taught him to read while they shared a cell. When Jimmy got released, a bunch of guys ganged up on Keeshon and beat him up badly. He's in Mass General now, in tough shape."

"What do you want, Debbie? Lay it on the table."

"Keeshon has about eighteen months left on his sentence. He's petrified to go back to Walpole. Is there any way he can get out early, maybe increase his probation time, or at least get moved to another facility?"

O'Malley paused and folded his hands in front of his face. "This is a new one on me, Deb. I'll have to work on this one. Never had anyone ask me for this before."

"If he's sent back, John, it's like sending a lamb to slaughter. There's something weird about this. Jimmy was his protector when he was in prison, and as soon as Jimmy was gone, Keeshon became a target. He told Jimmy the guards did nothing to protect him. He's a mess, physically and emotionally."

"He's a little guy, you say?"

"Yes, I'd say maybe 5'3"…a hundred, twenty pounds, I'd estimate."

"I'll have to get back to you. You have a business card?"

Reaching into her briefcase, she pulled out a small case. "Of course, I do."

He set it in the corner of his desk blotter. "I'll see what I can do, Debbie. No promises. I have a meeting with the governor later today. I'll find a way to weave it into our conversation."

"Thanks, John. I owe you one."

"Yes. But that's the way things work, isn't it? When you need something here on Beacon Hill, I help you out, and when I need something in your neck of the woods, you go out of your way for me."

"Something like that."

Debbie closed her briefcase, stood up and extended her hand, shaking his across the desk.

"Great to see you, O'Malley. Give my regards to that beautiful wife of yours, will you?"

"Indeed, I will."

As she left the office, she recalled how obsessed John O'Malley had been with her when they were in graduate school, and how he'd almost failed two classes when they had been thrown together to do joint projects. He'd shared with her that all he could think of was her and not the crux of what they were studying, and how dejected he was when he realized she wasn't interested in him. Instead, she was interested in being a power broker. "I'm going to change the world," is what she always said.

Changing the world was what she was doing.

One project at a time.

Today's project was Keeshon Washington.

Chapter Twenty-Seven

I trudge up the stairs at Kenmore Station on my way to Fenway Park. As nervous as I am, I know that I *can* get a job with the Red Sox, if I allow myself to do it. The only thing holding me back is *me*.

I walk over the bridge spanning the Mass Pike, or *the Pike* as we Bostonians call it, thinking about what they'd ask me. More than once, I pat my shirt pocket, making sure I have the letter from Tom Yawkey with me. It has been my lucky charm, something that got me through my prison days. The promise of a job with the Red Sox became something that kept me going during that time.

Jersey Street. On the left. Ticket office.

"May I help you?" a squeaky voice comes from behind the glass.

"Yes, ma'am, I'm supposed to see Ms. Malone in personnel. She said to ask for her here."

"Sure. Just hold on."

I hear muffled talk—can't make out what's being said, except that she's communicating. "She'll be right down, sir."

It's 1:55 pm. I'm not late. Whew.

I look around the room, checking every nook and cranny. Black-and-white, mural-sized photos of Jimmy Foxx, Ted Williams, and a very young Carl Yastrzemski. Portraits of both Mr. and Mrs. Yawkey. A black-and-white, aerial photo of good old Fenway. I can't find a place to sit, so I pace a little, waiting for Dorothy Malone herself—'*Ms.* Dorothy Malone, thank you very much'—to appear.

Fenway Park. Ticket office. Jersey Street. Boston, Massachusetts. My home team. My hometown.

I am daydreaming when I feel a tap on my shoulder.

"Mr. Bailey?"

I jump. "Yes? That's me."

"Dorothy Malone."

I turn around and offer my hand. "Pleased to meet you." Even though I'd planned to bring it with me, I left the sling at home; I wince a little when she touches my hand.

"Thank you. Follow me, please, and we'll go upstairs to my office to chat."

Silence as we walk up a flight of stairs, into a glass-enclosed, small office. "Hold my calls. I'll be busy for a short time," she says to the receptionist.

"Sure, Dorothy."

"Have a seat, Mr. Bailey." She gestures to two chairs opposite her desk. "Pick one."

"Thank you, Ms. Malone."

"Please… Call me Dorothy."

"Only if you'll call me Jimmy."

"Fair enough. You said you had a letter from Mr. Yawkey?"

I reach into my shirt pocket and hand her the well-traveled note, watching her eyes as they scan the late owner's words.

She sighs. "I need an explanation here, Jimmy. Let's start from the beginning. Tell me what happened that you ended up in Walpole State Prison."

I give her the entire story, all the way down to the day the Montreal Expos scout came to my house in Weymouth, sent me to Jamestown, New York, and then to the scene on the beach, where Paulie Donovan lost his life. "I had nothing to do with his death," I assure her, "but my lawyer couldn't find any witnesses, so he suggested I take a plea bargain. That's how I ended up in Walpole. I was so frustrated by the whole process. I always thought a person was innocent until proven guilty. Trouble was, I couldn't prove anything."

"You weren't being sarcastic when you said you wanted to be the starting pitcher for the Red Sox, then."

"No. No, I wasn't. That was always my dream when I was in Little League. But the Expos drafted me and that's where I went. When I was in prison, Bill Lee came to visit me and said there were other pitchers on the Red Sox who were supporting me. I saw him a couple of times. It meant a lot to me."

"I'll bet it did." She smirks a little. "Of course, Bill Lee visited you."

She pauses for what seems like a long time but is probably only about twenty seconds. "The problem is, Jimmy, I'm trying to figure out where to place you. What skills do you have? Did you have any jobs that might relate to what we do here? Do you have any summer employment skills or anything that you might have gotten in high school?"

"No, I was always playing ball, way back to Little League. My dad wouldn't allow me to work. My work was on the ball field."

"No jobs? Nothing?"

"Well, after my first season in the minors, I worked for a short time at Mister Donut, down the street from my house."

"Mister Donut? Did you work the counter?"

"Occasionally. But mostly I unloaded boxes and stocked shelves."

"I can work with that. I can put you into one of our concessions or as one of our ticket-takers. Remember, though, these are part-time jobs because the team's on the road half of the time. And this season's almost over."

"Yeah, I know. I'll figure something out. I'm living with my mother right now while I find a job and put some money aside."

"A wise choice. Do you remember the name of your supervisor from Mister Donut? It would be great to have a reference."

"Yes, his name was Al, and if you have a phone book, I'll look up the number for you."

"That's ok, Jimmy. I'm sure we can find it."

She stands; I follow suit. She reaches out her hand to shake mine. Again. I endure her strong handshake. *Can't wait to get back into the sling. Too much handshaking today.*

"Thanks for coming in, Jimmy. I'll call you in a couple of days. We'll find a spot for you. I just need to speak with my department heads to find out exactly where we can put you."

"Thank you *so much*! I really appreciate it. I can start any time you need me to."

"And Jimmy… I bet you *could* take to the mound here at Fenway. I bet you still can throw a ball and strike out batters."

"Maybe. It's been a long time."

Too long. And now I'm waiting for my wrist—my right hand, my pitching hand—to heal after that fall. Who knows if I can make it if I try to throw a ball from the pitching rubber to home plate without bouncing it? Who knows if I can even find the correct grip, the right feel? Would I fall apart if I were to walk onto any pitching mound, much less the one here at Fenway Park, the hallowed hall of baseball, the place where I dreamed of being a baseball star? Cesar's not here to urge me on. My dad's gone. My best baseball friend, Bud, is off pitching for a major league team. Now, the best I can hope for is a spot selling hot dogs. What would Bill Lee think?

As I take the elevator down toward the ticket office, I imagine Bill Lee when he visited me in prison, how he told me so many of the Red Sox pitchers were supporting me. The elevator doors open, and, as I look up, there he is… Bill Lee.

"Hey, remember me?"

"You look familiar, son."

"Probably look different when I'm not behind a plexiglass protection screen."

"Wait a minute! You're the guy I went to see in prison! How you doin,' man?"

"I'm better now. I'm out."

"I see that. What're you doing here? Trying to get on the pitching staff?"

"No, I'm just trying to get a job here at Fenway. I think my pitching days are done."

"Why do you think that?" he asks.

"Haven't pitched in more than four years. Then, last week I fell and broke my wrist. Pitching hand." I hold up my hand and wave it at him.

"That shouldn't stop you. I haven't pitched for a while, either. Got into a little altercation with the Yankees earlier this season and…well…you know…"

"No, I don't. I've only been out for about a week. I only just heard that Mr. Yawkey died. He sent me a letter while I was in prison, promising me a job here. I just showed it to Ms. Malone in personnel." I reach into my pocket and pull out the tattered note, handing it to Bill.

"Whoa, this is pretty cool, you know? Mr. Yawkey wasn't really a social butterfly. Not to me, anyway. Now, Mrs. Yawkey, she's something else. She's a lovely lady. Anyway, who'd you meet with in personnel, again?"

"Dorothy Malone. Seemed nice enough."

"Oh, *Ms.* Malone, eh? She treat you okay?"

"Yeah. She's looking for a place for me. Even part-time will be good. At least for now."

"Say, you want to go out on the field with me?"

"I… I can't throw a ball with a broken wrist… but I wouldn't mind walking around the field. Sure."

"Okay. I wouldn't mind that, either. Come with me."

As we walk through the players' entrance at Fenway Park, Bill puts his arm around me the same way my friends used to do when we played in Jamestown. He turns to the security guard, who's eyeing me with great suspicion.

"He's okay, Joe. He's with me," Bill winks. The guard tips his hat at us.

I feel myself grinning from ear to ear. My heart beats a mile a minute. Bill jabbers about something or other but I don't hear a word he's saying. All I know is that he is escorting me inside Fenway Park, *the* Fenway Park, into the locker room, up through the dugout, and onto the field.

I am almost paralyzed trying to walk up the dugout steps. The *home* dugout. Where the *Red Sox—my home team, my childhood idols*—had walked since 1912.

Are these the footsteps of Ted Williams? Bobby Doerr? Joe Cronin? Dom DiMaggio? Even Babe Ruth before he went to the Yankees? Such baseball history. The past and the present.

"Hey, kid! You wanna walk the field or what?" Bill snaps at me. "Wake up!"

"I'm sorry, I'm sorry. I was just thinking."

"I think you think too much. Too much thinking in baseball doesn't always lead to a great game. C'mon."

He puts his arm around me again and begins pointing out different things about the ballpark.

"You know," I tell him, "I did pitch here once when I was in high school. It was way different then, though. I was just a young punk, thinking the world was my oyster…that it'd be a walk in the park to make it to the major league."

"We're all young punks, you know, when we're eighteen, nineteen years old," he says. "Sometimes we're young punks when we should be old punks. Sometimes it works in people's favor to be a punk, sometimes it's best to leave punk-hood behind. Sometimes I don't know the difference. Do you?"

"Never learned the difference, not even in prison."

"Keep working on it. You'll know. In the meantime, let's get a ball and a couple of gloves. Even if we do some soft toss, I'll feel a lot better. Stupid Yankees. Ruined my summer."

"Didn't you ruin the season of someone on the Yankees, too?"

"Maybe."

"C'mon, let's go take in the aroma of this place and toss a little, white projectile for a few minutes. It'll do both of us a world of good."

"But I've got a broken wrist."

"Throw with your other hand," he says. "Even if it means you can't hit a target. Hell, I might be throwing with *my* other hand. We'll be two peas in a pod."

Chapter Twenty-Eight

Debbie Bailey didn't feel like answering the phone on her desk when it rang. She was exhausted, and in no mood to deal with anything. Her secretary had left hours ago.

She sighed after the third ring and picked up the receiver. "Deborah Bailey here."

"Debbie? John O'Malley. I have some news for you, some of it good, some not so good. Which do you want first?"

She yawned, knowing he probably heard her. "Okay…let's start with the bad."

"Let me ask you something first. By chance, did you have any kind of encounter with any of the guards at the prison the day you picked your brother up? Were you harassed in any way?"

"What do you mean by 'harassed?' Like what?"

"I mean, did one of them get out of line, or make an inappropriate comment toward you?"

Debbie paused, trying to remember that day. "Come to think of it, I did have to slap one of them when he tried to put his hands on me, and I gave him a piece of my mind, as well. Why?"

"I had a couple of investigators investigate the case of Mr. Washington at the jail. Seems like that guard might have been behind the beating your brother's friend got—he wanted to get back at you. He and his pals were incensed that you embarrassed them in front of other guards and some inmates, so they got a couple of tough guys to work over the

Washington guy. The guards looked the other way when he was getting beaten up."

"They did *what*?"

"I'm still investigating this, but that's what we've learned so far."

"Let me get this straight. Some pig in a guard uniform tried to paw me with his dirty hands, I stop him, so he decides to have someone beat up my brother's friend to the point where the guy's hospitalized, because *he* was embarrassed? Are you serious?"

"That's what my investigator at Walpole is saying. We've already asked that this guy be suspended until our investigation is complete."

"Do you know who the inmates were who did the beating?"

"We might have that information soon…that's what we're working on now."

"I can't believe this, John."

"I hate to be the bearer of this bad news."

"No… thank you for looking into it. But you said there was some good news, as well. What's that?"

"The governor thinks we need to complete this investigation and expand it so that we can put measures in place so nothing like this happens again at Walpole…and…"

"*And?* You mean there's more?"

"Yes. The governor thinks we should get Mr. Washington into an early release program when he's healthy enough, and then work on getting him clemency, once our attorneys can look into what got him into prison in the first place."

Debbie heaved a huge sigh. "That's more than we can ask for, John. Do you need to speak to my brother about any of this? He may have some information that could help this along."

"No, I think if I had any conversations with him, it might tarnish any chances I'd have with the attorneys. It's strictly related to the law and how they'll interpret it."

"My brother felt that Keeshon had less-than-adequate counsel when he was convicted."

"Could be true. I'll let the attorneys work on that. Right now, I'm working with the Corrections Department to find a halfway house placement for Washington. We need to make sure he'll be safe, and that any friends or connections this guard might have won't find him, and try to finish the job, if you know what I mean."

"Like, kill him?"

"Could be. From what I hear, this guard has been involved in stuff like this before, but he picked on the wrong woman when he tried to harass you, I'd say."

"John, never in my wildest dreams did I think standing my ground would lead to violence against anyone."

"You may have started something bigger than you could imagine. Or maybe this guard let the cat out of the bag when he decided to go after your brother's friend to get at you."

"You know I don't put up with crap like that."

"As well you shouldn't, Debbie."

"Isn't this rich? The Baileys of Weymouth try to do the right thing and it backfires on them. Again."

"Well, you did the right thing by bringing the governor into it, even if you didn't realize it at the time. This might even end up being a feather in my cap once this investigation is done."

"Are you still at your office?"

"Are you still at *yours*?" John replies.

"Yes."

"Well, me, too."

"Go home, John. I'm sure you have dinner waiting for you and it's getting cold."

"You, too, Debbie. I'll call you when I know more."

"Okay. And John—thanks for taking on this project. It means a lot to me."

"No thanks are necessary. Glad I could help. Have a good night."

"You, too."

Chapter Twenty-Nine

A*m I dreaming? Did I really just toss a few balls around the infield at Fenway Park with Bill Lee? Or is my mind playing tricks on me?*
My pitching hand is sore, but what would I expect from a hand whose wrist was broken when I blacked out and fell? I didn't throw the ball all that hard, but with a hairline fracture, I guess even soft tosses take their toll.

I don't care; it was worth it.

I leave Fenway Park and head up toward Kenmore Square to catch the trolley home. I think I'll get off at Charles Street Station after I change trains, then scoot in to see Keeshon. I won't stay long, but I think he'll appreciate my making a short appearance.

I'm still flying high as the inbound trolley creaks and swerves its way into Park Street Station, where I'll switch from a trolley to a train, and go to Charles Street. I'm beginning to remember what I need to do to get around this city. Debbie told me that each trolley or train car has a map of each line—all color-coded—near the doors. I can remember that.

Off at Charles Street, down the stairs and heading toward Massachusetts General Hospital, I'm energized by having set foot on a baseball diamond today. Can't wait to tell Keeshon all about it.

Walking into this hospital is like entering a community unto itself, a city within a city. The hustle and bustle of patients and hospital staff getting to where they need to be, plus security and visitors mixing in, make for an exciting, yet confusing gathering of people.

I know exactly where to go and which elevator to use, so I make a beeline for it. Can't wait to tell Key my news.

When I arrive at his room, the guard is gone. I look into the room. Empty bed. Where's Keeshon? Is he dead? What's going on?

"Debbie! Keeshon is *gone*!" I scream into the phone.

"What do you mean, *gone*, Jim?"

"Just what I said, gone! I went to the hospital on my way home from my interview, and he wasn't in his room. The room was empty. No guard. The bed was all made up, white and clean, like no one had ever been in it. I asked the nurse at the desk, and she said she had no information. No information, Debbie! Does that mean he *died*?"

"No. Wait. What? Let me think here, Jim." She pauses at the other end of the phone.

What the hell is going on? How could Keeshon have disappeared?

"Jim, are you home?" she asks.

"Yeah, and I'm panicking, I gotta tell ya."

"Okay. All right. I'm thinking. I'll call John O'Malley. Maybe he knows what's going on."

"Wait...Debbie?"

"Yeah?"

"Someone's at the door. Hold on a minute," I say, looking out the window. "I gotta go, Deb. It's the cops. I'm on parole. I gotta talk to them."

"Wait... what? Jim, do you need to have a lawyer with you?"

"No, they just said they had some news for me. I'll call you back. Okay?"

"Okay. Call me right back. In the meantime, I'm calling O'Malley."

~ ~ ~

Debbie dialed John O'Malley's number as quickly as she could.

"Mr. O'Malley's office. May I help you?"

"Yes, thank you. This is Deborah Bailey. I'd like to speak to Mr. O'Malley, please."

"Ms. Bailey, unfortunately, Mr. O'Malley is quite busy at the moment. May I take a message?"

"Yes. He has my number. Please tell him it's an emergency and I need him to call me as soon as he can."

"May I tell him what this is in regard to?"

"Yes. Tell him it's about Keeshon Washington."

"I will pass the message along, Ms. Bailey."

~ ~ ~

The governor's office was always chaotic, but John O'Malley felt the craziness of the day as soon as he walked through the door.

Phones were ringing off the hook. The secretaries couldn't keep up. A gaggle of reporters had gathered at the governor's door. He couldn't even get near the door of his own office without tripping over them.

He recognized one guy from WBZ radio but didn't want to make eye contact with him. He had no idea what they were scrambling to cover, but it had to be something big. Most times, they didn't congregate in a pack like this unless there was a huge story to cover.

After climbing over a couple of reporters, he made his way into his office and closed the door. Before he could sit down, a voice came across the intercom.

"John? I need you in my office. Now!" It was Valerie, the media relations manager.

"What's going on? This place is nuts."

"Yeah, yeah, it is, but I want to explain this to you in person. I think you may be involved."

"What do you mean? Involved in what?"

"Just get in here. I'll explain."

On a normal day, he would have organized his desk, methodically taken things out of his briefcase, set his coffee near his phone precisely the same way he always did. Today, though, he just threw everything willy-nilly onto the desktop and ran out the door to Valerie's office across the hall.

"Close the door. Fast," she said, pacing the floor. After she was certain the door was completely shut, she spoke.

"Does the name Keeshon Washington mean anything to you?"

"Why?"

"Just answer the question."

"Yes. He was attacked at Walpole by a bunch of inmates and is now at Mass General. He was the cellmate of the brother of one of my former classmates at Harvard. She asked me to bring the case to the governor's attention to see if he could be sent to a different prison when he is released from the hospital."

"Did you know the guards at Walpole had something to do with the beating of this man?"

"I'd heard that rumor, yes."

"Well, I heard you ordered the investigation."

"I didn't order an investigation. The warden did."

"The warden was killed last night, John."

"WHAT?"

"Yes, the state police are in there now. Walpole's on lockdown. The warden's secretary found him beaten to a pulp inside his office this morning. There was a note beside the body that said something to the effect of, 'This is what happens to snitches.'"

O'Malley was speechless. *The warden? Considered a 'snitch'? Had the guards killed him, or did they get inmates to do it for them?*

"For all I know, we may have to call in the FBI," Valerie continued. "Now we have all these reporters here, wondering who in the governor's office ordered an investigation."

"No one here ordered an investigation. As far as I knew, when I talked to the warden—with the governor's permission, I might add—he said it was standard operating procedure to investigate any attack on an inmate that leads to hospitalization, or even broken bones that lead someone to make a trip to the emergency room. The warden was professional about it. He seemed like a pretty cool guy. I'm so sorry this has happened to him."

"So now I have to handle this. We need to meet with the governor. Stat! Get ready," she said, opening the door wide to flashing camera lights.

"Valerie! Valerie! When will you give us a statement?" someone called out as they made their way through the throng of reporters.

"In due time," she replied. "We have no comment yet."

"No comment? A man is dead, for heaven's sake!" another reporter exclaimed.

Valerie threw an icy stare in his direction. "Don't go there with me, Dennis. You know better than that."

Silence overtook the room as they walked to the door marked "The Honorable Michael S. Dukakis." His secretary nodded. "He's expecting you."

Governor Dukakis sat with his back to the duo entering the room, staring at the wall behind his desk. His hands were folded in a semi-prayer position, fingertip to fingertip. When he realized they were in the room, he slowly swiveled his chair around to face them.

"John. Valerie...have a seat," he said, keeping his hands in the same position as he exhaled deeply.

"We have a big problem here. The public seems to think we had a hand in the death of a very experienced, well-loved employee of the Commonwealth. It also appears that our name is being dragged through the mud in connection with this tragedy. Seems we had a minor connection with a minor player in this catastrophe. Start from the beginning, John. Tell me the story and how we got dragged into it."

John reminded the governor about their earlier discussion but decided to go into even more detail.

He began with Debbie approaching him about the case and how she'd seen the shape Keeshon Washington was in at Mass General after having visited him with her brother, who'd been Keeshon's cellmate at Walpole. Initial evidence indicated the guards were upset by Debbie, who had put one of the guards in his place when the guard made inappropriate, sexual overtures toward her as she was leaving with her brother. To get back at the Bailey family, the guards allegedly convinced a bunch of inmates to attack Mr. Washington, and they looked the other way when the attack was underway.

"Why would they want to get back at the whole family?" Valerie asked.

"Debbie's brother had apparently been Keeshon's protector while they were in prison together," O'Malley explained. "During the time they shared a cell, Debbie's brother, Jim, also taught Keeshon how to read and helped him pass his GED exam. Keeshon's a little guy and he's Black. Debbie's brother's big and he's White. Keeshon was anxious, according to Debbie, that something would happen to him when Jim was released, and sure enough, it did."

"Wait a minute," the governor interjected, "Jim…Jimmy Bailey? Wasn't he a baseball player?"

"Yes, sir. Debbie told me he went to prison for a crime he didn't commit. At least, there wasn't proof that he did or didn't commit the crime, so he took a plea and served about four years in Walpole."

"I remember this case. A few of the guys from the Red Sox, including Bill Lee and Bill Monbouquette, filled me in. There wasn't anything I could do about it. I had too many other priorities at the time."

"Keeshon is at Mass General under guard, sir."

"Not anymore," Valerie noted. "We moved him early this morning to Deaconess, after the warden's murder. We also replaced the guards from the Department of Corrections with state police. We didn't want to take any chances with anyone else getting hurt."

"You think they'd come after Keeshon and try to kill him, too?" O'Malley asked.

"You never know," Valerie said. "That was the suggestion of the state police chief. He's been squirreled away at Deaconness. It's best to keep him out of the public eye while the investigation continues."

The governor buzzed the intercom. "Get me the chief of the state police on the phone. And tell him I want his public information officer on the call, too."

"Yes, sir."

"Now, John, this Keeshon is the one you want me to consider for a pardon, correct?"

"Yes, sir. My friend Debbie said her brother was worried that it would not be safe for him to return to Walpole."

"It probably won't be safe for him to go back to any prison in the Commonwealth, I'd say," the governor mused.

"You're probably right, sir."

"This is a multi-level problem. Valerie, here's what we need to include in the statement. First, we grieve for the loss of a valuable, dedicated employee, whose service to the Commonwealth will be recognized by flags being at half-staff for the rest of the month. Our hearts go out to his family. Second, we promise his family and friends that we will conduct a thorough investigation into this heinous crime. We will not tolerate this within our ranks, whether it was perpetrated by inmates or others within the prison system.

"Third, we will release details about this investigation as they become available, and we plan to press charges against those responsible for this terrible crime. Finally, we do not wish to discuss any background information about what may have prompted this horrific murder until we have all the facts.

"Does this sound like a good place to start? I'd rather Mr. Washington's name not come out at this time. If a reporter mentions his name, let's respond that we are investigating many different circumstances at Walpole State Prison and leave it at that."

"Yes, sir," Valerie replied.

"And you, John, I want you to know that I don't think for one minute any of this is your fault. There's something terribly wrong happening out there at Walpole, and this tragedy may help us get to the bottom of it. Understood?"

"Yes, sir, and thank you."

The intercom buzzed again.

"I have the chief of the state police and his PIO on the line for you, sir."

"Thank you."

The governor picked up the phone and gave a synopsis of what had just been discussed in his office. He nodded several times as O'Malley and Valerie listened in. When the call ended, he spoke to his aides, also in the room. "The chief is fine with what we're doing, and he's got a couple of good forensics out at Walpole. He's convinced we'll make progress soon. Valerie—you get to go out and take care of the sharks in the waiting room."

"Yes, sir," she replied, standing to leave.

When John and Valerie opened the door, they were greeted by a crowd of reporters waving notebooks and microphones at them, talking over each other, so that no one could understand what each other was saying.

"CALM DOWN!" Valerie shouted. "I'll have a statement for you in about twenty minutes!"

The roar became a dull thud, sounding more like a bunch of squirrels or birds chomping down new-found seeds in a feeder.

Chapter Thirty

Walpole Warden Bludgeoned to Death in Office:
Conspiracy or Isolated Incident?
That's the headline in *The Boston Globe* this morning. *The Record* is even more graphic:

Blunt Force Trauma:

Warden Pays Ultimate Price

Who knows what this afternoon's *Boston Herald* will say?

I was in shock when I read the story. The warden was always fair to us inmates. He wasn't nasty or anything. He made sure I got to go to Dad's funeral. He was polite to Debbie. He made arrangements for lots of things. His secretary must be devastated. Newspaper says she found him. Dead.

Yesterday, two members of the Weymouth Police came to the house and told Ma and me that Keeshon had to be moved from Mass General to another hospital because the state police were concerned about his safety. They said the warden had been killed, and they didn't know if it was inmates or employees who killed him. They also said that the state police were investigating, and the FBI would also be brought in, depending on what the troopers found.

They asked me if I knew of anyone who might have wanted to hurt Keeshon or me when we were cellmates in the prison, or if I knew anyone, especially inmates, who had vendettas against the warden.

"I really don't know," I told them. "Keeshon and me, we kept to ourselves. We just liked to read books because he was trying to work on his GED before he left prison. We tried to stay out of general as much as possible. Most guys thought we had a 'thing,' you know, but we didn't."

"A *thing?*" one of the officers asked. "What do you mean by that?"

"You know, a 'thing.' I don't want to say it in front of my ma, you know. It's like when two guys, you know, do things that normally only a man and woman would do together." I could feel my face getting hotter and redder.

"Come on, Larry, you didn't know *that?*" the other one chided. "You gonna embarrass this guy in front of his ma?"

"Geez! I'm dumb as a box of rocks some days, Donnie. Okay. Okay. So, what about the warden? Did you hear any rumors about him?"

"Don't think so. Some of the guards thought he was too soft on the inmates, though."

"The guards? Really?" one of the officers asked, writing something on his note pad.

"We have to check into everything."

"You guys know I'm on parole, right?"

"Yeah."

"This isn't going to interfere with my parole in any way, is it?"

"No, no, we just need to tell your parole officer that we spoke to you. You're not involved in this. We're just trying to get some info. That's it."

What a relief that is. I just want to follow the rules. Don't want to get in any trouble. Trying to keep my nose clean. Going to start working for the Red Sox. Like Mr. Yawkey promised.

"Hey, I just thought of something," I said. "The day I was leaving, one of the guards got a little fresh with my sister. She shot him down. Embarrassed the hell out of him in front of the other guards. Maybe that had something to do with it."

"I doubt it," one of the officers said. "But it's worth making a note of, I guess. You never know what will be made of some small comment. We'll pass it on."

One of the officers pulled out a small piece of paper and scribbled a phone number on it. "Here's how to reach us," he said, "in case you think of anything else—ya know, if something comes to mind after we leave. Me personally, I always seem to remember things early in the morning when I'm in the shower."

"If I think of anything, officers, I will call you. My sister has connections in the governor's office. I'll let her know we spoke, if that's okay with you."

"That's fine. See ya, Bailey. Thanks for taking time to talk to us."

As the cruiser drove away, I felt a sense of relief, yet simultaneous, unexplainable queasiness.

Chapter Thirty-One

The phone was in its cradle. Jimmy needed the courage to get up to use it.

Call her. What are you waiting for? She's most likely home from work now. Call her. CALL HER, DAMMIT!

He reached into his wallet for the crumpled piece of paper with a number on it, staring at the clear handwriting.

Debbie's right—a girl doesn't give out her phone number unless she wants the guy to use it. But what if she's not home? What if her roommate answers?

Dialing.

"Hello," came a woman's voice on the other end.

"Hi, may I speak to Eileen?"

"Sure. Hold on a sec."

Easier than I thought. She didn't even ask who was calling.

Clunk, clunk, clunk. Jimmy could hear footsteps in the background.

"Hello? This is Eileen."

"Hi, Eileen. This is Jim. Jim Bailey. Remember me?"

"Of course, I remember you, Jim. How are you?"

"I'm doing okay. How about you?"

"I've been busy at work. How's your job search going?"

"I'm pretty sure I have a part-time job at Fenway. I went for an interview a couple of days ago. Seems like it went well."

"That's what you wanted, right? Except I think you wanted to be one of their starting pitchers," she laughed.

"Yeah, but that was a joke. Don't even know if I remember how to hold a ball or step on a mound. Don't know if I could even throw a ball without bouncing it on the plate."

"I think you'd be surprised. It's kinda like learning to ride a bicycle. Once you learn how to pitch, it's kinda in your blood, right?"

In my blood. That's right. In my DNA, my brain, my fingers, my toes. It's there. Trouble is, I don't know if I remember how to capture it, bring it up to the surface.

"I guess so. But say, I called because I was hoping we could get together."

"I'd like that. When did you have in mind?"

"You tell me. You're the one with a work schedule."

"How about Friday or Saturday night? Either one would work for me."

"Either one would be fine with me, too. But…don't forget…I don't have a car," he said, stumbling across the words.

"But don't forget…I *do* have one," Eileen joked.

"So, you don't mind driving? I mean if we don't go too far?"

"Not at all. What time should I pick you up?"

"How about Friday at seven? You remember where I live, right?"

"I think I remember."

"Okay. I'll see you then."

"Sounds great. Looking forward to it."

"Me, too."

I have a date. With Eileen. In her Marina-blue Volkswagen. In two days. I'd better get my act together. Maybe we can go bowling or something. And to dinner. I'll need to consult with Debbie on this one.

~ ~ ~

"Hey, Eileen, who was *that*?" her roommate asked.

"*That* was someone asking me out on a date," she replied.

"A *date*? Was this the baseball player/felon/guy without a job and without a car?"

"Oh, stop…and be nice, but yes, the very same. I'll have to drive."

"Are you serious? He can't even borrow a car?"

"I don't mind. This puts me in charge more than I might be if he were driving, anyway."

"Okay, if you say so, Eileen."

"He's tall, handsome, with the dreamiest eyes."

"Hypnotic? Pulling you under his spell? Be careful."

"I will be. Don't forget, he lives at home with his mother."

"How many strikes can one guy have against him? No job, no car, lives with his mother, just got out of prison. And let's not forget the things you don't even know about."

"I want to give him a chance."

"And you always want to bring home stray dogs and cats, too, kiddo."

"I can tell he's different. He just seems to be down on his luck. I'm convinced it's temporary."

"You had one, two-hour conversation with him, and you know all this about him already?"

"I can feel it in my bones, I tell you. He's different. He can just sit and talk and doesn't seem to be pre-occupied with any of those hanky-panky ideas," Eileen replied.

"That was *before* he asked you out on a formal date. You still should be wary."

"Oh, I am. Trust me when I tell you, I am wary."

"Good. You need to be careful. I only know what I read in the newspaper about him. Don't let your guard down."

"I won't."

Eileen sat by the telephone for a short time, fielding the butterflies inside her stomach. She hadn't been this nervous about going out with a guy since her Aunt Tillie set her up on a blind date with a second-grade teacher from a private school in Milton. That turned out to be a disaster. She ended up drinking so much that he had to bring her home. Early. Very early.

But this time would be different. She'd already met the guy, seen his face, listened to his hearty laugh, breathed in his ear-to-ear smile. Heck, she'd even seen *inside* him, with her trusty X-ray machine.

Inside and out, Jim Bailey intrigued her. How many strikes did he have against him? It didn't matter. He wasn't playing baseball against her; this wasn't a game. Not to her.

Chapter Thirty-Two

Jimmy felt like a pinball machine, jumping from obstacle to obstacle. He wondered if he could find his old pals from Jamestown, Bud, and Bobby, to let them know that he was out of prison and hoping to land a job in baseball again.

And...he missed them.

He had a phone number for Bud but not for Bobby. He'd probably have to track him down through his job with the Mets—if he was still scouting for them. He was sure that Bud was playing major league ball now, based on the letters he'd received from him when he was locked up. But that was over a year ago.

Jimmy recalled a few postcards that he'd received from Bobby while he was on the road scouting talent. He laughed when he read that Bobby had everything down to a science—how to get in and out of hotel rooms with his wheelchair, how to disguise himself as a spectator when in the stands observing potential players, how to deal with issues of being physically handicapped while on the road. The guy who'd been the cocky, arrogant New Yorker had been transformed, through his disability, into a problem-solver who approached his life with dignity and patience.

I could have learned a great deal from the 1976 version of Bobby, whereas Bobby could have learned from the 1972 version of me.

Jimmy pondered where to begin. Would either of them even want to hear from him? If he got through to leave a message, would they call him back? Would they talk to a jailbird, although they were once on the same team?

Once upon a time, we all reached for the same brass ring that Major League Baseball represents for all Little Leaguers who dream of one day stepping up those dugout steps into the sun and seeing their names on the big scoreboard.

Whether they were accepting of him or not, he vowed to try anyway.

After my first real date with Eileen.

Chapter Thirty-Three

Debbie was concerned. She'd heard from her friends in the governor's office that the warden's murder was more complex than they'd originally thought.

Her contact was dropping hints that the reason the warden had been killed was he'd been in the process of uncovering a network of corruption within the prison—a complicated web involving a hierarchy of guards, inmates...even the head cook in the commissary. It was this group, not the warden, that oversaw the day-to-day operations of the prison. They also ran a multi-level drug and contraband distribution system behind the warden's back.

The warden had attempted to institute reforms within the prison walls, such as enhanced educational opportunities for inmates, and vocational counseling before parole. He'd brought mental health counselors into the prison to prepare prisoners for release back into the real world.

The guards who formed the network of corruption considered these innovations "coddling" the inmates and "interfering" with *their* operations. They talked behind the warden's back and tried to sabotage him at every turn. The guards looked down on the inmates and felt they should be treated with brutality, not with any sense of humanity or respect.

They viewed Jimmy and his success at teaching his cellmate to read as a direct threat, because it played right into the warden's hands. What

Jimmy did, in their eyes, showed the warden that increasing education for inmates would contribute to their being able to go in a positive direction when they left Walpole, rather than going back to the streets and returning to a life of crime, which in turn would return them to Walpole.

When Jimmy left, they decided to teach Keeshon a lesson that had nothing to do with reading. The crooked guards recruited four of their biggest, toughest prisoners and told them what to do.

Keeshon. Beat the crap out of him. Guards will not intervene. They also won't let anyone else near them while the walloping takes place.

The order was to not kill him but to do as much damage as possible to get their message across.

Those were the details the FBI and Massachusetts State Police had uncovered so far.

Debbie worried that the people who had killed the warden because he was investigating Keeshon's beating had contacts on the outside who might come after, not only Keeshon, but her brother as well. Her greatest concern was that her mother might be in danger, too, because Jimmy lived with her.

Debbie's concerns grew. How long would the good Commonwealth give Keeshon protection in a hospital? And was it possible that some of those law enforcement officials might be crooked, just like the guards at Walpole?

She once thought that her brother's two-bit, alcoholic friends, Terry and Eddie, were trouble. They were low lives, for sure, but the guys who had beaten Keeshon were professionals. Prison guards who had developed a multi-level network of protection, bribery, and drug distribution within the walls of a maximum-security facility, were cunning, violent, and merciless.

Debbie wondered if she was out of her league dealing with this. These thoughts from a woman who felt that she could solve every problem—a woman who earned her way from Weymouth High School into Harvard

University—who stood six-feet tall and carried herself as if she were queen of the universe—a woman who feared nothing.

Violence. Greed. Terror. Control. She had met her match.

Chapter Thirty-Four

The little, blue Volkswagen chugged over the Fore River Bridge, headed toward the Bailey house.

Eileen was anxious about picking Jimmy up, but she was also happy to do it.

She'd volunteered to drive. She wasn't bothered by this arrangement at all. What difference did it make, whether she drove, or he did? The important thing was that they would be spending time together, getting to know one another.

She'd tried on several different outfits and had decided on plain black slacks and a light-blue, sleeveless top, with a black unbuttoned cardigan. "I look like something out of the Sears catalog" she told her roommate.

"Maybe, but you also look ready to have a nice night," came the reply.

Ready to have a nice night was an understatement. She wanted to have fun, laugh a lot, and find out as much as she could about Jimmy.

Through Bicknell Square and down Bridge Street, she and her trusty car went, until it was time to make the right turn. She drove past Jimmy's house, then turned around so that she could park on the correct side of the street. Little did she know that Jimmy was inside, pacing, awaiting her arrival.

~ ~ ~

He kept looking out the window from the front hall, hoping to catch a glimpse of the Marina-blue VW. When he spotted her passing the house and making the turnaround, he took a deep breath, brushed off his shirt, and slowly walked down the stairs.

"Ma, she's here," he called out to the kitchen.

"Okay, baby, I'll be right out."

His mom dried her hands on the dishtowel and came to the front room, just as Eileen was coming up the walk. She fluffed up the back of her hair in anticipation.

Jimmy opened the door. "Come on in, Eileen. You've already met my mom, Mary Bailey."

Eileen extended her hand. "Please to meet you, again, Mrs. Bailey."

"It's my pleasure, dear. I hear you work at the hospital."

"Yes. South Shore. In the X-ray Department."

"Thanks for saving my Jimmy."

"I didn't save him, Mrs. Bailey. I just took his X-rays."

Jimmy sighed in the background. *How long will this small talk last?* he wondered. *I want to get out of here.*

"Well," he said, "we better get going."

"Where are you headed?" his mom asked.

"Debbie suggested the Red Coach Grille, down in Hingham."

"That sounds like fun, dear. You two have a great time."

"We will, Ma. We will."

Walking out the front door, he put his hand gently on Eileen's back and walked her around to the driver's side of her car. Although she was driving, he felt that he should be a gentleman and still open her door for her.

As Eileen climbed into her seat, she looked up at him and smiled. "How kind of you," she said.

Jimmy ran around to the passenger seat and pushed the seat back a little so that he could comfortably stretch his legs.

"I'll tell you how to get there. It's not very far. All you have to do is go back the way you came and take a right on Bridge Street."

"That's easy enough," she replied. Eileen had grown up in Hingham, so she knew exactly where the restaurant was, but she still allowed him to take the lead.

"That's where I had my very first job, after my first season in minor-league ball," he said, when they passed Mister Donut.

"Really? Did you have to wear one of those silly paper hats?"

"Sometimes. The place looks deserted now."

"Yeah, Mister Donut really never took off as a competitor to Dunkin' Donuts. I don't know how much longer they'll last."

"My boss there was a guy named Al. I learned a lot from him. I think he hired me because he knew I'd played ball at Weymouth High."

A moment of silence settled over the car.

"Hey, I told you I went for my interview at Fenway Park, right? I'd been carrying my letter from Mr. Yawkey around with me for a couple of years. But I found out that he died a few weeks back."

"Yeah, I think I heard something about that in the news."

"But they're going to honor the letter anyway. His wife still owns the club, and they say they're going to find me a job of some kind. It just takes so doggone long to get there. I had to take two buses, then the train to Park Street, then the trolley to Kenmore. I figure it'll take me about an hour and a half on a good day to get to work."

"It'll be worth it, don't you think, if you can get some job experience?"

"Yes, but all I wanted to do was…"

He paused.

"What?" she asked.

"I wanted to jump the fence, climb up on the mound, and see if I could still throw a baseball. I don't know if I can, but I sure wanted to try."

He didn't mention his meeting with Bill Lee. He wanted to save that story for later.

She turned briefly and glanced at him. It was almost as if he was in a daydream—like a Little Leaguer, ready to pitch in his first *real* game, not knowing if he had it in him to actually release a ball and make it to the catcher behind the plate.

"Oh, take this turn!" he said quickly. "Here's the restaurant. We almost missed it."

As she found a parking space, she couldn't help but feel sad for the young man who once had the ability—and the dream—of playing Major League Baseball.

They sat for a moment in the VW with the engine off. "I think you have a lot to tell me. I'm listening," she said, placing her hand on top of his.

"Yeah. I do. But I'm a good listener, too. A hungry one, at that. Let's go inside and we'll talk over dinner."

He popped out of the car and ran around to open her door, just as she was starting to emerge.

"No, no, madam, I will get the door for you."

When he was young, he thought the Red Coach Grille was the most elegant, elite place on the entire South Shore. He was about to take a young lady into this restaurant—on money he'd borrowed from his older sister—and see whether the inside lived up to its hype.

Chapter Thirty-Five

Keeshon looked around his hospital room and couldn't figure out what was going on. He was on so much pain medicine that he was drifting in and out of reality. He dreamed about going home to see his mother and talk to her again.

All she did in his dreams was cry. She cried when she saw his broken body. She cried because he wasn't in prison anymore. She cried because he had changed so much in the past four years. She cried because she hadn't protected him enough to keep him out of prison in the first place.

'My baby! My baby! My baby!' his mother screamed, over and over in his dreams—nightmares, really—and yet, when she reached out for him, he couldn't manage to touch her fingers. She was always out of his grasp, no matter how hard he tried. He lunged, he jumped, he dove toward her, but he never made it into her loving arms.

Whenever he awoke from one of those fitful experiences, he was drenched in sweat, the wounds from the beating he'd endured hurting more than ever, and the image of his mother's face...her outstretched arms, imprinted on his brain as he gasped for air.

He opened his eyes and realized he was in the hospital, attached to tubes and wires, with railings on his bed to keep him from falling onto the floor.

What am I doing heah? I'm not in the same place as I was a few days ago.

He pressed the call button.

"Can I help you, sir?" a voice came back over the speaker.

Suh? Someone's calling me 'suh'?

"Ma'am," he replied, "would it be possible fo' me to get some watta, if it's not too much trouble fo' you?"

"Yes, sir. Would you like anything else? Juice? Crackers? I don't think you ate much of your supper."

"Thank you, ma'am. I'm real hungry. If you could get me a Coke or Pepsi or something, that would be nice. And crackas, yes. That would be nice, too. Thank you, again."

"Yes, sir. I think maybe ginger ale or Sprite might be better. I'll get you a snack as soon as I can, and I'll bring you fresh water, too."

"Thank you. I appreciate that."

The voice from the speaker disappeared, but soon appeared in human form standing over him.

"How are you feeling right now?" she asked.

"I think I'll be betta once I have something to drink."

"You're soaking wet. Are you okay? Let me take your temperature to make sure you don't have a fever."

"Yes, ma'am. I feel like I'm swimmin' heah. Don't know if I have a feeva."

The nurse ran out of the room to get what she needed to check his vital signs, then burst back into the room. "I know it might not be easy, but could you open your mouth and hold this thermometer long enough for me to get a good reading?"

"I'll try, ma'am."

He opened as wide as he could and gently clamped his mouth down on the glass thermometer. His teeth ached around the instrument, but he focused on keeping it still while she wrapped a blood pressure cuff around his arm and pumped it up.

"Just as I thought," she said, removing the thermometer from his mouth. "You do have a fever. One hundred and two. I'll call the doctor. Your blood pressure's a little low, but I'd expect that with this fever. I'll tell the doctor about that, too.

"Mr. Washington, I think you'll feel better, though, if we can get your bed changed with clean linen, and if we can get a little food in your system. Let's get you up into your chair over here and I'll get someone from housekeeping to change your sheets."

"Yes, ma'am, whateva you think is best."

Woozy and unsteady, he followed her instructions to the best of his ability as she carefully moved his legs over one side of the bed and onto the floor. He watched as she pulled the string to communicate with someone at the nurses' station.

"Hello? May I help you?"

"Judy? It's Elaine. Can you or someone come to this room and help me? I need to transfer this patient to a chair and he's extremely weak and fragile. This is a two-person transfer."

"Okay, Elaine. Be right there."

A second nurse entered the room, and the two women worked together to ensure that Keeshon's pain was minimized as they moved him from his hospital bed to a vinyl recliner in the nearby corner.

"There you go," Elaine said. "Now the trick is to get that fever down while we get you some clean clothes, and fresh sheets on your bed."

Judy was heading out the door. "I'll call housekeeping and get someone up here."

"Thanks, Judy. And can you put a call into the doctor and tell him that Mr. Washington has a fever of a hundred and two?"

"Yes, I'll take care of that, as well."

Elaine went into the adjacent bathroom and soaked a washcloth with cool water. She came back and began wiping Keeshon's head, neck, and the top part of his chest. He sighed several times in approval as she stroked his head and neck.

"Am I hurting you?" she asked.

"No, ma'am. It feels good. Thank you."

"This is the best thing to do until I hear back from the doctor regarding your fever," she said. "When I was a kid and had a fever, this is what my mother used to do for me."

"My mama used to do this fo' me and my sistas and brothas, too," he said. "We didn't always have medicine when we had feevas. Maybe as'prin, but not always doctas to tend to us. My mama would get a bucket of watta and a wet towel, sing to us, and wipe us down with that wet towel ova and ova again until we felt betta. She'd rub the feeva right out o' us."

Only thing missing now is my mama's sweet singing voice.

He closed his eyes and tried to remember what his mother sang as she tried to rid her children of fever. Then, it came to him:

Wade in the water…wade in the water, children…wade in the water…God's gonna trouble the water…

His mother's voice became loud and clear when he closed his eyes.

I wish I could heah my mama's sweet voice.

Wade in the water…wade in the water, children…

He heard a cart with a squeaky wheel enter the room, bringing him back to reality. The person behind it knocked on the door but didn't stop to be recognized before they pushed right on in.

"Housekeeping," the man announced in a loud booming voice. Keeshon's head hurt from the noise.

"Keep it down!" Elaine snapped. "You'll disturb my patient. He's fragile with a fever."

"Uh, okay. Sorry," the man replied, as he went about attacking the sheets, removing them from the bed. It didn't take him long before he'd replaced the wet bedding with clean, dry sheets.

"Voila!" he declared, throwing the dirty linen into his cart. He exited as he had entered, with similar fanfare.

"Things will feel better now, when you get back into bed," Elaine said. "But I think I'll leave you in your chair until you eat something. I need someone to help me get you back into bed safely anyway."

Keeshon drifted off for a few minutes, sitting in the chair. His skin stuck to the vinyl in the back where the hospital gown opened. The chair swallowed up his entire body, his slight frame consumed by folds of beige, synthetic leather that would have accommodated someone three times his size. He was hungry but didn't want to eat much. He was thirsty and wanted to drink water —his choice, and a good one, but the nurse felt that ginger ale would help settle his stomach. He'd give it a try.

He nodded off again until he felt a soothing hand on his shoulder. "Mr. Washington? Are you awake?"

"Huh? Yes, ma'am, I am. Mostly."

"I brought you fresh water and a little ginger ale," Nurse Elaine said, "and a few saltine crackers. We'll see how you do with these then maybe we can graduate to something more exciting, like Jell-O and toast."

She pulled a chair over and sat next to him. "Don't drink too fast," she cautioned. "I know you're thirsty but take small sips until we're able to assess how you're handling it."

She watched him as he tried to manage the cup on his own. She could have helped him, but she wanted to see if he could do it without assistance. He was shaky, but he managed to get a few sips in before handing the cup back to her.

"Did I do it right, ma'am?"

"Yes, sir, Mr. Washington. You did just fine. Let's try a few crackers now."

She broke a Saltine cracker into three pieces and handed one to him. His fingers trembled as he grasped the tiny morsel and raised it to his mouth. She could hear his stomach growling. He looked up at her apologetically.

"That's a good sign," she said. "Means you're probably ready to eat something."

"Yes, ma'am," he managed to say, with Saltine crumbs in his mouth.

She broke several more crackers and placed them on his tray table. "Here's the rest of your gourmet meal," she said, with a chuckle. "This is all we're able to give you this time. How you handle this will determine if we can move on to something more complicated."

"Like Jell-O?" he asked.

"Yes. Like Jell-O," she smiled.

As she left the room, she reminded him that she would return shortly with assistance to help get him back into bed.

When she opened the door, she nodded at the guard standing outside. Keeshon could see his shoulder from the doorway. He understood then why they had transferred him from the other hospital. Someone was probably still trying to kill him.

Chapter Thirty-Six

Jimmy was restless.

He couldn't figure out why he couldn't sit still.

He felt a hand on his shoulder.

"Jimmy? Honey? Are you ready to eat some supper?"

"Huh? Oh, hi, Ma."

Her voice brought him down to earth—or at least, back into the living room.

"I made you a nice supper, dear. Meatloaf, mashed potatoes, and those nice Pillsbury rolls. The ones you always liked. And real butter, dear. No margarine tonight!"

"Real butter and Pillsbury dinner rolls! Yum! Can't wait, Ma." He jumped to his feet and made his way to the dining room table. The aroma of spicy, sizzling meatloaf, fresh out of the oven filled his nostrils, leading to hunger pangs in his stomach. He was certain his mother could hear the noises from where she stood at the stove.

"Yumm, yumm, yumm! Your home cooking is the best, Ma."

"I bet you said that to that Mrs. Anderson when you were in Jamestown," she purred.

"No, I did NOT!" he protested.

"You told me she made great blueberry muffins!"

"Are you jealous because I said Mrs. Anderson was a good cook?" he teased.

"No...well, maybe..."

"She was a good cook, but no one compares to my ma!"

She smiled and gave his shoulder a tight squeeze. "That's what I needed to hear!"

The comfort of her arms, though weaker than they once were, combined with the solace of what he knew would come from the meal she'd prepared, was almost electric, providing him with a charge of encouragement that only she knew how to provide.

She served a heaping chunk of meatloaf onto his plate, along with a steaming dollop of mashed potatoes—enough for two people, but she knew he could eat at least that much. He looked up at her approvingly before reaching for two Pillsbury rolls and the butter dish.

Ah, I'm in heaven. Ma's meatloaf, mashed potatoes with no lumps, Pillsbury dinner rolls, and real butter? Doesn't get much better than this!

"So, tell me dear," she said, as she sat across from him with her own plate, "does this lady, Eileen, know how to cook?"

He felt his face blush beet-red and knew right away that the heat wasn't from the piping-hot meatloaf.

"Uh—I dunno, Ma. We went out to the Red Coach Grille, thanks to Debbie giving me some money, so Eileen didn't cook. I suppose one of these days I'll find out if she cooks. That is, if she doesn't give me the boot for being a jerk or something."

"My Jimmy? A jerk? No chance, honey. You're a charming, young man, ready to find yourself a nice, young lady to keep company with. Seems like she's a nice, young lady. Maybe she'll show you that she has some cooking skills one of these days soon."

"I can't imagine she's able to cook like you, Ma."

"Well, she's not as old as I am. Takes a long time to develop skills like I have," she laughed.

"Maybe you could teach her a few tricks, Ma."

She broke into a full-fledged, belly laugh. "We'll see."

I haven't heard The Filly laugh like that since before my father died. This could be a good sign.

He put his hand over his mother's. "This is the hand of a cooking expert, the one that fed me and taught me what great food should taste like. You should write a cookbook, Ma."

"Maybe I will, dear. Would you use it if I did? Debbie doesn't cook. Would you?"

"I'd try, Ma. Maybe I could get Keeshon to use it, too. We could have fun with it."

"You always have such great ideas, honey. That would be great. Now, no more talk. Let's eat!"

Chapter Thirty-Seven

"Ms. Bailey, we need to take your statement. Do you mind if we sit down?"

Two FBI agents—one about 60, the other around 35—were all business as they entered her office to question her about what happened at Walpole State Prison on the day Jimmy was released.

"My name's Olson," the older guy said, "and this here's Fitzgerald. We're investigating the death of the warden at Walpole State Prison."

"I'm aware of that. Thank you for coming to my office, rather than asking me to come to FBI headquarters."

"Our pleasure," Fitzgerald said, smiling at her.

Olson asked for her permission to record the session. He placed the clunky cassette recorder on her desk, pulling out an electronic cord as he searched for a place to plug it into the wall.

"Before you begin recording, Agent Olson, would you mind giving me an idea of the kind of questions you plan to ask?"

"Of course, Ms. Bailey. We just want to know what happened when you went to Walpole State Prison to pick up your brother on the day of his release. Is that okay?"

"Yes. You realize, of course, that I am speaking to you without an attorney, so I would also like to request a copy of this recording when we're finished."

"Yes, of course."

Olson found an outlet and plugged in the recorder. He snapped a cassette into the chamber and pressed record.

"Now, Ms. Bailey, in your own words, can you tell us what happened on the day you entered Walpole State Prison to pick up your brother when he was released?"

Debbie recalled the day she and Jimmy met with the warden and how Jimmy asked to see Keeshon before they left. She also recounted how, as they were leaving, some of the guards greeted her with catcalls and lewd remarks. She explained how she had stood up to them, one in particular, who seemed embarrassed that she had done so in front of the other guards.

"Do you think that one guard may have been looking for revenge?"

"Revenge? On me? Probably. But he would have had to follow my brother and me to our mother's home to get it."

"Do you think he may have tried to get at you through your brother's cellmate?"

"I'm speculating, of course, but it's certainly a possibility."

"When you were speaking to the warden before your brother's release, did you discuss Mr. Washington at all?"

"My brother asked to see him prior to his release, yes, and the warden had one of the guards bring him to his office before we left."

"Was it, by any chance, the same guard who you might have encountered and possibly embarrassed?"

"To be honest with you, I cannot remember, Agent Olson."

"We have ways to check that, Ms. Bailey."

"I wish you would."

"Oh, we will."

"Thank you for your statement, Ms. Bailey," Fitzgerald said.

"You're welcome. If there's anything else you need, here's my card," she said, reaching across her desk.

Olson clicked off the cassette recorder, unplugged it from the wall, and packed it back into his briefcase.

"I will make a copy of this tape for you, Ms. Bailey, and will send it to you, per your request," he said.

"I'll be looking for it."

"And Ms. Bailey…" he began.

"Yes?"

"Tell your brother to be careful. We think this may be evolving into something more than an inmate beating. There may be folks on the outside looking for him, as well. We'll let you know if we get any specific details, but, as of now, we have some suspicions."

"Suspicions? Like what? Would they be after me? Our mother? Jim lives with her."

"We don't know exactly," Fitzgerald replied. "We should have more information soon."

"As I said, we will let you know as more information rolls in," Olson added. "Just keep your eyes open and tell your brother to do the same. Okay?"

"I will. Thank you."

She reached out to shake the hand of each agent and walked them to her office door. "Please keep in touch," she said.

Chapter Thirty-Eight

"Jimmy, does anyone from the prison know where Ma lives?"

"I don't know, Debbie. Why?"

"Just wondering. If anyone wanted to find you, do you think that's where they'd come looking for you?"

"I guess so. But why would anyone from the prison come looking for me? I had no friends there except Key."

"But did you have any enemies?"

"None I can think of. Key and me, we kept to ourselves. We just did our jobs and then studied because he wanted to get his GED."

"What about guards? Did you have any run-ins with them?"

"What are you getting at here, Debbie? What's going on?"

"I don't know, Jimmy. I just have a bad feeling about things. What about that guard, Rocco? The one who was being fresh with me when we were leaving?"

"You mean Rossi? Yeah, he's kind of a jerk, but I just ignored him. He had another guy he hung out with a lot, think his name was Jersey or something like that, or that might have been his nickname, but I never even heard him open his mouth. He just grunted a lot when he walked down the hallways."

"The silent guys, they're the worst ones," Debbie mumbled.

"Debbie, you're getting at something here. What is it?"

"These two FBI investigators came by my office today. They told me to be careful. They told me to warn you to be careful. They've got me looking over my shoulder now. They probably think you're this big tough guy because you've been to prison, but you and I know that's not true. We know you didn't kill that guy; I mean, you couldn't even kill a spider unless Ma asked you to. The investigators believe that these crooked prison guards might also have crooked friends on the outside. I'm worried that one of those guys who beat up Keeshon and killed the warden might come looking for you. I don't want Ma getting caught up in any of this."

"Ma? You think she's in danger?"

"I don't know what to think right now. I just know those investigators scared the crap out of me today."

"What about your friends in the governor's office? What are they telling you?"

"I have no inside information from them. I think they're just as shaken up by this whole thing as we are. They've got the FBI and the head of the state police on this thing."

"The FBI...The feds? Why can't the state handle this?"

"Sometimes the state brings in the feds when they need independent eyes to investigate. Sometimes state police have connections inside a prison, like, they put some of the guys on the inside into that prison, so they can't always be impartial...You know?"

"Yeah. I guess so. All I can figure right now is that everything must be in chaos out there in Walpole."

"I heard they named a temporary warden to take over the helm. Don't know anything about him except they brought him over from a maximum-security place in New York—Attica."

"Attica? Isn't that where they had that big prison riot a few years back?"

"Yeah. Hey, how did you know about that?" Debbie asked.

"One of the books Key and I read when we were inside. It was a history book or something. Very interesting. Thirteen-hundred inmates rioted. I'm surprised that book was in the prison library."

"Me, too. Don't want to give the Walpole inmates any ideas. Anyway, I think we need to be aware that there may be people on the outside who are involved in all this—guys who are friends with the guards or maybe even with the inmates who beat up Keeshon. This may be something big, Jimmy. Bigger than the both of us. Bigger than that piece of crap who put his slimy hands on me when I picked you up from Walpole."

Jimmy's head began to spin.

"Debbie, I can't protect myself from what you're calling 'something big,' much less protect Ma, especially if I'm working. I don't even have a car. It takes me loads of time to get to Fenway and back. I don't want to scare Ma, but with the FBI involved, will they give us protection?"

"I don't know, Jimmy. I'll try to find out. Just keep your eyes open. Promise me that. Okay?"

"Okay."

"That's all I can ask for. Those two investigators gave me the creeps. It was like I was watching something out of a movie."

Jimmy put his head in his hands.

That nightmare that I lived through in Walpole was like something out of a movie. I didn't know if I'd make it out alive, but somehow, I did. Now the guy who helped me is lying in a hospital bed, fighting for his life, all because my sister put some jerk in his place.

Chapter Thirty-Nine

Eileen strolled down a hallway at South Shore Hospital. She was early for work and even had time to stop at Dunk's for coffee on the way.

Memories of her date with the charming baseball player put a spring in her step. She couldn't get over how handsome he was. Tall. Unassuming. Interesting. Shy, though when he opened up, he was a good conversationalist. She still couldn't get over the fact that he'd been to prison.

Entering the X-ray Department, she began organizing her desk, staring at the giant brown envelopes containing X-rays that had come in the night before, when she was off. Looking at the names one by one, she methodically placed each in alphabetical order and found the correct filing drawer.

Still, even as she continued doing her job, the handsome, baseball player roamed inside her head, not in an X-ray film, but rather, a full-color photograph. She imagined him throwing a baseball from the mound at Fenway Park, striking out someone in a Yankee uniform. "Yes!" she said, out loud.

"Eileen, what the heck are you yelling about?" a voice from the doorway asked.

"Huh?" She looked up and saw her friend, Janet, snapping her back to reality. "Oh, hi, Janet. I was just thinking out loud."

"It sounded exciting. What were you thinking about?"

"I had a date last night."

"A date? Do tell!"

"Well…it was someone I met here. He came in for an X-ray, and then he needed a ride home. Don't tell anyone, though. I might get into trouble for giving a patient a ride home."

"Your secret's safe with me," Janet said, rubbing her hands together. "Tell me more! And hurry before another patient comes in here."

"Well, his name is Jim, and he lives in North Weymouth. He was a baseball player in the minor leagues. He's so handsome! He doesn't have a full-time job right now, but he does have a part-time gig lined up at Fenway Park. Remember Tom Yawkey who owned the Red Sox? The one who died? Well, Mr. Yawkey promised him a job when he became available for work," Eileen said, pausing to take a breath.

"Why wasn't he available when the guy gave him the letter?" Janet asked curiously.

"That's the catch…"

"What's the catch, girlfriend?"

"Well…"

"Well, what? Spit it out, girl!"

"He just got out of Walpole."

"Prison? Are you kidding me? Maximum security?"

"Yeah. He spent time there for a crime he didn't commit."

"Wait a minute. Was this about some guy who died at Wessagusset Beach a few years back?"

"How did you know that?"

"It's coming back to me now. Some guy was drinking with his buddies at Wessagusset, and this baseball player guy tried to join them when the first guy started a fight. The baseball guy…"

"His name is Jim," Eileen interrupted.

"Okay, so Jim...knocked the guy out and the guy drowned. There were no witnesses. Then Jim passed out on the beach. He said the guy who drowned had knocked him out, but since there were no witnesses, he was arrested for murder. Everyone knew the judge was going to make an example out of him and not let his famous name get him off. That judge was a real jerk."

"Did you ever meet him?"

"Oh, no, but he was kind of a celebrity around Quincy and Weymouth. He was a great pitcher! He even got to pitch at Fenway Park when he was in high school. I read about him in the newspaper. All the girls in my school had a crush on him."

"Not hard to see why. He's wicked cute. And soft-spoken, too. He's not the kind I would picture having been to prison. He said he taught his cellmate how to read while he was there."

"Well, that's admirable...and a good way to pass the time. You think you'll see him again?"

"If he wants to see me, yes, I'd like to see him again. He was a perfect gentleman. He doesn't have a car, though, so I'll have to pick him up again if we go on a second date. That part's a little awkward."

"X-ray Department! X-ray Department! Code 606!"

"Uh-oh! Car accident! I'd better get ready. We'll talk later, Janet. I have a lot more to tell you."

"I'm sure you do, kiddo. I'm sure you do." Janet grabbed a few charts from behind Eileen's desk and headed down the hallway. A code 606 multi-car accident meant that Eileen was about to get busy, quickly.

Chapter Forty

arden's Death Probed: FBI Enters Investigation.
Jimmy picked up the copy of *The Boston Globe* that someone had left behind and began reading.

'Special investigators from the FBI have joined the state police probe into the murder of Walpole Warden, Peter Miles, last month,' Massachusetts State Police Superintendent William Duquesne announced at a press conference yesterday.

Working in conjunction with Governor Michael Dukakis's office, Duquesne said his officers are collaborating with FBI officers who have expertise in forensic science.

'This is a special case,' Duquesne told reporters. 'Warden Miles was a respected member of the Department of Corrections here in the Commonwealth, and his death came as a shock to so many of us who worked with him over the past two decades. He was known for his compassion and commitment to inmate rehabilitation, and we promise that we will find his killer or killers and bring them to justice. We are confident that this collaboration with the FBI will strengthen our investigation.'

The article continued on page four, but Jimmy didn't have time to read it before he went into work. He folded the paper and tucked it under his arm. *I look like a real commuter now—a businessman on his way to work,* he thought, as he made his way to Fenway Park for training.

Jimmy was excited to learn what department he'd be working out of. Since the season was almost over, he assumed that he would be selling hot dogs or cleaning bathrooms, but he was grateful for anything they gave him that would earn him money. He wanted to start saving, and although he knew they didn't mind, he hated asking his mom and sister for money. He was young, healthy, and more than able to support himself.

And then there was Eileen. He couldn't get her out of his mind. He kept seeing her eyes and hearing her laugh. The memory of her hair and her voice drove him crazy. He didn't understand how a woman like her could see anything in a guy like him. He barely had a job, had no money, no car, and he lived at home with his mother. Most guys his age had their own apartments and supported themselves. All he had was a temporary, part-time job, one that would most likely end when baseball season did.

"KEN-MO-AH SQU-AH!"

Jimmy had reached his stop. The trolley screeched to a halt, causing him to lurch forward as he got up from his seat. Out the turnstile, up the steps, and over the bridge that spanned the Mass Pike, and he was at Fenway.

As directed, he found his way to Gate B and walked in, looking for Ms. Malone.

"Jimmy?" came a voice from behind him.

He spun around coming face to face with Dorothy Malone herself.

"Thanks for being on time," she said. "I thought about having you work in one of the concession stands, but we haven't had great attendance these past few days. So, I'm going to take you down to the players' laundry area. I hope you don't mind. It gets a little hot down there, but it's an important job as any other."

Laundry? She wants me to wash uniforms? I guess it could be worse—it could be toilets.

"Okay, Ms. Malone. Whatever you want me to do, I told you that it would be okay with me."

"Dorothy. Please call me Dorothy," she reminded.

"Okay, Dorothy, I'll follow you."

She led Jimmy through a maze of tunnels and places he'd never seen before. She greeted everyone she passed—ushers, ticket-takers, concession workers, even vendors getting ready to sell during the game—until they arrived at a huge room filled with steam and oversized washing machines.

In the center of the room, stood Eddie—an older woman who oversaw the laundry room. Dorothy introduced him.

"Eddie, this is Jimmy Bailey. I told you about him. He'll be working with you for the rest of the season."

Eddie wiped her hands on the back of her apron and greeted him with a smile that took over her entire face. She reached out her hand and shook his.

"Pleased to meet you, Jimmy Bailey. Do you go by Jim or Jimmy?" she asked.

Jimmy blushed. It could have been from the steam in the room, but he didn't think so. She had called him by name. "Either one," he replied, "whichever you like. I'm looking forward to working with you. Should I call you Eddie?"

"Everyone else does, so I hope you will, too."

Dorothy beamed. She was happy to facilitate the connection. A human resources person's dream was introducing people who would be working together, and who instantly hit it off.

Jimmy estimated that Eddie was between 45-50 years old. She was about 5'5, a little on the plump side, with chubby cheeks, dark brown eyes, and shoulder-length, black hair pulled back in a ponytail. He figured her to be of Italian heritage, not that it mattered. She bounced around the room, showing him the various machines and their functions.

Jimmy had always wondered how major league teams kept their uniforms so clean, especially when there was so much dirt, grass stains, base sliding, and the like. He was trying to pay attention to everything she said, but his thoughts let some of her words get right by him.

Dorothy Malone stood back in the corner, arms crossed, smirking at how fast Eddie was talking, and watching Jimmy's head spin, as he attempted to learn all that he could about the Red Sox laundry room.

"Don't worry, my friend, you'll get it. This is just the intro," Eddie said. "I'll show you all the different detergents and things we use to get the stains out. It's almost like science class. Did you like science class when you were in school?"

"Not exactly. I wasn't that great a student."

"Well, here you'll learn science according to Eddie, and it'll be fun."

"I'll leave you two to discuss that science according to Eddie, then," Dorothy Malone said, shaking her head and laughing as she walked out the door.

"Okay, kid, let's go over this stuff again. Everything's ready for today's game. I've got everything ready for tomorrow's game, too. What we'll do for the rest of today is work on the uniforms they'll take on their next road trip. The trick is to stay ahead of the game. No pun intended."

Jimmy laughed. Eddie did, too.

They continued walking around the room as she pointed out where everything went—the detergents, where the locker room attendants brought the uniforms after each game, where clean uniforms were placed, and where the towels were kept.

"We don't do the towels," she said. "They're done by a service."

"A service?"

"Yeah, it's almost like a diaper service. They get sent out. They use so many towels around here!"

We didn't get that kind of service when I played in the minor league.

"Our specialty here is the uniforms because we treat each player's uniform with the same type of individuality each player gets. Some guys slide all the time, so when their stuff comes in, it's covered with dirt and grass stains. Those uniforms take the most time to clean, so the faster you get the stain out, the easier it is. Capeesh?"

There's that word again—capeesh—just like what my catcher Russ in Jamestown used to say.

"Oh yeah, I get it. I used to play ball, you know. Did Ms. Malone tell you?"

"No, she didn't mention it. Tell me about it."

Jimmy shared with Eddie all about his friends, Bud Prescott, and Bobby Mangino in Jamestown, and how they were all pitchers, and how Bud was the only one of the trio who'd made it to the majors.

"We were drafted by the Expos, but Bud's with the Braves now," he explained. "I haven't heard from him in a while."

"No? You should write to him. Or you could try calling him," Eddie suggested.

"You're right. I should."

Eddie listened but continued to train him at the same time. "The away uniforms are gray, so they're a little easier to keep clean than the white home uniforms," she said. "But I don't like them as much. I like to see my boys in white."

Jimmy found Eddie to be extremely pleasant and he wondered if she loved her job. He wasn't sure if she'd ever had an assistant before, but she seemed happy he was there.

"Did you bring lunch with you, Jimmy?"

"No, I didn't pack one. I figured I'd just run up and buy a hot dog or something."

"I have a lot of food down here in my little fridge. We have coffee and some tonic here, too. Help yourself. Maybe I can save you a little money."

Saving money would be great. I don't have much to begin with, and saving a few pennies would help a lot, especially until I get my first paycheck.

"Thanks so much, Eddie. I gotta question, and I have to ask, is Eddie your real name?"

"I was wondering when you'd ask that. No, it's Edwina. But when I was a kid, I just couldn't go through life being called *Edwina*. My father called me Eddie and it stuck."

"Eddie it is, then. My father's name was also Jimmy Bailey, so I'm Jimmy Bailey, Jr. But my dad's no longer with us. He died about four years ago."

"Sorry to hear that, Jimmy. But life goes on, you know."

Yes, I know life goes on. Here in the Red Sox laundry room, maybe I can steam-clean some of the things that have been clogging up my mind and sanitize some of the thoughts that have been bogging me down since my dad left this world—and me—behind.

Chapter Forty-One

Keeshon was restless. He hadn't seen Jimmy for about a week. He began to doubt that he even knew where he'd been moved.

The knock on the door startled him and interrupted his thoughts. Two men walked in flashing badges that let him know they were police officers—in plain clothes. FBI.

"Hello, Mr. Washington. I'm FBI Agent Olson and that's Agent Fitzgerald," the older gentleman said.

Keeshon grabbed the call button lying on his bed. "I can't breathe," he said to the agents.

"You what?" Agent Olson asked.

"I can't breathe!" he repeated, clutching the hospital gown at his chest area.

The door flung open, and Nurse Elaine came flying in, brushing past the agents.

"Mr. Washington, what's wrong?" she asked.

"I can't breathe, Miss!"

"Could you gentlemen step back so that I can find out what's bothering him, please?"

The agents looked at each other and walked over to the door while the nurse pulled Keeshon's privacy curtain in front of the bed.

"Mr. Washington, tell me what's happening?"

"When they walked in," he said, pointing in the direction of the door, "I couldn't breathe. It was like they took the air out the room."

"They need to talk to you. If I stay with you and hook up some oxygen, maybe that would help."

"Okay. But I'm telling you, nurse, they took all the air out the room."

Nurse Elaine nodded and put her hand on his shoulder to calm him down.

"Let me speak to them, and I'll get the oxygen for you. We haven't had you on it for a couple of days, but I'll bring a tank in and hook you back up. It'll make you feel better."

He gave her a thumb-up.

She left the curtain closed and walked out of the room, gesturing for the agents to follow her.

"Agents, my patient is a little wobbly, and I need to get him some oxygen before he can talk to you," she explained. "It will only take a minute. I think you should wait out here until I get the oxygen and hook him up to it. I'm sure he'll be fine after that. Would it be okay if I sat with him while you spoke to him? He's not in the greatest shape."

"We'd rather speak to him alone," Officer Olson said, "but if you think he's too fragile…"

"Yes. Yes, I do," she replied. "I think it would be better if I stayed with him. Plus, with the oxygen…He's been on and off it for the past few days, so I'll need to monitor him."

"Okay," Agent Fitzgerald replied. "You can stay."

"I'll be right back," she promised, "with oxygen."

They looked at each other and shrugged.

When she returned, she had a tank and a collection of tubes. She rolled over to Keeshon and leaned into him.

"They're going to let me stay while they speak with you," she whispered. "If things get too uncomfortable, start coughing, and I'll make them leave. Okay?"

"Okay."

She pulled back the curtain. "Gentlemen, you may come in now."

"I'm FBI Agent Olson and this is Agent Fitzgerald," Olson said, pushing the curtain back. "We're working with the Massachusetts State Police to investigate the death of the warden of Walpole State Prison. We think, from the evidence we've collected, that the people who attacked you may be responsible for killing Warden Miles."

"Wawden Miles?" Keeshon repeated. "He's dead?"

"Yes, Mr. Washington. He was bludgeoned to death. We're trying to find out who beat you up, and who the guards were who turned away while the beating was going on. There may be a connection."

"I-I-I don't memba. It all happened so fast. They was all piled up on me. They took me by su'prise. Next thing I know, I was in the hospital."

"You can't remember anyone?"

"No, suh."

"Mr. Washington, are you afraid that if you tell us something, that someone may try to hurt you again?"

"They'll try to kill me."

"We won't let that happen, Mr. Washington."

"You can't stop them. I thought that was what the gawds was fo' in prison but look what happened to me."

"That's what they are *supposed* to be there for. That's why we are trying to figure this whole thing out. We want to bring them to justice."

"Ain't no justice in this world. I got put in prison wit'out justice. I got put in this hospital bed wit'out justice. So why would I believe that theah'll be justice fo' me now?"

"I wish you didn't feel that way, Mr. Washington," Agent Fitzgerald said.

"Can't help it. Been that way my whole life, suh."

"We try the best we can, Mr. Washington. We want to work with you to find justice, especially in this case."

"I'm so tired, suh," he said, starting to cough.

Nurse Elaine jumped up. "You'll have to leave now. I believe he's had enough for one day."

"Okay, sorry. We will come back when he's feeling better."

"Yes. That will be best," she said. "Maybe give him a few days. As I said, he's in bad shape."

"Thank you, ma'am," Agent Olson said.

"You're welcome," she nodded, walking them to the door to ensure they left.

"I can breathe again," Keeshon said, after they left. "You can take the oxygen now, miss."

"I'd be happy to, and, once again, you can call me Elaine."

"Thank you, Miss Elaine. You are so kind."

"It's my job."

"No, it's more than yo' job. It's who you are."

"Thank you, Mr. Washington."

"You can call me Keeshon."

"You rest now, Keeshon. Press the button again if you need us," she said before leaving the room.

When she made it back to the nurses' station, she looked at Keeshon's chart and the many injuries he was dealing with. So many broken bones and bruises. She wondered what he had done to deserve such a beating and why he still needed a guard at his door. There were many questions, with no easy answers in sight.

Chapter Forty-Two

Debbie worked late. Again. She had no time for a social life; she'd given that up, climbing the ladder of success. Brian wasn't just a substitute teacher; he was also substituting as her boyfriend. She was successful in the corporate world, while he drove a cab part-time to accommodate his love of teaching in the Boston Public School system.

She drove down Mass Ave, and with every stop light she encountered, she was reminded how much she hated traffic, while at the same time loving being behind the wheel of her Volvo. Smooth driving. Smooth braking. Smooth everything.

She looked in the rearview mirror and noticed a car following close behind her.

If this jerk hits my new car, I'll punch him in the face, honest to God! Stupid Boston drivers!

Because of the dark, she could only tell that it was a dark-colored car. Some kind of big sedan. No headlights. She couldn't see a face or even tell if it was a male or female driver, although for some strange reason, she assumed it was a man. She was only about a mile from her apartment, and growing more and more concerned that she was being followed, so she pulled away from the next light to be sure. The car behind her surged through the intersection to keep up with her. She tapped her brakes to signal that she knew they were tailgating, but the car crept closer and closer to her bumper.

What the hell? What are they trying to do? Where are the Cambridge Police when you need them?

She remembered the police station that was a mile past her apartment, so she drove past where she'd normally turn, aiming in that direction. The driver behind her turned on the headlights and began flashing the high beams, on and off, off and on. She flipped the Volvo's rearview mirror into night mode and kept going, hoping to lose them or make it to the police station first. After the fact, she realized that she ran a red light, but she didn't care.

Suddenly, she heard the clash of metal on metal. The car behind her had sped through the red light after her, but they weren't as lucky as she had been. Another car entering the intersection on a green light, t-boned the car tailing her, spinning the vehicle into the middle of the street. The sound was deafening, but Debbie kept driving in the direction of the police station.

She pulled into the parking lot, not concerned with how well she had parked the Volvo. Once she was at a complete stop, heart pounding, she flung her door open and ran up the steps, forgetting that she was wearing high heels.

"Help me! Can you help me?" she blurted, even before the door was fully open.

"Calm down, lady!" the officer behind the desk reprimanded. "What's wrong?"

Clutching her chest, she took a deep breath before she began to speak again.

"I'm sorry, sir. I'm Debbie Bailey. I live on Agassiz Street. I was driving home when I realized that someone was following me. Because he was tailing me so closely, he didn't stop when the light turned red. He crashed into someone coming through the intersection. I'm sure officers are on the scene by now."

"Where? When did this happen?" the officer asked.

"Just now! I came right here! I need to know who this person is and why they were following me!"

"What makes you so sure they were following you and not just a tailgater?"

Debbie took another deep breath to try and calm down. "He kept coming closer and closer, flashing his lights at me. I tried to lose him, but he got more aggressive in his pursuit."

"Ms. Bailey, I'm gonna see what's happening down the street so we can get this all sorted out. Why don't you have a seat…over there," he said, pointing to a wooden bench near the door. "Can I get you a drink of water or something?"

Debbie shook her head *'no.'* Her heartbeat was slowly returning to its normal rhythm, but she was sweating.

What's going on? Is this what those FBI agents meant when they told me I should watch my back?

Debbie watched the officer alternate between the phone and listening to the police radio as it squawked at him. Through the static, she could make out that both drivers were being taken by ambulance to local hospitals. One was in critical condition, but she didn't know which one it was.

"Uh-huh, uh-huh," he said into the phone. "Okay. I'll see if she's heard of him. I'll call you back.

"Ms. Bailey? Can you come over here, please?"

Jumping off the wooden bench, she was reminded once again, that she was wearing high heels.

"Ms. Bailey, do you know anyone named Rossi?"

"Rossi? No, I don't think I—wait a minute! Maybe I do! He was a guard at Walpole State Prison!"

"How would you have run into someone who works at bloody Walpole?" the officer asked.

"That's not important. Is that who was driving that car?"

"That's what we think. They're taking him to Mount Auburn. I'm bringing a detective down to take your statement. While you wait for him, try to remember everything you can regarding any interaction you've had with this guy, okay?"

"I remember. That won't be a problem."

"Good. Would you like some water now?"

"No, I'm okay."

When the phone on the officer's desk began ringing, Debbie turned back to the wooden bench.

Rossi. Oh, my God! Rossi! That guard from Walpole...following me?

A strange new voice pulled her from her thoughts. "Ms. Bailey?"

"Yes?"

"I'm Detective DeMarco. I'll be taking your statement. It seems like you've had quite the scare. We'll just go down the hallway here," he said, guiding her to a standing position, "where we can have some privacy. You can tell me what happened. Can I get you anything?"

These people are so hospitable.

"No, sir. I'm fine. Thank you, though."

"My pleasure." He held open the door to a small room with a wooden table and four chairs, inviting her to choose a seat.

Chapter Forty-Three

On the way to Fenway, Jimmy boarded the trolley for the last leg of his trip. Today he would receive his first paycheck, and he planned o take Eileen out for a nice dinner at some place other than the Red Coach Grille. He would ask Debbie for advice on where they should go.

The trolley car jogged back and forth. A sudden jolt landed a guy who'd been hanging on to one of the side poles into Jimmy's lap. The guy's sunglasses flew off his face during the lurch. He looked up into Jimmy's face and smiled.

"Sorry, man. That was out of my control."

"It's okay, man. I know it wasn't your fault," Jimmy replied.

They gave each other a nod as the man got back on his feet and brushed himself off. After retrieving his sunglasses from the floor, he moved to the end of the car.

Jimmy couldn't shake the feeling that he'd seen the man before, but he couldn't place where.

"KEN-MOAHHHH!" the driver yelled, as the trolley screeched to a halt.

Jimmy gathered his backpack, descended the stairs, and headed toward Fenway. The sun was highlighting azure-blue skies and marshmallow-white clouds, drifting high above Boston. It would not be a good day to work in the laundry at Fenway Park. He would have preferred to be out on the field, tossing a ball with Bill Lee, but his job was to get the uniforms in order, and that's what he was going to do, rain, shine, sleet, or snow.

As he began walking, he could feel someone following close behind him, so he picked up his pace.

Why would anyone be following me?

He crossed the bridge over the Mass Pike heading toward Jersey Street and began trotting toward Fenway. Now, he could almost feel whoever it was breathing down his neck.

Deciding to utilize a tactic often used by Boston drivers when someone was tailgating, he stopped dead in his tracks.

It worked. The person who was following him tripped and stumbled over the curb and onto the street. It was the same guy who had landed on top of him earlier on the train—the one he thought looked familiar.

"Hey, wait!" Jimmy shouted, as the guy picked himself up from the ground. "Why are you following me? Better yet, who the hell *are* you?"

"No one you'd know," the stranger replied.

"What do you mean? Why are you following me? What do you want?"

"Nothin', This is just a coincidence."

"So, it's a coincidence that you got off the train when I did? That you were walking so close to me when I stopped, you bumped into me, tripped, and fell into the street? Something's up, man. Tell me, what do you want?"

"Nothin'. Nothin' at all. Like I said, it's just a coincidence. I'm going to Fenway to buy tickets for tomorrow's game."

"Then why do I feel as if I've seen you some place before?"

"I dunno. I guess I've got one of those faces everybody thinks they know. Ya' know what I mean?"

"No. Actually, I don't," Jimmy replied snidely.

"That's what my mother says, anyway."

Jimmy didn't know what else to say. He extended his hand and helped the stranger to his feet, noticing the small tattoo above his wrist. The head of a cobra. He'd seen that before, too. But, again, he couldn't place where he'd seen it.

"Hey, what's that tattoo mean?" he asked.

"Oh, just something a few of my friends and I got together and did one night. I don't even remember why we did it."

Standing on his feet, the stranger made eye contact with Jimmy, just as they'd done on the trolley.

"Thanks for helping me out of the street."

"Yeah. Okay," Jimmy said, as he watched the stranger head back toward Kenmore.

Why is he going in that direction if he plans to buy tickets for tomorrow's game? Wait a minute! The team will be on the road tomorrow! That guy was walking the same way as me when he nearly ran me over.

Chapter Forty-Four

"Ms. Bailey?"

"Yes, this is Debbie Bailey. To whom am I speaking?"

"This is Detective Tony DeMarco. Do you have a minute?"

"Yes, of course, detective. Do you have new information about the crash?"

"Some. But I have more questions, as well. Any chance I could get both you and your brother to stop by the station sometime over the next couple of days?"

"I can't speak for my brother, detective. He's quite shy when it comes to law enforcement, as you can imagine. I don't know if he'd show up without an attorney, to be honest with you. As I told you, he's on parole, and he might need to check with his parole officer first before he even speaks with you."

"I understand that. I'll speak to his parole officer, if that'd make him feel better, before he comes in here."

"Again, I can't speak for my brother, but of course, I can speak to him and get back to you."

"That would be helpful. You still have my card, right?"

"I believe I do. I'll give you a call after I hear from him."

"This is important, Ms. Bailey."

"Please call me Debbie."

"Uh, okay, Debbie it is."

"Thank you, detective."

"Well, if I can call you by your first name, you should call me by mine. I'm Tony."

She could hear the smile in his voice. "Okay, Tony. Now, does this have anything to do with the warden's death?"

"I can't really say yet, but we're still working on it."

"This is all so creepy. Should I be afraid?"

"Afraid? No. Just wary and conscious of your surroundings, I'd say."

"Wary? That's a scary word."

"I don't mean to scare you, Ms.—er—Debbie. But if you're aware of what's happening around you, you don't need to be afraid. You have my card, and my number. If you see anything suspicious let me know right away, and I'll be there."

"That's reassuring. Thank you, Tony."

"Was that a bit of sarcasm?"

"No. I meant that sincerely. But I admit to being afraid of some of the guys who might have been involved in murdering the warden."

"I didn't mean to question your fear. I just want you to know you can call me or the station if you think you need help. They usually know where I am and can find me. I've got a radio in my car. They can track me down."

"I wouldn't want to disturb your family by calling in the middle of the night." Just as the words rolled off her tongue, Debbie knew that she had been too forward by mentioning his family.

"Not a problem, Debbie. I'm on call all the time. It's part of the job."

"Okay, that makes me feel better. I won't abuse your generosity, Tony. I will keep you posted."

"Yeah, and please try to convince that brother of yours that I need to talk to the both of you. We're still trying to gather some more facts about the guy in the accident."

"I'll work on him."

"I can't ask for more than that. Thanks, Debbie. Good-bye."

"Have a good afternoon, Tony."

She bit her lip as she hung up the phone.

What in the world am I doing? I was flirting with that man.

Chapter Forty-Five

I'd washed and hung up all the uniforms from last night's game, so that everything would be ready for this afternoon's contest. I'm proud that I'm getting the job done. Some days, I even like it.

What I like more than anything, though, is being in the same atmosphere as professional ballplayers. I can feel baseball in the air. Baseball on their breath. Baseball on their uniforms. Baseball in their hands, their legs, the very core of their being. Although they are adults, at heart they are still little boys, one step up from Little League or the neighborhood sandlot, inhaling the aroma of fresh-cut, outfield grass and infield dirt. They are not afraid to get filthy sliding into second to steal a base or leaping high in the air to catch an overhead ball.

They are just like me. Or, at least, just like I was before I went to prison.

Every now and then, Bill Lee would slap me on my shoulder and ask how I'm doing. One of the younger guys, Dwight "Dewey" Evans, would playfully bump into me, smile and say, "Whoa, sorry, man!" and we'd both laugh. Rico Petrocelli always had a huge grin on his face whenever I walked by him. He knew how lucky he was to be a grown man, getting paid to play a boy's game.

Lucky. Yes, they were all lucky, just as I was fortunate that Bill Lee stuck up for me and got Mr. Yawkey to promise me a job when I got out of prison. I often wonder if it hadn't been for Bill Lee, would I, as an ex-con, have ever found a job. I'm extremely grateful to him.

Do they know that I was once like them? That I once took to the mound in minor-league ball after working with my dad for years in a backyard that was only fifteen miles from this very park? I took the same journey they did. Did they know that I once signed a contract, listened to coaches, cheers, jeers, boos, and had programs shoved in my face by eager fans asking for autographs? That I was once an unknown prospect, highly regarded by the baseball writers who were now writing about *them*?

Did they know that I had blown it? Did they know about all the chaos that was happening in my life now?

Eddie knew everything. She's my confidante, my den mother. Had she told them?

My mind swirls like the industrial dryer I use to do their laundry. I can't help but be paranoid about what is going on in my life. I worry that something bad is going to happen to my ma or my sister because of their connection to me, or that Keeshon might end up dead.

I keep looking over my shoulder.

The only place I feel safe is in the bowels of Fenway Park—the laundry room. Or peeking out from the dugout when no one else is around.

Safe behind this team that is the 1976 Boston Red Sox.

Anywhere else in Boston is fair game and I feel like a sitting duck.

Chapter Forty-Six

Debbie thought back on her conversation with Detective DeMarco, and she didn't like where her mind was taking her. There were too many *what-ifs*.

She picked up the phone.

"Ma, have you seen anything strange around the house?"

"No, dear, why do you ask?"

"No specific reason, Ma. I just want you to be aware of your surroundings, that's all. Make sure the doors and windows are locked. Keep your eyes open."

"Do you have any reason to believe that someone might try to break into *my* little house? I don't have anything here that's valuable."

No, Ma, the valuable thing there is you.

"I don't know, Ma, I just have a funny feeling. This detective questioned me about some stuff that happened at the prison when Jimmy and I were leaving there. He thinks a couple of things might be related to what happened to that poor warden—the one who was so nice to Jimmy and me."

"What could that ever be? It all sounds so far-fetched to me."

"Ma, I'd rather explain it in person, when both you and Jimmy are there. Is he home?"

"No, he should be here in about an hour. That nice girl, Eileen, is coming over tonight. I made them dinner."

"Maybe I shouldn't come over if Eileen's going to be there. I don't want to explain this in front of her. I don't know if I should even tell my roommates about this."

"Then you'd better tell me NOW, Debbie. I don't like that you're being so secretive."

"Okay, but let me explain it to Jim myself, okay? The detective said he suspects some of the guards at the prison may have had an illegal *ring* of some kind going on inside the prison, and that the warden was getting close to discovering it. That's his theory as to why the warden was killed. He thinks the ringleader is this guy named Rossi. As Jimmy and I were leaving, he tried to touch me inappropriately and I slapped his hand away. I guess you could say that I embarrassed him in front of the other guards who were standing around at the time. That's why the detective thinks they went after Keeshon."

"He doesn't think my Jimmy was involved, does he?"

"Not at all, Ma, not at all. But he thinks Jimmy might be in danger because the guards involved might think that he knows stuff about their illegal activities. And Ma—that guy Rossi, the one who tried to get fresh with me...?"

"Yeah?"

"He was following me last night on my way home. I lost him by going through a red light, and when he came through the light after me, he crashed into another car. It was a pretty bad accident. He's in the hospital now, but he might know where I live. For sure he knows the kind of car I drive."

"Oh, dear! That means you and your roommates may be in danger! Can that detective protect you?"

"I don't know, Ma, but he gave me his card and told me I could call him any hour of the day or night."

"Debbie, you make sure your doors and windows are locked. And it wouldn't hurt for you to tell your neighbors in that apartment house what's going on, too."

"I will, Ma, I will. Just let me be the one to tell Jimmy about this, though. Okay?"

Her mom let out a deep, long sigh. "Alright, Debbie. I'll let you explain it to him. I have to go finish cooking dinner now."

~ ~ ~

Mary Bailey hung up the phone and walked into her modest kitchen, smelling the magical odors coming from aging pots she'd been using for more than three decades. Comforting food—one of the few things that gave her solace since her husband had taken his own life. He took so much of her when he pulled that trigger four years ago—part of her very soul. What he didn't take, though, was her passion for her children—one who God had just returned to her.

The little town of Weymouth, founded in 1622 by wayward Pilgrims, was her home—the place where she and her husband had built a life and raised their kids. And if those hooligans tried to come into it to hurt her boy, they'd feel the wrath of Mary Bailey.

Chapter Forty-Seven

I can't stop thinking about my conversation with Eddie where she suggested I call Bud and Bobby. She said if I don't call them, she's going to reach out to her counterparts at the Braves and the Mets and find them herself.

I can't let that happen. Eddie might be like a den mother to me, but I can't let her speak for me when I'm trying to find the guys. Guess I'll start with the Mets switchboard first.

"Hello, I'm trying to reach one of your scouts, Mr. Mangino."

"Mr. Mangino? I believe he's out on the road, sir. I can connect you to the scouting department and you can leave him a message."

"Thank you, ma'am."

"Scouting Department. Marie speaking."

I was expecting an answering machine.

"Hello, Marie. My name's Jimmy Bailey. I'm trying to reach or leave a message for Bobby Mangino."

"I'm sorry, sir. Mr. Mangino is out of town. May I take a message?"

"Yes, ma'am. Could you give him my home and work phone numbers? I work at Fenway Park. I'd appreciate it."

"Yes, indeed, sir, I will. Thank you."

One down, one to go. It'll probably be harder to reach Bud since he's an actual ball player. Lucky for me, though, Eddie gave me an insider number for the Braves.

"Atlanta Braves, may I help you?"

"Yes, ma'am. I'm trying to reach Mr. Prescott, one of your pitchers. Would you please connect me with your front office?"

"No, sir, I cannot do that. I can, however, connect you with our public relations office. They may be able to better assist you."

"Thank you, ma'am. I'd appreciate that."

Ring. Ring.

"Atlanta Braves Public Relations. May I help you?"

"Yes, ma'am. My name is Jimmy Bailey. I once pitched in the minors with one of your current pitchers, Bud Prescott. I'm wondering if you might be able to get a message to him for me."

"I might. What's the message, Mr. Bailey?"

"Would you please let him know that I'm working at Fenway Park in Boston? And also, would you give him these two numbers? I would love for him to return my phone call at his earliest convenience."

"You're working at Fenway? During daylight hours? Yes, sir, I will tell him that. It will be up to him as to whether he returns your call, though. The team is on the road right now. You stated that you played ball, so I'm sure you understand."

"I do, ma'am. And I appreciate your help."

I can't wait to get to work tomorrow to tell Eddie that I took her advice.

"Eddie! Eddie! I left messages for both Bobby and Bud yesterday! Aren't you proud of me, second mom?"

"Yes, I am! And I'll be even prouder if you actually talk to them when they return your call!"

"I'm confident both will call me back. I just know they will."

Out of the blue, Eddie breaks into song. "When you wish upon a star…makes no difference who you are…"

"Really? You're singing me a Jiminy Cricket song now?"

"Anything your heart desires, will come to yoooooouuuuu!"

She is so corny! But she makes it easy to work in the laundry room.

"Eddie, do you think the Braves will give Bud the message? I mean, if someone called the Red Sox and left a phone message for one of their players, would they pass it along?"

"It's possible," she says. "I guess it depends on what the person on the other end of the phone line said. Did you mention that you played with those guys in New York?"

"Yeah, I did. But I could be some sort of con artist, for all they know."

"Did you say you worked at Fenway? That would be a door opener in my book. Gives you some sense of legitimacy, you know?"

"I guess so. They work for major league teams, and so do I. They have no idea I'm here with my second mother in the laundry room."

"And a damned fine mother I am, too!"

We both laugh at Eddie's last comment because we know she's right. She brings me food, helps me save money, keeps me out of trouble, and makes sure I do a good job, so the players are happy.

Still, when I look out at that field, my legs ache to put on a pair of spikes, my right hand twitches to pick up a ball, my left hand feels for leather, and my head senses nakedness without a baseball cap to shield it from the sun. I have uniforms in my hands, but none carry my name or number on the back. I was once part of the game, but then again, I wasn't. I work for the Red Sox, but I didn't play for them. The gap between being on their payroll and being on their team is as wide as the Grand Canyon.

Eddie nudges me out of my daydream.

"Hey, you! Wake up!"

"Huh? Oh, yeah, I was just thinking about the weather."

"Game time weather or some other kind of weather?"

"Game time, of course."

"You mean you're worried about guys sliding into bases and getting their uniforms dirty?"

"Something like that. Yeah."

"Ain't no stain we can't get out, kiddo."

"Yeah, you got that right, Eddie."

Maybe not on the fabric, Eddie, but the stain I have on my soul that keeps me from playing baseball will never go away. My father is dead because of the choices I made. I can't get that out of my head, my heart, or my spirit. I look out on that field, and I yearn to play, ache to glance up into the stands and see him nodding at me as I take to the mound and throw a pitch the way he taught me. Those days are gone, Eddie. This is the stain I can't soak, brush, or bleach out. It will be with me forever.

Eddie waltzes around the laundry room, whistling, "When You Wish Upon a Star" again, as if she has the entire Red Sox team in her pocket—as if she could sit in the owner's suite with Mrs. Yawkey any day. Eddie loves her job and does it with grace and dedication. I wonder how she can be so close to the best game in the world and not want to play it.

"Hey, Jim, take those out to the locker room, would you?"

"Sure, Eddie."

Should I confess I want to steal one of these uniforms and put it on my body, roll over the mound, run the bases, shriek, and squeal like a stuck pig because I want to play so badly, that I hunger and thirst to do it?

Nah. I neither have the guts to do the deed, nor to tell her about my fantasy. When you wish upon a star…Yup. Sure.

Chapter Forty-Eight

When Jimmy arrived home, his sister's car was parked out front. He hadn't expected her to be there because his mom was cooking dinner for him and Eileen, and he had planned that night for his mom and Eileen to get better acquainted.

Debbie was sitting in her usual spot, reading a newspaper, and sharing her opinion on everything she read.

"Hey, glad you're here," she said, folding the newspaper in half. "We need to talk."

Uh-oh. Now what?

"You remember that guy, Rossi, from Walpole?"

"The guard? Yeah."

"Well, I had another encounter with him last night. He's now at Mount Auburn Hospital."

"Ha!" Jimmy laughed. "What'd you do? Slug him?"

"No, you brat! It's what *he* tried to do to *me*! He waited for me outside my office and started following me home. He tailgated for miles, so instead of going home, I headed toward the police station. I drove through a light that was about to turn red, and when he tried to come through the light after me, he was T-boned on the driver's side by another car. He's in pretty bad shape right now."

"What? He followed you?"

"Yeah. The cops think he had something to do with what's going on out at Walpole. He might even be involved in the warden's murder."

"What? Debbie, wait! What else do you know about what's happening at Walpole?"

"Not much. The Cambridge detective, who's *kinda* cute, by the way, says the state police brought in the FBI to investigate what's going on out there. He says they're tight-lipped, though—something about a contraband/bribery/drug ring that the guards and some of the inmates were involved in. The warden found out about it, and we know what happened to him. He's pretty sure Keeshon was just a pawn in all of this."

"So, he doesn't think it was all about Keeshon and me?"

"Not all about you, but the guards didn't like your friendship, either. They thought you guys were *an item*, you know."

"Yeah, I know that. But nothing like that EVER happened."

"You don't have to convince me. I believe you."

"Wait. Did you say the detective was *kinda* cute?"

Debbie winked. "Yeah, I might have *kinda* dropped that opinion."

"Were you flirting with him, sis? C'mon, be honest."

"Maybe. Maybe not. He's a straight arrow. But I told you before, he gave me his card and told me to call him at any time of the day or night if I thought any of us were in danger. Even Ma."

"*Especially* Ma, I'd say. They must think Key and I know stuff about the inside contraband ring. I know nothing about it. I bet Key doesn't, either."

"Probably not. But I wanted to tell you this myself to make sure you stay alert and watch for anything strange."

"Anything strange? As a matter of fact, there was something weird that happened today. A guy fell on top of me on the trolley, then followed me toward Fenway. I stopped walking just to see if he was really following me, and he tripped over me. When I confronted him and asked why he was following me, he said he was on his way to the box office to buy tickets, but then turned and walked in the opposite direction of the box office. He looked familiar to me, but I couldn't place him. Maybe he worked somewhere in the prison. I just can't remember."

"Do you remember what he looked like? Can you describe him?"

"Maybe. If I thought about it long enough."

"Then *think,* dammit! What did he look like?"

"Hmmm…White guy, not quite as tall as me, maybe 5'11' or 6 feet. Brown hair sticking out of a baseball cap. Wasn't a Red Sox cap, though. Green hat. Maybe a college hat. He had a tattoo on his wrist. I saw it at the end of his shirt. Red cheeks. Maybe an Irish-looking guy. That's the best I can do."

"Should I call DeMarco to let him know?"

"If you *need* an excuse to call him…"

"Oh, shut up, baby brother! I'm trying to protect you, you know!"

"I know, I know. What about Rossi?"

"As far as I know he's still in the hospital. His car's a goner, though. I hope the guy who hit him is okay. Rossi was the one who went through the red light, so he was at fault."

"Something's wicked fishy here, Debbie. I don't like it one bit. Someone following you crashes, almost gets himself killed, they move Key out of one hospital to another one with guards, some guy follows me to Fenway—what am I supposed to think about all this? Is it all connected to Walpole?"

"I think that's what DeMarco's looking into. They've got the FBI out at the prison. I bet the guards don't like having the feds out there. I heard through my friend in the governor's office that the governor's not too keen on it, either, but they'll get to the bottom of things, I'm sure."

"What should we do until they finish the job?"

"I guess we should just stay vigilant to what's going on around us. Stay awake."

"Stay awake? Like I wasn't having problems sleeping before this."

"I mean, stay alert when you're out in public. Maybe we should get some of those silly disguises."

"What?"

"You know, the ones with the fake noses, glasses, and moustaches."

"The silly ones that look like Groucho Marx?"

"Yes! Those!"

They laughed at the thought of walking down the streets of Boston wearing silly disguises.

"It's funny, but it's better than being mugged by one of those criminals," Debbie said.

Chapter Forty-Nine

"Hey, Bud, is that you?"

"Yeah, Jim. Great to finally catch you on the phone. Don't have much time, but I wanted to make contact. How's it goin,' I mean, after…"

"After prison? It's kind of a long story, but I'm back living with my ma, and I got a job at Fenway Park. It's not much, and it'll end soon. The Sox aren't going to make the postseason. But you already knew that!"

"I do. What a letdown after last year, eh?"

"Yeah. It's tough after last year. Say, how are things with you?"

"I'm in the bullpen these days. Got traded right out of Triple-A. I'm doing well here. Great bunch of guys. And Jimmy—I met a girl…"

"Well, that's a shock!"

"Not really. She works in the Braves front office. Her name's Emily. When the season's over, I'm going to propose."

"That's great, man! I met a girl, too, Bud."

"Really? Do tell!"

"Her name's Eileen. I met her at a hospital near my ma's house when I fell and broke my wrist. She's an X-ray tech."

"Don't tell me it's your pitching arm?"

"'Fraid so. But I'm not doing much pitching these days, anyway."

"You gonna try for a comeback?"

"Maybe next year. Right now, I'm trying to get settled in and make a little money. I'm just doing whatever work they have for me at Fenway. Concession stands. Cleaning. Wherever they need me. I'm in the laundry room at the moment. I'm actually having fun learning the science of cleaning dirty uniforms."

"So, in the off season, you'll get into a workout routine and get that arm back in shape, right?"

"That's the plan."

"I'll get back in touch in the offseason. We're getting ready to leave for San Francisco. Great talkin' to you, man. Oh—I almost forgot. I may see Richie out there. He's in the bullpen for San Fran! Isn't that cool?"

"Yeah, it's great. If you see him, give him my regards, okay?"

"Will do. And I'll tell you once I propose to Emily. We'll be setting a date for a wedding soon after. I sure hope you'll plan to come—and bring Eileen. It'd be nice to meet her."

"Yeah, that would be nice. Thanks, Bud. And you take care of yourself, man. Bye."

When Jimmy hung up the phone, he wondered how it would be if he and Eileen did attend Bud's wedding. Would everyone there remember him and look down on him because he'd *done time* in prison?? Would they expect him to walk in with his head hung in shame? Or would they simply ignore him the way most people in his hometown did?

Time will tell.

Chapter Fifty

Keeshon was feeling slightly better, but the pain medicine still made him groggy.

His favorite nurse came in to do what it seemed the nurses did every ten minutes—take his vital signs.

Automatically, he raised his left arm so she could take his blood pressure; it hurt less than the right one.

The nurse chuckled. "Mr. Washington, seems like you know the drill."

"Yes, ma'am, I do. How come you gotta do this so much? I mean, how much does my blood pressuh and tempachuh change, anyway?"

"You'd be surprised. We just look for patterns—like if it's high in the morning, right after you eat, right after you have visitors, right after the doctor leaves, things like that."

"Oh, okay. Don't get many visituhs. I wish my frien' Jimmy would come to see me. Haven't seen him fo' a while."

"They've restricted your visitors for now," she explained. "Seems like they're worried someone might come in here and try to hurt you again."

"Why would someone want to do that? I didn't do nothin' to nobody."

"I guess you forgot what the FBI agents told you."

"What?"

"Someone killed the warden at the prison two days after you got beat up."

"The *wawden*? *Dead?* Why would anyone want to kill him?"

"It's been all over the news and in the paper, too."

"Haven't seen a newspapuh in a while. Next time you see somethin' in the papuh, could you let me see it?"

"I'll try to remember to do that. Okay, your blood pressure looks good. Is there anything I can get for you?"

"Some ginguh ale. And somebody to talk to…read to me. I miss Jimmy."

"I can do the ginger ale. I'm not sure I can get you a friend, unless it's me. Probably the best I can do is turn on the TV…for now."

"Okay…Fo' now is good."

Chapter Fifty-One

On his way home from Fenway, Jimmy started thinking about what he would do when September ended. He'd be out of a job again, at least in the laundry room. He had no guarantee that the Red Sox would find another position for him in the off-season.

Jimmy didn't expect them to keep him on. Eddie said she liked taking the winters off because she had laundry to do in her own house and the time off also gave her time to re-charge for the next season. She also had a husband who brought in money.

Ma lives on whatever small pension Dad left, along with a Social Security widow's allowance. Ma says the mortgage is paid, but I know she has other expenses.

Jimmy paid his mother a little out of the paychecks he brought home, although they weren't big checks. He would also put a little to the side from each check, so that he could take Eileen out to dinner or a movie every now and again. He didn't spend much on himself at all.

Jimmy worried a lot. Worried that he wouldn't get another job and would have to dip into his meager savings. Worried the Red Sox would let him go after the season ended. Worried something would happen to his mother and he'd have to find another place to live. Worried he'd screw up his chances with Eileen by saying or doing something stupid. Worried his past would come back to haunt him. Worried he'd never pick up a baseball again.

His head spun with all the thoughts swirling around in it. He couldn't focus and couldn't resolve the anxiety.

When he stepped off the bus at the end of the street, he heard footsteps behind him, walking faster and faster. He stopped; so did the footsteps. When he turned to look behind him, no one was there.

He was sure he had heard footsteps.

Suddenly, everything went dark.

Chapter Fifty-Two

"What? What do you mean my brother is in the hospital? Where? Okay, I'll be right there!"

Debbie slammed the phone down and pushed the intercom button to her secretary. "Marcia, I've gotta go! Cancel my two meetings. My brother's been mugged!"

"What? Where is he?"

"South Shore Hospital. Someone beat him up near my mom's house! I'm leaving now!"

"Okay, okay, Debbie. Let me know what happens."

"His girlfriend works at that hospital. Marcia, call the Red Sox."

"The *Red Sox*? For what?"

"He works for them. Ask for Eddie in the laundry room. She's his boss."

"A *woman* named *Eddie*? Okay, I'll call now."

Debbie grabbed her keys and briefcase and rushed out the door, yelling over her shoulder as she passed Marcia's desk. "Call my mother, too, Marcia! Tell her what's happened and to lock all her doors and be careful!"

Once Debbie began pulling away from the parking lot, she heard a voice coming from the back seat.

"Well, well, well, Ms. Bailey, where are we going in such a hurry this afternoon?"

Startled, she looked up into the rearview mirror and saw a man wearing a baseball cap. He wore no disguise so she knew that he was White, but that's all that she could make out.

"Who are you, and what are you doing in my car?!" she screamed, terror evident in her voice.

"Doesn't matter who I am. The point is, I know who *you* are," the man replied.

"How?"

"Oh, you have quite the rep with some people I know."

"Are the people you know connected with Walpole State Prison?"

"How very intuitive of you, Ms. Bailey."

"What do you want with me?"

"You have an issue with one of my friends—someone you put into the hospital."

"That guy, Rossi?"

"The very same."

"He put himself into the hospital! He ran that red light when he was following me, when he shouldn't have been!"

"He only wanted to talk to you, you know."

"Didn't seem that way to me!"

"Doesn't matter, because now you're going to talk to me. On my terms."

Debbie noticed the deepness of the man's voice. There was no Boston accent. It was almost as if he had a voice trained for radio, or as if she'd heard him on the radio or TV or something.

"And what are *your* terms?"

"You'll find out. Wherever you thought you were going, there's been a change of plans. I'll tell you where to drive."

She had already made her way to Storrow Drive and was about to get onto the Southeast Expressway when he told her to turn toward South

Station instead. They drove down Atlantic Avenue, past Anthony's Pier Four restaurant and the fish market.

"Do you like fish, Ms. Bailey? It's my favorite food."

"Of course, I like fish. I'm a Bostonian. Everyone here loves fish," she replied, now attempting to remain calm while engaging him.

"Have you eaten at Anthony's?"

"Of course. Who hasn't? They have the best popovers."

"Then you really have eaten there. What about Jimmy's, down the road?"

"Yes."

As they crossed what she and her friends always referred to as the "rickety old bridge," she tried to maintain her composure and continue her conversation with the man. She had no idea where he was taking her or whether he had a weapon.

Her mind wandered to Jimmy, beaten up and in the hospital. He was waiting for her.

"You seem to be somewhat of a restaurant connoisseur," she said. "Any other favorites?"

"I also like to dine in the North End," he replied. "When not eating fish, I love Italian food."

Albeit strange, all Debbie could think of was "Wednesday is Prince Spaghetti Day" and the commercial where the Italian mother was hanging out of the window calling her son home. She chuckled.

"What's so funny?"

"Just thought of a commercial about Italian food," she said.

"I'm not laughing."

"Okay. I just never know what's going to cross my mind."

As they passed the Gillette factory, then through the rotary at Columbia Point, he told her to drive toward the L Street Bathhouse, then past it to Castle Island.

"Pull over," he commanded, "and get out of the car."

The day was windy, cool, and clear. A handful of people were strolling around the area, some walking dogs, some pushing baby carriages. Each seemed in a world of his or her own, looking at the straw-like grass growing near the ocean, kicking nearby sand, or just not paying attention to anyone else.

In years past, Castle Island was an entry point for immigrants who made their home in South Boston or Dorchester. The area was now a place where people came for leisurely strolls, or to get fried clams at the famous Kelly's, near the L Street Bathhouse.

As she left what had once been her refuge—the safety of her beloved Volvo—Debbie had no idea what was in store. If he had a gun, he could shoot her. Looking around, she wondered if the Boston cops patrolled the area. Hundreds of times before, she had driven through and seen a strong police presence. But where were they now?

Her eyes darted around the area, so expansive, so few people to hear her if she screamed. This place had once held prisoners during the Revolutionary War.

"Don't get any ideas," he whispered, noticing her surveying the area. "Just do what I tell you."

He stood behind her so that she couldn't get a good look at him. She still didn't know if he had a weapon. She could tell that he was taller than her because she could feel his breath on the back of her head.

They passed a woman pushing a baby stroller. Debbie made a face.

"Are you okay, Miss?" the woman asked.

"Help me. Call the police," Debbie mouthed, followed by, "Sure, I'm fine," which she spoke aloud.

"Uh, okay," the woman said, nodding, as she quickly began walking away. Debbie had no idea whether the woman would do anything with the mixed message she'd sent, or even if she had understood her, but she kept walking with the man behind her.

"Good," he said. "Keep walking."

It was painful to walk on the uneven grass in her work shoes. Even though the heels weren't all that high, they weren't made for walking on hills. When one of her heels broke, she reached down to grab it.

"What the hell are you doing?" the intruder demanded.

"My shoe came apart. I need to pick it up. I'll go barefoot, but I can't walk on this grass, not in these shoes."

"Fine. Go barefoot. No tricks. You hear me?"

"Got it. But I can't walk with one shoe on, and one off. Let me just take it off." As she reached down to remove her shoe, she noticed a patrol car coming around the circle. She tried not to react, instead pretending to fall off balance while removing the shoe, hoping he wouldn't notice the patrol car. Maybe the woman with the stroller had called for help after all.

With both shoes in hand, she stood up and started walking again. He was still right behind her, steering her to the water's edge.

He's going to push me into the water. That's what he has in mind. He's planning to kill me right here in the cold Atlantic Ocean. Maybe that's why he wanted to know if I liked fish.

They passed a few other oblivious people who were enjoying the afternoon at the park. None except the woman with the stroller seemed to think anything was strange about a woman dressed in a business suit, carrying her shoes, being followed closely by a man talking to her from behind, ordering her where to go.

They were about ten steps from the water when someone approached them from behind.

"Excuse me, sir, do you know this woman?"

"Huh?"

He turned around into the face of a police officer along with Detective DeMarco.

Debbie ran as fast as she could with bare feet, diagonally away from the trio.

DeMarco had the guy on the ground while the officer was putting him in handcuffs.

Debbie looked back. On the ground lay what could have easily ended her life. A gun. She didn't know what kind it was and that didn't matter. Any gun packed enough power to kill her and send her to the bottom of the Atlantic to sleep with the fish.

She ran back over to DeMarco and the other officer. "How did you get here? How did you know something was wrong?"

"Ma'am," the officer began, "a woman with a baby carriage flagged me down and told me that she thought you might be in trouble. She described you, so I came to check it out."

"And your secretary called me," DeMarco spoke up. "Marcia, right? She said something crazy was happening. I called the hospital where your brother is, and they said you never showed up. So, when I heard this on the police scanner, I just went with a hunch."

Her head was swimming as she tried to piece it all together. Jimmy had been beaten up. She had been kidnapped and almost killed. The warden was dead. Keeshon was still recovering from his attack.

"Come on, Ms. Bailey," DeMarco said. "Let's go get your car."

"I asked you to call me Debbie."

"Okay, Debbie, let's go get your car. Do you want to go barefoot, or would you rather wear your shoes?"

"I'll carry the shoes, thanks."

He escorted her by the elbow up the hill toward the parking area.

"Where's my car?" she screamed. "Someone stole my car! That jerk must have left the keys in it!"

"We'll find it. The most important thing right now is that you're safe."

"But my car! I love that car!"

"I'm sure you do, and you can get another one just like it. I'll give you a ride. Have you ever ridden in a fancy, detective car? I'm sure it'll be a thrill," he said, attempting to lighten the tension.

"This black thing? Really?"

"Beats walking barefoot to the South Shore Hospital."

Chapter Fifty-Three

Despite his head spinning, Jimmy could hear the familiar voice. "Jimmy? Are you there? I have to take you for a C-T scan. We already took some X-rays of your neck, and now…"

"Eileen?" he muttered. "Is…Is that you, Eileen?"

He could feel her hand gently touching his. Her touch was soft, soothing the bottom part of his body but he still felt as if he'd taken a Bill Lee fastball to the back of his head. He couldn't focus or hold his head straight. *Was she pushing him in a wheelchair?* He couldn't tell. All he knew for certain was that everything around him was moving, like Paragon Park's rickety, wooden roller coaster at Nantasket Beach. Up. Down. Dip. Slow. Fast. Faster.

Think, Jim. What happened? How'd you get here? Did someone hit you? Did you pass out again? What can you remember?

The chair stopped moving. Eileen squatted down to get closer to his face. "Jimmy, I'm going to need help getting you on this table. I've got a couple of guys coming to help me. We'll be as gentle as possible."

The room was cold and dark. Jimmy couldn't open his eyes for more than a second, and when he tried, his eyes blurred and wouldn't focus. He could hear male voices asking Eileen how they could help.

"I just need help getting him onto the table and maybe some help positioning him."

The duo looked at each other and shrugged simultaneously. "Okay," they said in unison, as they began their task.

Jimmy could feel someone at his feet, and someone else at his shoulders, as they manipulated him onto the cold,, metal table that would hold him for the duration of the test. He didn't know what to expect, but he trusted Eileen to make sure he wouldn't be hurt—or at least, the pain would be minimal—because she was involved.

Someone new entered the room as the two helpers exited. Another male voice. Jimmy strained to listen, still unable to open his eyes. As Eileen explained what was about to happen during the scan, he felt what seemed like a football helmet going around his head. "You might hear strange noises, but I need you to remain as still as possible," she said.

As the sounds began, Jimmy tried to identify them. Splat. Nerd. Uga-uga. That uga-uga sound kept coming up again and again, pounding against his already tender head. He tried deep breaths to minimize the sounds. No good. He could feel his feet wiggling at the end of his body. "Stay as still as possible," he could hear Eileen's warning prior to the test, but he couldn't help moving his feet. They had a mind of their own, as if they belonged to someone else, as they made circles back and forth.

They won't listen. No one and nothing's listening to me today.

After what seemed like a lifetime, the male voice told Eileen they were done, and she removed the football helmet. Now, all that was left was for the radiologist to look at the film and determine if that blow to his head caused permanent brain damage, a concussion, or just a big bump on his noggin.

Just as they got him on, an unknown male stepped in and helped Jimmy back into the wheelchair. They talked around him as they worked as if he wasn't in the room. Although he couldn't decipher exactly what they were saying, from Eileen's giggle, he had a sneaky suspicion that the unknown male was flirting with her.

He's putting moves on Eileen! Hey, pal, leave her alone! That's my girl you're flirting with, not just some random woman in a bar!

The more he focused on the guy and his flirty language, the more he felt his face grow hotter and redder.

Good thing it's dark in here or he'd know just how furious I am that he's flirting with her!

Millions of thoughts flooded his mind. From his dad's death to the interaction that was going on now between Eileen and the stranger, Jimmy had seen a lot in his lifetime. Making it all worse was his enormous headache, the source of which no one seemed to know, including him.

Chapter Fifty-Four

Detective DeMarco headed out with Debbie to the hospital, all the while noticing her picking at her fingernails. He sensed that she was proud of her impeccable appearance, so having uneven cuticles and pieces of cracked skin around her well-groomed nails would be out of character for her.

He glanced at her every now and then. She was silent as the radio played Elton John and Kiki Dee singing, *"Don't go breaking my heart...please don't go breaking my heart..."*

"Debbie...Are you okay?"

"Huh? Oh, I'm sorry, I must've dozed off."

"I didn't think you were sleeping, just lost in thought. What're you thinking about?"

"So many things, things you have no idea about."

"I'm a good listener, if you want to talk about it."

"Maybe...just until we get to the hospital."

"Okay. Go for it."

Debbie took a deep breath as if she was about to dive into turbulent water. She explained how her dad had the opportunity to play Major League Baseball, but her mother had been opposed to it and his being on the road, so she made him choose between her and baseball. She shared that she was the eldest child, with a younger sister, Donna, and her baby brother, Jimmy.

"My dad waited for a boy so he could teach him everything he knew about baseball," she said. "From the time Jimmy was about three, my dad would come home every night, dog-tired, and take him to the backyard to play catch. As Jimmy got older, my dad began to teach him the more complex parts of the game. Things he would have used himself had he played in the big leagues."

"Your dad had the opportunity to play with guys like Ted Williams and Mickey Mantle?"

"I suppose he did. But he was so head over heels in love with my mother, he gave it all up…for her."

"I mean no disrespect toward your mom, but I think it's terrible that she would give him such an ultimatum. I don't know too many men who would have gone along with that. He must have really loved her."

"He did. When he came home after a long day at the shipyard, his eyes would light up when he saw her. You could see an actual sparkle in his eyes. In fact, they met at the shipyard. He worked there during the winter, in the offseason when he wasn't playing ball, and she worked in the office as a secretary. She batted her eyelashes at him a couple of times, and that was that.

"Under Dad's wing, Jimmy became an all-star pitcher, just like my dad had been. He was champion this, champion that, the best in New England at one point. He was a little cocky sometimes, but we all knew he was the best. Donna and I teased him about it mercilessly, and his teachers in high school gave him a pass in most of his classes. Then the Montreal Expos drafted him."

"The Expos? Did he play for them?"

"Not exactly. His first year was playing for the Jamestown Falcons in Jamestown, New York…out in the boondocks. He played for one season and was shocked when he discovered that all the other guys had been the best in the regions they'd come from, too, and the competition was stiff. Jimmy had always been a starting pitcher, but the coaches turned him into a reliever out there. He got along well in his first year. He wasn't outstanding, but he was solid.

"Then he came home for the summer, got a job at Mister Donut down the street from where we live, and was saving money. But he got in with the wrong crowd—two jerks he barely knew from high school—and he started drinking. He would go out at night to the beach near our house and drink with those guys."

"That couldn't have been good while he was training."

"Not at all, and Dad got on him about it. They fought a lot about his going out with those guys. One night they had a big argument after dinner. Jimmy wasn't planning to go out that night, but after their fight, he stormed out and walked to the beach. Those *friends* were there, but three other people he didn't know were there, too. One of them was a guy named Paulie Donovan from Southie."

"Paulie Donovan? I know that name. He was a small-town hood, right?"

"Yeah. Anyway, Jimmy wanted a beer, and Donovan was the keeper of the beer that night. When Jimmy got there, those guys were already completely blitzed. As Jimmy tells it—and I have no doubt he was being truthful, Donovan threw a punch at him and they fought to the point that Jimmy passed out, right there on the beach. He never even had the chance to get a drink."

"Donovan was an amateur boxer, as I recall."

"That's what I heard, too. Jimmy hitchhiked back home, with his face all cut up and bleeding. He went to work the next morning, and it was there that the cops arrested him for the murder of Paulie Donovan."

"Wait a minute! I heard about this case! That was *your* brother? That's why he went to prison? What I heard was there were no witnesses, your brother insisted on his innocence, his friends wouldn't stand by him, yada, yada, yada—"

"Or couldn't stand by him because they were so drunk when he got there. Jimmy *swears* by all that's holy he didn't kill Donovan. He admits he fought with him, but he didn't kill him. He has no idea who the other two guys were at the beach that night. His lawyer hired a detective to try and find them but had no luck."

"Debbie, as I recall, your brother took a plea of manslaughter. Is that right?"

"Yes, after his lawyer tried so many options and angles to prove his innocence. There were no witnesses to prove or disprove anything."

"This case was a mess. It was presented at a conference I attended. The police who investigated it called it a 'Catch 22.'"

"If they thought it was difficult, they should have tried living it. My sister, Donna, essentially left the area and moved to Atlanta to get away from it all. My mother almost had a nervous breakdown. And on the day my brother went to Walpole…"

Debbie paused to fight back the tears but couldn't stop them from flowing.

"My dad—*our* dad—shot himself…killed himself…in our backyard shed."

DeMarco pulled over to the side of the road, put on his flashing emergency lights, and walked around to the passenger side, opening the door. He knelt by the curb.

"Debbie, I'm so sorry," he said, reaching out to hug her. She let her head fall into his chest and cried until his shirt was soaked. "Cry as much as you want," he consoled. "It's okay. I don't know the right words to say."

"There are no right words," she sobbed. "There never will be. Don't you see? We feel like a cursed family. We lost my dad, Jimmy went to prison, and all the other bad stuff that happened in between. And now this? I'm afraid…so afraid."

DeMarco helped her from the car, with her head still buried in his chest. They stood on the side of the road for what seemed like half an hour, his emergency flashers still blinking, forgetting about their destination.

Chapter Fifty-Five

"Hey, Prescott! Warm up!"

"Okay, boss."

The humid, Atlanta air hung like pea soup as the Braves tied with the Mets in the top of the seventh inning. Bud didn't mind the weather; after all, he'd learned to play ball not too far from where he stood, in even steamier conditions.

The team was having a bad year, sitting at the bottom of the National League West, and this game didn't mean that much to the standings. But Bud still loved every aspect of the game—playing for his hometown team and staying sharp from one season to the next. Just like when he was a teenager, he lived to play baseball.

Slow and steady, he gripped the ball and threw some easy warm-up pitches. He thought about his soon-to-be wife as he felt the stitches in his hand and released the ball into the bullpen catcher's mitt. He felt great. Reflecting on the situation he was in—and the great hand he'd been dealt in life—lifted any anxiety he might have felt as he anticipated entering the game.

He removed his cap and wiped the sweat from his brow.

"It's a mighty hot one today, Bud," came a voice from the bullpen bench.

"Yeah, I'd say so."

"How do you feel? Are you warm enough?" the bullpen catcher called out.

"I think so," Bud said, leaning over the fence waiting for the announcer's voice.

"Now pitching for the Atlanta Braves…Number twenty-seven…Bud…Prescott."

Bud opened the door and skipped onto the field.

High in the stands was a man approximately the same age as Bud, sitting in a wheelchair. He knew Bud well. They'd been teammates in Single-A baseball years before in an affiliate of the Montreal Expos. But Bobby Mangino wasn't playing baseball anymore after an accident took his legs. Instead, he was now a scout for the Mets—the team Bud was pitching against.

Bud had no idea he was there.

Bobby wanted it that way. He wanted to surprise Bud at the end of the game and had arranged to be taken to the locker room after the ninth inning.

It had been a few years since they'd seen each other, although they'd spoken on the phone a few times. Bobby had been on the road scouting, and Bud, playing ball. Bud said he would invite Bobby to his upcoming wedding, but Bobby didn't want him to make a fuss for the guy in the wheelchair. But he did want to say hello, even for a few minutes.

He watched Bud canter in from the bullpen and take a few warm-up tosses before facing the batter. He was the same old Bud Bobby had known way back when, with the same stance, same look, same way of touching his cap before he looked in for the sign. Bobby could also see that his confidence was still there.

As a Mets' employee, Bobby shouldn't have been rooting for a member of the opposing team, but deep down in his heart, he was hoping Bud would strike out the first batter he faced. The Mets' batter worked the count to three and two after fouling off a couple of pitches, then finally he struck out swinging. Bobby was happy. Now it was time to root for his own team.

Bud made quick work of the next two batters, with two quick groundouts, one to the third baseman, the other to the shortstop. He'd be back to pitch the ninth inning.

Bobby knew it would take a while to navigate his wheelchair down to the locker room. He asked for assistance from an usher, who led him to the freight elevator and down to the first floor. Then he'd be on his own to ask for more help.

He was used to asking for help. He didn't necessarily like it, but he'd become accustomed to it, nevertheless. He didn't want pity, but so many places like these big-league parks put major challenges in the way. He liked the minor-league parks more because they were smaller and easier to navigate in a wheelchair. He could get around those, as well as the college and high school parks, so much easier than these huge places.

He found a security guard, flashed his pass, and told him what he needed to do. He heard cheering and knew the Braves had most likely scored, taking the lead over the Mets. There'd be a top of the ninth Bud would pitch, but if he shut the Mets down, the game would be over. Bobby wanted to be in the locker room when Bud came in.

The security guard pushed his wheelchair into the locker room, much to the protestation of the Braves' trainer.

"Hey, get that guy out of here, Joe!"

"No, you don't understand. This guy used to play ball with Prescott. He wants to see him when the game's over. He has a pass."

The trainer looked down at the wheelchair. "*You* played ball with Prescott? Where? Memphis?"

"No, Jamestown, New York," Bobby replied. "Expos farm club. Single-A."

"Pretty far from here, I'd say. Why're you here now?"

"I'm a scout for the Mets."

"*The Mets*? This here's enemy territory!" he laughed. "Come on in, er—what'd you say your name was?"

"Bobby. Bobby Mangino."

"Okay, Bobby Mangino. You just wait here. Can I get you anything? Water?"

"No, I'll be fine. Just want to say a quick hello to Bud."

Cheers went up throughout the ballpark once again, as victory music played in the background.

"Won't be long now, Bobby Mangino. He'll be walking in soon," the trainer said.

Cleats clunked down the dugout steps as Braves players walked in, removing sweaty caps, and dropping gloves on benches in front of lockers. Bobby loved the smell of sweaty locker rooms. They brought back memories of days gone by when his legs worked, when he, too, tied his own cleats, ran bases, and stood on a pitching mound. He yearned for a day—one day—when he might do it all again, but he knew that was impossible.

He looked up and saw a familiar face, the one he'd seen from afar just a few minutes ago.

As Bud came through the door, he got a glimpse of the wheelchair and had a brief clue of who might be in it.

"Bobby? Is that you, Man-GEEN-o?" he yelled, running over to hug his old buddy.

"Bud! How're you doing? I watched you pitch. Man, you look great!"

"I feel pretty good for a guy who's getting on in years. Hey, what're you doing here in Atlanta?"

"I'm still scouting for the Mets. I've got a couple of kids to look at over the next couple of weeks. Got to go to Savannah and then over to Charleston. You guys turn out some great ballplayers down here."

Bud smiled. "If you say so, you're the scout. But hey, what're you doing for dinner? I'd love for you to meet my fiancée. She'd love to meet you. I talk about you and Jimmy all the time."

"I bet you do. But I don't want to barge in on you."

"Not a problem. Let me grab a quick shower and then I'll call her. If there's a problem going out for dinner, I'll grab something on the way home. Emily's going to be so excited!"

Bobby was glad Bud had mentioned her name as he couldn't remember it from their past conversations. He sat in a corner of the locker room, listening to the guys' banter and watching them flick towels at each other, taking in the sights, sounds, and smells of a life he'd dreamed of having, an elite fraternity he'd yearned to join, if only he hadn't taken a certain bus ride to Buffalo one night.

Chapter Fifty-Six

"No concussion," the doctor proclaimed, "but you've got a big egg on that head of yours. You must have a pretty thick skull."

"That's what my father always said," Jimmy replied. "Always told me he couldn't get much through my thick skull."

The doctor chuckled. "You have no idea what someone hit you with, or why they wanted to hurt you?"

"No, they came up from behind. I didn't even see who it was. Thought I heard someone in the bushes but couldn't tell if it was the wind or my imagination. Just walking home from the bus stop."

"The police said it didn't seem as if they took anything from you. Were you missing anything?"

"I don't know. Don't have much for anyone to take."

"I'm sure they'll be around to ask you questions. I'd like to keep you here overnight and check you in the morning. Think that'd be the best thing."

"Has anyone called my mother? Or my sister? I worry about my mother."

"Is there any particular reason you have to worry about your mother?"

"It's a long story, and I've got a headache, but I need to know if my sister is on her way here."

"You can check with the nurses. In the meantime, I want you to stay here overnight. I'll check on you again in the morning."

"Okay, doc—what did you say your name was?"

"Dr. Costa. I'm a neurologist. My office is in the professional building across the street. I'll probably want to see you in a week to ten days after you're discharged."

"Fine with me. And I should expect to hear from the police soon?"

"I can't speak to when they'll come by to talk with you," the doctor replied, extending his hand. "Mr. Bailey, I'll see you in the morning."

He whisked out of the room, chart in hand, his white coat flowing as the door closed behind him.

Jimmy looked over at the empty bed next to him all made up, hospital style, with the sterile, white sheets tucked in just so, the back of the bed tilted at a ninety-degree angle with a thin pillow leaning against it.

Dizziness and a headache took over as he tried to recall exactly what happened before someone knocked him out. He remembered getting off the bus and walking up the street toward the house. He vaguely remembered feeling that someone was following him and turning to look back. When he didn't see anyone, he remembered continuing to walk, and then nothing else until he woke up in the hospital.

The doctor said he didn't have a concussion, but it still hurt.

Keeshon flashed through his mind.

If my head is hurting this badly, I can't even imagine what his pain was like after the beating he took.

A knock at the door caused Jimmy to raise his head.

Owww! More pain!

"Who's there?"

"Jimmy? It's Eileen."

Finally! My guardian angel has arrived.

Chapter Fifty-Seven

"I'm not going to put on the siren, if that's what you're worried about," DeMarco joked.

Debbie chuckled. She'd stopped crying a few miles back, but anyone who looked at her face would have known she'd shed tears.

"So, you don't want to make a grand entrance, detective? You don't want everyone in the hospital to know that you're a big man in the Cambridge Police Department?"

"How do you know that I'm a big man in the Cambridge Police Department?"

"Do you think for one second that I'd get into a car with someone I hadn't checked out beforehand? I've got friends in high places, too, you know."

"You mean, like the governor's office?"

"Exactly."

"I bet you do. I bet you like it that way."

"Indeed, I do. I worked hard to make those connections, and I respect them. It's a two-way street."

Debbie was in full-flirt mode. She had a boyfriend, but DeMarco was smooth as silk, handsome, confident, strong, and knew the right things to say at exactly the right time. She'd never run across anyone like him before. It felt like she was in a movie—he was an Italian version of Ryan O'Neal, and she was the unknown ingenue who had made a life for herself and never thought she'd find someone like him.

He pulled into a parking space, got out, and walked around to open her door. He reached his arm out to hers as she slipped her feet out of the car. He smiled when he noticed her blushing.

"Why, thank you, sir. You're too kind."

"I wondered how you'd react if I opened your door. I don't mean to insult you, but this is how I was raised to treat a woman."

She smiled back at him and extended her hand.

"Then, whoever taught you how to treat a woman, raised you right."

They walked into the hospital hand in hand.

Chapter Fifty-Eight

Alone, Mary Bailey puttered around her kitchen, humming an old tune. When she heard banging in the back yard, Debbie's words came back to her:

Ma, be careful. This whole situation with Jimmy, his friend from prison, Keeshon, and the warden is serious stuff. Make sure the doors are locked, and don't leave the windows open, no matter how hot it is outside. I mean it, Ma. This isn't the time to let your guard down.

Mary grabbed her rolling pin and moved toward the back door. Jimmy had a baseball bat on the cellar landing. Maybe she could get that if she moved quietly. With the rolling pin in one hand, she leaned toward the baseball bat and slowly picked it up with her other hand. She gripped both tightly.

When she leaned against the wall near the entrance to the cellar, trying to make herself invisible, she saw the back door handle wiggle.

Someone was trying to get in.

Her mind sprang into action. The bat would probably be a better weapon, but the rolling pin was in her right hand. If she put one of them down, she'd make a noise. She had to stay as quiet as possible.

Suddenly, the door flung open, and when it did, she began swinging. She used both of her hands to slam the intruder over the head as hard as she could. Once he was on the floor, knocked out cold, she took the bat and hit him once again. "For good measure," she said, standing over him, wondering what to do next.

She had to get to the phone. She didn't know how, but she quickly stepped over the intruder lying on her floor and hurried to the living room. When she stopped for a moment, she thought better of that decision. Still gripping the bat and rolling pin, she ran out the front door, crossed the street, and began beating on her neighbor's door.

"Mary, what the hell?"

"Let me in, Doris! NOW!" she said, pushing her way past her neighbor.

"Lock the door, Doris! I have an emergency. Call the police! NOW! Where's your phone?"

Doris gave her a blank stare.

"I'm not kidding! We need to call the police! Someone broke into my house, and I hit him over the head with Jimmy's bat!"

Doris was speechless but pointed to the phone.

Mary dialed 911 as fast as she could, giving them her address and explaining everything that had happened. She shared that she was across the street at her neighbor's and would be staying there until they arrived.

Minutes later after hanging up the call, they saw flashing lights in front of her house. Mary jumped out of Doris's front door waving and screaming. "Over here! I'm over here! Thank God you're here! I was so scared!"

"Calm down, ma'am. Are you the one who made the call?" the approaching officer asked.

"Yes! Yes, it was me! I was alone in my house and..."

"You say you hit the guy who broke in with a baseball bat? On the head?"

"I-I-I think it was the bat. Or my rolling pin. It all happened so fast!"

The officer put his hand on her shoulder. "Okay. Try to calm down a little. Go back inside your friend's house. We're going over to your house to check it out. With any luck, he's still out cold. We'll come get you when everything is clear."

Mary nodded and headed back to Doris's house. Doris's husband had woken up from where he'd fallen asleep in front of the TV and wanted to know what all the racket was about.

"Oh, shush, Harold, I'll explain it to you later," Doris scolded.

One officer went around the back of the house and the other entered through the front door. The flashing lights atop the police cruiser continued to flash, attracting a crowd from houses all along the street.

Neighbors came out dressed in an assortment of clothing—women in crinkled housecoats with their hair bound in curlers and kerchiefs, and men in shorts and bulging T-shirts that really didn't fit anymore.

Standing on her neighbor's porch, Mary could hear the faint sound of banging, but no gunshots.

The two officers emerged from around the back with an unidentified man in handcuffs and put him in the cruiser. One of the officers approached Mary.

"Ma'am, do you recognize this man?"

Mary peered into the car and took a long look. "Did I put that big egg on top of his face?" She looked at the man again, this time right in his eyes. "I'm so sorry, but you were breaking into my house, and you scared me," she said.

The officer frowned. "Ma'am, he had a gun, and since you didn't invite him, I'm quite sure he was prepared to use it. You shouldn't be apologizing to *him*."

"But I hurt him. I didn't mean to. I was just all alone..."

Doris cut in. "Officer, you don't know Mary Bailey like I do. She'd have a hard time killing a fly if it was infesting her food!"

"I understand. I really do. But what I need to know is, ma'am, do you know this man? Have you seen him before?"

Mary tried ignoring the huge bruise on top of the man's head. "No, sir, he doesn't look familiar to me. Maybe my son, or my daughter might recognize him, but neither of them are here now. I was expecting them both to come home, but they're late. I don't know where they are."

The other officer turned off the cruiser's lights as people began heading back inside their homes. "Hey, Johnny, we gotta go. Another call. And we gotta get this guy to the station first," he said.

"Yeah, right. Ma'am, here is my card. If you could have your son and daughter call me, that would be great."

As the cruiser began pulling away, the man in the back seat made an obscene gesture at her through the window. She gasped.

"And I was nice to him," she muttered.

She looked down at the card: Officer John T. Howell, Weymouth Police.

"But he was a nice young man," she said out loud. "A nice young man."

As she walked back to her house, she realized Doris's husband was following her.

"Just want to make sure your house is all locked up, Mary."

"Oh, Harold, that's kind of you."

They walked around to the back door. Mary thought she had heard banging while she was standing in front of Doris's house. She now realized what the banging had been. The guy who'd tried to break in had used her screen door for batting practice, until the police officers found him.

"Good thing you came over, Harold. I wouldn't want to walk in here and find that on my own."

Harold grunted and began picking up pieces of door debris. He knew it would be a long night. Good thing he was retired.

Chapter Fifty-Nine

Keeshon was restless. He was also lonely. He hadn't heard from Jimmy in quite a while, and he'd read all the books he'd left when he'd come to visit him in the other hospital.

His current hospital was not as nice as the other one. The nurses were nice, but he had no idea why he had to have 24/7 security outside his hospital room.

I'm just a low-level, Black boy from Roxbury who's spent time in prison. I'll probably be going back. And I probably won't make it out alive the next time.

He wanted to see another face, hear another voice, one that wasn't on the television. How many times could he listen to the Sweathogs on "Welcome Back, Kotter," or the theme song from "The Jeffersons?" He'd never seen either of these shows before he was beaten to an inch of his life, but that's all he'd done since being in the hospital. Watch TV. Shows like "Sanford and Son" and "Barney Miller" made him laugh. Now that he had no more books to read, when he wasn't watching television, he slept.

He wanted to be like Steve Austin, the fictional "Six Million Dollar Man" and get all his parts replaced so he could run like the wind.

I wish I had bionic strength when those goons at Walpole had come afta' me. I'd have shown them who was boss.

Keeshon didn't like most police shows, but every now and then he watched "Hawaii Five-O." He'd always wondered what it would be like to go to an exotic place like Hawaii. Palm trees. Beautiful beaches. Surfers riding the waves. It seemed like such a peaceful place.

Sometimes he simply counted the tiles on the ceiling to make sure his bed was in the right position. Four tiles to the back for the head of the bed. Twelve from the left, sixteen from the right, ten from the foot. If they used the bed to take him for an X-ray or something, he would always know if it was out of position when they returned him, simply by counting ceiling tiles. If anything was off, he would ask the orderly to put him and his bed into their proper position.

He was drifting off to sleep, thinking of Hawaiian beaches and surfers, when he heard a scuffle outside his door. He quickly sat upright, causing a sharp pain to shoot from his abdomen to his chest. When he heard the guard yelling, he pressed the nurse call button.

He could hear some of the hospital staff outside his door talking in hushed tones, but he couldn't figure out what was going on. He turned the TV off and gripped the side rails of the bed.

Something's not right! What's happening out there?

The room started spinning as he tried to pull himself together. Gripping the bed rails tighter and tighter, his heart monitor began to scream. A nurse flung open the door and rushed in.

"CODE BLUE! Get the crash cart!"

Over the loudspeaker, he barely heard the announcement.

"Code Blue, third floor, A Wing," grew fainter and fainter.

Keeshon couldn't figure out what was happening to him, as an army of medical figures swarmed around him. It felt as if his chest, arms, and legs, were being bounced all over the place.

He felt as if he were floating above all the chaos, as they continued frantically poking and prodding. Then, he saw her face— the woman he'd once worked for whose family had accused him of stealing money. The lie that had sent him to prison.

"I'm so sorry, Keeshon," she whispered. "You were such a nice companion to me. I don't know why they didn't believe that I gave you that money. I'm so sorry you went to prison." She reached her hand out to touch his before her image faded away. He tried to find her again, but she was gone.

Tubes and paddles. "CLEAR!" Paddles again. "CLEAR!" He was back in his body again. His chest hurt, but his head hurt more.

"Mr. Washington, can you hear me?!" the doctor leaning over him shouted.

Keeshon nodded his head.

"Good. You've been through quite an ordeal. Your nurse will try to make you more comfortable now. We'll move all this equipment away. You should be able to breathe better now."

He heard clattering and squeaky wheels as medical staff removed carts and various paraphernalia from the room. He couldn't tell how many people had been in his room, but when all was said and done, he was with his favorite nurse and one orderly.

Elaine put her hand in his. "Mr. Washington, you had a close call. I thought we were going to lose you," she said.

With a breathing tube up his nose and a tube down his throat, he couldn't speak. He felt out of control, even more so than the day he was put in prison.

"It's okay," she said. "I know you can't talk. They'll come back in about an hour to remove the N-G tube. We're going to keep you as comfortable as possible. Maybe we can get one of the books your friend brought and read to you for a while. I'll see if I can find one."

Keeshon's head was still spinning. He didn't know what to think, much less what to do.

Chapter Sixty

"Do you think I'll ever see my car again?" Debbie asked, as Detective DeMarco drove toward the Fore River Bridge.

"Probably not," he replied. "But your insurance company will pay for a new one. Maybe you can even get next year's model."

"Do you always try to make lemonade out of lemons in situations like this?"

"The missing car is the least of our worries here, Debbie. The car can be replaced. I'm more concerned that something may be happening with your mother and brother. These guys aren't fooling around. There's a lot more going on here than we know about. The FBI is on site at the prison but they're pretty tight-lipped about what they've found."

"Yeah, my source at the governor's office isn't spilling any beans, either."

"How do you know this guy from the governor's office?"

"Why do you want to know?" she asked.

"Because he called me this morning. Said he wanted to know what my 'relationship' with you was."

"And what did you tell him?"

"I didn't tell him anything. I asked him about *his* relationship with you. He didn't respond."

She laughed. "I met him when we were in grad school. We worked on a few projects together. He had a crush on me—or so my friends thought. I was pretty clear that I was only interested in a professional relationship. He's married now to someone else we were in school with. She's nice—and wicked smart, too, I might add."

"In school? You mean Harvard?"

"Yeah... *That* school."

"So... He had a crush on you... I guess he and I have something in common, then."

Debbie felt her face flush red. Again.

"And just what does *that* mean?" she asked.

He sighed. "You don't know? You haven't figured out that I've got a crush on you? Except I think for me it's gone up a step further than the crush phase."

Now her face was on fire—scarlet. She wasn't the blushing type or one to become silent when confronted with comments such as this. Yet she was dumbfounded. Speechless. Tongue-tied.

"Uh—uh—uh..." she stumbled.

"Oh, I don't mean to embarrass you," he said. "I've just been looking for just the right way to tell you that I like you."

"You mean, more than saving my life?"

"Saving your life is in my job description," he said. "That's not the point. The point is, I want to spend time with you without having to save your life. As in, have a normal life without all these crazy people who seem to want to kill you, your brother, and his former cellmate."

"So, you would have saved my life even if I'd been just some jamoke in Cambridge who had found someone waiting in the back seat of her car?"

"Yes, I would have. That's my job. Most of the time, I don't get involved with the people I work with through law enforcement, but you—you—I haven't been able to get you out of my mind since the first time I laid eyes on you."

"The old 'love at first sight' line, huh?" she teased.

"It's not a line, and it's not just your physical beauty," he insisted. "Your presence overwhelms me. Who you are. How you carry yourself. You know yourself and where you want to go in life. I find those things attractive."

"I hope so. I've been planning my life since I was in the second grade."

"Do you have room for me in your plans?"

No one had ever asked her anything like that before, at least, not in those words. She didn't know how to respond. In the space of fifteen minutes, she was once again speechless.

As he drove around the corner toward her mother's house, they could quickly see that the street was filled with neighbors wandering around two police cars with their lights flashing.

"What's *this* all about?" DeMarco asked. "Looks like we're walking into another fresh hell."

Debbie didn't wait for the car to come to a complete stop before she opened her door and jumped out.

"Ma!!! Where's my mother," she shouted into the throng of people.

Chapter Sixty-One

Eileen sat next to Jimmy, explaining that she'd tried several times to contact his mother, but her calls had gone unanswered.

"She's not answering, Jimmy. Do you think she could be at one of the neighbor's houses?"

"Not likely. Something's wrong, Eileen. I just know it. She's a homebody. She stays home all the time. She doesn't drive and she even needs someone to take her to the grocery store. She wouldn't be out at the grocery store now, anyway."

"Do you think I should try the police?"

"Maybe. I hate to think so, but maybe."

"Okay. I'll be right back."

Eileen walked into the hallway to make the call to the Weymouth Police. If something was wrong, she did not want to alarm him.

She called the police non-emergency number, gave Jimmy's address, and asked if there had been any police calls to that part of North Weymouth.

"Hold on, please, Miss. I think you should talk to the desk sergeant," came the reply. The words left her uneasy.

After what seemed like a lifetime, another voice came on the line. "Sergeant Waters here. To whom am I speaking?"

"My name is Eileen Maloney. I'm an X-ray tech at South Shore Hospital. One of my patients has been trying unsuccessfully to reach his mother at her home. He's concerned that something may have happened to her. She lives in North Weymouth."

After giving Sergeant Waters the address, Eileen heard an audible sigh at the end of the phone. "What's your patient's name, ma'am?"

"Jim Bailey, sir."

"Well, nothing happened to *her*," he said. "But she did something to someone who tried to break into her house. Hit 'im over the head with a baseball bat. Did a job on 'im, but we arrested the intruder, not her. She's fine. She's with her neighbor across the street now. She told the patrol officer she's waiting for her son and daughter to get there before she goes back home."

"Wait—what? She hit someone with a baseball bat?"

"Yup. That's what I said. At least that's what's in the report I have on my desk. You should probably tell Mr. Bailey about this. Has he been admitted to South Shore for something?"

Eileen explained Jimmy's situation and told the sergeant that she'd pass the information along to him.

"Thanks, Sergeant Waters. I appreciate your help. I'm sure Mr. Bailey will be happy to know his mother is safe."

"Anytime, Miss, anytime. Call me if you have more questions, or you can have Mr. Bailey call me himself. Just tell him to ask for Sergeant Waters."

"Yes, I will. Thanks again."

Chapter Sixty-Two

Barefoot, Debbie raced through the crowd.

"Where's my mother?!" she screamed, as the gathered crowd of mostly elderly neighbors moved out of her way. "Where's my brother?! What's happened here?!"

"Calm down, Debbie!" one of the neighbors called out. "Wait until you hear what your mother did. She's the neighborhood hero!"

"Hero? What?"

Blocking part of the street, DeMarco got out and walked toward Debbie with the shoes she'd removed at Castle Island in his hands.

"Yours?" he asked, with a smirk.

The crowd standing within earshot chuckled.

"Don't embarrass me," she said, while taking the shoes back from him. "I'm trying to figure out what's going on here. These people are telling me my mother's a hero. I have no clue what that means..."

"What that means," came a voice behind a screen door, "is that I beat up an intruder with your brother's baseball bat. He tried coming in the back door, but I stopped him."

"Ma? Is that you?"

"Yes, Debbie, it's me," her mother replied, voice quivering a little. "I don't know how I did it, but I did it. Maybe your father's ghost guided my hand. I had Jimmy's bat in one hand and my rolling pin in the other. To be honest, I don't know if I hit him with the bat or the rolling pin."

"It was definitely the bat!" one of the neighbors yelled out. "If you saw that guy's head, you'd know it was the bat!"

Her mother came down from the neighbor's porch.

"Dear, let's go back to the house and I'll show you the back door and tell you exactly what happened," she said, linking her arm through Debbie's. "And who is this handsome, young man?" she asked, looking up at DeMarco.

"Ma, this is Detective DeMarco. He's been working on the case of those men who have been stalking me in Cambridge. He just saved my life in Castle Island. But that's another story for another time."

"*Detective* DeMarco? I see. Well, you can tell me your story of running from the bad guys and I'll tell you mine, my dear. It all feels so 'Hawaii Five-O-ish,' doesn't it? And it's nice to meet you, *Detective* DeMarco. I can fix you something to eat and…"

"No, no, Mrs. Bailey, that won't be necessary but thank you. I just need to re-park my car. I was a little sloppy when I pulled up the street," he said.

"Yeah!" someone from the crowd yelled. "Didn't you take driver's ed?"

Laughter erupted from the crowd.

"Take it? I *taught* it!" DeMarco replied, jokingly, as he raised his keys high in the air and skipped up the street toward his car.

Debbie and Mary Bailey chuckled as they walked into the old homestead, elbows locked as if they were schoolgirls heading to a teenage dance.

"He's awfully cute, Debbie."

"Yes, he is, Ma."

"Italian, I guess?"

"So his name would imply."

"I bet his mother's a great cook."

"I bet mine's a better cook."

"I bet his mother never decked someone over the head with a baseball bat."

"I wouldn't take *that* bet," Debbie said, leaning into her mom with a giggle.

Debbie had never felt this way before. Ever.

She was used to having any man she wanted, winding him around her finger, having him at her beck and call. But Detective DeMarco was someone who intrigued her. He was unlike anyone she'd ever met. Now he was meeting her mother.

They were seated in the living room when DeMarco rang the doorbell.

"Come on in, the door's open," Mary Bailey called out.

"Did you put your baseball bat away?" he teased, as he eased the door open.

Mary Bailey laughed.

"I think I like you, Detective DeMarco," she said.

"I hope so," he replied, "but please, call me Tony."

"Okay, Tony, come on in. All baseball bats and rolling pins have been safely put away."

The three sat down and exchanged tales of how Debbie had escaped the guy who caused her Volvo to be stolen on Castle Island, while Mary Bailey gave details of her Wild West encounter with the guy on her back porch.

After they regaled each other, Tony became somber.

"I'm afraid we need to get serious," he said. "I'm not sure we're completely done with these shenanigans. There's something dangerous about this conspiracy the FBI is investigating, and I'm not quite sure where it's going. Debbie, you, and your roommates need to be careful and take extra precautions. Mrs. Bailey, you need to be wary, as well. I don't know what their next move will be."

Debbie smiled. The conversation between Tony and her mother was endearing.

"Speaking of being careful, Debbie, where is your brother? Maybe we should call his girlfriend over at the hospital," Mary suggested, making a beeline for the phone book to find the hospital's phone number.

Debbie excused herself to the ladies' room. She'd already had a trying day and did not want to be around when her mom got the news about Jimmy.

"South Shore Hospital? Please connect me to the X-ray Department. I'm looking for Eileen…No, I don't know her last name. Just Eileen. Yes, I'll hold…"

"Ma'am, I'm putting you through," the voice on the other end of the line said.

"Hello, this is Eileen Maloney. Can I help you?"

"Eileen, this is Mary Bailey, Jimmy's mom. We're trying to find him. Have you seen or heard from him?"

"Oh, hi, Mrs. Bailey. I left a message about him with a police officer. I guess you didn't get it. He's here at South Shore. Someone attacked him from behind as he was walking home."

"Attacked him?!" Mary screamed into the phone. "Is he okay?"

"He has a bump on his noggin, but he will be fine."

"Can we come over and see him now?" Mary asked, covering the mouthpiece on the phone when Debbie returned to the room, as her mom motioned that she was talking to Eileen.

"You can come now. I'm pretty sure seeing both of you will relieve some of his anxiety."

"Tell him we're on our way," Mary said, hanging up the phone without waiting for a response from Eileen.

The trio headed to Tony's car, with Tony in the middle and one Bailey woman on each arm.

"Are both your back and front doors locked, Mrs. Bailey?" he asked.

"I think so," she replied.

"I'll go back and check," he said. "Don't want any surprises when you come home."

Around the back, he saw where the intruder had jiggled the screen door open, but Mary had reinforced the door leading into the house with a second lock. The key lock was also secured. As he walked to the front, he heard noises around the side bushes. Hand on his holster, he crept to the front, eyes scanning from left to right in the dark.

He rounded the corner to find a couple of kids around eleven or twelve on the front steps, whispering to one another.

"Is this where the old lady bonked the guy who was trying to break in?" one asked.

"Yeah, I think so. The cops were here," the other one said.

"Keep ya voice down, ya dummy!" said the first one. "She might be in there. She must be one big, ole lady!"

"Yeah, maybe."

Realizing that they were kids, Tony stood up. "Hey! You two!"

Startled, both boys jumped about two feet in the air when they heard him yell.

"WHAAAA!!! Who are YOU?"

"I'm a cop," Tony said, "and I want you out of here. You think the old lady is strong? You don't want to mess with me."

The duo went barreling down the street, looking back to ensure that Tony wasn't hot on their heels.

Tony snickered as he walked back to the car, shaking his head and clicking his shoes on the pavement. Debbie and her mother were laughing when he approached the car, but stopped abruptly when he got in.

"You had a couple of visitors, Mrs. Bailey," he said. "No one dangerous, just a couple of kids—teenagers, maybe—who wanted to meet 'the old lady who bonked a guy with a baseball bat.' It seems you're growing a fan club."

"Did you get a good look at them?" Debbie asked.

"No, but I got a kick out of scaring the daylights out of them. Listen, I'm worried about you staying here in this house, Mrs. Bailey. The real bad guys—the ones we're trying to find—know where you live. Do you have anywhere else you can go? A relative's house, or a friend's?"

"I can't think of anywhere," she replied. "Besides, wherever I go, Jimmy has to go with me. He has nowhere to go, either."

"Jimmy. That's right, Jimmy. He needs to be safe, as well. We'll get something figured out," Tony said. "But now, we have to head over to the hospital to see how Jimmy's doing."

"Do you know how to get there?" Debbie asked.

"Of course," he replied. "Police officers have a sixth sense when it comes to finding hospitals."

Chapter Sixty-Three

"Was I really dyin', Miss Elaine?" Keeshon asked.

"You came close this time, my friend. We're glad you're still here, though. We want you to live a long time."

"I've neva had no one to care fo' me the way you do, Miss Elaine. Wanna know a secret?"

"Of course. I'll keep it between you and me."

"Good. When I was dyin,' I saw Miss Kittel, the lady I used to look afta. She gave me some money so I could git a place to live. It was a gift. When she died, hah family accused me of stealin' it, so that's why I was in prison. She told me she was sorry that hah family got me sent away. She said I didn't deserve none of the way they treated me. Then she disappeared."

"Do you feel better, now that you saw her?"

"Maybe. But was I just imaginin' that? Do you think I really saw hah?"

"You were very close to death, Keeshon. I don't know what that means. I do know you're back now and you're going to get better. Her family can't hurt you anymore."

"You sure? Do they know I'm heah?"

"No. We're keeping that a secret, too."

"Does Jimmy know I'm heah?"

"That I don't know. Maybe you could call him in a couple of days. We would have to ask the guard if it's okay first."

"Okay. But now I think I will sleep. You been too kind to me, Miss Elaine."

She put her hand on his shoulder. "And you're a fine human being, Keeshon. You deserve so much better than what you've been through."

"I been lucky to find people like you and my frien',, Jimmy, to look out fo' me."

"It's my pleasure to help you get better," she said, pulling up his sheet and blanket so that he'd be warm. "You let me know if you need anything. I'll be here until eleven." She dimmed the light over his bed and touched his shoulder once again. "Sweet dreams, Keeshon."

Chapter Sixty-Four

Tony dropped Debbie and her mother off at the hospital's front door. They asked the front desk volunteer where Jimmy's room was and made their way down the hallway. Before they knew it, Tony had caught up with them and again was escorting them, one on each arm, to see Jimmy.

Debbie knocked lightly. "Come in," she heard Eileen call out softly.

TV remote control in hand, bandage on his head, Jimmy glanced up and saw the trio come through the door. "Ma! You're here! I was hoping you'd come!"

"I told you they were coming," Eileen said.

"Yeah, but since I got this bump on my head, I'm not myself. I forgot just that quickly."

"Good excuse," Debbie said. "What was your excuse before you were hit on the head?"

"Haha, sis," he replied sarcastically.

Mary Bailey was already at Jimmy's side, hugging him. "We have a lot to tell you, Jimmy," she said. "For starters, let me tell you that I've never been so thankful for one of your baseball bats before in my life."

Tony pulled a chair up for her to sit right beside Jimmy's bed. She related the tale, complete with the flashing lights from the police cars in the street, and the attention she got from the neighbors. "And Jimmy," she added, "it was a good thing your bat was there. He had a *gun*."

"What? A gun?!"

"Yeah. I had my rolling pin in one hand and your baseball bat in the other. To tell you the truth, dear, I don't know if I hit him with the rolling pin or the bat. I think it was the bat, though, because I knocked him clean out. Then I ran across the street to the neighbor's house."

Jimmy glanced around the room. "Who are you?" he asked Tony.

"Detective Tony DeMarco, Cambridge Police," Tony replied. "And your sister has a tale of her own to tell."

Debbie explained what she'd been through at Castle Island, how her car had been stolen, and how close she'd come to "sleeping with the fishes." She added that Tony had been alerted through the MDC Police after a woman passing by realized that something was wrong.

What she didn't tell him, though, was how she was developing feelings for Tony, and how she was trying to figure out how to dump the guy she was dating. She also left out the part about how afraid she was that this conspiracy had put their family in danger.

"Tony says Ma shouldn't stay in her house because these people know where she lives," Debbie said. "That means we need to find a place for both of you to stay until this thing is settled."

"Rossi is still in Mount Auburn Hospital after he tried to run your sister off the road. That's how I got involved. He followed her from her job," Tony explained. "We think he's running part of the operation to get at you—through your family—from his hospital bed. We'll get to the bottom of all of it. The investigation is already underway."

"Wow. That's a lot to digest," Jimmy said. "So, we need to find somewhere else to live? What about my sister and her roommates?" Jimmy asked.

"I'm concerned about them, too. They're in my precinct, so I've got them on our radar," Tony assured him.

A long silence blanketed the room.

"So, this is why they went after Keeshon?"

"We think they went after him to get back at your sister after the incident at the prison the day you were released. But we have arranged for him to be guarded in his hospital so that no one will be able to harm him there. In fact, that's why we moved him from Mass General to another hospital," Tony said.

"You sure he'll be safe?" Jimmy asked.

"As safe as we can make him. He's in tough shape after what they did to him," Tony said.

"And that's all my fault—"

"No, Jimmy," interrupted Debbie, "it's all *my* fault. If I had just ignored Rossi's behavior, they might have left Keeshon alone."

"I wouldn't necessarily say so," Tony said. "Those guards had something in mind for him as soon as Jimmy left prison. The warden was on to them. He'd already begun an investigation that was supposed to be confidential, but somehow the guards found out. When they attacked Keeshon, they figured that would send a message to the warden, but when he wouldn't back off, they killed him."

Eileen sat in silence during the entire exchange but suddenly felt the need to clear her throat. "Excuse me, Detective. Because I'm friends with Jimmy, do you really think that my roommates and I could be in danger, too? Do you think they know what kind of cars we all drive, my roommates and me?"

"I don't know how to answer that question, but I'd say yes, you should be concerned," Tony replied. "Anyone who's connected to Jimmy and his family should be worried in some way. I just need to find a place for Jimmy and his mother to live until this blows over."

Debbie looked at Tony while he was speaking. His confidence, his dapper, outgoing manner, stature, and perfect features impressed her more than any other man had. He was the total package. True, there had been other handsome men in her life, but none compared to the way Tony DeMarco made her feel.

And he'd saved her life.

Chapter Sixty-Five

Jimmy wondered whether he should let the people he worked with at Fenway know about all that was going on.

Did Eddie need to watch her back? What about Ms. Dorothy Malone? Would those guys go after Bill Lee if they knew he had a connection to me? And what about Keeshon? Hell, someone tried to kill Debbie. With a gun, no less.

Jimmy didn't want anything to happen to anyone else, especially Eddie.

No, especially Eileen.

How can you pick and choose the ones you want to protect, Jim? You've got to worry about them all.

His eyes wandered around the ceiling, but for once he wasn't counting tiles. His foggy mind was trying to inventory everyone who might be in danger because of him. He didn't notice Eileen tiptoe into the room and gently put her hand on his right arm. His *pitching* arm.

"Who's there?" he asked, startled.

"It's just me, Jimmy, Eileen."

He tilted his head toward her voice and tried to focus his blurry vision in the darkness. "Could you turn the light on so I can see you?"

"Of course, but I'll put the low lighting on first," she replied. "Don't want to give you a jolt."

She reached behind the bed, pulled a string, revealing a soft light toward the ceiling. "Is that better?"

"Much."

"I don't know what I'm going to do with you, Jimmy Bailey. What are you doing, trying to keep this hospital in business or something? I mean, we don't usually have problems finding patients…"

"Well, you know, Eileen Maloney, I'd rather we met at the Red Coach Grille or someplace like that. The Cameo Theatre down the street, maybe?"

"Or watching a baseball game at Fenway Park?" she asked, through a chuckle.

"That would be ideal. I know someone who might even be able to find us a couple of tickets. I'd like to be able to smell that new-cut grass in the outfield and just get drunk on it. I'm never gonna drink beer again, but that aroma is enough to make me lose my mind. I'd love to share that with you."

"Better than dinner at the Red Coach Grille?"

"Better. When it's with you."

She laced her hand into his and put her arm around his back. "Anywhere—even a hospital bed—is better with you, you big lug. Just quit letting people use your head for target practice!"

"Hey, speaking of that—what'd'ya think of my ma bonking somebody over the head with my baseball bat?"

"She's something else. Bravery must run in the family."

Chapter Sixty-Six

Safely back at her mom's, Debbie called her roommates in Cambridge.

"You girls need to be careful," she warned, after relating the story about Castle Island. "My car was stolen, and our address is on the registration. I have no idea if someone will try to come to the apartment. Tony says…"

"Tony? Who's Tony?" asked her roommate, Carol.

"Oh, that's Detective DeMarco," she replied. "Tony says he's having the Cambridge Police patrol the area around the apartment, but they can't be there all the time, so you guys should be extra careful, and always aware of your surroundings."

"You know I take the bus to work," Carol said.

"Yeah, I do. Maybe someone can give you a ride home."

"I've got to go to school at night. I have class until 9."

"Yikes, I forgot about that. I have no car. And I don't know when I'll be getting another one."

"Oh, no, Debbie! You love that car."

"Past tense, Carol. I'll just have to learn to love another one. The police say I'll most likely never see my car again. Right now, Tony's trying to find a place where my mother and Jimmy can stay until this all blows over."

"You're on a first-name basis with this detective, Debbie? Sounds kind of chummy to me."

"Well…" Debbie replied.

"Well, what?"

"Well, he saved my life, you know."

"And?"

"And if you saw him, you'd know why I'm getting chummy with him. He's tall, dark, and handsome. Cliché, huh?"

"Deb, you have a boyfriend."

"Maybe not…"

"What'd'ya mean by *that*?"

"Anything I'd seen in Brian is eclipsed by Tony. Tony's all class. Brian's minor league by comparison. And my ma loves him already. She was lukewarm at best with Brian."

"Oh, the parental approval thing. Ten points for that."

"If you saw my ma with him, you'd give him fifty points!"

"That good?"

"That good. Oh, and Jimmy's back in the hospital. He was mugged on his way home from work. Then someone tried to break into Ma's house, but that's another story. It's been quite a night."

"Wow. Nothing surprises me about your family, and I'm sorry to hear that your brother is back in the hospital. Do you think Judy and I should leave the apartment? Maybe go home to our parents for a few days?"

"I'll ask Tony and see what he says about it. For now, be careful. I can't stress that enough. And, yeah, there's never a dull moment with the Baileys."

"Let me know if you need anything. If you need me to gather some of your clothes. Judy can drive them out to you—wherever you are."

"Thanks, Carol. I'll keep in touch."

When Debbie hung up the phone, she could hear Tony and Mary laughing in the kitchen. Debbie was pleased that they were getting along and enjoying each other's company. Tony was such a nice guy. She sat back and smiled, but before the smile could settle on her lips, it was booted out of the way by her worry of when the next shoe would drop.

Chapter Sixty-Seven

FBI Agent Mike Dahl sat down with John O'Malley in Governor Dukakis's office. He tapped on his notebook and wiggled his foot with a nervous twitch.

"Okay, Mr. O'Malley, I have the full story now on Jimmy Bailey and everything surrounding his release and the subsequent events. Thanks for helping with that."

"Detective DeMarco from the Cambridge Police Department has more information on this case. You might want to meet with him, too," O'Malley replied.

"One of our other agents is meeting with him this afternoon."

"That's great. Agent Dahl, if we can help you with anything else, please let us know."

"We will. I hope that everyone involved will stay alert until we can get a handle on this situation."

"I will be sure to relay that message again to Ms. Bailey."

"Here's my card. If you think of anything else, give me a call."

"I will, sir."

"Thank you for taking the time to meet with me. I know how busy you are."

"Likewise."

Chapter Sixty-Eight

Angela DeMarco hadn't had houseguests since her husband, Vincent, passed away five years ago. She was excited when her son asked if a young woman he knew, along with her mother and brother, could stay with her for a few weeks.

The reason they needed a place to stay didn't matter to her. She had a huge house with five bedrooms, three bathrooms, and only a small dog to keep her company. Every day she rattled around the place, bouncing from room to room, keeping each space neat and precise, the same way she did when she had four children and a husband. How she missed those days—the clamor and chaos of people running up and down stairs, laughing and jostling with each other. Tony, the youngest, caused the most trouble, but she never minded. Her husband always called Tony "the apple of Angela's eye." He was right; Tony could do no wrong as far as Angela was concerned.

Three girls preceded Tony in the DeMarco household: Mary Ann, Gloria, and Barbara. Angela and her husband thought they were finished, but then, "God sent them the miracle of a son.."

Angela doted on him and pampered him to the point that one day Vincent said, "Angela, you're going to make a wimp out of him."

"Vincent, you're wrong! He's a miracle boy! He will be strong and confident. I prayed to the Virgin Mary for this boy to be born, and she will give him the health and resolve he needs to be the cream of the crop."

True to Angela's predictions, Tony grew strong and confident, excelling at everything he did. He was valedictorian at Matignon High School, captain of the baseball and basketball teams, and earned a full academic scholarship to Boston College, where he graduated *magna cum laude*. Somewhere along the way, he decided he wanted to pursue criminal justice, leading him to study at Northeastern. He almost went to law school but decided against it. Instead, he took the test for the Cambridge Police and his law enforcement career began.

Angela was proud of her three girls, but Tony remained the apple of her eye. When Vincent passed away, he came home to live with her for a while. She relished the chance to cook for him—all his favorite dishes, including *pasta al forno*. After nine months, though, he went back to apartment living. He was, after all, an eligible bachelor. She knew he couldn't live with her for the rest of his life, but oh, how she loved having him there.

But now, three people were coming to visit. And they were going to stay for a while. It would be Christmas, the Fourth of July, and Thanksgiving all wrapped up in a bow for Angela. She began cooking. Lasagna. Meatballs. *Pasta al forno*. Chicken *cacciatore*. She called Mary Ann in Gloucester. "I'm so excited, Mary Ann," she said. "Tony's bringing company to stay with me!"

"What do you know about these people, Ma?"

"Not much. Just that it's his friend, her mother, and brother. The mother's a widow, like me. The girl knows people in Governor Dukakis's office! And the son works at Fenway Park!"

"How does he know these people, Ma? It sure sounds like one of Tony's schemes."

"Why do you say that, Mary Ann? I am so happy to have company over."

Mary Ann knew her mother would be over the moon to entertain these people, whoever they were. But she worried they'd take advantage of her and make off with some valuable, family heirloom.

"I'm just naturally suspicious, Ma. You know, Tony. Always picking up strays."

"These are not stray dogs! These are people!"

"Okay, okay, Ma. Let me know after they're in the house. I'll stop by and meet them."

Angela's heart was racing. She'd have to wash a few sets of sheets. Dig out pillows and comforters for the beds. Vacuum the rooms. Dust the blinds and bureau tops. Clean out the extra bathrooms. Maybe even wash the curtains. There was so much to do, but she was excited about it all. She'd been rattling around her big Victorian house by herself for so long. She was lonely.

This house. This house had been part of her from the day her late husband picked her up after their honeymoon and carried her over the threshold. She'd given birth to five children—three girls and two boys—and lost the one boy when he was just five years old—hit by a car. Just thinking of him—her little Vincent, Jr.—brought tears to her eyes. Such a sweet, round-faced boy, her first-born, named after her husband. After he died, she didn't know if she could even bear to have another child. But then…Gloria, Mary Ann, Barbara, and Tony. They filled the house from top to bottom, from turret to basement, with laughter, non-stop arguments, incessant footsteps, and a whirlwind of challenges she faced with dedication that came from deep within her.

This house. Her children. Her husband. The food that bound them together. Everything had been so quiet lately. Maybe, just maybe, these houseguests would help her shine again, return conversation and joy to the walls, and creativity back into the dormant pots and pans tucked away in the kitchen.

Angela DeMarco wouldn't be watching reruns on television. She was on a mission.

Chapter Sixty-Nine

John O'Malley had great news for Debbie.

"I'm sorry, Mr. O'Malley, Ms. Bailey isn't in the office today," her assistant told him. "I'm not expecting her for a couple of days. Can I take a message? I expect her to call in shortly."

"Of course. Please have her give me a call at the office. She has my number."

"I'd be glad to pass that on, Mr. O'Malley. It's always a pleasure to speak with you."

"Same here, Marcia. Hope to run into you again one of these days."

"Likewise. Thank you, Mr. O'Malley."

He picked up the South Shore phone book and looked up Mary Bailey's phone number, listening as the phone rang more than ten times. No answer.

"Mr. O'Malley?" his secretary asked, interrupting his thoughts. "May I come in?"

"Of course. What's up?"

"The governor will be back in half an hour. He wants to meet with you and the PR staff. Are you free about that time?"

"I'm always free when it comes to meeting with the governor. The only thing is, if I get a call from Debbie Bailey when I'm in that meeting, please find out where I can reach her. Okay?"

Chapter Seventy

Debbie and Tony walked around the Volvo dealership in Newton. "I don't want to do this," she said. "I want my old car back."

"That's water under the bridge," he replied. "You'll have to get a new one. You won't be able to tell the difference."

"*You* won't be able to tell the difference. *I* will," she replied. "I had that one broken in exactly the way I wanted it. The seats were the way I wanted them to be, the mirrors…you know—it takes a while to get everything to your liking."

"Picky, picky, picky," he said. "At least you're not sleeping with the fishes!"

She shook her head and lightly punched him in the arm. "Yeah, some detective stopped *that* from happening."

He slipped his arm around her as they walked around the showroom, looking at each car sticker until a salesman approached them.

"May I help you find something?" he asked, directing the question at Tony.

"Actually, Ms. Bailey is the one who's car shopping," Tony explained.

"Oh?" The salesman was taken aback. "I see," he said. "What did you have in mind, Ms. Bailey?"

"My car was stolen," she explained. "It was almost brand new—only about 15,000 miles on it—264 GL Volvo sedan, white, four-door, leather interior. I want to replace it. Do you have one in stock that fits those criteria?"

"Why don't you come over to my desk and we'll see what we have, Ms. Bailey. And Mr. Bailey?"

"No, I'm Mr. DeMarco," Tony replied. "I'm Ms. Bailey's—er—friend."

"Okay…Ms. Bailey…Mr. DeMarco…My office is this way."

Chapter Seventy-One

"Blue? You bought a blue Volvo?" her roommate Judy asked.

"Yes. It's kind of sexy, isn't it?"

"Debbie, you don't *need* anything else to make you sexy," she replied. "You've got a patent on that. At least that's what it seems like to me."

"Cut it out," Debbie blushed. "I wanted to get another Volvo, and Tony suggested…"

"Tony? Who the heck is Tony?"

"Uh—Detective DeMarco. His first name is Tony—Anthony if you want to be formal about it."

"And since when did *you* start taking advice from a guy?"

"Well, I had no car and he drove me to the dealership. On the way, he suggested that I get a different-colored car. He thought it might throw off those goons who've been following me."

"You mean, the ones who have been following *us*, don't you?"

"You've seen stuff around the apartment?"

"Yeah. Stupid things. My dog has been growling at the windows. If I look out, nothing's there. When I walk him, seems like he's on high alert, looking over his shoulder. Usually, I walk him for a while, but now, as soon as he does his thing, I bring him in."

"Good thing he has a Rottweiler bark instead of a dachshund bark, eh?"

"Debbie, I'm serious. How scared should we be? How scared should the rest of the people in this building be? After all, some guy was waiting for you in your car. He had a gun, for God's sake! He could have killed you! No dachshund is a match for a gun. You know that."

Debbie flopped down on the rundown, paisley sofa. "Yeah. I know. According to Tony, the Cambridge cops are supposed to be increasing patrols over that way, overnight, especially."

"I mean, should I go stay with my parents for a while? I could do that. But I don't know about Carol. I'd hate to have to commute to my job again from the South Shore, with that stupid Southeast Expressway and all. But fighting traffic is better than trying to evade a guy with a gun."

The 32-pound, wirehaired dachshund jumped on the couch next to Judy and started licking her face. "Yeah, yeah, Schnitzel, I love you, too, and I wish you were as fierce as you let on when a stranger comes in. And that big bark of yours! Decibel city!"

Debbie was rarely flummoxed, but this time she had no answers. The dog rolled over on his back, signaling that he wanted a belly rub. Without thinking, Judy obliged, as if perhaps rubbing the canine's fur might bring her the response she needed.

"I have no clue, Judy," Debbie said. "I don't know what we're going to do. But what's scarier is I don't know what these guys might do to people I care about, just to get to me."

"Debbie, I'm scared."

Debbie knew something had to be done to stop these guys. Now. But could she depend on the FBI or the Cambridge Police to do it? She trusted Tony, but what was the plan? There *had* to be a plan.

Chapter Seventy-Two

Mary Bailey wondered about leaving her house unattended for a week. "My Jim wouldn't like this," she said to herself out loud. "He'd want to stay here and fight, fight, fight! But that's what a man would do…" She rolled her eyes back, thinking of him, and fighting back tears.

"Why did you leave me, dammit!" She looked up at the ceiling. "What did I do to deserve this? What did I do to you that made you leave me here to deal with all the messes you made, the messes Jimmy made, even Donna? Only Debbie's on the right track. You should be here to help me!" She slammed her fist on the kitchen table so hard, it sent pain up to her shoulder. She looked skyward again, shaking the throbbing fist in the air. "Damn you, Jim Bailey, Damn you!"

Mary was angry. So angry, she was in full-blown, crying mode, wiping tears on the sleeves of her dress. She stumbled to the counter, half-blinded by a combination of streaky tears and anger over her husband's absence in the house they bought *together*. The house they brought their children home from the hospital *together*. The house where they shoveled snow, fought off hurricanes, dealt with a presidential assassination, worked hard—*together*. Every battle fought, every victory won, they'd done it hand in hand, as a couple, because that was the decision they'd made for their life…*together*.

She was old-fashioned in the "Father Knows Best" kind of way. The man of the house was the bread winner, the woman stayed home, cooked, cleaned, and cared for the children. Her job was also to look good for her husband when he came home from work. That's how Mary Bailey was raised, and that's who she still was on the day after she'd taken a baseball bat and slammed a potential intruder in the head to keep him out of her home.

Her house seemed a lot worse than *our* house, in Mary's mind. To her, this should be a place with children running around, asking for something from her as grandchildren do. "I need a drink," "When will my mom be home?" or "Where's Daddy?" Those were questions she longed to be asked. She was old enough to be a grandmother. Where were the grandchildren?

She would be a terrific grandmother, she thought, smiling, drying up a few tears. She imagined babies with cherubic faces, just like those of her own babies decades ago, cooing and smiling as she walked by. She knew how to change diapers, could sing "Twinkle, Twinkle Little Star" with the best of them, and she knew, she just *knew*...that one day, this house—*her* house—would see some action. Baby action. Toddler action. Running-up-the-stairs action.

The guy she'd hit over the head was not going to stop her from that action. She hit him once, and she'd do it again if she had to.

But what she wouldn't give for one last hug from the love of her life, Jim Bailey. Yes, she was angry at him for leaving her alone, taking his own life and leaving hers intact, but really in tatters. She still loved him. Truly loved him. His caress, his warmth, his strength. His ability to bring a smile to her face with a light touch on the small of her back.

Mary realized she was wrapping her arms around herself and rocking back and forth as if he were hugging her. The living room window was open about two inches, and the chiffon curtains began waving in the breeze, originating from the beach. She tasted the salt from the Atlantic, felt the near-weightless wind through the gossamer fabric, almost as if it were a sigh, someone breathing on her. She closed her eyes and imagined he was there with her—her Jim, the love of her life, and she felt his presence, smelled the shampoo and soap he used. *Head and Shoulders. Dial.* Her arms wrapped around her tighter and she danced.

She waltzed and whirled around the living room, still feeling his presence. She'd never experienced anything like this before. She enjoyed the sensation of what seemed like a full dance at the place where they used to go when they were dating. When the music in her head stopped, the curtains weren't moving anymore. In fact, the window had closed on its own.

She looked at the hallway clock, which hadn't moved at all as she danced through the house, drinking in his aroma. She shook her head. "Back to reality," she said aloud to herself again, walking up the stairs. She was supposed to be packing for herself and Jimmy so they could stay with Tony's mother for a few days.

As she made her way to the top of the stairs, she detected the faint scent of *Head and Shoulders* shampoo and *Dial* soap on her hands.

Chapter Seventy-Three

"Mr. O'Malley, Ms. Bailey's on the phone for you."

"Oh, great, put her through."

O'Malley dusted himself off and straightened his tie, as if he were expecting to see Debbie walk through the door. For some strange reason, he wanted to look good for her, even as they chatted over the phone.

"John O'Malley here."

"Hi, John, it's Debbie Bailey. I hear you've been trying to reach me. What's up?"

"As a matter of fact, I have been trying to reach you. Where've you been?"

"Car shopping."

"Car shopping? Wait a minute! Don't you have a new car?"

"It was stolen. I was kidnapped, and…"

"Wait…You WHAT?"

"Let me finish and don't interrupt, okay?"

"Okay. But start from the beginning."

When she finished giving him every detail, his mouth was open as he held the phone. "This sounds like something straight out of a movie! Are you okay?"

"Well, I am now, but when I was taken at gunpoint, the keys were left in my car, and someone stole it. It was a sitting duck with the keys in it. I'll never see it again. So, I bought a new one. Same car, just a different color."

John was glad she couldn't see him. He was shaking his head and wondering what other trouble she might find herself in. "Do you have any idea why this guy did this?"

"No. But there's a detective from Cambridge working on the case, and he thinks it's all related to the warden's murder. My brother was mugged again on his way home from work and is back in the hospital. And get this, someone tried to break into my mother's house, and she hit him over the head with my brother's baseball bat!"

"Now I've heard it all! Is your mom okay?"

"Yes, she's fine."

"Well, I'm happy to know that everyone's okay. Now that that's over with…I have good news for you from the governor himself about Mr. Washington."

"Keeshon? You do?"

"Yes. The governor has arranged to have his sentence commuted to time served. He's going to make sure that Mr. Washington goes to a secure residence when he's out of the hospital, although we have no idea when that will be. He's a long way from a full recovery."

"Wow, Jimmy will be so happy! Is it okay if I tell him?"

"Yes, but it's not for publication with the press. If anyone asks you questions about this, refer them to our press office. They'll handle it."

"Let's get back to my family situation for a minute. The detective who's working on this case thinks that my mother, Jimmy, and I need to get out of our respective residences for a week or two. The FBI agrees."

"Who is this cop, Debbie? Would I know him?"

"You don't know him? But you gave him a call asking about me. His name's Tony DeMarco."

"I may or may not have called him, but just to check him out for your sake."

Debbie smiled, then changed the subject.

"John, thank you for your help with Keeshon. It will take a load off Jimmy's mind."

"I'm glad we could help. 'Course, we had no idea what a hornet's nest this all was when you and I first met about it."

"No, we didn't."

"Where are you, Jimmy, and your mother going to stay? In a hotel?"

"No, we'll be staying in Arlington with a relative of Detective Demarco."

"Really? How did that arrangement come about?"

"It was DeMarco's idea. I guess he figured that's the last place any of these goons would be looking for us."

"How can I find you if I need to reach you?"

"I'll call you when I get the phone number at the place. We're going over there later today. Detective DeMarco is on his way to pick up my mom, then he'll swing by and pick me up."

"Okay. Just don't forget about the number. And let me know about your brother's reaction when he hears about Keeshon. The governor's got a lot of compassion for things like this, you know."

"As does his chief of staff. Thanks again, John. I owe you one."

"At least one," he joked. "At least one."

Chapter Seventy-Four

Keeshon was feeling better. He was eating more than he had over the past week, leading to encouraging words from his favorite nurse. He sat up on his own and felt confident for the first time since he'd been attacked at the prison.

Aiming the remote control at the screen, he turned on the television to the local news station.

"We have breaking news today in that ongoing investigation of the murder of Warden Peter Miles at Walpole State Prison. Let's go to Hank Nichols outside the jail. Hank, what's new?"

"Well, Joe, here's what we have...Governor Dukakis has commuted the sentence of Keeshon Washington, the prisoner who was brutally beaten and hospitalized a few days before the warden was killed. A statement from the governor's press office today indicated that the governor decided to reduce Washington's sentence to time served. We still have no information on Washington's condition or the hospital he's in. The Department of Corrections is staying mum on that bit of information."

Keeshon pushed the nurse call button. Again. And again. *Had he heard correctly? His sentence had been commuted?* He pressed the button again, this time harder.

The nurse came running in. "Mr. Washington! Are you okay? What's wrong?"

"I have to tell somebody the news, Miss! I just saw on TV that the govna's not gonna send me back to prison! He commuted my sentence! I can't believe it!"

"This is great news for you. Is there someone you'd like to call? A family member?" the nurse asked.

"No, just my frien' Jimmy. I have to find his numba. I have it heah someweah…"

"I need you to calm down for a minute. I'm looking at your heart monitor and it's going haywire. I know you're excited but just take it easy for a little bit. We'll find Jimmy's number and place the call. But take a deep breath first. Maybe drink some water."

"Okay, okay. Deep breath. Deep breath." He pursed his lips, leaned his head back into the pillow and closed his eyes, taking another deep breath. He still had wires and tubes attached to his arms and felt pain throughout his body, but the news he'd heard was as much of an analgesic as any pill he'd had since he came through the hospital door.

Chapter Seventy-Five

Mary grabbed her clothes and was still deciding whether to bring some of her favorite kitchen tools when Tony arrived with Jimmy.

She'd barricaded the front and back doors. When they tried to enter, the clanging began.

"Ma! Ma! What the hell? Where are you? I can't get the door open! Are you okay?"

Tony went around back, only to find she'd done the same there.

"Mrs. Bailey! We can't get in!"

"That's the point, you two! I wanted to make sure NO ONE could get in…unless I wanted them to! My days of slugging people are over!"

Jimmy stopped in his tracks. He kept playing the scene over in his head. His ma, the mild-mannered Mary Bailey, baker of cookies, comforter of neighborhood kids, prayer of the Rosary, knocking a guy out because he was trying to break into her house.

Chapter Seventy-Six

When Tony brought Mary and Jimmy up the walk to the DeMarco house, Angela could hardly contain her excitement. She'd been cooking since Tony had asked if they could stay with her, and the house smelled like Tuscany—a combination of oregano, capers, ricotta cheese, and simmering, homemade tomato sauce.

She'd rushed around the house, changing sheets on beds and fluffing pillows, as if she'd just opened the newest bed and breakfast in the neighborhood. The sheets had been dried in the sun, on the line in the backyard, smelling sweet and defying any relationship to a clothes dryer.

This tiny woman with dark hair and sparkling, brown eyes, energized by the thought of having guests in her home, flitted about the room as if wearing ballet slippers when she heard them coming up the front steps. She was the Pearl Bailey of Arlington, the entertainer of the year in her own home again.

Tony put his hand on the carved, brass knob, but the door flew open before he could turn it.

"Come in, come in! Welcome, welcome!" Angela said, reaching out and hugging Mary, as if she were her long-lost friend. "How nice it is to meet you! Welcome to my home!"

Tony rolled his eyes back at his mom and her excitement. "Hi, Ma. This is Mrs. Bailey…"

Mary interrupted. "Call me Mary, please. I'm just Mary."

"Yes," Tony said, "and this is her son, Jimmy. Her daughter, Debbie, will be here shortly. She's driving from Cambridge."

"So pleased to meet you, Mrs.—I mean, Mary. And Jimmy! So handsome! Thank you for coming to visit. I haven't had any overnight visitors for a while," Angela exclaimed. "I am excited to share my home with you!"

"It's lovely of you to have us," Mary said. "Is there anything I can do to help? In the kitchen or anything?"

"Oh, no, I have it under control but thank you so much."

"Everything smells great, Ma," Tony added. "I feel like I'm in the North End or something. I can't wait to eat!"

"Tony, mind your manners. We'll wait for Debbie," Angela said.

"Thank you, Angela," Mary said, with a smile.

"Of course! And Jimmy, my son tells me you played professional baseball once and now you work at Fenway Park?"

"Yes, ma'am, I did play for a while. My job at Fenway will end when the season ends. I do love baseball," Jimmy replied.

"I love watching baseball," Angela said. "The Red Sox are not very good this year, but I still watch them or listen to them on the radio. It keeps me company when I'm doing things around the house."

She motioned to everyone to follow her into the parlor, a room with a formal air about it. "Why don't you all sit here while we wait for Debbie. I'm going into the kitchen to set everything out."

"I'll go with you," Mary said.

"So, Tony, do you think they'll get along okay while we're here?" Jimmy asked.

"Looks to me like they will. They both like to cook, it seems. My ma just loves to cook for gobs of people. The aroma in here probably tipped you off to that."

"Yeah, it did. I'm salivating already. You have no idea how much I longed for good home-cooking while I was in…"

He paused without finishing his sentence.

"I get it, Jim. No need to explain."

"Between your ma and Eddie at Fenway, I'll probably gain ten pounds before baseball season is over!"

The sound of the doorbell announced Debbie's arrival. Tony jumped up to let her in.

"Hey, welcome to the DeMarco Resort," he said, leaning in to kiss her cheek.

"Are you the *maître d'*? If so, I'd like a table with a view," she said.

"Will I get a good tip if I can arrange that?"

"Of course. But first, you'll have to get the bellhop to take my suitcase to my room."

She reached out and gave him a mighty hug, then stepped back and looked into his eyes. "I feel safe now, Tony," she said, laying her head on his chest, knowing she was in the right place.

He took her hands, slowly lacing his fingers between hers. "Don't worry, you are," he whispered. "But there's the matter of meeting my ma and having some Italian food before you collapse. You're going to love her cooking!"

"If you say so."

Angela and Mary came out of the kitchen, in step with one another. "She's here, Angela! This is my Debbie!"

Before she spoke, Angela took notice of Tony and Debbie's intertwined hands.

She's the one I've been praying for. She's perfect for him. She's so tall and beautiful, just like her mother. Statuesque. Yes. Somehow, fate has brought her to us. Vincent, from up above, are you listening? Did you have anything to do with this? Our 'little Tony,' who was never serious about a woman— I think he has found the one.

Angela snapped back from her thoughts and shepherded them to the dining room and served a gourmet Italian dinner, family-style, complete with lit taper candles throughout the table. The restaurants in the North End of Boston—the ones where the lines were long, and no reservations were taken—had nothing on Angela DeMarco.

Chapter Seventy-Seven

Eileen worried about Jimmy and where he might be. He said he'd call her when he was settled and give her the number where he could be reached, but so far, no call had come through. She had seen the news story of the governor commuting his friend's sentence, but she wouldn't be happy until she spoke to Jimmy.

She had definitely fallen for him. She thought he felt the same way about her, but he seemed shy when it came to saying it out loud. Some days he treated her like a friend, and on others, he made her feel extra special.

As she sat cross-legged on her bed, with a pen in her mouth and a pad of paper on her lap, her roommate Trisha walked in.

"What are you doing?" she asked.

"What do you think I'm doing? What have I been obsessing over for the past couple of months?"

"Oh, the baseball player," Trisha said, rolling her eyes.

"Yup. He's got a lot going on with his family, and I'm just a little worried, that's all."

"Wow, Eileen. Are you sure you want to get further involved with this guy and his family? Sounds like a full-time job—you've already got one of those."

"You're right, but I really like him, and I know he's worth it."

"How about we go out to the Dairy Queen and get an ice cream or something? It'll help take your mind off things. We can walk. It's not too late, you know."

"Sounds good. Let me grab my shoes," Eileen said, as she hopped off the bed.

"Well, let's get cracking!"

Eileen and Trisha sat on wooden picnic tables outside the Dairy Queen around the corner from their apartment, slurping away at cones filled with soft ice cream, dipped in chocolate that covered and hardened around the twirled, vanilla treat.

"Nothing like DQ on a night like this," Trisha said. "Do you remember a few years back when we came here to get autographs from Tony Conigliaro and Dalton Jones? The place was swarming with crazy girls hoping to get a look at those two hot Red Sox players."

"Crazy girls just like us, Trisha. I took a couple of photos of them. No one could even get near the window to get ice cream that day."

"Hell, no one wanted ice cream! They—we—all wanted Tony and Dalton. It's too bad what happened to Tony, though."

"Yeah, hit in the eye with that baseball from that Jack—Hamilton, was it?"

"I think so. Tony had such a great career ahead of him. Then he didn't. Such a cute guy, too, him and his red Corvette."

"Yeah, all those ballplayers were cute. I'm pretty sure they're all still cute."

"Kinda like *your* baseball player, Eileen?"

Eileen blushed at the prospect that Jimmy was *hers*. "Well, he's not exactly *mine*, Trisha. We're just sorta dating. I don't even know where he is right now."

"Just because you don't know where he is at the moment, doesn't change his cute status, though," Trisha said, with a chuckle. "Have you ever seen him in a baseball uniform? He'd probably be even cuter then."

"No…But I'm sure he'd cut a handsome figure in just about any baseball uniform and cap—unless it was a Yankee uniform!"

"You'll get no argument from me on that, Eileen."

They giggled and wiped drips from their cones, enjoying the coolness of the night. The streetlights were on, their yellowish glow illuminating the side streets near the Dairy Queen.

They didn't notice the two, black-clad figures skulking behind the dumpster.

Chapter Seventy-Eight

Mary was surprised at how well-kept the "DeMarco Mansion" was, even the parts of the house that hadn't been used for many years. She was impressed with how well Angela had kept every nook and cranny free of dust bunnies, every bathroom immaculate, every armchair doily snowy white. She'd expected this old Victorian to have a musty aroma through and through, like so many historical New England homes she'd visited over the years in Plymouth and Quincy—some of which had once belonged to presidents and founding fathers.

But this place, despite its age, had no flaws that she could see or smell. It almost seemed like something out of a Hollywood movie set. Was it "Arsenic and Old Lace?" No. Maybe "Rebecca," or even "Meet Me in St. Louis." When watching one of those old classics on TV, she'd always felt there had to be an odor of some sort trailing the heroine while she was inside the house.

She was impressed that this tiny Italian woman kept this huge house spotless and so welcoming, all by herself. With little advance notice that Mary and her two adult children were coming to invade her space, Angela had also cooked a gourmet-worthy meal for them.

For her own part, Mary still loved to cook and bake, and she kept her own house spotless. But her house could fit into this mansion six or seven times. As she wandered around, she continued to revel in the wonder of Angela and the DeMarco mansion, taking in all the wall-mounted, family photos, and admiring the grain of the wood the builders had used on the staircase.

"Mary, why don't we go and sit for a minute?"

She jumped at hearing Angela's voice behind her.

"I'm sorry, I didn't mean to startle you."

"Oh, Angela, I was just taking in the atmosphere of your beautiful home. I live in a small bungalow in North Weymouth, and I'm simply amazed at the workmanship and the great touches that went into building this gorgeous house."

"It *is* quite beautiful, a jewel, really. I've been so fortunate to have been allowed to stay here," Angela said, wiping tears from her eyes. "When my Vincent died, I just didn't think I'd be able to keep up with this house. He did so much around the place. You know, old houses have old innards—plumbing, electricity, and all. But he left an insurance policy that allowed me to have all that modernized and brought up to code. And my son Tony helps me when I have any kind of disaster here in the house."

"Your Tony, he's such a nice boy," Mary piped up. "You raised him good, Angela."

"Oh, it wasn't just me," she blushed. "It was Vincent and our girls, too. Tony's the youngest. The girls teased him all the time, but when it came to sticking up for him in school, no one—I mean, no one—could ever pick on Tony and get away with it as far as they were concerned."

"My Jimmy's the youngest, too. I have two daughters. You've met Debbie…"

"Yes, and my goodness, she is so gorgeous. Looks just like you, Mary. And so tall! You and your husband both…"

"Yes, Angela, my late husband was also tall. My other daughter, Donna, is tall as well. She's a nurse in Atlanta. She left town shortly after—my husband's death."

"It's so hard, isn't it, Mary, losing the men we loved and still love to this day?"

Tears welled up in both their eyes as their minds returned to the days when they had fallen in love with their now-deceased husbands.

"I can still picture him, Angela, walking into the Quincy shipyard where I worked. He was so handsome. Of all the men who worked there, I knew he was the one. It was truly love at first sight. I never thought it was a thing…That is, until I saw my Jim."

"It wasn't exactly that way for me, Mary. I worked at the Fanny Farmer candy store in downtown Boston. I was putting candy in a box for this elderly woman when this GI came bouncing into the store. He had so much energy, and I knew he was in a hurry, but the elderly woman was taking her time picking out what she wanted. He took off his cap and stood in the corner for about five minutes. Someone else offered to wait on him but he told her he wanted me to help him. He stood there and watched me pack the chocolates, tie the bow on the box, and take the woman's money.

"Then he stood there, grasping his flat hat between both of his hands, until I asked if I could help him. He picked out three pieces of chocolate and paid for them. Then he said, 'One is for my mother, one is for me, and the third one is for you. Will you meet me at Swan Boats when you get off work? I would like to get to know the beautiful Fanny Farmer chocolate girl.'

"I told him I'd think about it, but of course, I knew I would. I couldn't wait for work to be over. I tried to keep myself busy and keep my mind off the dark-haired GI, but it was hard. When I left the store, he was waiting for me. 'I knew you'd do it!' he told me. Then we went over to Swan Boats and talked for about three hours. That was it."

"What a romantic story, Angela. We could write books about our love stories, couldn't we?"

"I suppose we could, Mary. And while we're on the subject of love stories, what's up with your Debbie and my Tony? Is something going on there?"

"Could be. But Debbie doesn't share much with me. My Jimmy met a girl recently, and he tells me more about her than Debbie ever says about her personal life. But I see the way Debbie looks at your son. I think there is something happening."

"My sentiments exactly. But we must not let on that we know. We have to—what is it my daughters say? Play it cool."

"Deal," Mary agreed.

~ ~ ~

Angela had unearthed her best tablecloth—the one she'd embroidered for her twenty-fifth wedding anniversary with Vincent. As she smoothed it on the rectangular, oak table, she recalled so many dinner parties with their friends over the years. Candlelit dinners on Christmas Eve, when she served the traditional Feast of the Seven Fishes, while all the in-laws squished in with chairs of all sizes to get a better view of the food. A 28-pound turkey in the middle of the table on Thanksgiving, when she always put little white coverlets on the big bird's drumsticks, as if he were wearing special booties. A huge ham on Easter, with cloves inserted into crosscut knife markings.

She also remembered a few romantic dinners with just her and Vincent, and his hand holding hers under the table in case one of the kids stumbled down the stairs. 'It's alright if they see us, Angela. They know how much we love each other,' he'd say.

'Yes, Vincent, but they don't need to be let in on everything.'

They'd lean in and share a little peck of a kiss and then finish dinner. The rest would come later. As dessert. That's how she liked to think of it, anyway.

She stood and looked at the table. It could seat at least ten comfortably, fourteen if you packed a few in on the sides. They had twenty people at one time, but most of the latecomers had to hold their plates on their laps that day. Angela hated it when her guests were uncomfortable.

Today, it would be five—Tony, Debbie, Mary, Jimmy, and herself.

Should Tony sit at the head of the table, the way his father always did, or should she, as the current head of household, sit there?

"I will sit there," she heard herself say out loud. "I am the eldest. This is my house. I will be the head of household today."

"Ma, what did you say?" Tony asked, as he plowed down the stairs. "Do you need me to help you set the table?"

"Huh? Oh, yes, Tony. I was wondering who was going to help me set the table."

"You've done enough for today, Ma. I'll take care of the plates and silverware. How do you want the table set up? Two on each side and you at the head?"

"That's what I was thinking," she replied. "Maybe you and Debbie on one side and Mary and her son on the other."

"That makes sense," he said, skipping toward the kitchen as if he were still eight years old searching for table settings for a family dinner.

"Hey, Tony, aren't you a little big to be skipping in the house?" a voice came from the stair landing. "Your feet sound like concrete!"

He looked up to see Mary descending the stairs, all made up and dressed for dinner. "Maybe so, Mrs. Bailey, but every time I come home, I feel like a little boy again, and I can't help it."

"Mary," she said. "You should call me 'Mary,' not 'Mrs. Bailey.' It just sounds so formal, like you're taking my statement down at the police station."

"I would be happy to call you Mary, Mrs. Bailey. Oops. Force of habit. I'll do better next time."

"Can I help with anything?" she asked.

"Oh, no," he replied. "This has been my job since I could reach the top of the table. Sit down and relax. Dinner will be ready shortly."

Angela had given him the "good" China, the kind she didn't use every day, so he treated it gently, placing each plate delicately and deliberately in front of a chair. He'd also received instructions to use "the good silver," which meant the stainless-steel tableware had the night off. He opened a rosewood box lined with velvet, where Angela's pattern *Chateau Rose by Alvin* (or so it said on the box's metal label) and carefully selected knives, spoons, salad forks, and regular forks were stored. His mother loved the tiny roses carved into the handles.

Chapter Seventy-Nine

Giggling and chatting, Eileen and Trisha strolled down the street to their apartment. "Nothing like chocolate-covered DQ on a night like this," Eileen said.

Two shadowy figures followed behind them, although not too closely, stopping every few feet to hide behind a hedge or a bush. Dusk had taken most of the daylight from what had been a spectacular, blue-skied afternoon. The stealthy beings were careful not to broadcast their presence; instead, they made sure the women remained unaware.

As Eileen paused to put the key into the front door, she felt something around her neck pull her backwards down to the pavement. Trisha, too, experienced the same thing. Both screamed, but their screams were short-lived. The women were quickly thrown into the back of a VW Vanagon, where a third person was waiting. The two grabbers slammed the women on the floor, shoving scarves into their mouths. They tied Eileen and Trisha by their hands and feet and left them to roll around on the back of the vehicle floor.

"Wonder what lover boy will think when he finds out we got his girl," the driver said.

"Yeah, which one is she? Do you know?" one of the accomplices asked.

"No, but we got two for the price of one!" The driver laughed as the van chugged along. "No one will ever suspect this little four-cylinder thing as a getaway car."

"What about Rossi? You think he knows which one is Bailey's?"

"Nah. He's still so knocked out in the hospital by that car accident, he can barely see. Besides, who'd'ya think is more Bailey's type? The redhead or the blonde?"

"I vote redhead," one replied.

"Yeah, me, too," said the other.

"That's what I was thinking," the driver agreed. "We can mess her up pretty badly unless she tells us where Bailey and his sister are hiding out. We oughta get his mother, too. She cracked Louie over the head real good with that baseball bat."

In the back of the van, Eileen and Trisha were petrified, sweating, trying to undo the knots that bound their hands. No sounds came from their mouths, only phlegm and choking gulps. They were able to make eye contact, each feeling the other's fear.

Dear God, please protect us. Eileen's heart sank as she looked into Trisha's eyes, knowing she was responsible for the terror projecting from her roommate's retinas.

Eileen felt one of the strands on her hands loosen. She managed to get it off and set her hands free. She looked at Trisha and put her finger to her lips to quiet her as she carefully turned around and liberated her. They remained in the position they'd been placed in while they worked on freeing their feet. When those restraints were loose, they went back to the positions they'd been placed in. They didn't want their captors to realize they were no longer under their control.

Meanwhile, the three guys kept rambling on about how much money they were going to get for bringing in Jimmy's girl, and how the friend would be a bonus. As they laughed, they had no idea what was happening in the back of the van. Without speaking, Eileen and Trisha were mapping out a plan.

"When they open the back end," Eileen whispered, "we jump out and run. Got it?"

Trisha nodded as Eileen put the scarf back in her mouth.

Neither one had any idea where they'd be when the van stopped, nor what kind of environment they'd be in. But the one thing they were certain of was that their only chance of staying alive would be to run.

Chapter Eighty

"Eileen's not answering her phone," Jimmy said to Debbie. "I told her I'd let her know that I was safe, but so far, no answer."

"Maybe she went out for dinner or something," Debbie replied.

"She was waiting to hear from me. I've got a funny feeling about this."

"What's up, Jimmy? You think something's wrong?" Tony asked.

"I'm not sure, but she told me she'd be waiting by the phone."

"Well, here we are, all stuffed with great Italian food, thanks to your mother, and we can't find Eileen. And for the record, you're always suspicious, Tony," Debbie teased.

"Most of the time, I'm suspicious with good reason. Where does she live, Jimmy?"

"Quincy Point. Near the Dairy Queen by the Fore River Bridge." Jimmy reached into his pocket and pulled out a crumpled piece of paper. "Here's her address and phone number."

"Give me a sec," Tony said, heading for the telephone.

"Hey, this is Detective Tony DeMarco from the Cambridge Police. I'm wondering if you could check on someone for me…Yeah, she lives in Quincy Point over near the Dairy Queen…and here's her address… Yeah, I can get a description for you. Hey, Jimmy, how would you describe Eileen?"

"About five-foot-six, red hair, green eyes, medium build, I'd say. Freckles, too. She drives a Marina-blue VW bug."

Tony relayed the description, provided his contact information, and said he'd wait to hear back from someone.

"It's probably nothing, but they're sending a patrol car over to check things out," Tony said, returning to the room.

"Of course. Better safe than sorry," Debbie chimed in.

A nagging feeling began to stir in Jimmy's gut, and it had nothing to do with Angela's lasagna or the bump on his head. When his pulse accelerated and the room began to spin, he took a seat on one of Angela's brocade side chairs and put his head in his hands.

"I have a bad feeling, sis, and it's not going away. I won't feel better until I hear from Eileen."

"Relax, Jimmy. It's probably nothing, but let's wait a bit. You need some water? An aspirin? Would that help?" Debbie asked.

"No, but thanks for asking."

When the phone rang, Tony pounced. "Oh, I see…Did you go into the apartment? Okay…Yeah… Keep me posted…Thanks again."

"What?" Jimmy jumped up.

"They found keys in the lock to Eileen's apartment. The apartment was empty, and her car was still there, but no sign of her or her roommates. They're canvassing the neighborhood now to see if anyone saw anything."

"We need to go out there, Tony. NOW!"

"Calm down, Jimmy. I need to think for a minute. Let me piece a couple of things together first."

"What's to piece together? Someone took her to get to me! That's what this is all about! Nothing more, nothing less! She doesn't even know where I am!"

Tony put his hand on his brow as if some miraculous thought process would lead him to Eileen. "I need to call the Arlington Police," he said, "because if you and I are going to the South Shore, I can't leave my mother, your mother, and Debbie unprotected. This is important. I also need to call my contact at the FBI. He needs to be aware of what's going on."

Tony went into the kitchen to use the phone, while Jimmy and Debbie sat, practically paralyzed at the thought that Eileen might have been kidnapped.

"All I ever wanted to do was to play baseball!" Jimmy shouted. "Now this! I meet someone I really like, and those goons take her?"

"I don't know why these things happen, but some days I think our family has a cloud overhead," Debbie replied. "I wish I had an answer for you, Jimmy. Just know that Tony has good connections, and I know that he will do everything in his power to find her."

"I know, I know, but I still hate it, sis! I hate the whole thing. My life is out of control! I have no career, no prospects, no nothing! And if something happens to her because of me, I don't know how I could live with myself."

"Don't go talking like that! We'll figure it out. Just try to keep your head screwed on straight."

Tony returned to the parlor. "The Arlington Police are sending someone over here, my guys at the Cambridge Police are going to Agassiz Street to watch your apartment, Debbie, and my contact at the FBI is looking into what they've found in their investigation. He can't share everything with me, but he's willing to pull together his resources and act on them. Jimmy, let's go. You and I are going to Quincy."

As the two bounded down the front steps, Jimmy vomited his dinner onto the sidewalk. "I'm so sorry, Tony. Truly, I am."

"Don't worry about it. Better here than in the car. Let's go."

Debbie shut and locked the door behind her and walked back into the sitting room. She could hear movement coming from upstairs. She knew that what she was about to explain would send both mothers into a tizzy.

Chapter Eighty-One

The Vanagon bumped around a little but finally came to a stop. The driver hopped out and talked to someone outside the vehicle.

"Yeah, yeah, we got two of 'em, boss. They were together—couldn't figure out right away which one was Bailey's girl, but we figure it's the redhead. The other one's a bonus. When we're done with them, they'll tell us where he is. You can be sure of that."

The two abductors came to the back and began unlatching the door. After finding an old tire iron rolling around in the back of the van, and with the pepper spray Eileen remembered was in her back pocket, the adrenaline rush between the two women was high, and they were ready to attack. When the doors opened, the kidnappers did not have a moment to think before one was hit over the head, hard, then stumbled before he fell to the ground, and the other was doused with pepper spray, right in the eyes. With a quick look back to ensure that their attackers were not on their heels, Eileen and Trisha dashed down the hill into a heavily wooded area. Neither of them knew where they were, only that it was dark and somewhere out in the country.

"My eyes! My eyes!" yelled the guy who had been sprayed. "They're getting away!"

"They *what*?" the driver yelled back. "Where the hell did they go?"

"I dunno! Into the woods someplace!"

"They won't get far. Besides, we've got guns," the driver said, as he walked around to the back of the van. "But, we can't forget, the whole purpose here is to find out where Bailey's hiding. We can't shoot 'em just yet. They can't hide from us forever. Besides, girls have to, you know, use the facilities a lot more than men do. We can be on the lookout for that. Get your flashlights and go looking for 'em."

"Got it!"

They looked like a bunch of bounty hunters searching for escaped prisoners.

Eileen and Trisha stuck together and hid behind rocks and trees, as their captors aimed their lights around the forest. Eileen figured they were in the Blue Hills near Milton. She'd gone horseback riding there when she was in the eighth grade. She thought she'd caught a whiff of horse manure a little farther from where they were hiding. That meant they weren't too far from the stable where she and her schoolmates had rented horses back then.

They spoke in muted whispers, almost just mouthing words to one another, hoping that the men wouldn't be able to locate them. A couple of times, they just touched each other lightly on the arm to indicate a direction to try. They were fighting mosquitoes and tree branches that scratched their exposed flesh, but they didn't want to slap the insects for fear of being heard.

They continued plodding through dead leaves, twigs, squirrel carcasses, and acorns.

"Shush," Eileen whispered. "I think I hear someone coming this way."

They froze in their tracks.

A hulking man grabbed Trisha from behind, causing her to nearly faint. "Quiet, both of you. I'm with the FBI. Don't move. We're after those guys who kidnapped you. If you stop fighting, I'll show you my ID."

Eileen, standing in flight position, was wary. "How do we know if you're really here to help us, or if you're part of their gang?"

"Well, you can decide that on your own, but I'm all you've got right now. Do you know a detective from Cambridge named DeMarco?"

"No, but I think my friend knows him."

"This friend here?" the agent asked, nodding his head down at Trisha, still flailing about in his arms.

"No, another friend. How did you know we'd been abducted?"

"We've been following these guys for a while, so we saw them when they grabbed you. They're just a bunch of low-level punks."

Eileen still had her doubts. She'd seen enough police dramas on TV to know that sometimes the FBI was just as corrupt as the criminals. She remained cautious until they came to a clearing, and Jimmy was waiting for her.

She wanted to scream, yell, beat on his chest, but instead, when he held his arms out for her, she jumped into them, seeking the comfort only he could give.

"I've never been so happy to see someone in my life!" he said, pulling her hair back from her face.

Trisha grabbed the FBI agent and gave him a big hug as well. "Ma'am," he said, "we're not allowed to give hugs when we're on the job."

"Like hell you're not!" she replied. "You're getting a big one from me now and I want one back! You saved us!"

The agent grinned then hugged back.

Tony shook the agent's hand. "Thanks, man. I didn't quite know how serious this all was."

"Serious is an understatement," the agent said. "These guys were prepared to do these ladies significant harm if we hadn't gotten here. They're just a bunch of punks, but they're ruthless."

"So, where do we go from here?" Tony asked.

"Detective, all I can say is, your instincts were right on target. We'd love to get you into the FBI one of these days. You've contributed a great deal to our investigation. The three guys who kidnapped these ladies will be going away for a long time. Kidnapping's a federal offense."

They shook hands again, and Jimmy followed suit. "Sir, I thank you from the bottom of my heart."

"Agent Summer," he said. "That's my name."

"Okay, then, Agent Summer," Jimmy replied. "You're a hero in my book."

"Just doing my job."

Chapter Eighty-Two

"What's keeping them?" Debbie asked. "I need to know what's going on."

"Oh, Debbie, calm down. I'm sure if something big happened, it would be on the news," Mary said. "Do you think Jack Williams on Channel 4 would miss it if it was big news?"

"Oh, Ma, you and your TV news guys!"

"But he's such a hunk, Debbie, and with that beautiful voice! If there is something we need to know, Jack will tell us."

"So, let's turn on the TV."

Angela obliged, but there was nothing on about Eileen, Trisha, the FBI, Tony, or Jimmy.

"Guess you can relax, Debbie. Our boy, Tony, didn't make his appearance with Jack Williams tonight," Angela said.

"Guess you won't get to hear him say Tony's name tonight, Ma," Debbie laughed.

Mary smiled. "No, but someday I'd love to meet that hunk of a news anchor!"

As the ladies waited for the Johnny Carson show to begin, they heard two car doors slam. They jumped from their chairs, almost in unison, and ran to the front door. There stood Tony and Jimmy, but they weren't alone; they had two women with them.

"*Two* women?" Angela asked. "I thought they went looking for Jimmy's girlfriend."

"One of them is Eileen," Mary said, "but I don't know who the other one is."

"Strange that Tony would bring two people I don't know here without asking my permission. He knows better than that."

"There's a story here," Debbie chimed in. "Fasten your seatbelts."

As the four walked in the front door, Tony began to apologize. "Ma, I'm sorry to bring you a couple more guests, but when you hear what happened, you'll understand…"

"Here we go," Debbie said, as Tony and Jimmy tripped over each other talking. And so began the tale of the Dairy Queen abductors.

Chapter Eighty-Three

Jimmy had two weeks left to work in the Red Sox laundry room. He kept thinking about what other jobs he might be able to find. He and Eddie talked about this all the time.

"How about working in a pharmacy? Do you live near one?" Eddie asked.

"Yeah, there are a couple nearby, but they seem to be set for employees. Maybe Bradlees. They're close... Or Zayre. They're a little farther away. I still have to take the bus, you know. I don't have a car."

"You've got that cute little redheaded chauffeur to drive you around, though."

"She has a job, too. Besides, I don't want to wear out my welcome in that department. I usually just do that when we go somewhere together. I'd like to start saving for my own car. On another note, Ma and I love staying with the DeMarcos. Especially the food! Mrs. DeMarco and my ma could open their own restaurant! They make quite the pair in the kitchen."

"Seems like you're at least having a good time. So, tell me, what's the deal with your sister and the detective?"

"I dunno. She seems to like him a lot. But she doesn't talk to me about that kind of stuff. She's too busy with important stuff at work. She's always running around from here to there. I never know where she is. But the good thing about Tony is that he doesn't seem bothered that she's into the women's lib thing, you know?"

"Yeah. That's such a turnoff for some guys."

"Tony's a take-charge kinda guy, but he doesn't seem to mind if Debbie's in charge half the time. The one thing I don't know is, if they get together, does he want kids? Debbie doesn't, for sure."

"Oh, big Italian family? Kids are a big deal. They'll have to work that out. And you and Eileen? How serious are you two?"

"Eddie, I can't get serious with anyone until I have a permanent job. I love working here with you, I really do, but it's temporary. I'm so happy that Mrs. Yawkey and Ms. Malone gave me this job, but I couldn't possibly do what I'd want for Eileen without a full-time job."

"You're right to think that way, Jimmy. Hey, no one's stalked you or bonked you on your bean for at least a week. Must make you feel better."

"Yeah…I still look over my shoulder, though, wherever I go. Per that FBI guy, they're getting close to wrapping up that prison investigation. He swore us to secrecy that we wouldn't say anything to anyone about it until an announcement is made."

"Well, you did a good job with that. I couldn't weasel anything out of you here in the laundry room, Jimmy. I don't think that even Bill Lee himself would get any secrets from you."

"That's what we promised, Eddie. I don't go back on my word."

"No. No, you don't. Not from what I've seen. You're a good kid, Jimmy. I've had fun working with you this year. You kept my spirits up the past few weeks. Even though people kept bonking you on the bean and you kept ending up in the X-ray Department. You were just looking for opportunities to see that Eileen, weren't you?" she laughed.

He peered over a big pile of folded towels and grinned. "Yeah, guess that's why I let people come up behind me and knock me out—just so I can go to the hospital and see Eileen. I must look good on those films."

"You look good no matter what, kiddo!" She hugged him for a minute. "Now get back to work!"

Chapter Eighty-Four

Keeshon was finally ready to leave the hospital. He'd come in with so many injuries that the nurses thought he'd never make it. Knowing he didn't have to go back to prison was a relief, but he still had lots to worry about. He had no place to live. He wasn't in any shape to work yet, and although he now had a GED, he worried that no one would hire a Black guy who had been to prison. Especially one whose face had been plastered all over the news.

One of the nurses suggested he try to work with the social worker in the hospital, but Keeshon had no confidence that would help.

He knew that he could call Jimmy for advice. Jimmy knew everything there was to know about him after spending hours with him locked up in a tiny cell. Jimmy taught him to read and helped him earn his GED when his public-school teachers had given up on him.

After he learned to read, new horizons opened to him. Science. History. Even learning about the Constitution and things that happened in Boston—things that involved Black men. Crispus Attucks. He'd never heard about that guy until Jimmy brought him a book. All he'd learned before then were stories about White people. Jimmy had taken the time to find books about the civil rights movement and people like Martin Luther King, Jr., and the march on Selma. He'd cried when he learned about the four young girls who'd been blown up in a church in Birmingham, Alabama, simply because they were Black. So many other things had happened in the country and were still happening to people just because they were Black, and sadly, he was just learning about them for the first time.

Jimmy never treated him like he was trash because of the color of his skin. The lady he took care of never did, either. To them, he was just a person, another human being. But to the police, prison guards, and people on the street, though, that was a different story. He didn't want a handout; he just wanted a place to live and a way to make a living on his own.

All the nurses advised him to take it easy for a while, until he was sure he was fully healed. He didn't have a doctor to follow up with, so they gave him the name of a clinic he could go to, free of charge.

He wondered where Jimmy could be. He hadn't heard from him in a while. He didn't know if the hospital released people out onto the street, with no place to go.

I don't have to go back to prison, but my problems sho' ain't ova.

Chapter Eighty-Five

"Ma, I don't know what to do about Debbie," Tony said. "She's simply the woman I've been looking for, but…but…she's so…different."

"I know what you mean. She's a women's libba, isn't she?"

"I guess you might call her that. But she's also strong, confident, self-assured, and courageous. What would she see in a guy like me? I've always been a take-charge guy, a protector, a…"

"Knight in shining armor? Yes, that's what you are. Now it's time for you to learn to be a partner, not a guardian angel. It's not easy, but it's a mountain you can climb if you want to. You gotta want it. It's a decision only you can make."

"But was that what Dad was to you? A partner? Not the *man of the house*? He always came off as the king around here."

"That's because he was the king of some things, but I was the queen of others. We had respect for each other in so many ways. That's why relationships last, Tony. That's how two people can stay married for a long time and get through the rough patches. God knows we had our share of those…. Rough patches. Life isn't always easy. I bet Mary Bailey would tell you that, too."

"Debbie hasn't had an easy life, Ma. Her brother just got out of prison. Her father committed suicide when her brother went to prison. Mrs. Bailey's been a widow since then. Her sister took off for Atlanta and doesn't even speak to Debbie or her brother. It's a sad situation all around."

"That girl in Atlanta will rue the day that she stopped talking to her family, Tony. But how sad is it that their dad felt so bad about their situation that he killed himself rather than face life? Life is hard, but the only way to deal with it is to just, well, deal with it."

"Suicide's not that easy, Ma. Someone's got to be mentally ill to go through with it. If I had to guess, Mr. Bailey was just that disappointed in Jimmy for doing something that would get him locked up. He was living through his son's baseball career, and that would all end with him in prison. I never met the man, but I'd guess he thought his life was over with his only son locked away in a cage, because there'd be no more baseball for him. And the sister in Atlanta? She blames Jimmy for everything."

Sitting together on the Italian-style loveseat in the parlor, Tony took his mother's hands in his.

"Ma, how ironic is it that Dad would have given anything to live longer, and Mr. Bailey cut his own life short?"

He watched tears well up in her eyes and reached to bring her close to him in a full-blown hug. "I didn't mean to make you cry," he said.

"I know. It's just that I look in your eyes and I see him. Every time I look at you, I see him. If you're sure you love this girl and want a relationship with her, you need to realize that it will be give-and-take every day. You need to tell her. Because that's life. Don't worry about her father. Her brother. Her runaway sister. All that matters is you and her. But Tony…"

"Yes, Ma?"

"Can she cook?"

He laughed, letting out a full-belly guffaw. "I doubt she can cook like you, Ma, but her mother cooks great. The two of you ought to open a restaurant. You take care of the main courses, and she'll do the desserts. That restaurant would be a winner!"

"I'm too old for that now, but I don't mind cooking for you and her family. I like having them around here. It's not so lonely when they're here. And they're not as nosy as your sisters."

He rolled his eyes back, remembering his meddling three sisters and how they were always in his business. "They're all right, Ma. They're just looking out for you."

"Uh-huh," she replied. "But they do like to talk. I bet they've already got you and Debbie walking down the aisle at St. Anthony's Church, even though they haven't met her."

"Probably so. But maybe they're not so far off."

Chapter Eighty-Six

Debbie knew that Brian Riggi expected that he'd soon be her husband, but one day she called him and said they were done. She told him that she had a lot of family issues and that her job was just too busy.

He was too furious for words.

"What the hell's more important than your own relationship?" he demanded.

"Brian, don't lose your temper with me. That's happened more times than I'd like to remember," she said. "And maybe that's part of it, too."

"Oh, so that's it? You're telling me that I'm the bad guy here?"

"Not exactly. It's a combination of things," she replied.

"Oh, yeah? So, what's his name? You found someone else, right?"

"I owe you no explanation, Brian. We've only been dating for a few months. If this is the way you're going to react when I tell you I have family and work issues, forget it!" she yelled, slamming the phone down. She could feel her face burning red.

Jerk! How dare he? I haven't even seen him in a couple of weeks, and I've hardly spoken to him over the phone, so, why is he acting so shocked... like he didn't see this coming. Some guys just don't appreciate it when you try to let them down easily. Oh, well. Bye-bye, Brian.

~ ~ ~

Brian was substitute-teaching in a middle school in the Boston Public School system, which had recently been de-segregated via decree of the Boston School Committee, Louise Day Hicks, and Judge John Sirica. The effects of that decision were that many White parents took their kids out of the schools and sent them to parochial schools, while Black parents were excited to see their kids going to better schools than they had before.

In other words, the school system was in complete chaos.

Even teachers had to be bused into the schools, where they were greeted by stone-throwing residents and jeers. Some teachers took leaves of absence while they waited for things to calm down.

There were few, if any, White children left in Boston Public Schools—a reverse segregation, really. Brian was not adept at teaching anyone, let alone Black children who were essentially illiterate and had been passed on from grade to grade because some teachers were afraid of them.

He drove a cab at night to supplement his income. One night he answered a call for a fare outside of the Howard Johnson's restaurant on Morrissey Boulevard. It turned out to be an interesting ride.

"Hey, you," the guy in the back said, "can you take me to Cambridge Police Headquarters?"

"Uh, yeah, but it's going to be expensive, all the way from here."

"I didn't ask how much it was going to cost, idiot. I asked if you could take me there. Capeesh?"

"Uh, yeah, okay."

Brian started the meter.

After they got onto the Southeast Expressway, the guy started grumbling and talking. "Hey, aren't you the one who was going out with that dame, the one whose brother was a baseball player from Weymouth?"

Brian looked up into his rearview mirror. "How do you know that?"

"Well, are you that guy?"

"Umm…Yeah, but we broke up."

"You know she's seeing a cop, right? A Cambridge cop."

"A cop? No, I didn't know that." Brian felt his blood pressure rise and his face and neck turn red. Sweat began pouring from his head.

"Yeah. Guy named DeMarco. You could go into headquarters with me and have a *conversation* with him. Ya know…about taking your girl and all."

"She was not my girl, whoever you are, and I'll just drop you off after you pay your fare."

"Whoa, kinda sensitive, aren't we? I have a proposition for you, though."

"Why? And why do you think I'd do anything for you? I don't even know who you are. You're just some random guy who called for a cab."

"*Au contraire,* pal. I specifically asked that *you* be my cabbie. See, we're trying to get to this Cambridge cop and your girl Debbie's brother. We tried kidnapping her to get to the cop, but someone saw the kidnapping in progress over on Castle Island and we failed."

"Who *are* you?" Brian demanded.

"Does it matter? Don't you want to get back at the guy who stole your girl? Didn't it make you mad when she broke up with you?"

"How do you know she broke up with me?"

"We have our ways, Brian."

Brian looked at his livery license on the glove compartment door. He wanted to believe that was how the guy knew his name, but he had a sneaking suspicion that wasn't the case.

"Who are you working for?" Brian asked.

"That's none of your concern."

"It is if you want me to listen to your proposition."

"Let's just say I have friends who have a beef with this Detective DeMarco guy. And your girlfriend put one of my friends in the hospital. Wouldn't you be upset if that happened to one of your friends?"

"I guess so. But couldn't you just get a lawyer and sue *him*?"

Peals of laughter hurled from the back seat. "You can't be serious, Brian! Sue a *cop*? For putting my friend in the hospital? You should be a comedian!"

"Listen, what do you want from me?"

"I want you to find out where your girl is staying."

"Well, we aren't on speaking terms these days."

"Do you know her brother? Her mother?"

"I haven't met her brother. He just got out of prison..."

"Yeah. We know. How about her mother?"

"I met her a couple of times. She's a nice lady."

"You might not think that if you saw her with a baseball bat in her hand."

"What are you talking about? A baseball bat?"

"She beat up one of our guys at her house. He was trying to, well, you know, have a *conversation* with her."

Brian didn't like the way he said conversation. "What *kind* of conversation?"

"That doesn't matter. We need to know where the Baileys are staying. You can help us with that, Brian."

"And if I don't?"

"I'm not answering that question, Brian. I think I've shared enough to let you know that we are serious people."

The cab pulled in front of the Cambridge Police headquarters.

"Here's your money, Brian. There's a note inside with a phone number. Call me if you have questions."

He handed Brian $250 wrapped around a small piece of scrap paper.

"Call me, Brian. We do know where to find you. It would be a shame if your students needed a new teacher."

Brian looked at the money and tried to get a glimpse of the person who'd handed it to him. Of course, he could use the cash, but what about all this cloak-and-dagger stuff? Should he call DeMarco himself and tell him about this cab encounter? Should he tell Debbie about it? Or should he just cooperate with the guy who had just threatened him so that he could save his own skin? This was the guy who said his collaborators had tried to kidnap Debbie. *Kidnap* her!

He found a spot in the parking lot. He was going to find this DeMarco guy, in or out of the police station. First, he'd give him a piece of his mind about stealing his woman. He hadn't decided if he would tell him about the guy in the back of his cab.

With sweat pouring down the back of his neck, and his usually olive-colored skin transformed beet-red, Brian Riggi walked into Cambridge Police headquarters with a wad of fifty-dollar bills in his wallet.

"Do you have an officer here named DeMarco?"

"Who wants to know?" the desk sergeant replied sternly.

"I have some information he might need for…a case he's working on."

"Which one? He's got a bunch of cases going."

"The one with the tall woman from Cambridge."

"DeMarco ain't here. He's out on the streets somewhere. You wanna talk to one of the other guys who's working that case? What's your name again?"

"Brian, but never mind. I'll come back again. I'm driving a cab. There are probably some fares waiting for me."

"Yeah, probably so. What's your last name, Brian? I'll tell him you were here."

"Ruggierio," Brian lied, using the name of someone he went to high school with. "Brian Ruggierio. I drive a cab. I'm all over the place, you understand."

"Yeah, I get it. I'll tell him you were here."

"You do that."

Brian shook his head as he walked down the steps to his cab, relieved that DeMarco hadn't been in. He had no idea what he would have said to him anyway. He felt like a coward.

Chapter Eighty-Seven

"You're going to need a little cash when you leave here," she said. "This is what I call some seed money for when you need to buy some food or some clothes so you can look for a job."

The nice nurse had given Keeshon fifty dollars. *Fifty whole dollars!* He thought he'd inherited the moon.

He was speechless.

"I-I-I... don't know what to say. No one eva did that fo' me befo'."

"Did what?" she asked.

"Worried about me. Most folks just wanted to get rid of me. 'Cept that nice lady I used to work fo.' She was nice to me, too. She gave me money, but then, when she died, hah family 'cused me of stealin' from hah. Honest, ma'am, I didn't take nothin.' She gave me money as a gift. Like you doin' now."

"People can be cruel," she said. "I don't believe in that. You know what?"

"Ummm... no."

"I'm going to tell you something that no one else knows, even in this hospital. I used to be a nun. I left the convent because I couldn't stand it anymore. I couldn't take being isolated from people, knowing that the priests had all kinds of privileges, while we in the convent had very strict rules. I just woke up one day, after a long night of praying, and said, 'God,

I don't think this is what you had in mind for me.' I packed up what few things I had and went to Mother Superior and told her I was leaving."

"You was a nun? You mean one of them ladies who weahs big veils and long dresses all day, and teach in Catholic schools?"

"Precisely. But I wasn't a teacher. I was a nurse, just like now. I'd gone to nursing school before I entered the convent. I'd expected to be sent to places overseas, like Africa, India, and Haiti, where the church needed nurses. Instead, they kept me here in Boston to work in the Catholic hospitals. Mother Superior said the need was great here, as well."

"So...let me get this straight. You went to nussin' school and then into the convent. You 'spected to be sent to fah away places to be a Catholic nuss but instead the chuch kept you heah. But you left the chuch..."

She cut him off. "No, I didn't leave the church, just being a nun in a convent. I am still a Catholic and attend Mass every Sunday. That didn't change. What changed is that I live in the community and my paycheck is my own. I give away parts of my pay to people who are in need. I'd say you're in need right now. I set aside money from every paycheck I make as a nurse so that I can help others. It's better to be an action-oriented person, in my opinion, than to be in a convent somewhere, praying all the time."

Keeshon scratched his chin. "I kinda undustand this a lil mo.' I need to find a safe place to live, and I need to find my frien,' Jimmy. I just hope the goons who beat me up won't be waitin' to kill me once I'm outa heah."

"I can set you up with a social services agency that can help you, Mr. Washington."

"Please call me Keeshon or Key fo' shawt, ma'am."

"Okay, Key. I have several connections in the community that could be helpful to you regarding getting a place to live. I can make those calls now. Would you like that?"

"As long as you can trust the people," he warned. "I don't want to git involved wit nobody who might be caught up wit the ones who killed the wawden and almost killed me."

"I would never, ever, put you in danger," she assured him. "I don't know those kinds of people."

"Thank you, ma'am. And thank you fo' the money. It's a godsend."

"Great. I'll be back after I finish with the rest of my patients and have had time to call some of my contacts at the social services agencies. Stay put, okay?"

"I'll be heah."

Something didn't feel right to Keeshon, but he couldn't put his finger on it. She had an answer for everything. He wondered if he could trust her.

~ ~ ~

Keeshon still didn't know where Jimmy was. Luckily, the social worker he had been connected with had lined up a place for him to stay.

"Now, Mr. Washington, I want you to promise me you'll be careful," the social worker said.

"Yes, ma'am."

"You will be receiving rental assistance, and I will have someone check in on you."

"Yes, ma'am."

"You will also need a phone. Basic service. I haven't set that up yet, but I will."

"Yes, ma'am."

"Is that all you can say? Yes, ma'am?"

"Yes, ma'am—I mean, no ma'am. I'm just thinkin' 'bout what it might be like to live on my own agin without nobody else. I was in prison fo' a long time befo' I got beat up. This a big change fo' me."

"Yes, indeed, it is. I can't imagine. We'll get you some furniture from the St. Vincent DePaul Society, through the big church over there. You should go there sometime. It's quite beautiful. The paintings on the ceiling are breathtaking."

"Thank you fo' gettin' me things fo' my place."

"It's been my pleasure. And Mr. Washington…"

"Yes, ma'am?"

"Don't go looking for any trouble over there. Things have been strained since the school's desegregation a couple of years ago. Sometimes thugs from Southie prowl around Mission Hill looking for trouble, if you know what I mean."

"Yes, ma'am."

"Well, good luck to you. Here's my card if you need help anytime."

He looked at the fancy embossed business card. *Kitty Price, MSW, Social Worker.*

"Is that yo' real name, ma'am, Kitty?"

She laughed. "Oh, no, it's really Katherine, but my brother always called me Kitty, so that's what I go by."

"Well, then, ma'am, if it's good enough fo' yo' brotha, it's good enough fo' me."

As he walked away, she thought about the hard-luck world he was about to face, but she also recognized that when he saw her name, it was the first time she'd seen him smile since she'd met him. Maybe he was hopeful and more optimistic for himself than she was for him.

For his part, Keeshon hadn't heard from his friend in a while, so he was on a mission—to find Jimmy. Boston was a big town, but Keeshon decided that once he was settled in his new place, he'd visit North Weymouth where Jimmy had grown up.

Chapter Eighty-Eight

Not ten minutes after Brian left the Cambridge Police Station, Tony popped up the stairs.

"Some guy was looking for you, Tony—Brian Ruggiero or Ruggieri or something like that. He said he was a cabbie and that you might have a couple of mutual friends."

"Hmmm... I don't know anyone with that name, or at least it doesn't ring a bell. Maybe someone on the team knows him."

"Nope," the sergeant said. "I asked if he wanted to talk to someone else on the team. He said only you, DeMarco, only you."

"Did he mention what case he wanted to discuss?"

"He said something about the case involving the tall woman from Cambridge." He handed the pink slip to Tony that he'd jotted Brian's information on and turned to answer the phone. "This blasted thing never stops ringing, ya know!"

Tony looked at the note. He was sure that he didn't know anyone named Brian Ruggierio or Ruggieri. He didn't know many cab drivers, either. Then it hit him... Debbie's ex drove a cab.

He trotted back to his office and picked up the phone. After two rings, Debbie answered.

"Hello? Tony?"

"Hey, Debbie. How's it going?"

"Ummm… Okay… I'm just looking over some material for a meeting I have in the morning. Did you just want to hear my voice, or do you have some other fresh hell to warn me about?"

"A little bit of both, actually." He could almost feel her eyes rolling in the back of her head.

"And here I thought it was just because you wanted to talk. Okay, spill the beans."

"Your ex, the cab driver—his name's Brian, right?"

"Yes… But what does that have to do with the price of potatoes?" she joked.

"What's his last name?"

"Riggi. Brian Riggi. He's from Long Island."

"But he has a Massachusetts hack license, right, to drive a cab in this state?"

"As far as I know. I don't know if he can drive a cab in New York or the City. Why all the questions?"

"Some guy came looking for me at the station a little while ago. Told the desk sergeant that his name was Brian *Ruggiero* and said he was a cab driver. He also said he had a message to deliver to me about the case involving the tall woman from Cambridge."

"Hmmm… I wonder what that's about."

"I thought maybe it was your ex, you know, trying to make a point."

"Trying to tell you to stay away from me? Oh, no, Tony, all he'd have to do would be to take one look at you and he'd know he was outclassed. Besides, I told him not to contact me anymore. I think I made myself abundantly clear to him."

"Does he know where your mother lives?"

"I think so. We went to her house once and then took a ride to Wessagusset Beach. We didn't stay at Ma's house for long, though."

"Do you think he could be mixed up in this stuff we're investigating?"

"Brian? He's such a wimp! No, I don't see any way he could be. The only thing he's capable of doing might be if he'd seen my Volvo parked at Castle Island with the keys in the car, he might have driven off with it. Other than that, no. But Tony, are you coming home soon? I mean…to your mother's house?"

He hesitated. "Okay. I'll be there just as soon as I figure out a couple of things. And Debbie?"

"Yes?"

"I miss you."

Debbie was speechless for a couple of seconds. She wasn't used to anyone being this sweet to her. She didn't know what the correct response should be.

"Then come home. I don't like it when you're not here."

"I will. I promise. Let me handle some things here first. Don't go anywhere. Keep the doors locked and stay alert."

"I will. I promise that back," she said, looking over her shoulder as she heard her mother and his mother's giggles coming from the parlor. The two of them had become fast friends.

Tony hung up the phone and ran down the hallway past the two interrogation rooms to where the clerk for motor vehicles sat.

"Hey, Joe, how can I find out about a cabbie here in the good old Commonwealth?" he asked, trying to catch his breath.

"What is it you wanna know, Tony? I may have to make a phone call or two, but I can usually figure things out."

"Can you find out if a person with a certain name actually has a cabbie license?"

"Oh, *that's* a piece of cake. What's the name?"

"Brian Ruggierio. I think it's spelled…"

Joe cut him off. "I can figure it out. I do this stuff all day long."

He opened a binder, approximately eighteen inches long and twelve inches tall, containing green-and-white slotted paper from the dot-matrix printer. He shuffled pages until he came to the letter R.

"Here are the names of all cabbies with the last name beginning with R, Tony."

They scanned together and found no one with the last name Ruggierio.

"The closest I can find to that name, Tony, is Riggi. Are you sure the last name was Ruggierio?"

"Thanks, Joe. Maybe Stan at the front desk misunderstood the name. What's this Riggi's medallion number?"

Joe grabbed a slip of paper and wrote down everything he could find on Brian J. Riggi— his date of birth, place of birth, and his current address.

"Hope this helps," he said, handing the information to Tony. "What d'ya want him for, anyway?"

"Not sure, Joe. I'll think of something."

Chapter Eighty-Nine

"I feel like I'm in a witness protection program or something," Jimmy said to Eileen, as they sat on the sofa in Angela DeMarco's parlor. "I'm sure you feel that way, too. I'm sorry. Every time I think about those guys taking you, I get angry."

"I wasn't too keen on it, either," she replied, "but the most important thing is that we found a way out of that situation. It put a little adventure in our normally dull lives, I guess."

"You don't need adventure. You get that in your job every day, what with all the accidents and stuff that come in. Don't you?"

"Some days. But so many days are just, well, dull. The worst days are when we have a big auto accident and people come in after they're rescued from crushed cars, and they're in bad shape."

"Yeah. Guess you don't need all that excitement. I wonder, though, Eileen, if the guys know where you live, they might also know what kind of car you drive. I mean, that guy was waiting for Debbie inside her car when he took her to Castle Island."

"I never thought of that, Jim. Maybe I should see if I can trade cars with my dad for a couple of weeks. They'd never think I'd be driving a 1970 truck, would they?" she giggled.

"Wow, you're braver than I am!"

"Jim—that little caper at the Dairy Queen made a believer out of my roommate. She doesn't doubt me now when I tell her about the adventures of the Bailey family. She thinks you should write a book."

"Me? Write a book? Fat chance. Maybe when I'm old and gray and look back at all this stuff. Hey, I'm wondering what's happening with Keeshon. I know he can't find me here. Don't know how to reach him at the new hospital. They kept that location a secret for his safety. Don't know how he's doing or even if his health is better. Don't know if he has a place to live, either, when they release him. Hell, Mrs. DeMarco could fit him in here! This place is a palace compared to Ma's. Debbie calls it elegant. I just call it huge. Lots of nooks and crannies to hide. Bet that's what Tony did when he was a kid—hid from his ma and his sisters. We haven't met them yet."

"You mean they haven't popped in to check out the girl their brother is dating?"

"Nope, not yet."

"They do have a *thing* for each other, don't they? Your sister and Tony?"

"Yes, he and my sister have a *thing* for each other. I'm sure of it."

"And you? Do you have a *thing* for anyone?"

"If I did, Eileen, you know it would be for you."

Scarlet red swept over her freckles and forehead, matching her hair color. He smiled as she blushed; his words had achieved the desired effect.

Chapter Ninety

Tony made his way to Beacon Hill, looking for Brian at the Revere Street address.

The parking was almost non-existent. The cobblestone streets were too narrow for his big, black car. He had to drive up and down the streets until he located a spot he could squeeze into. He placed his police credentials on the windshield, even though he was out of his jurisdiction, then walked up Mount Vernon Street and over to Revere. Not much of a hike, but an inconvenience.

He arrived and saw Brian's name on the mailbox. He stood there for a few minutes, contemplating what he'd say to Debbie's ex-boyfriend.

As he stood in the vestibule, someone else walked in.

"Hey, man, what are you doing here?"

"I was looking for someone who lives on the second floor. Brian Riggi."

"Who are you?"

"I'm Detective Tony DeMarco from the Cambridge Police Dept. I have a couple of questions for him."

"I'm his roommate. I think he's out driving a cab. I doubt that he's home. Stay here. I'll check. I'm not letting you in, though."

Tony flashed his badge so the roommate could see.

"You can show me that thing until the cows come home, but if you don't have a search warrant, I'm not letting you in."

"Slow down, man. Have I asked you to let me in?"

"No."

"Then relax. Just see if Brian's home. Okay?"

"Just wait here."

He bounded up the steps, taking them two by two, and slipped the key into the door lock. Tony heard him yell, "Hey Riggi, you home?" but he got no response.

Tony could make out footsteps as the roommate walked from room to room looking for Brian. Finally, he returned to Tony.

"Sorry, man. Don't know why you're looking for him, but he's not here."

"He was looking for *me* earlier today. I don't know why but I figured I'd return the favor."

"Oh. Does this have anything to do with Debbie? Because, man, Brian's been a basket case since she broke up with him."

Tony shrugged. "Like I said, I don't know. He came looking for me." He reached into his pocket and pulled out a business card. "Just give him this when he comes home, okay? Let him know I was here."

"Yeah. I will. Sorry, I couldn't help you. He could be anywhere in the city right now. He's trying to make some extra money. You know how it is."

"Yeah. I sure do."

When Tony returned to his car, he found that someone had slashed his tires and left a note on his windshield: "Go back to Cambridge, PIG!" He wondered if it was Brian or someone else.

He would have to get this monstrosity of a vehicle towed—before the City of Boston did it for him. Parking on Beacon Hill was not for the faint of heart.

Chapter Ninety-One

Brian picked up fare after fare, traipsing all over Boston and Cambridge.

Every time someone new got in the back, he worried it would be the guy who wanted information about Debbie and her family.

Tonight's take had been great—nearly $80 in tips—but he still had that $250 he'd gotten from the mysterious passenger. He didn't dare spend it. He knew it was a *quid pro quo*—something in return for something else. He also knew he had to have information for that guy to earn that money. *Was it blood money?*

How could he betray Debbie? He *loved* her. At least he thought he did, until she told him to get lost. Why would she throw him out, like yesterday's garbage? She was a special person—the first woman he'd ever met he could bring home to his mother and know the family would approve. Even some of the snobbier parts of his family would have found Debbie classy, smart, and sophisticated.

She overwhelmed him in every way. She fascinated him with her conversation, her knowledge of any topic anyone could throw her way, her manner of walking, her sense of perfection. And her exquisite looks. Never a hair out of place. Perfect yet understated make-up. She wasn't model-thin. She was a real woman, curves, and all. She rarely strayed far from his mind.

And yet...

She told him she didn't want to see him anymore, that they were done. The reasons she had given were vague…nothing too specific. What had he done? He'd always been respectful, polite, and tried to cater to her every need. When he went to her place, he followed her rules. He never left the seat up on the toilet. Never put a dirty dish in the sink without rinsing it. Never used the wrong cups when he made coffee. He always took his shoes off at the door when he entered, always hung up his coat in the hall closet, and always opened the door for her as she entered her car.

What else could he have done so that she wouldn't have shut him down?

Now he had the opportunity to get back at her by finding out where she was staying and turn her over to the guy who was looking for her. He didn't even know who the guy was or what his reasons were for wanting to see her. He didn't even know if this was legitimate or if the guy wanted to hurt Debbie and her brother.

As he sat in a line of taxis at the Parker House Hotel in downtown Boston, anxious thoughts filled his head, most of which focused on Debbie. What had he done so wrong to ruin his chances with her?

His thoughts were interrupted by a brusque knock on his window.

"Hey, buddy, can you take me over to MIT? I need to get to Mass Ave, near where the entrance to the MIT Coop is. Can you do it?"

He looked up and replied, "Sure. Do you need help getting your luggage in the back?"

"No, no luggage. Just me."

"Okay, then," he muttered half to himself, as he flipped the meter down and pulled out into traffic once the guy was settled in the backseat.

"So, uh, Brian, any news? About the whereabouts of the Bailey family? I mean, we gave you enough time to get us the info."

Here we go again. Brian looked into his rearview mirror. "Who *are* you?"

"Doesn't matter who I am. What matters is I need to know where they are. I've got a score to settle with your girl, Debbie."

Brian was tempted to correct him; she was no longer *his* girl. But he held his tongue.

"She must've really done something bad, if you're this focused on getting to her," he replied instead.

"Let's just say," came the voice from the back, "she insulted me as a man. Then she threw a few of my good friends under the bus. Know what I'm sayin'?"

"Oh, I have an idea. Sure do."

"So, give me a progress report, Brian. We don't have oodles of time here."

"I've got a few clues but not a specific place yet. All I've been able to figure out on my own is that she's staying just outside of Cambridge, maybe Arlington, maybe even Watertown; staying with a family that has a big house. I'm asking around, though."

"Did you get to that detective yet, that DeMarco guy? He must know."

"I went to the Cambridge Police Station looking for him, but he wasn't there, and I got nowhere with the desk sergeant. He was dumber than a box of rocks."

The MIT dome came into view.

"Where exactly do you want me to drop you off?"

"Right at the crosswalk, where the main MIT building meets Mass Ave. And Brian—you got another week. That's it. If you don't get the info by then—well, I make no promises, but I'll tell you to watch your back, if you know what I mean."

A chill went up Brian's spine. "I have a good idea. I'm working on it. Trust me, I am," he said, pulling alongside the curb.

"Oh, I believe you. It's just gotta be faster. We got business to take care of."

The man hopped out of the cab, threw a roll of money through Brian's window, slammed the door, and ran up the steps that led to MIT's main corridor.

As he pulled away wondering what business the man had at MIT, Brian could still feel the chill.

Now he was really in a predicament. Debbie wasn't taking his calls anymore. He debated telling DeMarco what was going on at the risk of incurring his wrath. On the other side of that coin, was it all worth him risking his own life if he didn't deliver what these shady characters wanted him to?

Chapter Ninety-Two

Keeshon looked at the $50 the nurse had given him and tucked it back in his pocket.

"This all the money I got in the world," he muttered to himself.

Something inside him kept him from going to the place the social worker had found for him, so he left the hospital in search of his friend instead. He decided that he would locate Jimmy first and then they could find him a job and a place to live. He trusted Jimmy. Maybe they could even become roommates again.

He walked up to the MBTA booth.

"'Scuse me, suh, can you tell me what trains and buses I need to take to get to Nawth Weymouth?"

"North Weymouth? Why you wanna go there?"

"Got a frien' who lives theah. Lives off Bridge Street, I think, neah a Mista Donut. You know wheah that is?"

"Yeah, near St. Jerome's Church. Okay. You get on this train here and go to Park Street. Park Street. Got it?"

"Yeah."

"Then wait for a train that says 'Braintree' or 'Quincy' on it. Don't take the other train to Dorchester. Understand?"

"Yeah."

"Get off at Quincy Center, then take a Hingham bus to Weymouth. You go over the Fore River Bridge. Tell the driver to let you off at the Mister Donut or St. Jerome's. They're close to each other."

"Thanks."

"Hey kid—does your friend know you're comin'?"

"No. I haven't been able to git ahold of him on the phone."

"Just be careful. Not too many of...your kind down there on the South Shore. You know what I mean?"

"Yes, suh, I do. Thank you. Now how much do I need? Tokens?"

"Two tokens for the train, two for the bus." He slid four gold-colored coins, embossed with the MBTA logo, under the window. "One to get on the train, one to get off. Same for the bus."

"Thanks, suh. I'm glad I met you."

"You take care, son."

"Oh, I will."

The darkened screen behind which he spoke didn't reveal that the man in the booth was also Black, with a deformed nose and punched-in left cheek. Seemed he'd seen some action for the color of his skin during his lifetime and was happy to be protected behind the plexiglass and locked door of this booth. Seemed he was glad to have a job in this city. Seemed he was concerned about Keeshon.

~ ~ ~

Keeshon's $50 felt like a million to him. He was determined to find Jimmy, no matter where he was. North Weymouth? Near a church? St. Jerome's? Maybe the priest knew his address. He vaguely remembered Jimmy saying that he lived near a Mister Donut. Good thing it wasn't a Dunkin.' They were all over the place.

He arrived at Park Street Station, not even knowing what or whom to ask for help. Finally, he heard some guys talking about making sure they got onto the Braintree train downstairs so they could get to Weymouth.

"'Scuse me, guys, you going to Weymouth? I'm new in town and I need to git to Nawth Weymouth. I think I gotta take a train and a bus. Or maybe a coupla buses. You know how to do that?"

"Yeah," one of them replied. "You gotta get a Braintree train and go to Quincy. Not North Quincy. QUINCY. Then get on a Hingham bus. Takes you over the Fore River Bridge into North Weymouth. Whattaya looking for?"

"St. Jerome's Chuch," Keeshon said. "'Posed to meet somebody."

"It's a big one," the other guy said. "Just tell the driver to let you off at St. Jerome's. It'll be on the left. Can't miss it."

"Thanks. 'Preciate it."

One of them tipped his Red Sox hat. "Anytime," he said. "Glad to help." They went down the stairs to wait for the train.

Keeshon decided to grab a quick donut and cup of coffee at the Dunkin' inside the train station. As he stood in line, he couldn't shake the feeling that someone had eyes on him. He ordered a Boston crème donut and a small regular coffee, then headed downstairs himself, still convinced he was being followed.

He told himself he was being paranoid, that he just needed to keep going to find Jimmy. He chalked it up to being locked up for so long where people watched you twenty-four, seven. Nevertheless, he still felt closed in and hoped the train would come soon.

He finished his donut and coffee without spilling a drop or getting any chocolate on his mouth. He was proud of himself for that. When the train came along, he got on it without checking to see if it was going to Braintree. He soon discovered he'd taken the wrong train and began to panic a little.

He sat down next to a teenager and asked how he could fix his mistake. At first, the only response he got was, "I dunno."

"Listen, go to Fields Corner. Take a bus to Quincy Square, then get another bus to Hingham. It'll take longer but you'll get there," came a voice from behind.

Keeshon turned around. "Thank you, Miss. I 'preciate yo' advice."

"Not a problem. I've made the same mistake more times than I can count. But I get off at Quincy Square now. I don't live down in North Weymouth anymore."

The teenager glanced Keeshon's way. "Yeah, what she said," he replied, putting his hands firmly on top of his backpack.

At Fields Corner in Dorchester, he left the train behind and looked for the correct bus. He hadn't asked the woman which bus to take. He went to the token booth and asked the person inside.

"'Scuse me, suh. But which bus would I take to git to Quincy Square?"

"Whad'are you, stupid or somethin'?" the guy in the booth asked. "The banner will say 'Quincy Square.' Now get outta here!"

Keeshon jumped a little when the guy screamed at him but realized it was par for the course. He saw other Black people around, but most had their heads down as they waited for their buses. He put his hands in his pockets and waited, too.

As the Quincy Square bus pulled in and passengers began to load, he noticed the Black people automatically went toward the back of the bus, even though buses were no longer segregated. Force of habit, he guessed, but he sat in the middle, close to the exit door. A few White people gave him dirty looks; he didn't care. He was going to find Jimmy.

He began to sense, once again, that someone was watching him. He looked around the bus and tried to find someone—anyone—who might look familiar. Nothing. No faces matched those in his memory. No Walpole guards. No members of the woman's family who'd put him in prison. None of his old friends from Roxbury. He scanned the bus like an old lighthouse, repeatedly. Still nothing.

People boarded and left the bus at regular intervals. He heard the bus driver's gravelly voice announce each stop, but he couldn't differentiate what each declaration meant. Sounded like "MO—FFFT" or WOL—STN." He could smell the ocean from his seat, that distinctive aroma of low tide in the Atlantic Ocean—wet sand, rotting clamshells, dockside barnacles—as the waves retreated out to sea. Some may have found this to be a foul smell, but to Keeshon, it was just another thing he'd missed when he was behind bars at Walpole State Prison.

They passed the North Quincy train station, which Keeshon would have seen firsthand had he taken the Braintree train. Traffic increased through this area, slowing the bus in near-bumper-to-bumper conditions. While other riders complained, he didn't mind. He was getting closer to finding Jimmy. He just knew it.

End of the line: Quincy Square.

Everyone who was left on the bus departed, walking into a rundown station that once had only catered to buses. Inside, the train station was clean and well-kept. Where the buses parked, on the other hand, trash was strewn all over the pavement, as careless commuters dumped their debris when they departed the bus on their way out.

Keeshon kicked a Dunkin' coffee cup out of the way, as well as a Twinkie wrapper, as he stood and waited for a Hingham bus.

Ten minutes, fifteen minutes, twenty minutes went by.

Finally, a bus with a Hingham banner arrived. He entered and asked the driver to let him off at St. Jerome's Church. The driver nodded and pointed to the token compartment to remind Keeshon that he needed to deposit one to ride the bus. The driver never uttered an actual word, only pointed to the machine; Keeshon obliged and headed for a seat a few rows behind the driver.

He'd only heard about the Fore River Bridge from Jimmy. He'd also heard about the shipyard where Jimmy's dad had worked. He didn't know much about either except for Jimmy's stories about how the bridge opened sometimes to let big ships either in or out of the shipyard. *A drawbridge*, it was called.

The bus made its way out of Quincy Square, remaining on the main thoroughfare, picking up and dropping off passengers along the way. He was enjoying the ride, taking in the scenery, and making mental notes; Montillio's Bakery, several churches, Dairy Queen.

After a rotary, where it seemed the bus took the circle on two wheels, there was the Fore River Bridge. Up the bridge ramp it went, going over a grated metal part in the middle, then into North Weymouth.

Welcome to Weymouth. Established 1622, the sign read.

The driver turned around. "Get ready," he said to Keeshon. "We're almost to St. Jerome's Church."

Keeshon jumped up and went to the front door.

"I will let you out the other exit door," the driver said. "Don't you know nothin' about riding buses?"

"No, I don't know much," Keeshon replied. "I haven't been on a lotta buses in my life."

"Well, you've ridden the best since you've ridden mine," the driver said, relaxing his attitude, as he pulled over to the bus stop across from St. Jerome's.

"Thank you, suh."

"You're welcome."

Keeshon jumped off the bus wondering what he should do next. He wanted to cross the street and go to St. Jerome's, but this Bridge Street he was on had no crosswalk, no light, and cars were whizzing by. The next corner had a streetlight. He decided to walk up there and cross, then he'd come back up to the church.

He was about to press the walk button when he saw Mister Donut. He opted to go there instead of the church.

Again, he had the feeling that someone was watching him. He couldn't explain it, but he just had the notion that near him, someone, for some reason, had eyes on him.

He pressed the walk button and headed for Mister Donut.

'Scuse me, ladies," he said to the women at the counter, "I am trying to find a frien' of mine who lives close by heah. Wonda if anybody could help me."

A woman came up to the counter. "Who are ya' trying to find?"

"Jimmy. Jimmy Bailey. He told me he worked heah once. It was a while ago, but he told me he could walk heah."

"Yeah…He could…How do you know him?" asked a woman whose name tag read, "Candy."

"We was…roommates…fo' a time."

"He lives with his mother up the street," Candy replied. "I don't think he's there now, though. He's in protective custody."

"Protective what?"

"Protective custody. The police put him and his mother there after some thug tried to break into Mrs. Bailey's house."

"What? Do you know wheah he is now?"

"No, but they do come back from time to time to get clothes and stuff."

"Do you know the address? I will drop a note off fo' him in the mailbox."

"Sure." Candy wrote the address down on a Mister Donut napkin. "And what's your name, if I might ask?"

"Keeshon Washington."

"Nice to meet you, Keeshon Washington." She reached out her hand to shake his.

"I hoped to be able to stay the night with Jimmy and maybe he could help me wit a job," he said.

"I wouldn't necessarily go up there by myself," Candy warned. "The cops patrol there all the time ever since that baseball bat thing happened. If it's a job you need, you can talk to my manager, Al, about that. He's always looking for people."

"That's kind of you to offa, Miss. But if I don't know wheah I'm going to live, I don't think it would be right of me to take a job heah."

"Talk to Al anyway. Tell him you're Jimmy's friend. It can't hurt."

"Okay, I will. But let me drop this note off at Jimmy's house fust. I'll come back. I promise."

Candy came out from behind the counter and walked him to the door. "You can stay with me for the night," she said. "I don't mean any romantic thing, by the way, but I do have a couch you could sleep on until you find Jimmy and straighten out your living situation."

"That's mighty kind of you, Miss. I would 'preciate it."

"Fine. Then it's settled. Drop off your note and come on back."

"Thank you, Miss. Yo' name from yo' name tag says 'Candy.' May I call you that?"

"Of course. And may I call you Keeshon?"

"I would be 'aunawd if you did."

"It's a deal, then."

Keeshon smiled as he left to find Jimmy's house, just up the side street and to the left. Maybe he and Jimmy would finally connect after all.

Chapter Ninety-Three

Debbie and her mother were comfortable at the DeMarco's. They had everything they needed—and more: their own bedrooms, a private bathroom, and all the food they could eat.

Angela cooked the entrees, and Mary made dessert and snacks for everyone. They were quite the pair, Debbie thought. Two septuagenarians who loved being in a kitchen together, sharing recipes and breathing life into flour, sugar, vanilla, a pinch of this, a dash of that, with the help of measuring cups, well-seasoned pans, and years of skill they'd cultivated. It was as if they'd worked together for decades. Their creations were never dull.

Jimmy loved the food aspect, but he wasn't all that keen on being in Arlington. He wanted to be home. Home. His own bed. His squirrely rug under his feet as he trudged to the bathroom half asleep. His chenille bedspread—the one he'd had since seventh grade—all wound up around his now-adult body, the one where the threads were unraveling. He loved it all even more, after being released from prison. Arlington was closer to Fenway Park so it was easier to get to work, but it was only about a week longer that the Red Sox would keep him working. No postseason place for this guy.

He missed Eileen most of all. She and Trisha had left the DeMarco's and gone back to their home, to their lives. He couldn't just call her and ask her to stop by after work. To get to Arlington would take a good hour with traffic.

Stupid Expressway! Whoever named it that, had a sick sense of humor.

Traffic was always bumper to bumper. His head spun thinking of the traffic she'd have to go through just to see him.

Eileen. In Jimmy's mind, she became more and more beautiful every day he didn't see her. He thought about her brush with danger with Rossi's men. He wanted to kill Rossi. *Really* kill him. More for what he did to Eileen than for what his boys almost did to Debbie. Debbie could take care of herself, but Eileen and her roommate were innocent bystanders. They should not have been involved.

Rossi was out of the hospital, Tony said, but he didn't know what kind of shape he was in. Only that he'd been discharged. Even if Rossi couldn't walk, he could order his gang to take care of business. Jimmy knew that all too well.

Jimmy hadn't talked to Keeshon for a couple of weeks. He didn't know if he was still in the hospital or if he had been released. There was just so much going on.

Chapter Ninety-Four

The blinding sun almost obliterated the golden dome atop the Boston State House as reporters set up their gear near the front steps. The governor's office had already provided a podium in the middle of the ascending stairs, along with an electrical outlet for the governor's microphone and a box the radio reporters could plug into.

They were expecting the governor, and representatives from the FBI, the Department of Corrections, and the state police.

The print and wire service reporters wrangled their way to the front, keeping their eyes open for still photographers who'd been assigned to cover the story and enhance their writing with accompanying pictures.

The people below in the Boston Common were oblivious to the gaggle assembling within their sights, too involved in their own little worlds to be concerned with what was happening with the guy they'd elected to lead their state.

As Governor Dukakis and other officials descended the State House stairs, grim-faced and serious about what they had to announce, the reporters gathered as if they'd been called to order. TV camera operators scuffled behind their lenses. Print writers squinted as they prepared to fill their special reporters' notebooks with quotes from this imposing rally. Photographers appeared from out of nowhere, taking positions from up and down the steps, changing lenses to get better angles.

The crisp, cloudless sky provided a perfect backdrop for what would be a somber announcement of corruption, crime, murder, and mayhem behind the walls of one of the Commonwealth's maximum-security prisons.

John O'Malley, assistant to the governor, stepped to the microphone first. "Thanks for your patience, everyone. We have updated copies of the press release available for you. I'll have them passed out as soon as the governor makes his announcement. It's my pleasure to introduce the Honorable Michael S. Dukakis."

A couple of passersby clapped, but the press remained silent.

"Thank you, John," Dukakis said, in his full-blown Boston accent. "Today's a solemn day here in the Commonwealth. First, I wish to remember the late warden of Walpole State Prison, whose family is here today. He was killed in the line of duty by the people who were involved in one of the worst corruption scandals in the history of the Department of Corrections. Let's take a moment of silence in his memory.

"Thank you. We happened upon this discovery in what some might call a strange way. My assistant here, John O'Malley, came to me about a Walpole prisoner who'd been beaten by a group of other inmates. My first instinct was to hand the incident over to the state police and the commissioner of corrections, but a few days later, the warden was murdered, with a note left beside his body that read, 'This is what happens to snitches.' As it turned out, the warden had been doing his own investigation into strange happenings at the prison. I'll let Commissioner Richard Mandel explain what the warden had discovered."

"Thank you, Governor Dukakis. Yes, let me just say we lost an amazing man when Peter Miles was killed. He was a champion for prison reform and had instituted many innovations for rehabilitation with prisoners who were on their way to release, to minimize recidivism. After his death, we found an underground ring of drug and contraband distribution, run by guards and inmates alike, with connections to organized crime on the outside. The guards had favorite inmates whom they allowed to brutally beat and punish those not in their inner circle, while simultaneously bringing drugs into the place and distributing them among the ones who did favors for them. They found out about the warden's investigation and knew it would end their crime spree. We worked with the state police, who recommended we involve the FBI, as well," Mandel said.

The state police representative took over at the podium. "Thanks to everyone here. Yes, we joined in as soon as the warden was murdered. We went into the prison and were not welcomed by any stretch of the imagination. Corruption went from drivers who picked up the inmates, to those working in the kitchen, the laundry, and the infirmary. The only place we didn't find corruption was in the classrooms where inmates studied for GEDs or other things. The guards left the teachers out because they all came from the outside. Now, I'd like to step aside as our FBI representative explains why we wanted the feds to join the investigation."

The FBI investigator cleared his throat as he made his way to speak. "Thank you all. I'm Agent Summer and I was involved at the grassroots level. I worked on the ground in this investigation and even caught a couple of the people incriminated directly with this scheme. We made the connection between organized crime and a few of the guards who worked at Walpole. Direct connection, even with some people in South Boston. I won't identify the people in Southie, though. That's another ongoing investigation."

Reporters began shouting out questions. "Hold on a minute, guys! We'll call on you. Raise your hands! O'Malley yelled, without benefit of a microphone. "Okay, *Boston Globe*. Go ahead."

"I heard there was a detective from the Cambridge Police involved, too. Is that correct?"

"Yes," Agent Summer replied. "Detective Anthony DeMarco had a peripheral involvement."

"This is explained in the timeline you have in the updated press release," O'Malley leaned into the microphone. "If you have questions after you see that, let me know." He then pointed to the reporter from WBZ Channel 4.

"Was there something I heard about a guy who was severely beaten just before the warden was killed?"

"Yes. The guards wanted to get back at his cellmate who'd been released. This was their way of sending that old cellmate a message. Next question," O'Malley said, pointing to the reporter from *The Boston Herald*.

"Wait a minute! Was the cellmate Jimmy Bailey, the former baseball player?" the reporter yelled out.

"Yes, and that's all we have for now. Many of your questions will be answered in the press release. Thank you and have a great day," O'Malley said, as he turned away from the podium.

~ ~ ~

The story was headline news everywhere. *The Globe* read: *Crime, Corruption, Contraband at Walpole: Guards, Inmates Collaborated with Organized Crime*; *The Herald* read: *Guards the Real Criminals at Walpole*; and *The Record-American* screamed: *Drugs, Death at Walpole*.

Debbie picked up *The Globe* and *The Herald*, reading the articles carefully. She saw Jimmy's name and Tony's but not hers.

What a relief. Nothing about our bat-wielding mother, either. Whew.

She could only imagine the rumors swirling around North Weymouth. She hadn't seen the hometown paper, *The Patriot-Ledger*. There'd probably be something in the weekly paper, *The Weymouth News*, as well.

She flung her back onto her swiveling office chair on wheels, going backward across the room. She leaned her head on the headrest and looked skyward, bringing her hands together fingertip to fingertip, deep in thought. She had planned her entire life, and thought she was in control of it all. What a crazy life it had turned out to be.

Chapter Ninety-Five

Brian couldn't stand it any longer. He picked up the phone and called Debbie's office.

"Hey, Marcia, this is Brian Riggi. You know, Debbie's friend?"

"Yeah…Brian…I recognize your name. Debbie's asked me to hold her calls."

"Marcia, this is important. I mean, *really* important. It may be a matter of life or death. Debbie needs to know what I have to say. Is there any way you can interrupt her for a couple of minutes?"

"I'll try. Hold, please."

Brian drummed his fingers along his desk. He'd called in sick to work at the school. It was the only way he figured he could contact Debbie—when she was at work—and talk to her about the mystery guy who kept getting into his cab. He couldn't call her at night since he didn't have a phone number where she was staying.

Marcia returned. "Hold on, Brian. She's finishing up with someone on the other line. She'll be with you in a couple of minutes."

"Thanks, Marcia," he said, breathing a sigh of relief.

The drumming became louder and more intense. He started tapping his feet, heel to toe. He was anxious about what he would say.

"What do you want, Brian?" Debbie came on the line. "This better be important."

"Debbie, it is. I know you don't want to hear from me, but I have to tell you that some strange guy has been jumping into my cab and trying to find out where you are. He says that he has some score to settle with you."

"What?"

"Yeah. He's tried to pay me off with a big wad of money. I told him I had no idea where you are, but he thinks I'm lying. He said if I don't tell him where he can find you within five more days, I better start watching over my shoulder because he will have some serious business with me. What's this all about, Deb?"

"If I tried to explain this, you wouldn't believe it. But I can't tell you where I'm staying. I'm in protective custody at my office and staying with friends. That's about all I can reveal."

"So, what should I tell this guy when he hops into my cab the next time? He might have weapons or something! I have no one to protect me!"

"Brian, I don't want anyone to hurt you, honestly, I don't. Is this why you went to the police station in Cambridge looking for Detective DeMarco?"

"Well...yeah..."

"Let me talk to the people involved in the protective custody. Are you home?"

"Yeah..."

"Okay, Brian, I will have to call you back. Stay put until you hear from me. When are you supposed to get back in the cab?"

"Not until six tonight."

"Hang tight. I'll get back to you."

Debbie was glad she had accepted Brian's call. *It really was a matter of life and death.*

She quickly dialed Tony's direct line, bypassing the sergeant's desk.

"DeMarco here."

"Tony, it's Debbie."

He could hear fear in her voice. "Debbie, are you okay? You're at work, right?"

"Yes. I'm okay. Sort of. I just got off the phone with Brian. My ex."

"Yeah. I know who he is. I went looking for him on Beacon Hill and someone slashed my tires while I was there. What's up?"

"He said some shady guy has been getting into his cab throwing money at him, trying to get him to tell him where my family and I are staying. The guy said Brian has five more days to get that information or something bad will happen to him."

"Wait, what?"

"That's what he told me. He said the guy randomly got into his cab. He hasn't gotten a good look at him, but hes given him big tips. What do we do? I know I broke up with him, but I really don't want to see him hurt because of me. I hurt him enough. We know what these people are capable of."

"Yes. Yes, we do. I'll call you back in five minutes. Tell Marcia to let me get right through, okay?"

"Absolutely."

"And Debbie…everything will be okay. Don't worry."

"I'm trying not to, Tony."

~ ~ ~

Tony drummed his fingers on his desk. He knew that most of the people involved in the drug ring had already been arrested. How was it possible that some shady guy was popping in and out of Brian's cab, trying to get information about Debbie's whereabouts?

The detective's brain was spinning at a hundred fifty miles per hour, taking the curves on two tires. He drummed. He swiveled in his chair. He tapped his feet. He bit his lower lip. Looking for something—anything—to come to his head. Clues. Connections. Anything.

He leaned back in his chair, almost to the point of falling over, closing his eyes, trying to picture Brian in his cab with a shadowy figure in the back seat. It couldn't be Rossi; he was in a rehab facility after his accident and had a twenty-four-hour guard watching him. Must be one of his friends.

Tony had to find Brian to see if he had any information that could lead him to the mystery people who kept popping up on him.

Chapter Ninety-Six

Keeshon wrote a note on the back of a Mister Donut napkin and walked toward Jimmy's house.

He looked around the neighborhood and noticed how well-kept the lawns were and how flowers were still blooming in people's yards in September. His old neighborhood in Roxbury didn't have green spaces like this. The buildings were constructed by the government at subsidized rents...the projects. This—this was nice. Calm. Quiet. Serene.

Jimmy's house was surrounded by yellow, crime-scene tape, guarded by a Weymouth cop. Keeshon didn't know what to do. He'd just been pardoned. He didn't know if he could even approach this police officer and ask if he could put the note in the mailbox. Although it was in the process of healing, his face was still banged up from the beating.

From outside the yellow tape, he called out. "'Scuse, me suh, can I speak to you fo' a moment?"

"Wha'dya want?" came the reply.

"Suh, I have a note I would like to place in the mailbox fo' my frien' who lives heah. Would you please take this and place it fo' me?" he asked nervously.

"Who are you? Why are you here? Ain't no one like you around here."

"I know. I know. But Jimmy Bailey is my frien' and I just need to get a message to him."

The cop drew his gun and approached Keeshon ever so slowly. "Hands up where I can see them."

Keeshon complied. "I mean no harm, suh. Jus' want to give you the note."

The cop began patting Keeshon down to see if he had a weapon. When he found none, he put his gun back in the holster.

"Where's this note?" he asked.

"In my shuwt pocket. It's on a napkin. A Mista Donut napkin."

"Is that the best you can do, if this guy Bailey is actually your friend?"

"It's all I had at the moment, suh."

The officer unfolded the napkin and quickly read the note.

"Okay, okay. I will put it in the mailbox. But I don't know when he will get it. The house is vacant. The family is staying elsewhere."

"Yes, suh."

The cop walked backward from Keeshon to regain his post on the steps. "Now don't try any funny business, you hear?"

"I won't, suh. I'm just walking back to Mista Donut. Thank you fo' puttin' the note in the mailbox."

"Humph."

~ ~ ~

Keeshon returned to the donut shop as he'd promised and waited for Candy's shift to end. He still wanted to find Jimmy, but at least he had a place to sleep.

He knew the social worker from the hospital said she'd found him an apartment in Roxbury, but he was trying as hard as he could not to return to his old neighborhood. Old "friends." Right. Friends who had abandoned him when he was sent to prison. Friends who laughed at him for his small size when they were in school together. Friends who had even beaten him up because they *could*. Who needed friends like that? Jimmy had shown him what a real friend was like when he stood by him at Walpole, and always protected him from the goon squad.

Now this woman, Candy, was standing by him enough to offer him her couch for the night. She didn't even flinch because he was Black.

As these thoughts filled his head, he noticed Candy taking off her Mister Donut hat and saying goodbye to her coworkers.

"I am outta here!" she said, walking towards Keeshon. "C'mon, let's take off. My car's outside."

She had a rickety, old, 1965, green Plymouth Valiant that could have used a paint job on the outside, but the inside was as clean as a whistle. The upholstery was faded chartreuse—at one time, it had probably been a bright pine or mossy color. With use, the seats had picked up a little brown here, a little yellow there, adding to their character.

She opened the door and motioned to Keeshon to get into the passenger seat.

"You're a little shy," she observed. "Don't be. We're all in this life together."

He wiggled his way into the passenger seat, still feeling pain from some of his injuries.

"So, what happened to your face?" she asked.

"It's kinda a long story," he said. "Once Jimmy left me in prison…"

"Wait, you and Jimmy were in Walpole together?"

"Yeah. I was lucky to have him as a cellmate. I was convicted fo' a crime I didn't commit, just like Jim. He taught me how to read while we was inside. When he got released, some of the gawds let a few of the otha prisonas beat me up. Jim was my protecta."

"Did this have to do with that drug ring they just broke up at Walpole?"

"I think so, ma'am, but I don't have a TV or radio and I haven't seen a newspapuh, eitha."

"Wait, are you the guy the governor pardoned?"

"Yes, ma'am."

"Oh, it's becoming clear to me now. And Jim's sister, Debbie—did you know she'd been kidnapped and almost killed?"

"What? Oh, no! I didn't heah about that!"

"Yeah. That's why the family went into hiding. None of us here in North Weymouth know where they are. Seems like they're safe, though. But, what about you…are you okay?"

"When I was in the hospital, I had a twenty-fo'-owa gawd. Now I'm on my own."

"I'd say you are. Well, they don't know where I live, so you should be okay tonight. I'll try to make some calls tomorrow. It's my day off. We'll try to figure this out. Okay?"

"Yes, ma'am."

"We'll be better if you cut out the 'ma'am' stuff. It's Candy, like I told you at the donut shop."

"Okay, Candy. Thank you."

She continued asking questions until she arrived at an apartment complex in Braintree.

"It's not much, but it's mine as long as I pay the rent," she said.

"I'm so grateful," he said. "So grateful."

Chapter Ninety-Seven

Tony trudged up Beacon Hill again, this time having left his car in the Mass General garage.

He arrived at Brian's Revere Street address again, knocking on the door.

The same roommate who'd greeted him before did again.

"Oh, it's you," the roommate said.

"Were you expecting the Avon lady?" Tony asked.

"Oh, come on, detective! When you came the last time, it wasn't funny, and it's not a joke today. But you're in luck. Brian's here."

"That's good. I really, really, really need to talk to him."

"I'll tell him. Just don't come in."

He stood in the vestibule until heavy steps stomped down two flights of stairs.

"DeMarco? Is that you?" Brian asked.

"The very same. You got a minute, Riggi?"

"I guess so. What's this all about?"

"I talked to Debbie a while ago. She said…"

"She told you what I told her?"

"Yes. But I need to know more."

"What's to tell? I told her everything. This guy keeps getting into my cab. He seems to know where I am, when I'm driving, the works. He gets in the back seat and wants to know where the Baileys are hiding out. Says he has a score to settle, especially with Debbie. Says if I don't tell him where they are, I'll have a hefty price to pay myself. Like what was almost done to Debbie."

"What if we do this? What if I give you the location where they're staying?"

"Oh, no! I don't want anything to happen to Debbie. Or her mother. Even though I get the impression you stole her away from me."

"I did no such thing. I'm working a case."

"Yeah. Right. Big, bad detective comes swooping in to save the lady in distress, and *voila!* She falls for him. Seems like I've seen this movie before."

"Before you jump to conclusions, that's not how anything went down. But I want to warn you, these guys aren't playing around. If you don't cooperate, they *will* do something to you. I can't predict what, but it won't be pretty. And you know Debbie doesn't play the femme fatale, right, Brian?"

"No, she doesn't. Not for a minute. So, how did it go down?"

"I don't have time for that. We need to come up with a plan to save your ass."

Tony and Brian sat on the stairs and devised a scheme to throw off the mysterious backseat guy, and maybe even trap the rest of those involved in the ruse at the same time.

~ ~ ~

As Tony rambled down Beacon Hill's cobblestone streets, he tried to remember where he'd seen a pay phone. He needed to call Debbie and let her in on the strategy he and Brian had worked out. She played a pivotal role in the plan despite the fact she had no input into it. She'd probably be upset for that reason, but they had to make fast decisions.

Chapter Ninety-Eight

Brian hopped into the well-worn front seat of his cab. He felt comfortable there. In control. Behind the wheel. *His* cab. *His* city. *His* roads—until he encountered the mystery visitors who'd been putting the squeeze on him about Debbie.

Debbie. He sighed when he thought of her. Why did she have to meet this cop? He had to admit, DeMarco was a good-looking guy. Confident. Intellectual. Problem-solver. A guy with a career and not just a job. He could see how Debbie might have fallen for him.

He was jolted back to reality when someone knocked on his passenger side window.

"Hey, kid! Is your cab available? The light on top says it is."

"Sure, sure. Go ahead and get in. Do you need help with luggage or anything?"

"Nope. No luggage."

"Where are you headed?" Brian asked, head down, writing on his clipboard, recording the first trip of the night.

"MIT. The crosswalk by the main entrance. You've taken me there before."

Brian tensed up. "I have? Unfortunately, I don't remember every fare, you know."

"You'll remember this one, Brian. Do you think we're playing around?"

"Ahhh…Now it's coming back to me. No, I don't think you're playing at all," he said, clicking the meter down and making a U-turn toward Cambridge.

"Do you have my information, Brian? I'm counting on you."

"I do. But do you want it now or when I drop you off at MIT?"

"Now is fine."

"The Baileys are staying at that detective's mother's house. She lives in Arlington. I have the exact address on a piece of paper in my back pocket. I'll give it to you when I drop you off. I can't reach it now."

"If you're trying to pull somethin' on me, Brian, there'll be hell to pay. I think you know that. Right?"

"Right, but like I said, it's on a piece of paper in my pocket. If you want me to pull over and give it to you now, I will. If you want to wait until you get to MIT and pay today's fare, that would be best."

"I'll wait."

"Say, who do you know at MIT? You just kinda disappear into the air when you get out of the cab."

"None of your beeswax, Brian. That's a private matter. Let's just say I know many people in high places. Some day you might be able to say the same thing."

Brian laughed out loud. "At the rate I'm going, driving a cab and substitute teaching, I doubt it. But if you say so…"

"Ya' gotta have faith in yourself, Brian. Ya' gotta start hangin' with the right people. Ya' gotta set goals and reach for them. That's when you meet people in high places. That's how it happened for me."

"Really? That simple, huh?"

"That simple. You do what you're told, you climb the ladder, you learn things. You stay loyal. It's kinda like that old song, 'Save the Last Dance for Me,' you know? Dance with the one who brung ya."

Brian chuckled again. "A Jay and the Americans reference. Very good. Keeping me on my toes, are you?"

"That's right."

Brian saw that they were coming up on Mass Avenue, right where he had to turn to get in front of the main MIT crosswalk. He drove slightly past the crosswalk, pulled over to the side of the road, put on the cab's hazard lights, and stepped out of the vehicle. He reached into his pocket and pulled out a handwritten note with an address scribbled on it. He handed it to the mystery man.

"Well? Where's the cost of my fare?" he asked, as he handed off the piece of paper.

"How much is it?"

"Seven-fifty."

The mystery man reached into his pocket and took out a ten-dollar bill. "Here. Keep the change."

"And Brian…"

"Yes?"

"If this is a scam, you can bet I'll be back. Only this time, I'll have reinforcements. Capeesh?"

"Oh, yes, I understand. You don't have to tell me twice. But that's the address I have for them. Detective DeMarco hangs around there a lot, so you may have to get through him."

"DeMarco, Deschmarco! We can handle him and his two-bit police force! Now get outta here! I have business to take care of."

Brian got back into the front seat of his cab, knowing full well he might be followed by someone from mystery man's entourage. He drove over the Mass Ave bridge to the fancy Copley Plaza Hotel. He might be able to pick up a fare or two there.

Chapter Ninety-Nine

Their plan was in place. Brian found a pay phone and called Tony.

"I gave him your mother's address. He said he had business to take care of," Brian reported.

"I bet he does. Okay, thanks, Brian. I'm headed to my mother's place to watch for him and his cronies. I'll keep you posted if anything happens."

"Glad I could help. I wish I knew what they had in mind."

"These are dangerous guys, Brian. Creative and dangerous. A bad combination. I'd better get going. Thanks again."

Tony flew out of the police station, stopping briefly to tell the desk sergeant that he had to leave. "Gotta go. Got a tip to follow up on."

"Sure. You bet..." was all the desk sergeant could get out before Tony was down the front steps and in his vehicle.

The big, black monster he drove responded like the devil trying to steal a soul as he flew down city streets through traffic, deftly avoiding pedestrians and double-parked cars. He only needed ten minutes to arrive at his mother's house, but he decided to park in a back alley so that no one would realize he was home. He patted his right hip where his holster held his trusty gun and went in the back door.

He found Angela and Mary preparing dinner, laughing, and joking about some television show they'd watched earlier in the day.

"Tony, what are you doing home so early?" Angela asked. "I wasn't expecting you for at least another hour or two."

"Ma, we have a situation. Everyone in this house might be in danger. I'm not sure how, but those guys who kidnapped Debbie? They found out that she's staying here."

"How? Who told them?" Angela asked nervously.

"It's a long story, and I'll explain it all to you later. I want to secure all the windows and doors to prevent them from getting in."

"Too bad Mary didn't bring her baseball bat!" The ladies broke into peals of laughter, holding their sides because they couldn't stop.

"This is serious, Ma. The guy who kidnapped Debbie had a *gun*. A big one. He was *this close* to killing her and dumping her in the ocean."

A somber look came over Mary's face. "I guess he's not just kidding us, Angela. Seems like when your Tony talks like a cop, he means business."

"Yes. Yes, he does. So, tell us what to do."

"Okay. I will make sure all the windows and doors are locked. I may even come up with a booby trap for the back door. I want you both to stay out of sight of the big windows. That's a big ask, I know, since there are so many big windows in this house. I want all the shades and blinds drawn. I'm going down to the cellar next to secure the cellar door out to the backyard. After that, I'll meet you back here in the kitchen for further instructions. Jimmy should be coming home soon, right? I hope they're not following him home."

"Jimmy! They know what he looks like, Tony!" Mary said. "He might be their first target."

"Yes. I'm going to call the station and have someone escort him from the bus stop. That's the best I can do right now."

He flew down the cellar steps at about the same speed as he'd run down the steps at the police station, fiddling around with the lock on the cellar's bulkhead doors. The lock was a little rusty from not being used in a long time, but Tony grabbed a can of WD-40 and loosened it up. He was able to lock and unlock it, then re-lock it.

He took the cellar stairs two at a time to return to the kitchen, where the two women now looked like a pair of deer in headlights. "Okay, now let's do the first floor." He moved like a pinball in action, from window to window, ensuring that each one was locked. Then to the back door, where he not only secured it, but also placed a rod against the door handle to make it more difficult to turn.

Upstairs he repeated the same process on the windows and the door that led to the huge balcony on the front.

When he finished securing the house, he plopped down on a couch in the front room. "Okay, that's done," he announced. "Come on in here and we'll talk about what might happen if they actually get into the house."

Mary and Angela entered the room and sat quietly opposite him.

"Here's what I want you to do if they do get in. Try to sneak out of whatever room you're in. Get in a closet or anywhere they can't find you. Better if you can get out and go to a neighbor's house. If you can do that, call the police. Tell them who you are and why you need them immediately. Don't try anything stupid, like argue or try and fight with them. Okay?"

The ladies looked at each other and nodded in agreement.

"I'll have the same conversation with Jimmy when he gets here. I'm going to call Debbie now. Maybe it would be best if she didn't come back here at all tonight."

"But…" Mary protested, "won't they be following her from her office? Where would she even go?"

"That's one of the things I have to discuss with her," Tony replied. "I haven't figured that out yet. I was most worried about you two. You're the centers of our universes, you know."

Angela thought she saw tears forming in Tony's eyes. It wouldn't be the first time.

She didn't have to mention it, but Mary noticed it as well.

"Okay. Continue to make supper as usual and we'll wait. That's all we can do now." He ran off to call his friends at the police station to arrange for an escort for Jimmy, and then to call Debbie.

"Ms. Bailey's office," Marcia announced over the phone.

"Hi Marcia. This is Detective DeMarco. Is Debbie available?"

"No, sir. She just stepped out of the office. She should be back in about five minutes. I can have her return your call if you'd like."

"I'm at my mother's house. Would you please tell her it's urgent?"

"Yes, sir, I certainly will… Oh, wait a minute. She's coming through the door right now. Please hold while she gets into her office."

He tapped his fingers for what seemed like forever but was only about twenty seconds.

"Hi!" she said. "What's going on?"

"Debbie," he began, "I'm afraid they know where you and your family are hiding out, and I believe they're going to come looking for you tonight."

"NO! How did that happen?"

"It's a long story. I don't want to tell you on the phone. I am sending someone to escort you home because I don't want to leave our mothers here alone. I've got someone waiting to escort Jimmy from the bus stop. Or you could go somewhere else for the night."

"No. I'm not going anywhere you won't be. Not tonight. Not anymore."

"Umm…Okay then. So, I'm sending the officer escort."

"That's fine. Just give me a specific name for this officer so that I know I can trust him or her."

"I'll work on that. And what did you mean, 'not tonight, not anymore?'"

"You're the detective. You figure it out. Call me back when you have the name of the person you're sending."

"I will. And Debbie…"

"Yes?"

"I don't want to be anywhere you aren't, either. Not tonight. Not anymore."

"So we are on the same page, right?"

"Same page. Same chapter. Same book."

"You are a Renaissance man, after all, Detective DeMarco."

Chapter One Hundred

Jimmy stepped down from the bus in Arlington Heights and heard his name called.

"Jimmy Bailey? Is that you?"

He looked up and discovered a Cambridge Police Officer in full uniform.

Oh, no, what did I do now?

"Yes, sir, that's me."

"I have a patrol car here. One of our detectives asked me to escort you home. Detective DeMarco. Do you know him?"

"Yes, sir, I do."

"Good. Let's go."

Jimmy was hesitant but got in the car anyway. The officer told him he could sit in the front if he preferred, so he did. He introduced himself as Officer Toomijian and said he would be taking Jimmy straight home but didn't explain why. They chatted about the weather, how bad the Red Sox were that year, the Celtics and Bruins, and any other minor things the officer could think of.

They pulled up in front of the DeMarco house. Officer Toomijian got out of the vehicle and took Jimmy by the elbow, walked him up the steps and rang the bell. They were greeted not by Tony but by two other Cambridge detectives Jimmy didn't know. Toomijian told Jimmy that when he escorted someone, he delivered them directly to the person who'd asked for the escort.

One of the detectives, Jason Bell, told Toomijian that Detective DeMarco had to leave for a short time, so he and another detective were guarding the family until he returned.

Jimmy entered the house, looking around for his mother.

"Ma, what's going on here? Where are Tony and Debbie? And why the guards?"

"Well, Jimmy, it seems like those bad guys have discovered where we're staying. Tony thinks they're going to come after us tonight."

"What?! The goons figured it out? If I find out who told them, I swear I'm gonna kill 'em!"

"Now, now, Jimmy, don't say that, especially in front of these nice detectives…Come into the kitchen. Angela and I are finishing making dinner."

Jimmy was hot. His face was beet red, and he could feel his blood pressure rising. This was supposed to be a safe house, a place where they could relax and feel secure until every one of those goons were caught. He only had one more day of work at Fenway Park. Now this.

Angela puttered around the kitchen, putting the finishing touches on yet another pan of lasagna, humming a tune Jimmy did not recognize. The aroma of her cooking filled his nose and calmed him, though not completely. She gave him a huge hug for a small woman, and he lifted her up into his arms.

"Mrs. DeMarco, you are a magician in the kitchen. But what is happening here? Why do we always have to be afraid?"

"I don't know, Jimmy, but my Tony will figure it out. He always does. I'm just sad because when it's over, I won't have my new friends living with me anymore."

He put her down on the ground. "Maybe so. Maybe not. You never know. So, it's lasagna again tonight? What's Ma making for dessert?"

"I'll never tell," Angela replied. "It's a secret."

As they sat worrying about Debbie and Tony, they heard a crash in the front of the house, as if a battering ram had collided with the solid oak door with leaded windowpanes on top.

The detectives drew their guns. Angela and Mary remembered the instructions Tony had given them. Run. Get out of the house.

Angela ran down to the basement. When she looked behind, Mary wasn't with her, so she hid in an old, tool locker where her late husband had kept his woodworking gadgets. She found an old rag nearby to sweep out the cobwebs and crawled inside. She was tiny enough to fit. She pulled the cover over her head and waited.

Mary ran for the back door, removing the rod Tony had used to reinforce the door. Before she could make her escape, someone grabbed her and forcefully pulled her back inside.

"Put your guns down, pigs, or I'll shoot this one!" the man shouted to the officers. Feeling the gun in her back, Mary fainted on the floor, while her son looked on helplessly.

"Ma!" Jimmy shouted.

All Angela could hear was commotion coming from upstairs. She was slightly comforted that she didn't hear any gunshots or screams, although there was a lot of banging and other noises she wasn't familiar with. She prayed to the Virgin Mary that no one would be hurt, or worse. She prayed that her Tony was okay.

The masked gunmen had taken guns away from the detectives and tied them up. Jimmy was also bound to a chair, while Mary was still out cold on the floor.

The one who seemed to be in charge kept asking Jimmy where Debbie was. "We know she's been living here," he said. "We looked all over this place—in the attic, all three floors—and we can't find her. Did she take off with the lover-boy detective? Is that why we have these two bozos here?"

"She never came home from work," Jimmy said. "I haven't seen her since this morning. Is my ma okay?"

The guy slapped Jimmy across the face.

"You can do better than that, Jimbo!"

Jimbo? I hadn't heard that name since I was in prison. One of the guards called me that, but I can't remember which one.

"I'm telling the truth. I expected both her and Tony to be here when I got home," Jimmy replied.

"You're lying, Jimbo! But then again, you lied all the time when you were in Walpole! We knew you and that little guy had a thing going. You just wouldn't admit it."

"No, we did NOT have a thing going, Edwards! Is that your name? Or is it Ellis?"

"I'm not telling you my name. All I'm telling you is that we want that sister of yours to teach her a lesson about respecting men. Capeesh?"

"I *capeesh*. Do you *capeesh* when I tell you I haven't seen her since we both left for work this morning?"

That comment earned Jimmy another slap across the cheek, even harder than the first one.

"Don't play with me, Jimbo. Your sister's gonna learn, even if it means we take out you and the old lady. Your old lady put a friend of ours in the hospital with that swing."

"Good for her."

Another slap. "You better start talkin,' Jimbo, or that face of yours ain't gonna be so pretty for that little, X-ray tech friend of yours."

Jimmy was seething. He didn't want Eileen to be involved in this, any more than she already had been.

"I'm telling you once again! I haven't seen Debbie since we left for work this morning. We walked out the door together, she gave me a ride to the bus stop and that was it!" he hissed at the man.

"About that bus stop…We waited for you there tonight, but you didn't show. Why weren't you there?"

"I had a police escort tonight. Don't know why."

"A police escort, is it? That's why we missed you. We were on the lookout. Who arranged that?"

"Must have been Detective DeMarco."

"And where's he?"

"I don't know that, either. Maybe he's with Debbie."

The two, bound-and-gagged detectives made eye contact with one another.

"So, which one of you are going to answer my questions? Huh? Is the detective with his sister right now? Is he?" He snatched the gag from the female detective's mouth and ran his gun up and down her left cheek. "Honey-pie, you have something you wanna tell me?"

"I don't know where they're going," she said, "but I believe they are together."

He slapped her in the face. "Don't think that because you're a woman I won't get physical with you," he said. "In fact, there are more ways to get physical with you because you are a woman. Catch my drift?"

She nodded.

"So where are they going, honey-pie? Here or somewhere else?"

"I told you, I don't know if they're coming here or going somewhere else. Both options were discussed."

He hit her again. "I'm not playing here, I promise you," he said, forcefully stuffing the rag back into her mouth.

Tony and Debbie drove past the house. Tony noticed his mom's front door barely hanging, and shattered glass on the front porch. And her once-well-groomed flower bed had been trampled over—a big clue that something had gone wrong.

"Oh, no, Debbie, we may be too late!" he said.

"Don't say that, Tony! Our moms are in that house! It's me they're looking for!" she yelled.

"Why don't I just walk in and let them take me? That would solve all our problems with these guys!"

"Let them take you? You can't be serious! I can't let that happen!"

"No, listen to me, Tony. Then you could rescue me like you did at Castle Island. It could work! We can't just do nothing!"

"It doesn't work that way, Debbie! Not when you're dealing with goons like these. And they've got guns!"

"Don't the detectives you left behind have guns, too?"

"Yeah, but if they were taken by surprise, which looks like a strong possibility from what I can see, they've probably been stripped of their weapons."

"So now what?"

"I need to drive around the back and assess the situation. Just try and calm down. Please."

With his headlights off, Tony drove around to the alley behind his mom's house, while simultaneously radioing for police backup.

"Stay in the car," he cautioned Debbie, once he'd cut the engine. "I don't want anything to happen to you."

"I don't want anything to happen to *you*," she whispered back. "What good will I be in the car?"

"I don't want them to see you. It might give them an incentive to do something to someone who's already in there."

"I'll try to stay in the car. I really will. I'll try."

"That's all I can ask for," Tony replied.

With gun drawn, he crept up to the back door and discovered it open. He looked through the window and saw Jimmy and the two detectives tied up. Mary was on the floor. Had they done something to her? Had she fainted? He noticed her feet were beginning to twitch, but no one was paying any attention to her. All their attention was focused on Jimmy.

The female detective seemed to notice him outside looking in. As if to indicate how many were in the room, she looked around the room, then turned in his direction and blinked three times slowly. Three guys. Okay. It would be tough. One against three. One gun against three guns. No backup. Yet.

One guy was pacing, letting his gun flop in his hand as if he had no intention of using it. Tony took that as a good sign, but he couldn't see the other two and what they were doing with their weapons.

He tiptoed in through the back door, thankful that he'd recently sprayed some WD-40 on the hinges. He knew where all the squeaks were on the kitchen floor and gingerly avoided those spots. He slithered around the appliances and cabinets until he was behind the guy who was pacing and pounced on him, hitting him with his gun, knocking him over. His head hit the floor so hard that he was knocked unconscious. Now he had to contend with the other two.

They were so startled, one shot at Tony, nicking him on his left forearm. Tony shot back at him, hitting him in the knee and down the guy went. The third one rushed at Tony with all his might, leading Tony to believe that he did not have a weapon.

They punched and kicked each other, sweat and blood taking up permanent residence on the carpet.

Still in the toolbox, Angela heard gunshots and burst out of hiding. She could not sit still any longer not knowing if Tony and the family she'd come to love needed help.

Bounding up the stairs, she grabbed a spare lasagna pan from the cupboard on her way into the living room. She noticed Tony tussling with one guy, so she ran over and whacked the guy over the head as hard as she could.

"Get off my son, you brute!" she said, before dealing a second blow. The guy was knocked out cold. And although the other guy was out already, she rushed over and whacked him on the head, simply because she could.

Debbie came running in through the back door, just as her mom was attempting to lift herself off the floor.

"Ma, are you okay?"

"Yes, dear, I am," Mary replied, still a bit woozy. "Please go and help your brother. He's tied up in there," she said, pointing into the living room.

Debbie slowly and quietly inched her way a few feet into the other room, not knowing what she would find. She could see the three intruders all on the floor, two of them knocked unconscious and one with a gunshot wound to the knee, lying in a puddle of blood. Before untying anyone, Debbie stopped and looked over at Tony. "You are a mess!" she said, with a chuckle.

"But I'm *your* mess,"

"I guess you are," she replied. Looking at him a little closer, she yelped. "Wait, you've been shot!" she screamed, when she realized there was blood on his shirt.

"It's only a scratch. Believe me, it's not that bad."

Debbie untied Jimmy and then the detectives. Mary made her way to one of the Queen Ann-style chairs to gain her composure.

Although Angela was shaken by the experience, she knew she'd done the right thing by whacking the men on their heads.

As the rest of the police force showed up to take the criminals away, Angela announced:

"Dinner is served. Take your place at my table. My son will lead us in saying grace."

They made their way to their respective places at the dining room table. No one spoke, as members of the Cambridge Police Department cleaned up the mess in the parlor.

Tony cleared his throat. "Okay, Ma, let's not act like nothing happened tonight. We're all a little shaken."

Debbie interrupted. "No, we're all a lot shaken up, Tony. First, Jimmy's been stalked and bonked on his head, leading to emergency room visits. Keeshon's been in the hospital. Eileen and I have been kidnapped. We had to involve my ex to lure these guys here. We don't know if any more of them are out there. We don't know if this is over. We don't know when it will be. I feel like we're living in a bad TV show."

"That about sums it up," Jimmy agreed. "The only good thing about all this is that I met Eileen. Oh, and you met Tony. That is good. Right?"

Debbie nodded her head.

"Everyone, calm down," Angela said. "We need to eat. Italian food—especially the kind that I cook—is comfort food. We all need some comfort food about now."

Mary laughed. "And wait until you see the dessert I made. I confess, it's one of Jimmy's favorites."

"It's not the Red Coach Grille, is it, Ma?" Jimmy asked.

"Or Anthony's Pier Four," Debbie added.

A collective sigh rose throughout the dining room.

A police officer poked his head in. "Uh, Detective DeMarco?"

"Yes, do you need something, officer?" Tony asked.

"We're almost done, sir, but we'd like you all to stay out of the parlor. We'll be over with another crew in the morning to make sure everything's completed. We're all going to the station so that we can make sure those punks—er, those men—have been booked and are in their cells."

The assembled group muttered. One by one, each promised they'd stay out of the parlor until the police returned the next morning.

Chapter One Hundred and One

The following morning, six people gathered in the DeMarco dining room in silence. Eileen had just arrived. They couldn't help looking at the leftover debris from what had happened the night before with the fighting and jousting. What had once been a prim living room, complete with snow-white doilies on the arms of each chair, perfect carpeting on gleaming hardwood, and everything arranged just so, was in turmoil.

Today, they hoped they'd be able to return the room to that pristine setting, once the police were finished.

But would anything ever be the same as it had been before Jimmy left Walpole State Prison? Would anyone be able to forget the kidnappings and stalkings they'd endured? The actual muggings and fearmongering from those who had followed them around the Boston area? And, above all, the death of the warden?

Tony finally broke the silence.

He sat down at the head of the table, on what had been his late father's favorite chair and let out a long sigh.

"So…Everyone…How does it feel to know the guys we've been looking for are all in police custody and we can sleep peacefully tonight?"

Silence.

"Come on, you all must feel some sense of relief. I mean, look at us. We've all been changed by this experience. As I look around, I'd say we've benefited from our brushes with those professional punks. Haven't we?"

"Well…I made a new friend. Not the guy I hit over the head with the lasagna pan, though," Angela said.

"Yes," agreed Mary Bailey. "I'd say Angela and I are kitchen cousins."

A few chuckles responded to that.

"We've got the cooking and baking covered," Angela said. "There's not a recipe in the world the two of us can't conquer. I think we could even do our own cooking show!"

Jimmy looked at Eileen and laced his left fingers into her right hand. "I remember that day I left Walpole," he said. "I didn't know what my life would be like or what direction I'd be taking. Then I bumped my head and met this amazing woman here. She even fought her way from the clutches of kidnappers. I think I believe in fate now."

Eileen smiled and looked at the floor. She had no words but was obviously pleased that he'd spoken those on her behalf.

Tony excused himself to answer the phone.

"Hello, Detective DeMarco here…Yes…He's here. Hold on just a moment, please. Hey, Jimmy, the officer who's guarding your house in Weymouth has a message for you."

"Hi, this is Jimmy Bailey. Yes, I know Keeshon Washington. He's been released from the hospital? Oh, I see. He left a message at the house? Hey, can someone get me a pen? And a piece of paper? Yes, sir, please hold on…Uh, huh…Okay. Got it…Thank you, sir…Yes, I will call him."

Jimmy walked back into the living room. "Hey, everyone. Keeshon left a note on a Mister Donut napkin at the house. He talked to my former coworker Candy. She took him to her apartment overnight and he's staying there until I get in touch with him."

He hung up the phone and dialed the number the officer had given him. A faint voice answered.

"Hello?"

"Key? It's Jim. Just got your message."

"Hey! Where are you? That cop said you're someplace secret."

"I am. But where are you? At Candy's apartment?"

"For sure. She so nice. She let me sleep on her couch las' night. Those social service people got me a place in Roxbury, but I dunno. Lots of the old neighborhood guys I went to school wit' live there, in that area. I gotta go look at the place before I take it. Ya' know?"

"I get it. Don't want you to get in any trouble."

"And that Candy? She said some guy Al might hire me at the Mistah Donut. Where you used to work. But I can't work there if I live in Roxbury."

"No...That wouldn't work."

"Can I see you, ole frien'?"

"I would love that. I'll be going back to Weymouth tonight."

"Sounds good. Maybe Candy can take me to yo' house?"

"Let's count on it. I'll call her at the Mister Donut and make arrangements."

"Can't wait!"

"Wow, that was good fortune for you, baby bro," Debbie said, as Jimmy hung up the phone.

"We train our law enforcement guys well, you know," Tony added.

"Well, detective, do you have anything to add to this conversation?" Mary asked.

"I do," he replied. He moved closer to Debbie and put his arm around her shoulder. "When I first met your daughter, I was only doing my job. It took about fifteen minutes before I fell in love with her. I hope she feels the same about me."

Debbie blushed. "Well, you saved my life, didn't you?"

"Maybe, but you saved mine, too."

"So…Mary…Do you think we should start talking about catering a wedding?" Angela asked.

"Not really," Mary replied. "We'd have other obligations if your son married my daughter."

"True. So, we'd be busy, then?"

"Angela, shall we tell them our plan now?"

"Might as well," Angela agreed.

"Well," Mary announced, "I've decided to move in here with Angela and leave my house in Weymouth. Jimmy can move into the house. He could have Keeshon move in with him if he wants to. They have to keep the house up, like mow the lawn, stuff like that. It's all paid for. They'll only have to pay for the utilities."

"Ma," Debbie asked, "are you sure about this? I mean, you love living near the ocean. Arlington is pretty far from Weymouth, and you don't drive. All your friends are in Weymouth…"

"I have made a friend here, Debbie. Angela and I will have fun living together, cooking, and baking together, going to the soup kitchens, and serving food to the homeless. It's what I want to do."

"When were you going to tell me your plan?" Jimmy asked. "I mean, it's great for me and Keeshon. He could work at Mister Donut and walk to work. I'm going to be looking for a job closer to home than Fenway Park, until I can save enough for a car."

"There are still lots of details to work out," Mary explained. "But I'm excited about all this. And also, about the prospect of the developing love I feel in this room."

"Me, too," Debbie said. "But how ironic is it that my ex-boyfriend, Brian, helped Tony and the Cambridge police catch those guys? He put his own life in danger."

"He did," Tony agreed. "But he did it because he wanted to make sure you didn't get hurt, Debbie. He didn't want to see anyone in your family get hurt, either. It took courage for him to do the right thing.

"You all realize that we'll be called to testify against these guys in court when their trials come up," he continued. "We're all witnesses. We're all victims of these punks. They might have friends in the community, so we still have to watch our backs. The FBI's investigation is ongoing. Who knows what else they'll uncover?"

"Wait a minute. You mean we're still basically under their thumb?" Jimmy asked.

"Most likely," Tony replied. "But we still need to go about our lives. My hunch is that the worst of them are in custody, but there may be some strays, so, again, let's remain vigilant."

"Do we need to learn how to use a gun? Go to a gun range and practice?" Debbie asked.

"Well, as a convicted felon, Jimmy can't own or touch a gun," Tony responded.

Taking it all in, Angela looked around the room. "I have an idea," she said. "Each one of us should get a baseball bat and a lasagna pan and keep them by our bedside. We don't need permits for those. And if you need to learn how to use one, Mary here is pretty handy with a baseball bat."

"And my friend Angela wields a mean lasagna pan."

~THE END~

Acknowledgements

This book is a work of fiction. **4WillsPublishing** edited the manuscript. The author extends her thanks to them for their creativity and attention to detail during the process.

Thanks also go out to Bill Fischer for his patience and support while this manuscript was being developed. Such an endeavor takes much time and effort, as well as time away from usual social activities, and this novel was no exception.

Thanks to the exceptional services of **WordRefiner** for final, final proofing.

And finally, I remain indebted to my English teacher, the late Ed White, from Bicknell Junior High School in North Weymouth, Massachusetts, who encouraged me many years ago to become a writer. By the way, Bicknell Junior High School has been converted into condominiums these days. I'm sure the spirit of Ed White roams through the hallways.

About the Author

Following more than forty years in public relations/marketing/media relations for not-for-profit and governmental organizations, **Wanda Adams Fischer** decided to try her hand at writing fiction. Her award-winning debut novel, *Empty Seats*, is a coming-of-age book with baseball as its foundation. That novel earned her interviews by various publications, as well as on several radio stations, including the nationally syndicated *Only a Game*, produced at WBUR in Boston.

Born in Kingsport, Tennessee, Fischer was raised in the Boston area and graduated from Weymouth High School and earned a bachelor's degree in English from Northeastern University. She began singing when she was four years old and sang at coffeehouses in the Boston area when she was in college. She still plays the guitar and sings occasionally, and has produced one CD, "Singing Along with the Radio," aptly titled, because she has hosted a folk music program on public radio for more than four decades. Her radio career began in Worcester, Massachusetts, at a small station, and, for the past forty-two years, she's hosted a critically acclaimed show, "The Hudson River Sampler," on WAMC, the Albany, New York-based National Public Radio affiliate. In 2019, Folk Alliance International inducted her into its Folk Radio Hall of Fame. In 2023, the Proctors Collaborative inducted her into its Thomas Edison Music Hall of Fame.

She and her husband, Bill Fischer, who met at a coffeehouse at Boston College, have been married for more than fifty-one years. They have two adult children and seven grandchildren. They live in Schenectady, New York, with their dachshund, Oscar.

Still Doing Time is Wanda Adams Fischer's third novel. Her prior novels are *Empty Seats* and *A Few Bumps*. She also has published several short stories, available only as eBooks on Amazon.com.

Made in the USA
Middletown, DE
11 October 2024